The Time Machi

Liverpool Science Fiction Texts and Studies

General Editor DAVID SEED

Series Advisers
I. F. CLARKE, EDWARD JAMES, PATRICK PARRINDER
and BRIAN STABLEFORD

The Time Machines

The Story of the Science-Fiction Pulp Magazines from the beginning to 1950

The History of the
Science-Fiction Magazine
Volume I

MIKE ASHLEY

LIVERPOOL UNIVERSITY PRESS

First published 2000 by
LIVERPOOL UNIVERSITY PRESS
4 Cambridge Street
Liverpool
L69 7ZU

British Library Cataloguing-in-Publication Data
A British Library CIP record is available.

ISBN 0 85323 855 3 cased
ISBN 0 85323 865 0 paperback

Typeset in Meridien by
Koinonia, Bury, Lancashire
Printed and bound in the European Union by
Redwood Books Ltd, Trowbridge, Wiltshire

Table of Contents

Preface

It has been over twenty-five years since I first prepared my *History of the Science Fiction Magazine*. Much has happened in the science-fiction world since then. Blockbuster movies such as *Close Encounters of the Third Kind*, *Star Wars* and *ET* have made science fiction popular and accessible. Computer games have brought an interaction between humans and technology greater than ever before. Now we are into virtual reality, where we and our simulated dream worlds can become as one. To many of us the worlds of science fiction are alive and all about us.

To a large extent the science-fiction magazine has become a strange anachronism in this world. Its demise was already being predicted 20 years ago, and yet it lives on. In those past 20 years magazines have been issued in tape format, back issues are available on microfilm and CD-ROM, and magazines have developed on the internet. Yet there is still a desire for the written word in magazine form, and for as long as that desire is sufficient to make the magazines pay for themselves, they will, I believe, continue to appear.

Unfortunately, whenever the science-fiction magazine receives any form of press coverage (and that isn't often), it tends to reflect the garish and sensational aspects. This attitude has not changed in the past 20 years, and much of my argument in the preface to the first volume of my *History* published back in 1974 remains valid. Science fiction is still not regarded as literature by most of the literary establishment, although it has achieved slightly more respectability in recent years as we have entered the high-tech age, and as its leading lights, especially Isaac Asimov and Arthur C. Clarke, have been acknowledged for their craft and predictions. In addition the more literary aspects of science fiction have been championed from both within, through writers such as Brian W. Aldiss, Robert Silverberg and Harlan Ellison, and without, through Kingsley Amis, Colin Wilson and Angela Carter, so that it has developed a veneer of respectability, although that respectability tends to cling more to the writer than to the subject.

Most science fiction is regarded as puerile and of low quality and, unfortunately, Sturgeon's Law that 90 per cent of everything is rubbish holds as good today as ever. But most of that rubbish, I believe, appears in books and in low-grade movies. The science-fiction magazine remains the haven of quality science fiction and the cauldron from which much new talent emerges.

On the quality front it is sad to reflect that this was not always so. In their heyday (the 1930s to the 1950s), the science-fiction magazines published far too much rubbish. At that time little sf appeared in book form and there was not the proliferation of paperbacks that there is today. What has happened is that the original paperback novel has become the main focus for science fiction, for all ages and tastes. The science-fiction magazine, however, remains the primary focus for short stories, and is today as much the training ground for new recruits as it ever was.

I began my preface in 1974 by asking 'who are your favourite science-fiction writers: Robert Heinlein, Arthur Clarke, John Wyndham, Isaac Asimov, Frank Herbert, Clifford Simak, Michael Moorcock …?' Although only two of those are still alive today, all of their names live on and they retain their popularity, and to them we can add a host of new names: Orson Scott Card, Kim Stanley Robinson, Robert Holdstock, Lucius Shepard, David Brin, Lois McMaster Bujold, maybe even Terry Pratchett … and many, many more. And the chances are that, with very few exceptions, all these major writers first appeared in science-fiction magazines, often continuing to contribute to them. Many of their best short stories being published today in book form probably first appeared in the magazines, and some of the novels may first have been serialized there.

Science-fiction magazines are now entering their eighth decade and, as I write, the first of them, *Amazing Stories*, is still with us (though going through significant changes as I write) as is its first rival, *Analog*, though back in the winter of 1929 when the latter first appeared it was called *Astounding Stories*. In the intervening 70 years magazines have come and gone, several hundred of them, amongst them *Wonder Stories, Startling Stories, Galaxy, If, Other Worlds, Imagination, Worlds of Tomorrow, Galileo, Odyssey* and *Venture*. Some have survived, including *The Magazine of Fantasy & Science Fiction* and the resilient *New Worlds*, and others, such as *Isaac Asimov's SF Magazine* and *Interzone*, have emerged to take their place.

This book, the first of three volumes, tells their story, focusing on that first flush of exuberance, the pulp magazine. It traces the infant genre from its birth in the technophobic years after World War I, through the cosmic thirties into the atomic shadow of the forties and the decline of the pulps at the start of the fifties. The second volume, *Transformations*, continues that story through the Cold War, the paperback revolution and the dawn of the space age. The final volume, *Gateways to Forever*, looks at the way in which the magazines have survived following the new wave of the sixties, the punk era, the computer age, and the astonishing popularity of the big budget blockbuster sf movies.

Since I wrote my *History* nearly thirty years ago there has been much academic interest in the genre and much research into science fiction. Little of that research has been aimed at the science-fiction magazines themselves, and the only major contribution has been *Science Fiction, Fantasy, and Weird Fiction Magazines,* which I produced along with Marshall Tymn and a number of stalwart contributors. I use the word 'major' not as a sign of conceit (though I regard the work as the most thorough book yet produced on the sf magazines), but in reference to its size – it is almost a thousand pages long. However, the book is now some fifteen years out of date.

For the current three volumes I have completely rewritten my introductions to the original series and then doubled the length of overall text with new material. These books are intended to be the latest word on the entire history of the science-fiction magazine.

Mike Ashley

Acknowledgements

The early days of my research were inspired by two men: Sam Moskowitz and Robert A.W. Lowndes. They will both be encountered in this book as editors and writers, but it is their work as researchers and historians of science fiction that I acknowledge here. Sam Moskowitz delved deeply into the nooks and crannies of science fiction from the magazine viewpoint and conducted more original research into the genre than most other researchers and academics combined. He inspired and influenced me more than I can say and I acknowledge here my indebtedness to his work. Robert A.W. Lowndes, known affectionately by me as RAWL, his editorial insignia, slaked my thirst for knowledge in a series of articles he wrote in *Future Science Fiction* about the early sf magazines, and he continued to provide nuggets of fascinating facts throughout his magazine editorials, reviews and articles. I was delighted when RAWL and I became regular correspondents and we worked together on my detailed history of the early days of the sf magazines, *The Gernsback Days*.

My early research for the original series, back in the 1970s, was helped considerably by Philip Harbottle and the late, and very sadly missed, Walter Gillings. Since then my research has been undertaken almost entirely on my own, including amassing a near-complete run of all magazines and conducting research with most of the magazines' editors and publishers over the years. I must thank Alistair Durie, who still has a bigger collection of sf and fantasy magazines than my own, and who is frequently pestered by telephone enquiries into the minutiae of magazines.

The bibliography at the back of this book lists all those books that I have consulted in my research for both the original series and these revised volumes. I have consulted these books liberally, although in the majority of cases I have checked facts and opinions separately.

The end results are all my own, including any errors or omissions. I thank Atsushi Hori at The English Agency for encouraging me to bring this *History* up to date and publishers Tokyo Sogensha for their interest. And finally I thank all those editors, writers, publishers and collectors who, over the past 20 years, have put up with my persistent enquiries. They, and others, made this history. I am merely retelling it.

CHAPTER ONE
Before the Creation

Britain and Europe

When *Amazing Stories* appeared on the news-stands in America in March 1926[1] it was by no means a bolt from the blue. Science-fiction readers were doubtless delighted, but they should not have been surprised. A magazine devoted entirely to science fiction was the next logical step in the progression of science fiction in the magazines, and in the development of specialist genre magazines. Hugo Gernsback, the founder of *Amazing Stories*, said: 'the concept of *Amazing Stories* in 1926 was not a haphazard undertaking. Its groundwork had been well prepared for 15 years!'[2]

Fifteen years takes us back to 1911, but we can go still farther back. As we shall see later, 1911 was the year in which Gernsback began publishing science fiction. It was not called science fiction then. Gernsback would not coin that term until almost twenty years later.[3] His term was 'scientifiction', but more popular at the time was 'scientific romance'. However in this history I shall refer to it throughout as science fiction, or by its most popular abbreviation: sf.

By way of background perhaps we should be clear about what magazines are, and when they first appeared. The word 'magazine' is of Arabic origin, and meant a place for stores – the French for shop is still *magasin*. The French developed that concept of a place holding a variety of articles during their literary renaissance in the seventeenth century and launched their first *magasin*, *Le Journal des savants*, in Paris in January 1665. Its purpose was to collect together

---

1. The first issue was released on 10 March 1926 with the cover date April. From the second issue the publication date moved to the 5th of the month preceding the cover date.
2. From a guest editorial by Hugo Gernsback in *Amazing Stories*, 35 (4), April 1961, p. 7.
3. The term 'science-fiction' had been used first by a British writer, William Wilson, in his monograph *A Little Earnest Book Upon a Great Old Subject* (1851) and his definition is similar to that of Gernsback, though his single example, *The Poor Artist* by Richard Henry Horne (1844), is a poor one.

articles by scientists and learned men of Europe. *Le Journal* was edited by Denis de Sallo, a magistrate and the founder of modern periodical criticism. It was weekly and lasted for 13 issues before French censorship brought about its suppression. It was revived the following year and prospered. It was taken over by the State in 1702, later switched to a monthly publication and, though it ceased publication in 1792, was revived in 1816 and continues to appear to this day, though on a quarterly schedule.

It was in a French magazine that the first fantastic fiction began to appear. This was not science fiction by today's criteria, but most certainly vivid works of the imagination which also chose to satirize society – one of the frequent purposes of science fiction. Today we know these works as fairy tales, for it was in the pages of *Le Mercure galant* that Charles Perrault's fairy tales first appeared. *Le Mercure galant* was a court and society magazine, founded in 1672 and much favoured by Louis XIV. It was an ideal medium for the type of *salon* fairy tales that were being created by Madame d'Aulnoy and Charles Perrault, and it was in *Le Mercure galant* for February 1696 that one of the first and best known of all fairy tales, 'La Belle au bois dormant' ('The Beauty Sleeping in the Wood' or 'The Sleeping Beauty') appeared.

Although the characteristics of a magazine should be obvious, we shall encounter time and again developments by which magazines and books become almost indistinguishable. The obvious magazine features – a mixture of fiction or non-fiction, artwork, editorial and reader columns – can appear just as easily in a book. What tends to distinguish a magazine more readily is a periodic publication. That may be daily, weekly, monthly or even annually, and quite frequently it is irregular. But even that element applies to regular anthology series. Quite clearly, then, the distinction between magazines and books, though ostensibly straightforward, can often be confusing, and that is an important point to bear in mind throughout this history. Although primarily it is a history of science fiction in magazines, it cannot cover that without considering the impact of other publishing media.

Periodicals, more as newspapers than general magazines, began to make their mark in Britain once the Licensing Act, which regulated (and almost wholly suppressed) the press, expired in 1695. By 1709, with the appearance of *The Tatler*, edited and almost entirely written by Richard Steele, the newspaper began to come of age. At that stage *The Tatler* was a single broadsheet of news and political comment which circulated around the then fashionable society coffee houses. Its success spawned many imitations and successors, and by degrees led to the first proper British magazine.

This came about in 1731 with *Gentleman's Magazine*, founded by London printer Edward Cave and for which Dr Samuel Johnson was a frequent reporter. It was due to this publication's popularity that the word 'magazine' passed into the English language. It was followed soon afterwards by *London Magazine* (1732) and *Scots Magazine* (1739). These all had one thing in common: they were magazines of literary and political comment and criticism. Few of them are readable today except for specialist study, although of passing relevance was *The Adventurer*, a twice-weekly paper that ran for 140 issues between November 1752 and March 1754. This was produced by John Hawkesworth, who had succeeded Samuel Johnson as parliamentary reporter for *Gentleman's Magazine*. Hawkesworth was an able political satirist but used the medium of fantasy to make his point, particularly the oriental tale which was then in vogue following the popularity of the *Arabian Nights*. Hawkesworth published several oriental fantasies in *The Adventurer*, of which the best was 'Amurath' (January 1753) about a wicked sultan who fails to obey a genie and is transformed into a series of animals.

The shift from magazines of political and literary review to ones with more general coverage happened only gradually, but a major change came with the appearance of *The Monthly Magazine* in 1796. This broadened the coverage to science and philosophy and allowed for a wider discussion of the arts. It attracted contributions from many of the literati of the day including William Hazlitt the Elder, Robert Southey, Dr John Aikin, William Godwin and Thomas Malthus. It was Malthus who was one of the first to think seriously about future trends and the extent to which population growth would outstrip agricultural production.

The Monthly Magazine continued until 1825, but in 1814 it spawned a competitor, *The New Monthly Magazine*, from publisher Henry Colburn. Colburn was one of those individuals who ingratiated himself into society and, as a consequence, was everywhere and knew everyone. This allowed him and his publications to become a focus for much literary activity, and he increased the popular coverage of society events.

However, the most influential magazine to appear came from Scottish bookseller William Blackwood who founded *Blackwood's*

Magazine (initially *Blackwood's Edinburgh Magazine*) in 1817. Although primarily a literary review, it was in this magazine that fiction became a regular feature, particularly the works of James Hogg, John Galt and William Maginn, writers who influenced, amongst others, Walter Scott and Edgar Allan Poe.

We should perhaps pause at 1817/18 because it is a pivotal period. Although prior to this there had been a number of science-fiction novels (by later definition), these were mostly imaginary voyages, whether on Earth (as epitomized by Jonathan Swift's *Gulliver's Travels*, 1726), or to the moon (as in Francis Godwin's *The Man in the Moone*, 1638), and they were frequently satires on society. Their popularity is attested by the appearance of the first English-language science-fiction anthology, *Popular Romances* (1812), anonymously edited by Henry Weber, consisting of five imaginary voyages. Anthologies feature frequently later in this history, and it is interesting to note that their history is older than that of the sf magazine. There were, in fact, French anthologies of imaginary voyages published in the 1700s.

The year 1818 saw the publication of *Frankenstein, or the Modern Prometheus* by Mary W. Shelley which has been credited by many, most notably by Brian W. Aldiss in his *Billion Year Spree*, as the first genuine work of science fiction. It brought scientific experimentation rather than supernaturalism to gothic horror, and encouraged consideration of the power of science for good and evil.

Thus we find that magazine fiction and science fiction arose at the same period and were allowed to develop together, albeit slowly. One interesting item resurrected by Peter Haining in his anthology *The Shilling Shockers* (1979) shows one of the fruits of this birth. 'Five Hundred Years Hence' by the anonymous 'D' appeared in the *Pocket Magazine* in 1818, and compared a dying Britain with a prosperous United States. Meanwhile, the only other story to be published as a result of that literary competition between Lord Byron, Percy Bysshe Shelley and Mary Shelley which spawned *Frankenstein*, 'The Vampyre' by Byron's physician Dr John Polidori, appeared in the April 1819 issue of *The New Monthly Magazine*. Science fiction and the supernatural were growing healthily together, and they will remain intense competitors for the rest of our history.

The real growth in magazines in Britain started in the 1830s with the appearance of *Fraser's Magazine* (in 1830) as the London equivalent of *Blackwood's* and of *The Metropolitan Magazine* (in 1831) which pioneered the serialization of fiction. *Chambers's Edinburgh Journal* appeared in 1832 as a weekly rival to *Blackwood's*, and the *Dublin University Magazine* took them all as a model for its launch in 1833. Charles Knight began his *Penny Magazine* in 1832, intending the 'diffusion of useful knowledge' to a much wider range of readers. There was now a growing army of 'popular' writers (as distinct from 'literary') who were contributing to these magazines, amongst them Edward Bulwer (later Lord Bulwer-Lytton), Captain Frederick Marryat, Joseph Sheridan Le Fanu, William Harrison Ainsworth and, above all, Charles Dickens. Some of these not only were contributors but also served as editors.[4]

In 1860 came George Smith's *Cornhill Magazine*. Under the editorship of William Makepeace Thackeray, this was the first magazine to reach the magnificent circulation of 100,000, still a watershed amongst popular magazines. By January 1865 there were 544 magazines appearing regularly in Great Britain and Ireland. Perhaps the biggest single influence in this, apart from the rise in educational reform, was the expansion of the railways, which meant that people spent more time on trains, and a popular way to pass the time was by reading. In 1849, William Henry Smith secured the privilege of selling books and newspapers at railway stations. Inevitably the production of magazines and books expanded to meet the demand.

Science fiction in these magazines in Britain was rare. One of the few examples from this early period is the anonymous 'Anti-Humbug' (*London Magazine*, February and April 1840), an early Gernsbackian extravaganza set in the fortieth century and featuring a catalogue of wonderful inventions. Another is the anonymous anti-gravity robinsonade[5] 'Tale of a Chemist'. This was written as early as 1824. It was a popular story, being reprinted many times. William Tegg included it in his volume of table-talk, *The Story-Teller*, in 1836, and Charles Knight reprinted it in his *Penny Magazine* in 1846.

4. Bulwer edited *The New Monthly* from 1831 to 1833, Marryat edited the *Metropolitan* from 1832–1836, and Dickens was the first editor of *Bentley's Miscellany* (from 1837 to 1839), launched as a rival to *The New Monthly*. Ainsworth (1805–82) started his own *Ainsworth's Magazine* in 1842 whilst Dickens's *Household Words* followed in 1850.
5. A 'robinsonade' (from *Robinson Crusoe*) relates an individual's fight for survival in an alien terrain, and the term has grown to include extravagant travel books such as *The Adventures of Baron Munchausen* and *Gulliver's Travels*.

Fantastic fiction was much more common. The first magazine to specialize in gothic and supernatural fiction was *The Marvellous Magazine* published in London in 1802. It featured heavily edited versions of popular gothic novels and stories such as Ann Radcliffe's *Mysteries of Udolpho* which was cut by one tenth as 'The Veiled Picture'. A similar compendium was *The Romancist and Novelist's Library* edited by William Hazlitt the Younger, except that the reprint of gothic novels and stories was authorized, and the series included many new stories. It ran as a weekly part-work from January 1839 to December 1840 before converting to book format in 1841 and running for six volumes to 1842. It published no science fiction but was immensely popular in making available what was, at that time, the widest selection of imaginative fiction for the public.

It is perhaps surprising that, with this upsurge in magazine fiction, scientific fiction did not feature more regularly. But in Britain it remained the exception. Lord Bulwer-Lytton's 'A Strange Story', which attempts to explain supernatural events rationally and scientifically and includes as a key feature the discovery of an elixir of life, was serialized in *All the Year Round* from August 1861 to March 1862, but the same author's more profound sf novel, *The Coming Race*, was published first and only in book form, by Blackwood's, in 1871. At that same time *Blackwood's Magazine* published anonymously in its May 1871 issue 'The Battle of Dorking'. The author was George Tomkyns Chesney, who later became the Conservative Member of Parliament for Oxford. The story told of the invasion of Britain by Prussian troops, and the successful defeat of the British army at Dorking in Surrey. Appearing within a month of the Prussian success in the Franco-Prussian War the story evoked much reaction among *Blackwood's* readers. Many imitations followed, making 'The Battle of Dorking' the godfather of the future war story which became so prevalent in the magazines in the 1890s.

The next major break in Britain came in 1891 when George Newnes started *The Strand Magazine*, the first magazine of its kind to sell for just sixpence. (*Cornhill's*, for example, had been twice that price 30 years earlier.) The emphasis in *The Strand* was on easy-to-read stories and a variety of factual articles on every facet of life, all heavily illustrated. Most British magazines hitherto had carried solid pages of text rarely broken by any form of artwork. The *English Illustrated Magazine* had started the move in October 1883, but *The Strand* took it much further, with illustrations and photographs on every page, many dramatically portraying exciting scenes from the stories. *The Strand* took the reading public by storm, its first issue selling out instantly and its circulation rising dramatically, particularly during the publication of the Sherlock Holmes stories by Arthur Conan Doyle.

Success breeds imitation. *The Ludgate Monthly* (using the name of another popular London thoroughfare) followed in May 1891, *The Idler* in February 1892, *Pall Mall Magazine* in May 1893, *The Windsor* in January 1895, *Pearson's* in January 1896, *Harmsworth's* in July 1898 and *The Royal* in November 1898, to list but a few of the more obvious imitations.

This profusion of markets for popular fiction was the main stimulus for the publication of science fiction in Britain. The genre particularly lent itself to clever ideas for new inventions which could now be comically illustrated rather than laboriously described. *The Strand* was quick to take advantage of this and, within its first year, began a series under the general title of 'The Queer Side of Things'. A number of authors contributed to this series, but the stories with the most scientific slant were written by James F. Sullivan. 'Old Professor Willett' (December 1892) is an ingenious story about a professor who invents an implosive (rather than explosive) that happens so rapidly that people disappear. 'The Dwindling Hour' (January 1893) is a fascinating exploration of the mystery of time and entropy, whilst 'The Man with a Malady' (July 1894) is about precognition.

The December 1895 *Strand* contained 'An Express of the Future', attributed to Jules Verne though subsequently discovered to have been written by his son, Michel. It allows us to bring into this account the more significant development of science fiction on the continent, in particular the work of Jules Verne, generally regarded as the father of science fiction. It is important because much of Verne's significant work appeared in magazines.

Jules Verne had trained as a lawyer but had little interest in the profession. He was fascinated with the exploration of the world, but not being a great traveller, he undertook these voyages in his imagination. It was his desire to describe to his readers all the corners of the known and unknown world, including the centre of the Earth and the Moon. His early stories, such as 'A Voyage in a Balloon' (*Musée des familles*, August 1851), sometimes called 'A Drama in the Air', and 'Winter amid the Ice' (*Musée des familles*, March–April 1855), are really adventure travelogues, and had only been moderately successful. Verne almost quit writing and took up work as a stockbroker. He tinkered with a manuscript about the history of ballooning, but his interest waned and he tossed the manuscript on the fire. It was rescued by his wife, and soon after Verne presented it to the publisher Pierre Hetzel. Hetzel suggested that Verne revise the manuscript, reducing the historical aspects and developing the adventurous. The result was *Cinq semaines en ballon* (Hetzel, 1863), published in America as *Five Weeks in a Balloon* (Appleton, 1869). Hetzel arranged for Verne to sign a contract promising two novels a year for the next 20 years! He released a publisher's announcement that firmly placed Verne's work in the development of science fiction, stating that 'the day has come when science must take its rightful place in literature', and adding, 'His [Verne's] plan is to sum up all the information gathered by modern science in the fields of geography, geology, physics and astronomy, and to rewrite ... the history of the universe.'[6]

Hetzel was planning a magazine that would appeal to the young, providing education whilst remaining entertaining. As we shall see, this was exactly the same premise upon which Gernsback issued *Amazing Stories*, making Hetzel's *Magasin d'éducation et de récréation* a direct literary precursor to the science-fiction magazine. The first issue appeared on 20 March 1864 on a twice-monthly schedule, and was heavily illustrated. Verne's novels became a regular feature starting from the first issue, with 'Les anglais au pole nord', which ran to 20 February 1865, followed immediately by 'Le désert de glace' and 'Les enfants due Capitaine Grant' (better known as *In Search of the Castaways*). But perhaps his most popular was '20,000 Leagues under the Sea', serialized in the magazine from 20 March 1869 to 20 June 1870.

Not all of Verne's fiction appeared in *Magasin d'éducation et de récréation*. Hetzel had launched another magazine aimed at a higher age-group, called the *Journal des débats politiques et littéraires*, which was similar to the literary reviews. It was this that serialized 'From the Earth to the Moon' (14 September to 14 October 1865) and the sequel 'Round the Moon' (4 November to 8 December 1869).

Hetzel had arrangements with magazines outside France, most notably the American *Our Young Folks* (started in 1865) and the British *Boy's Own Paper* (started in 1879) and through these and

---

6. From Jean Chesneaux, *The Political and Social Ideas of Jules Verne* (London: Thames & Hudson, 1972), p. 23, as quoted in Edward J. Gallagher, Judith A. Mistichelli and John A. Van Eerde, *Jules Verne: A Primary and Secondary Bibliography* (Boston: G. K. Hall, 1980).

others Verne's reputation spread. Verne's influence upon science-fiction, particularly voyages of discovery, is immeasurable. There is no doubt that his work attracted the youthful Hugo Gernsback who would have encountered it both in bookform and in the *Magasin d'éducation et de récréation*.

In Britain the development of science fiction was in the hands of others, amongst them Arthur Conan Doyle, Grant Allen, George Griffith and increasingly, H.G. Wells. All of these were writing regularly for the weekly and monthly magazines. Some of Doyle's early work treads the borderline between science and the super-natural, particularly in the unknown realms of mesmerism. In 'John Barrington Cowles' (*Cassell's Saturday Journal*, 12-19 April 1884) a young girl seems to have the power to will people to death, whilst in 'The Great Keinplatz Experiment' (*Belgravia*, July 1885) experiments in mesmerism lead to a personality exchange between bodies. Grant Allen, a close friend of Doyle, was contributing to *Belgravia* at the same time. 'Pausodyne' (*Belgravia Annual*, Christmas 1881) is about the creation of a painkiller that brings about a cata-tonic trance and results in suspended animation. 'A Child of the Phalanstery' (August 1884) projects a regimented society in the next century. Both Doyle and Allen would continue to write science fiction throughout the 1890s, and Doyle's major contribu-tions were yet to come. Their work, however, was eclipsed by the emergence of George Griffith and H.G. Wells.

Griffith was a regular contributor to the publications of C. Arthur Pearson, the main rival to George Newnes, and his forte was the future war story. The first to be published was 'The Angel of the Revolution', serialized in *Pearson's Weekly* (21 January–14 October 1893) followed by 'The Syren of the Skies' (23 December 1893–4 August 1894). The future war story is a significant sub-genre within science fiction and was a major part of pulp science fiction, particularly in the years after the First World War. As we see, it had its antecedents in the popular magazines of the previous century. H.G. Wells added his own war stories, first with an alien invasion, in 'The War of the Worlds' (*Pearson's Magazine*, April–December 1897), and later a global war in 'The War in the Air' (*Pall Mall Magazine*, January–December 1908).

Wells's contribution to the development of science fiction is incontestable. Unlike Verne, who was primarily concerned with imaginative voyages aided by scientific developments, Wells was interested in the detail of discovery. His early stories, however, bear some comparison with Verne's in that they consider the discovery of unknown lands and species. Some, such as 'Aepyornis Island' (*Pall Mall Budget*, December 1894) and 'In the Abyss' (*Pearson's Magazine*, August 1896), take us to remote parts of the world or the ocean depths to witness strange creatures. Others, for example 'The Flowering of the Strange Orchid' (*Pall Mall Budget*, 2 August 1894), 'In the Avu Observatory' (*Pall Mall Budget*, 9 August 1894), 'A Moth – Genus Novo' (*Pall Mall Gazette*, 28 March 1895) and 'The Sea Raiders' (*Weekly Sun Literary Supplement*, 6 December 1896), bring those creatures to us.

All of Wells's significant sf short stories appeared first in magazines as did most of his novels (the most notable exception being *The Island of Doctor Moreau*, published by Heinemann in 1896). 'The Time Machine', his first substantial work, had a tortuous history, all traceable through magazines. The final version (edited slightly for book publication) ran in *The New Review* from January to May 1895. Wells was eventually captured by George Newnes and also became a regular contributor to *The Strand*. His first appearance there was with the highly successful 'The First Men in the Moon' (November 1900–August 1901) and the magazine was the market for several of his better known later stories, including 'The New Accelerator' (December 1901), 'The Truth about Pyecraft' (April 1903), 'The Land Ironclads' (December 1903) and 'The Country of the Blind' (April 1904).

By the turn of the century popular magazines were proliferating in Britain. In addition to the general magazines printed on high-quality china-coated stock, there were cheaper fiction magazines printed on lower-quality newsprint or pulp paper. The British pulps are less well known than their American counterparts, perhaps because they were less sensational, and their true value has yet to be fully assessed even though they carried the bulk of short fiction published in Britain in the first 40 years of the twentieth century. They included *The Novel Magazine* and *The Grand Magazine*, both launched in 1905, *The Story-teller*, started in 1907, *The Red Magazine*, started in 1908, and *The Weekly Tale-Teller,* launched in 1909.

Whilst these magazines featured a wide range of fiction, of which romance, adventure and mystery were the main attractions, science fiction was never too far behind. Certainly more science fiction appeared in these magazines than has ever been fully accounted for or subsequently reprinted in book form and this is still a major area for research. To give some idea of the writers who contributed in addition to the continuing work of Arthur Conan Doyle and H.G. Wells, we must list M.P. Shiel, William Hope Hodgson, George C. Wallis, Donovan Bayley, James Barr, A.E. Ashford, Coutts Brisbane, Owen Oliver, Barry Pain and Sax Rohmer.

Hodgson, Rohmer and Shiel remain the best known, though perhaps more for horror and supernatural fiction than science fiction even though they all produced their fair share. Time has treated the others less well, almost certainly because so little of their work survived in book form, which emphasizes the ephemeral existence of magazines and the fact that they are so readily overlooked in the history of fiction, even though their influence at the time can be significant. George C. Wallis is worth a further mention because we shall encounter him again in our history. He had one of the longest careers in science fiction at this early stage, as he started writing in the 1890s and was still producing in the 1940s. He had two profound stories in *Harmsworth's Magazine*. 'The Last Days of Earth' (July 1901) has a Wellsian image of a dead sun and a frozen Earth. Earth's final inhabitants, a man and a woman, propel their space-ship away from the Earth at twice the speed of light in the direction of the nearest star known to have planets. The story leaves their fate untold. 'The Great Sacrifice' (July 1903) is similar in mood. The Martians sacrifice their own planet in order to shield Earth from an approaching giant meteor swarm. These stories would have compared well with the material Gernsback published in the early *Amazing Stories* and even with some material in the early *Astounding Stories*.

James Barr is surprisingly neglected today although he was producing science fiction for at least the last 20 years of his life. Much of his work focused on future societies, projecting from current trends, such as the suffragette movement in 'When Women Won' (*The Red Magazine*, 15 April 1911) or the threat of aviation in 'Lord Hagen's Dress Shirt' (*The Red Magazine*, 15 August 1911). His most striking story, though, is 'The World of the Vanishing Point' (*The Strand*, March 1922), an incredible adventure into a microcosmic world full of monsters. It is one of a number of stories prevalent at the time taking the subatomic world as their theme.

Perhaps the most unjustly neglected of all these authors is the Australian Coutts Brisbane. His real name was Robert Coutts Armour, but he wrote usually as Coutts Brisbane and sometimes as Reid Whitley, and possibly under other names. He was a very prolific writer for many magazines, including boys' periodicals, and specialized in mysteries and science fiction. His work was often humorous, sometimes rather too light-weight to have much impact, but his imagination was fertile and he utilized all of the then prevalent science-fiction concepts, many of them for *The Red Magazine*. Drugs send a man into the past in 'The Generations of his Forefathers' (15 March 1911) and into the future in 'The Triumph' (15 July 1916); antigravity features in 'A Matter of Gravity' (1 January 1913) and extracting gold from the sea in 'A By-Product' (15 June 1914) – the by-product being giant crabs; invasion by giant ants occurs in 'De Profundis' (15 November 1914), robots in 'The Fall of Podunkey' (15 March 1916), television in 'Better Dead' (1 December 1917), a Wellsian dying Earth in 'The Little Bit of Fat' (1 April 1921), atomic disintegration in 'The Almighty Atom' (17 March 1922) and giantism in 'Growth' (8 June 1923). He was particularly good at interplanetary adventures and creating bizarre alien life-forms, something which was later developed with great success by Stanley G. Weinbaum. Starting with 'Take it as Red' (15 February 1918) Brisbane had a series of stories in *The Red Magazine* exploring the solar system and encountering a variety of aliens.

Over the past few pages I have only skimmed the surface of the wealth of science fiction produced in Britain between 1890 and 1923. It is perhaps surprising that no enterprising publisher considered issuing a magazine specializing in science fiction, but that direction was not taken in Britain and would not be until 1934. In fact there were no specialist magazines in Britain, not even for crime and romance stories, which were the most popular, until the publisher Sir George Hutchinson, seeing the developments in the United States, launched *Adventure-Story Magazine* in September 1922 and *Mystery-Story Magazine* in February 1923. These were under the able editorship of E. Charles Vivian, whose name will bring a glow of recognition amongst devotees of lost-race fiction because of his novels *City of Wonder* and *Fields of Sleep* which were serialized in *Adventure-Story* in 1922 and 1923.

The closest any periodical publication came to producing a science-fiction issue was *Pears' Annual*. Annuals are a strange hybrid of books and magazines. Because they appeared on a regular annual basis, usually at Christmas but sometimes in the summer, they are regarded as periodicals, but they have rather the character of books than magazines, lacking most editorial features and usually focusing on a theme. Some annuals contained single novels and were later reissued as books. The best known of all annuals is

Beeton's Christmas Annual for 1887 which featured the first Sherlock Holmes novel, 'A Study in Scarlet', and is now highly collectible. An earlier *Beeton's Christmas Annual*, for 1880, had been entitled 'The Fortunate Island' and had included several stories within a frame device of an idyllic island where the tranquillity is spoiled by British visitors. Most of these sub-stories are science fiction or fantasy, particularly Henry Frith's 'What It Must Come To' which features a series of inventions four centuries hence. However, that volume also included some non-fantasies.

Pears' Annual for Christmas 1919, on the other hand, is based wholly on the premise of future prediction, both articles and fiction, forecasting what life would be like 'Fifty Years Hence'. It included contributions by A.A. Milne, G.K. Chesterton, W.L. George, F. Britten Austin and Mary Cholmondeley. As pointed out by book-dealer George W. Locke, who rediscovered this item, it has some grounds for being regarded as the first genuine British sf magazine, borderline though it is.[7]

The real developments towards science-fiction magazines were not happening in Britain but in the United States, where 1919 was also an important year. But before crossing the Atlantic let us just consider developments elsewhere in Europe.

As we have already seen, the work of Jules Verne had a significant impact on the development of science fiction. His work was readily available throughout Europe as was much British and American fiction in translation. All European countries had their magazines, some more colourful and adventurous than in Britain, but because there was only limited translation of stories from European countries into Britain, the full impact of European sf has yet to be fully explored, despite much original research by Sam Lundwall, Darko Suvin and Franz Rottensteiner.

Science fiction was perhaps most deeply rooted in Germany, going back as far as Johannes Kepler whose dream-trip to the Moon, *Somnium*, appeared in 1634. It was in Germany that the early museums developed, called the Cabinet of Curiosities in English but known by the Germans most evocatively as the *Wunderkammer*, or Chamber of Wonders. The concept of a room full of curiosities easily lent itself to the book or magazine form. Eberhard Happel, a German novelist and miscellaneous writer, who lived in Hamburg in the late seventeenth century, was himself a collector of literary

7. George W. Locke, *A Spectrum of Fantasy* (London: Ferret Fantasy, 1980), p. 4.

curiosities and was noted for his extravagant and greatly embel-lished stories. Starting in 1682 Happel began to compile *Grösseste Denkwürdigkeiten der Welt oder so-genannte Relationes Curiosæ* or *The Things of Greatest Consideration in the World or the so-called Curious Tales.* This was a compendium of scientific and fantastic facts as well as fairy tales and extravagant stories. It was issued as a weekly part-work, a common practice throughout Europe at that time, and thus was technically a magazine, though it is arguably as much an anthology or even encyclopædia.[8]

The real development of sf in Germany came with the writings of Kurd Lasswitz whose novels and stories appeared at the end of the nineteenth century, most notably *Auf zwei Planeten* (1897) about the interface between human and Martian cultures. The influence of Verne made itself known through the work of Robert Kraft, who was actually marketed as the German Jules Verne and wrote a series of short adventure novels issued in the same serial format as the American 'dime novels'. Dime novels are not magazines but, because they often featured the same characters and appeared on a regular weekly or bi-weekly schedule, they are sufficiently borderline to take into account. We shall explore them more fully in the next section. One of Kraft's early series bore the serial title *Aus dem Reiche der Phantasie* (*From the Realms of the Imagination*), and ran for 10 issues in 1901. It can claim to be the first serial science-fiction series in Europe. It may also have been read by a teenage Hugo Gernsback.

The longest-running dime-novel series in Germany was *Der Luftpirat* (*The Air Pirate*) – a theme popular in the later sf magazines. It ran for a total of 165 issues between 1908 and 1911, and featured the adventures of Captain Mors, a fugitive from justice (like Verne's Captain Nemo), who used his advanced airship to fight evil. Although strongly influenced by Verne and the American dime novelists, *Der Luftpirat* (or *Kapitan Mors* as it is sometimes called) had a strong influence in Germany. It is a direct forerunner of the immensely popular *Perry Rhodan* series that we shall encounter in the 1960s. The author of *Der Luftpirat* has never been discovered, though it was probably the work of several.

A magazine rather like *Magasin d'éducation et de récréation*, but focusing more on technical developments, appeared in tsarist Russia

---

8. For more details about this publication see Ahrvid Engholm, 'A Magazine of the Fantastic from 1682', *Foundation*, 72, Spring 1998, pp. 88–93.

in 1910. This was the legendary *Mir Prikliuchenii* (*World of Adventures*). In the original volume of my history I quoted Willy Ley from the February 1963 *Galaxy*, where he referred erroneously to this magazine as first appearing in 1903, and running till at least 1923. According to Ley, 'the early issues consisted mainly of translations of Jules Verne, but with a sprinkling of Russian authors, one of whom was a lady [*sic*] specialising in interplanetary romances'.[9] According to Moskowitz: '*Mir Prikliuchenii* was an adventure magazine, like *The Argosy*, that also ran science fiction. In the twenties it sometimes had a cover illustrating a science-fiction story, but almost never more than one story or serial instalment per issue.'[10] Nevertheless this is a higher sf content than many other general magazines and shows the interest in Russia in technical developments. The publishers had contact with Hugo Gernsback in the 1920s (and possibly earlier) as the magazine reprinted fiction from Gernsback's publications. In turn, Gernsback was to use a story from *Mir Prikliuchenii* ('The Revolt of the Atoms' from the March 1927 issue) in *Amazing Stories* in April 1929. (I suspect more dedicated research would find further examples.)

Sweden has also laid claim to having the first sf magazine. *Stella* had four scattered issues between April 1886 and August 1888, reprinting short stories in translation from various European writers plus some indigenous material. Again its qualification as a magazine is limited as it bears comparison with a short anthology series. *Hugin*, which ran for 82 issues between April 1916 and December 1920, may have a slightly better claim, although it was more a technical science magazine, written single-handedly by its editor and publisher Otto Witt and espousing every possible idea of scientific advance that Witt could imagine in both fictional and factual form. It is unfortunate that Witt's work was not made available outside Scandinavia, for he would undoubtedly have had a greater impact on the history of science fiction than he did.

Perhaps the most deserving claimant to the title of the world's first fantasy magazine is the German *Der Orchideengarten* (*The Orchid Garden*), published and edited by Karl Hans Strobl in Munich. This ran for 51 issues between April 1919 and May 1921 and featured a beautiful array of artwork, together with work by a wide range of

---

9. I have never been able to find issues of this magazine, though Sam Moskowitz has told me about copies he has seen in the Library of Congress. Even if I did see them I doubt I would understand any of the contents.

10. Letter, Moskowitz to Ashley, 24 April 1975.

writers, with most of the fiction being reprinted. It contained little by way of science fiction, but much fantastic and surreal fiction which was popular in Europe at that time.

Despite all this interest in science fiction and fantastic adventure in Britain and elsewhere in Europe, the catalyst to unite this into a single publication did not happen there but in the United States. I have deliberately avoided discussing the development of magazine sf in the USA so far, but it is to that country that we must now turn.

The American Dawn

The development of magazine publishing in the United States was as tortuous as it is fascinating, but it closely resembled that in Britain, where its origins can be traced. Andrew Bradford's *American Magazine* and Benjamin Franklin's *General Magazine*, which appeared within days of each other in January 1741, were modelled closely on the *London Magazine* and *Gentleman's Magazine* respectively, though neither survived a year. Perhaps the most relevant magazine from this early period was *The Columbian*, founded by Mathew Carey in Philadelphia in 1786. It carried the first work by America's first professional writer, Charles Brockden Brown, who had an interest in scientific and psychological fiction, and it concentrated on not only general information but also scientific development.

The first detailed utopian fiction published in America was 'Equality; or a History of Lithconia', a novel clearly inspired by *Gulliver's Travels*. It was serialized in *The Temple of Reason*, a Philadelphia weekly, from 15 May to 2 July 1802, but did not appear in book form until 1837. This emphasizes the importance of knowing the original magazine publication details of stories to ensure they are set in their proper chronological and influential context.

The American short story proper began with the works of Washington Irving, especially his influential *Sketch Book of Geoffrey Crayon, Gent.* (1820) which contained the classic 'Rip Van Winkle'. Irving was heavily influenced by German writers, particularly Ernst Theodor Hoffmann whose short fiction had been appearing in German periodicals since 1809. A similar story to 'Rip Van Winkle' was 'Peter Rugg, the Missing Man' by Boston lawyer William Austin which appeared in the *New England Galaxy* for 10 September 1824.

American short fiction was soon to take a giant step forward with the appearance of two of its greatest early exponents: Nathaniel Hawthorne and Edgar Allan Poe.

Poe has every right to claim to be the father of the short science-fiction story. Although he is best remembered as a writer of horror stories, his literary genius caused him to craft his work not only in the realms of psychological and supernatural horror but also in scientific and detective fiction. His first story, which brought with it all the residue of the gothic influence, was 'Metzengerstein', published in the *Baltimore Saturday Courier* for 14 January 1832. Most of his submissions at that time, though, were rejected, until he entered a contest sponsored by the *Baltimore Saturday Visitor* which offered $50 for the best short story. Poe submitted several stories and won the first prize with 'Ms. Found in a Bottle', published in the 19 October 1833 issue of the *Visitor*. It is a powerful story of a sinking ship's encounter with a ghost ship and the two becoming trapped in an icy current pulling them towards the Antarctic and a craterous entrance into the Earth. It launched Poe's writing career. As we shall see, story competitions became a feature of Gernsback's sf magazines.

Poe soon moved to Richmond, Virginia, where he became associated with the *Southern Literary Messenger*. The June 1835 issue featured his story of a balloon flight to the Moon, 'The Unparalleled Adventures of Hans Pfaal'. Poe took over the editorship of the *Messenger* in December 1835 and his essays and stories rapidly established a reputation for himself and the magazine, the latter's circulation increasing seven-fold. He soon fell out with the proprietor, although the magazine did start serialization of Poe's most significant sf story, 'The Narrative of Arthur Gordon Pym of Nantucket' (January–February 1837). This short novel falls into the category of the fantastic voyage and strongly influenced Jules Verne whose *Le Sphinx des glaces* (*Magasin d'éducation et de récréation*, 1 January–15 December 1897; sometimes called *An Antarctic Mystery*) was his own attempt to complete the story.

For the remaining 12 years of his life, Poe became associated with most of the leading magazines of his day. He briefly edited *Graham's Lady's and Gentleman's Magazine*, which published his noted 'A Descent into the Maelstrom' (May 1841). *Godey's Lady's Book*, a highly prestigious magazine renowned for its coloured fashion plates, published his tale of mesmerism and temporal displacement, 'A Tale of the Ragged Mountains' (April 1844). His last great sf story, 'The Facts in the Case of M. Valdemar', also dealing with mesmerism and survival of the soul after death, appeared in the *American Review* for December 1845.

At this same time Nathaniel Hawthorne was contributing his tales and fables to various New York and New England magazines. His contributions to science fiction are less potent than Poe's but no less significant. Interestingly the two great writers came together in a short-lived magazine, *The Pioneer*. This only survived for three issues, between January and March 1843, but the first carried Poe's 'The Tell-Tale Heart' and the last Hawthorne's 'The Birthmark'. This serves as a reminder that even the shortest-lived magazines can feature work of lasting value.

Poe did not live long enough to see the emergence of the major American magazines, otherwise his life may have been different. The 1850s saw the appearance of *Harper's New Monthly Magazine* (1850), *Putnam's Monthly* (1853) and *Atlantic Monthly* (1857). *Harper's* became the leading American magazine, its circulation rising to over 200,000 by 1860. It later met healthy competition from *Scribner's Monthly*, which appeared in 1870, and it was these two rivals that provided George Newnes in England with the model for *The Strand Magazine*.

Harper's frequently carried the stories of Fitz-James O'Brien, including his story of mesmerism, 'The Bohemian' (July 1855), and the classic story of an invisible creature, 'What Was It?' (March 1859). It was *Atlantic Monthly*, however, that carried his most influential story, 'The Diamond Lens' (January 1858), one of the earliest tales about sub-microscopic life. *Atlantic Monthly* also carried Edward Everett Hale's short novel about Earth's first artificial satellite, 'The Brick Moon' (October–December 1869), and its sequel, 'Life in the Brick Moon' (February 1870).

These stories did much to raise the circulation of their magazines, and science fiction rapidly became entrenched in American popular fiction earlier than it did in Britain and the rest of Europe. Much of this can be attributed to the inevitable pioneering spirit of the immigrant Americans, and to the desire to strive for social bliss. But it was also due to the greater democratic and radical nature of the American free spirit which was still stifled in Europe. In America, any fiction that explored social or scientific advance was not only welcomed but encouraged. It is no surprise, therefore, that one novel about a utopian society attracted immense interest. Edward Bellamy's *Looking Backward, 2000–1887* (Ticknor, 1888) tells of an insomniac who is put under hypnosis and sleeps to the year 2000. There he encounters a socialist utopia which Bellamy describes in considerable detail. This work had an immense influence not just on science fiction – Wells's 'When the Sleeper Wakes' (*The Graphic*, 9 January–6 May 1899) being the obvious one, projecting an alternative capitalist dystopia – but also on politicians and reformists. Several communes based on Bellamy's principles were established.

The novel's significance here, though, is its influence on the magazine world. *The Overland Monthly* had been founded in San Francisco in 1868, modelled on *The Atlantic Monthly*, and had shot to overnight success with the popularity of the stories by its editor, Bret Harte. The magazine declined after Harte left in 1870 and folded in 1875. It was revived in 1883 in a rather more substantial form. The magazine responded to the success of Bellamy's *Looking Backward* with a special 'Twentieth Century Number' with its issue for June 1890. It contained a mixture of stories and articles looking forward over the next two centuries, including a reprint of Kurd Lasswitz's 'Bis zum Nullpunkt des Seins' (1871) as 'Pictures out of the Future'. This marked the first magazine issue devoted solely to the study of the future, and was 30 years ahead of the British *Pear's Annual* and any of the other European contenders.

Interestingly, this special issue of *Overland Monthly* appeared at just the same time as the first American pulp magazine began to emerge, but before we follow that strand to the birth of the science-fiction magazine, we need to pick up one other thread.

In 1860, brothers Erastus and Irwin Beadle began to issue a series of yellow-backed short novels selling for a dime (their slogan was 'a dollar book for a dime'). The term 'dime novel' soon followed. (Britain had its equivalent in the penny-dreadful.) The early successes came with novels of pioneer life, but soon they proliferated into all fields of writing, often the more sensational the better. The boom period was the 1870s, and the prominent publisher was Frank Tousey. Tousey published a regular juvenile story-paper called *The Boys of New York*, first issue dated 23 August 1875. In 1876 he commissioned Harry Enton to write a dime novel to emulate the success of Edward S. Ellis's *The Steam Man of the Prairies* (*American Novels*, 45, 1868), which had been reprinted in 1876 as *The Huge Hunter*. Enton produced 'Frank Reade and his Steam Man of the Plains', which ran in *The Boys of New York* from 28 February to 24 April 1876 and was published under the house

pseudonym of Noname. Reade is a New York teenager and mech-
anic who builds a giant man-shaped steam engine. Reade and his
cousin take the steam man out onto the Missouri plains and
encounter a string of adventures. The novel was extremely popular,
especially amongst teenage readers, and started a succession of
adventures featuring Frank Reade. These were written initially by
Enton before he and Tousey parted company.

A few other writers turned a hand before the series passed to a
young Brooklyn writer of Cuban descent, Luis Senarens. Senarens
moved on a generation with Frank Reade's son and a new selection
of pals. He started his series with 'Frank Reade Jr. and his Steam
Wonder' (*The Boys of New York*, 4 February–29 April 1882), but with
the next novel moved into the age of electricity with 'Frank Reade
Jr. and his Electric Boat' (*The Boys of New York*, 12 August–21 October
1882). Thereafter the inventions became increasingly more creative,
the adventures more daring, and the readers more excited. Senarens
later came to be christened 'the American Jules Verne' (in a tribute
in Gernsback's magazines[11]), and there is no doubt that the adventures of Frank Reade Jr. were every bit as inventive and exciting as
those of Verne's heroes. Tousey started a second series, this time
featuring Jack Wright, the Boy Inventor, again mostly written by
Senarens and based closely on the Frank Reade Jr. stories. The first,
Hunting for a Sunken Treasure, appeared in *The Boys' Star Library* for
18 July 1891.

With the success of the Frank Reade Jr. series, Frank Tousey took
a historic plunge. His gamble was a regular weekly publication
devoted entirely to 'invention' stories. Entitled *Frank Reade Library*,
its first issue appeared on 24 September 1892. Although this was
strictly a series of paperbound books, there is no denying that it was
the first regular publication of science fiction in a serial format. The
issues usually contained 32 pages of demy-octavo size (about $8\frac{1}{4}$
by $5\frac{1}{2}$ inches). The series was a mixture of new stories and reprints,
mostly the work of Luis Senarens, who by now had become the
first prolific writer of science fiction. It remained weekly until 5
February 1897 when it went bi-weekly. Its last edition appeared in
August 1898, 192 issues after the first issue was published. By then

---

11. Uncredited article in *Science and Invention*, 8 (6), September 1920. The article may have
    been by Gernsback himself or one of his editors, but may also have been by Charles I.
    Horne who had been editing a complete set of the works of Jules Verne and had
    contributed an article, 'Jules Verne, the World's Greatest Prophet', to the August 1920
    issue of *Science and Invention*.

there was increasing hostility by parents to the quality of fiction in dime novels and to the extent to which they were harming their children's education.

Nevertheless there was one final episode in this chapter. In 1902 Sinclair Tousey carried out his father's wishes to reprint the Frank Reade Jr. series in magazine form. Starting with the issue of 31 October 1902, Tousey began the *Frank Reade Weekly Magazine*. It ran until 26 August 1904, and was all reprint, but it was a genuine magazine composed of invention stories. The Frank Reade stories, therefore, can lay claim to giving birth not only to the first regular sf series, but also the first regular sf *reprint* series!

Although the dime novel was entering its decline, it would still survive until the First World War. At that point it gave way to the immense popularity of the pulp magazine which began to emerge in the 1890s.

The Birth of the Pulps

The forerunner of the pulp magazine was technically *Munsey's Magazine* not *The Argosy*. Frank Andrew Munsey, of Mercer, Maine, had moved to New York in 1882 where he began publication of a children's weekly story-paper, *The Golden Argosy*, first issue dated 9 December 1882. The magazine was profitable but Munsey's interest in the children's market, then dominated by *St Nicholas Magazine*, waned. He decided to shift towards an adult audience, and his first move was to disassociate *The Golden Argosy* from the 'golden' name, shortening its title to *The Argosy* from 1 December 1888.[12] It continued to run juvenile stories for some time, however. Munsey then created *Munsey's Magazine* in February 1889 to test the adult market. *Munsey's* was a high-quality magazine modelled on *Scribner's*. It tended to feature society stories with very little fantasy or science fiction, and though initially printed on high-quality paper this became lower-grade book paper in later years. The magazine sold well and Munsey then upgraded its partner. In April 1894 *The Argosy* shifted to a monthly schedule, and in 1896 Munsey began to

---

12. The word 'golden' was used increasingly in children's papers of the 1880s since it seemed evocative to parents of some kind of golden age. The model for Munsey was almost certainly *Golden Days*, which had been published by James Elverson in Philadelphia since 6 March 1880. *Golden Hours* would start in January 1888 and in November 1889 *Young Men of America* would be retitled *Golden Weekly*.

print it on the lower-quality wood-pulp based paper used on his newspaper, the *Daily Continent*. Technically *The Argosy* became the first adult *adventure* pulp magazine with its issue dated December 1896. It was the standard pulp size (7 by 10 inches) and carried a range of short stories, serials and features. That first pulp issue carried only one sf story, 'Citizen 504' by Charles H. Palmer which had first appeared in *Munsey's Magazine* for December 1892. Written in the wake of interest in Bellamist futures, it was a dystopia about a regimented society in the twenty-third century.

Science fiction did not feature strongly in *The Argosy* at this time, though each year would see half a dozen or so stories and serials. These were by authors now mostly forgotten, although Tudor Jenks and Frank Aubrey became regulars, and there were some lost-race adventures by W. Bert Foster and Jared L. Fuller. Most of the stories still betrayed a juvenile dime novel background, but the occasional more adult story appeared, such as Harle Oren Cummins's 'Martin Bradley's Space Annihilator' (which despite the cosmic-sounding title is actually about radio) and James B. Nevin's 'The Whereabouts of Mr Moses Bailey', about invisibility. Both of these appeared in the September 1901 issue.

It is rather ironic that scientific fiction, which experienced such a burst of development in Britain, remained relatively stagnant in America in the 1890s, even though the seeds for its future were slowly taking root. It is worth pausing in the development of the Munsey story to consider two other magazines, often listed in bibliographies of science fiction, which require some brief coverage here, if only to dispel the belief that they were magazines of science fiction or fantasy. These are *The Black Cat* and *The Clack Book*.

The Black Cat first appeared in October 1895 in the same format as the dime novels (and the new nickel weeklies) selling for five cents. It did not convert to pulp format until 1913. Its title may suggest a magazine of weird fiction, but that was far from the truth, though it was certainly idiosyncratic. Its publisher, Herman Umbstaetter, had set out to establish a magazine of unusual stories, in which the writers would strive for originality and the unique. In that sense it was a spiritual ancestor to *Weird Tales*. Over the years it has earned a legendary status for publishing stories of the weird and gruesome even though the publisher said, in one of his policy statements, 'While writers may choose their own themes we especially desire stories in the handling of which the morbid, unnatural and unpleasant are avoided rather than emphasised.' This meant that by and large horror stories were out, although in their ingenuity writers created many stories of illusion, madness and the bizarre. The most famous of these was 'The Mysterious Card' by Cleveland Moffett (February 1896) which set a trend for baffling stories with no rational solution (and usually best left that way). One such borderline-sf story is 'A Hundred Thousand Dollar Trance' (May 1896) by Eugene Shade Bisbee in which a hypnotist demonstrates how he can age a man through suggestion. The reader is left with the dilemma of whether the man really aged or whether all the members of the audience were under hypnosis.

The tally of full-blown sf stories in *The Black Cat* is limited, falling far short of the number in the later Munsey magazines. Perhaps the best known is Jack London's first sale, 'A Thousand Deaths' (May 1899), in which a scientist succeeds in reviving a dead body many times over. Others are mostly invention stories such as 'The Caves of Fire' by Burt Leaston Taylor and Edward Ward (May 1898) about a powerful microscope which reveals the subatomic world; 'Under-water House' by Frank Bailey Millard (March 1899), which includes the invention of the television; 'The Horn of Marcus Brunder' by Howard Reynolds (June 1899) about a machine to nullify sound; and 'Ely's Automatic Housemaid' by Elizabeth Bellamy (December 1899), a humorous story about robots.

A number of tales are slightly more adventurous. They include 'My Invisible Friend' by Katherine Kip (February 1897), which is very derivative of Wells's *The Invisible Man*, and the more creative 'A Human Chameleon' by Newton Newkirk (October 1900) with its protagonist's ability to blend into his surroundings, which is a taster for the later super-hero stories of the thirties. 'The Transposition of Stomachs' by Charles E. Mixer (April 1900) is an early story about organ transplants, whilst 'In an Unknown World' by John Durworth (November 1900) is a clever story in which the auditory and optical senses are switched.

Most of the writers were transitory. Two of the more regular contributors of imaginative stories were Don Mark Lemon and Frank Lillie Pollock, both of whom contributed sf to later pulps. Lemon's unusual stories started with 'Doctor Goldman' (December 1900), in which tissue transplanted from a dead man transfers his memories to the recipient. 'A Bride in Ultimate' (May 1903) is about a woman who, when struck by lightning, finds herself trapped in a diamond crystal. 'The House that Jill Built' (March 1907) is an amusing satire on the perils of living with an inventor.

'The Mansion of Forgetfulness' (April 1907) is about a ray that can eradicate memory cells. Lemon's ideas were always imaginative, and we shall encounter him again in the Gernsback magazines.

Pollock had contributed imaginative stories to *The Black Cat* since 1901, starting with the surprising 'The Invisible City' (September 1901) about a scientist/hypnotist who is able to establish a city which he succeeds in disguising from the world as the hypnotic illusion of a lake. Pollock was intrigued by the idea of vibrations, a theme which emerged strongly in later sf. In 'The Skyscraper in B Flat' (June 1904) he explores the way in which certain vibrations will establish a resonance that is highly destructive. He would also write one of the best early stories for *The Argosy*, the Wellsian end-of-the-world short story 'Finis' (June 1906).

After Umbstaetter's death *The Black Cat* published hardly any scientific stories. The last of note was 'John Jones's Dollar' by Harry Stephen Keeler (August 1915). Set in the year 3221 it considers many wonders of the future, including teaching by television, though its main plot revolves around the accumulation of interest in a bank account that has passed down the generations and is now enough to buy the solar system. This story was later reprinted by Hugo Gernsback in *Amazing*.

A final note of interest with regard to *The Black Cat* is that it published two early oriental stories by Clark Ashton Smith – 'The Mahout' (August 1911) and 'The Raja and the Tiger' (February 1912) – 15 years before he began to build his reputation in *Weird Tales*. *The Black Cat* itself continued until October 1920. It had a short-lived revival in 1922, and was even resurrected as a fantasy reprint magazine in 1970 by George Henderson of Memory Lane Publications in Toronto, Canada, but financial problems stopped this final incarnation lasting more than one issue. This *Black Cat* therefore scarcely had three lives.

The Clack Book was something else entirely. It was a small literary magazine modelled to some extent on the British *Yellow Book* and specializing in bohemian poetry and fiction. Its first issue, dated April 1896, was under the editorship of Frank G. Wells, and was in chapbook form, running to only 26 pages with a mixture of poetry and short prose, mostly anonymous. The magazine attracted some of the leading artists and poets of the day, amongst them Edgar Fawcett and Elia Wilkinson Peattie. It published a number of short fantasies and weird stories, including 'Giles Furness, Ghoul' by Gardner Teall (August 1896), 'In the Cave of Dreams' by Percival

Pollard (September 1896) and 'The Expiation of Scrooge' by John Kendrick Bangs (December 1896), but it carried no genuine science fiction. It folded with its twelfth issue, dated June 1897.

At the end of the nineteenth century science fiction had still not taken hold in the pulps, though it remained evident in the leading popular 'slick' magazines, mostly because of the American serialization of the novels by H.G. Wells. *Harper's Monthly*, for instance, ran 'The Great Stone of Sardis' by Frank R. Stockton (June–November 1897). Set 50 years in the future, the story includes a wealth of inventions and discoveries including the first submarine voyage to the North Pole and a journey inside the Earth to discover that the centre of the planet is a massive diamond. A more scientific journey through the Earth is experienced in 'Through the Earth' by Clement Fezandié (*St Nicholas Magazine*, January–April 1898). Fezandié was a teacher and popular writer who later became Gernsback's first leading sf author. One of the writers who kept his science fiction relatively light-hearted was Robert W. Chambers, the renowned author of *The King in Yellow* (Neely, 1895). His later book *In Search of the Unknown* (Harper, 1904) concerned a zoologist's exploration for rare creatures. Some of the stories included were sf and many had made earlier magazine appearances, including 'A Matter of Interest' (*Cosmopolitan*, June–July 1897) about the resurrection of a dinosaur and 'The Harbor-Master' (*Ainslee's Magazine*, August 1899), featuring a merman.

By the turn of the century, however, apart from the inevitable invention story, science fiction appeared less frequently in the slick magazines and became more the territory of the pulps. By 1902 almost every issue of *The Argosy* carried a story of some scientific or fantastic development. Two distinct fields had emerged: stories that explored the idea of a new invention, and those that were an extension of the dime novel, featuring sensationalistic fantastic adventures.

In the first category are the humorous stories by Edgar Franklin about an eccentric inventor, Mr Hawkins. Humorous invention stories would become a feature of the early Gernsback magazines, and they were common in many magazines in the first years of the twentieth century, indicative of the growing fascination with technology. The series began with 'The Hawkins Horse-Brake' (May 1903) and ran through to 'Hawkins-Heat' (July 1915). Similar to these are the biological creations of Professor Jonkin in the stories by Howard R. Garis. The first was 'Professor Jonkin's Cannibal Plant' (August 1905).

The second category is best exemplified by the work of William Wallace Cook, a prolific and experienced dime novelist, noted for his imagination. His first sf in *The Argosy* was the serial 'A Round Trip to the Year 2000' (July–November 1903), combining time travel with a future travelogue, a catalogue of adventures and some fairly blunt satire. Cook had five sf novels serialized in *The Argosy* including the interplanetary adventure 'Adrift in the Unknown' (December 1904–April 1905). All of these bore the trademark of the dime novel with simple characterisation and fast-action adventure, but had a veneer of sophistication in setting the stories in a social and political context.

Science fiction received a boost when Munsey started a new magazine called *All-Story* in January 1905. It was here, under the strong editorial guidance of Robert H. Davis, that pulp science fiction began to develop. One of the earliest significant events was the reprinting of Garrett P. Serviss's short novel 'The Moon Metal' in the May 1905 issue. Serviss was a journalist but also a writer and lecturer on popular science – almost the forerunner of Isaac Asimov. While working as a reporter on the *New York Evening Journal* Serviss was commissioned to write a sequel to Wells's *The War of the Worlds*, of which an American adaptation was running in the *Evening Journal* to tremendous acclaim. Serviss used Wells's novel as a base only for his own 'Edison's Conquest of Mars' (*Evening Journal*, 12 January–10 February 1898), in which Thomas Alva Edison is able to develop an antigravity device and build an armada which defeats the Martians.

This story was extremely popular in its day and it is worth noting the hero-status that Thomas Edison achieved. The inventor was revolutionizing American technology. Ever since he had established the first industrial research laboratory at Menlo Park, New Jersey (known colloquially as the 'invention factory'), he had become a legend in America. Edison more than anyone before or since inspired Americans to explore the wonders and possibilities of technology, and it was he who provided the boost to the many invention stories that proliferated in the magazines at the turn of the century. He was also the direct inspiration for Hugo Gernsback, as we shall shortly see.

Serviss's 'The Moon Metal' is the story of the discovery of a new metal, artemisium, which is brought to Earth from the Moon by matter transmitter and replaces gold as the financial standard. Serviss would soon become a regular contributor to the Munsey magazines and his stories were extremely popular. In 'A Columbus of Space' (*All-Story*, January–June 1909), his inventor hero, Edmund Stonewall, discovers the secret of atomic energy and uses it to power a spaceship in which he and his friends explore Venus. The novel still has overtones of the dime-novel, but it was right for the time and was very popular. Even before it had finished, Serviss had another serial in *The Scrap Book*, a new Munsey magazine. 'The Sky Pirate' (April–September 1909) is a Vernian-like adventure story about a master criminal and his magnificent air-yacht, the *Chameleon*. Perhaps Serviss's best story, and in later years one of his best remembered, is 'The Second Deluge', serialized in *The Cavalier*, another Munsey pulp, from July 1911 to January 1912. Earth enters a spiral nebula and is subject to a second global flood. This had been foreseen by scientist Cosmo Versal, whom few believed, and he creates his ark from a new metal, and saves a few thousand believers and animals.

Between 1905 and 1911, *All-Story* published over 60 stories of scientific or fantastic extrapolation. *The Argosy* published another 50, *The Cavalier* published 40, and there were a dozen more in *The Scrap Book*, making over 150 in the Munsey magazines alone. A number of regular writers appeared, but the most important was George Allan England, a prolific writer of a wide range of stories, who brought much creativity to his science fiction. This began with 'The Time Reflector' in the non-Munsey *Monthly Story Magazine* (September 1905), and included 'My Time Annihilator' (*All-Story*, June 1909), which uses the same gimmick as in Verne's *Around the World in Eighty Days*, the bizarre 'The House of Transmutation' (*The Scrap Book*, September–November 1909), which considers advances in plastic surgery, 'He of the Glass Heart' (*The Scrap Book*, May 1911) about an artificial heart, and the remarkable 'The Elixir of Hate' (*The Cavalier*, August–November 1911) about an elixir of life that reverses growth and causes the taker to grow younger.

And so we come to 1911, the year Gernsback cited as the genesis of *Amazing Stories*. As I have demonstrated, though, by then science fiction had become a major part of the content of popular magazines and many of the features and story-lines that Gernsback would develop had already been explored by the growing generation of writers fascinated with the possibilities of science.

Enter Gernsback

Hugo Gernsback was born in Luxembourg City on 16 August 1884. At a very early age he became fascinated in the power of electricity, particularly in the development of the battery. He also took a delight in science fiction which, as we have seen, was strongly in evidence in Europe at that time. Gernsback's father worked in the wine business which did not interest young Hugo and, following his father's death, Gernsback emigrated to the United States which he believed was the land of scientific opportunity, as was being ably demonstrated by Edison and his rival Nikola Tesla. Tesla was born in Croatia of Serbian descent and had emigrated to the States in 1884, for a while working for Edison. The two, however, fell out and thus started the rivalry that inspired scientific research for the next 20 years.

It was to this creative culture that Gernsback emigrated in 1904 to establish his dry-cell battery business. He met with mixed success, but Gernsback had an 'easy-come easy-go' attitude to life and moved without concern from one problem to the next triumph. Before arriving in New York he had been working on a small portable radio transmitter and receiver but it was taking some time to perfect and make marketable. Once in New York, he found that many of the radio parts were not available so he established The Electro Importing Company (called Telimco from the company's initials) to import and distribute scientific equipment from Europe, especially Germany. Gernsback completed his portable radio set and wrote about it in the *Scientific American* as 'The New Inter-rupter' (29 July 1905) with the by-line 'Huck' Gernsback. This was Gernsback's first appearance in print, a few weeks short of his twenty-first birthday. Gernsback's promotion of his radio-set caused some scepticism and he was charged to prove that the radio worked, which he did with no problem. Nevertheless he was astonished at the general ignorance of technology amongst the American public: 'It rankled me that there could be such ignorance in regard to science and I vowed to change the situation if I could. A few years later, in 1908, I turned publisher and brought out the world's first radio magazine, *Modern Electrics*, to teach the young generation science, radio and what was ahead for them.'[13]

13. Hugo Gernsback, '50 Years Hence', speech delivered before the joint meeting of the Michigan Institute of Radio Engineers and the American Radio Relay League at the Henry Ford Auditorium, Dearborn, Michigan, 5 April 1957.

Modern Electrics appeared in April 1908 and was an immediate success, its first issue of 8,000 copies selling out. The circulation rose rapidly over the next few years. It was evident from the start that Gernsback was aiming the magazine at the young experimenter or hobbyist. The bulk of the contents comprised details about new developments, particularly in radio, but Gernsback soon began to provide speculative articles, starting with 'Harnessing the Ocean' (December 1908). In the same issue he began a column to stimulate interest in more imaginative areas of science, though it was written in a humorous style so as to avoid scepticism. The first considered 'Wireless on Saturn', showing that Gernsback was already keen to take his readers' interests beyond earthly boundaries.

Perhaps the most significant of Gernsback's early articles appeared in the December 1909 issue: 'Television and the Telephot'. Gernsback explained in simple terms the principle of television and put forward his own contribution on how television might be realized. He called his own technique the 'light-relay', but he considered the device 'too complicated for general use', so he did not patent it. This method, though, was more akin to the way television works now than the scanning-disc system which John Logie Baird promoted and which caused him to be recognized as the inventor of television.

Gernsback also established the Wireless Association of America in January 1909, and *Modern Electrics* became its official magazine. It demonstrates Gernsback's desire to promote and organize people, and he would repeat this 25 years later when he founded the Science Fiction League.

Of greatest significance, however, is the April 1911 issue of *Modern Electronics*. This carried the first instalment of Gernsback's serial 'Ralph 124C 41+'. The series is only loosely a novel, though it clearly developed as Gernsback became more creative. Essentially it was a forum to explore a catalogue of inventions through the character of Ralph, one of ten great superminds in the year 2660. The story continued through 12 instalments to the March 1912 issue. By this time we have had a travelogue of New York and seen many of Ralph's inventions. These include a 'hypnobioscope', a machine which transmits impulses to the brain whilst the person sleeps. Gernsback later patented this invention as a 'learn-while-you-sleep' process, but in the story the machine may be seen as a precursor of modern-day virtual-reality technology, since Ralph is able to experience a film-tape of Homer's *Odyssey* in his dreams.

The most remarkable element in 'Ralph' was Gernsback's pre-diction of radar. It occurred in the issue for December 1911, in which Ralph's spaceflyer is pursuing Martians who have kidnapped Alice, Ralph's fiancée. Not only does Gernsback describe its opera-tion in detail, he provides a diagram which shows accurately how it would work. The word 'radar' did not come into existence until 1935 when Robert Watson-Watt perfected the method of tracking an airplane by the reflection of short-waves. Watson-Watt was knighted for his invention of radar and no credit passed to Gerns-back. When Gernsback's prediction was later shown to Watson-Watt he was astonished and thereafter maintained that Gernsback was the real inventor.

It is important to note that in his introduction to the story Gernsback emphasizes that 'while there may be extremely strange and improbable devices and scenes in this narrative, they are not at all impossible or outside the reach of science'. Gernsback always believed that any scientific extrapolation in his stories had to be possible, otherwise it was relegated to the realms of fantasy. In later years he let this premise slip, but in these early days he was strict. As a result his readers became subject to a succession of 'invention' stories which at the time may have seemed remarkable but are now extremely pedestrian.

The reception accorded to the serial by the readers caused Gerns-back to encourage others to contribute similar stories. The first was by Jacque Morgan, who had already contributed several articles to the magazine. He began his 'Scientific Adventures of Mr Fosdick' with 'The Feline Light and Power Company is Organized' (October 1912). The series explored a variety of humorous inventions just like Edgar Franklin's Hawkins' stories in *The Argosy*, though with far less literary skill.

Shortly after this Gernsback sold his share of *Modern Electrics* to his new business partner, Orland Ridenour. Gernsback's last issue was that for March 1913, though the magazine continued as *Modern Electrics and Mechanics* for two years before merging with *Popular Science Monthly* in April 1915.

Gernsback started over again with a new magazine, *The Electrical Experimenter*. The format allowed for greater development of photo-graphs and illustrative material and was all round a more stimu-lating magazine. Aimed even more directly at the young hobbyist Gernsback went all out to encourage and stimulate interest in scientific advance. This initially took the form of speculative articles but before long fiction started to appear. The first piece came about as a consequence of a competition on how to accomplish new things with old apparatus. Story contests became a feature of Gernsback's magazines as we shall see. The first prize of $5 went to Thomas W. Benson for a piece about how to set up a range of electrical equipment to play a trick on his sister's boyfriend. It was written in fictional form under the title 'Mysterious Night' and appeared in the June 1914 issue. It introduced a character who became a regular feature in *The Electrical Experimenter*, the Wireless Wiz. The stories are barely definable as science fiction, being scientific instruction in narrative form, but clearly demonstrate the direction that Gernsback was seeking to take.

He added impetus to this with a series of his own stories, 'Baron Munchhausen's Scientific Adventures', starting in May 1915. Through the miracle of wireless the narrator contacts Munchhausen on Mars. In each succeeding episode (which ran intermittently to February 1917), Munchhausen describes his own adventures starting with his suspended animation from the eighteenth century, his work in World War I, his journey to the Moon, and the many wonders of Mars.

Gernsback rallied his readers to write their own stories and speculative articles in a powerful editorial, 'Imagination versus Facts' (April 1916). It was in this editorial that he acknowledged the inspiration of Edison, remarking:

> No real electrical experimenter, worthy of the name, will ever amount to much if he has no imagination. He must be visionary to a certain extent, he must be able to look into the future and if he wants fame he must anticipate the human wants. It was precisely this quality which made Edison – a master of imagination – famous.

The first to respond to Gernsback's challenge was George F. Stratton, an engineer and writer of boys' adventures. His stories, which featured the millionaire entrepreneur Ned Cawthorne, were on the same level as the dime novel, but were ideal for Gernsback's purpose. In 'Omegon' (September 1915), Cawthorne invests his money and trust in a young inventor who has plans to develop a submarine that will disable ships with no loss of life. The war theme remained throughout the series, of which the most striking instalment is 'The Poniatowski Ray' (January 1916) with its description of something remarkably akin to laser.

The war was a powerful incentive to seek scientific supremacy over the enemy. Gernsback delighted in quoting the American Secretary of War who had said that 'one scientist very probably may do more for the United States than any admiral or general ...'. Despite censorship Gernsback encouraged speculative articles in his magazine. These include 'Warfare of the Future' (November 1915), an anonymous illustrative feature probably written by Gernsback, and 'The Mystery of Gravitation' (May 1916) by H. Winfield Secor, which inspired a super-scientific cover by Vincent Lynch depicting an antigravitation ray lifting a battleship out of the sea. The idea of new warfare devices continued in two stories by Charles Magee Adams, 'Eddy Currents' (May 1917), and 'The Radio Bomb' (August 1917), but by then censorship had taken hold and scientific speculation was muffled.

Censorship in fact allowed sf in *The Electrical Experimenter* to move ahead. 'At War with the Invisible' by R. and C. Winthrop (March–April 1918) substituted Mars for Germany and envisaged a war between the alliance of Mercury, Venus, Earth and Jupiter, and the Red Planet. The Martians have no compunction against destroying whole cities but their method of invasion, through invisibility, is discovered and they are routed. 'At War with the Invisible' is not very well written but it includes a fascinating series of scientific concepts, such as portable telephones and private planes. This was the most advanced piece of genuine science fiction yet published in Gernsback's magazines. It was also the first piece of fiction to be illustrated by Frank R. Paul. Paul had been working for Gernsback since 1914 utilizing his technical skills, but his imaginative vision was never fully exploited in *The Electrical Experimenter* and did not emerge until *Amazing Stories*.

After the war *The Electrical Experimenter* began to expand its features to cover all aspects of science and it moved away from the hobbyist. This change resulted in the magazine being retitled *Science and Invention* with effect from the August 1920 issue and this allowed Gernsback a much wider scope. For radio enthusiasts he established a separate magazine, *Radio Amateur News*, started in July 1919 and soon retitled *Radio News*. This magazine featured a regular series of radio stories but most are only of marginal science-fiction interest, being more along the lines of Benson's Wireless Wiz stories.

Science and Invention, however, strove for a bolder speculative content. Its covers, mostly now in the hands of Howard V. Brown, became bolder and more adventurous. The first retitled issue carried a feature on Jules Verne, and a later issue looked at the prophecies of Luis Senarens. The stories moved slightly beyond the basic invention mould, although Gernsback's desire that the stories should all be rooted in solid science meant that the opportunity for major imaginative leaps was limited. A few strove for originality. Both 'The Golden Vapor' by E.H. Johnson (February 1920) and 'The Transformation of Professor Schmitz' by George R. Wells (September 1921) gave original twists to the concept of matter transmission. 'The Deflecting Wave' by Herbert L. Moulton (June 1921) sought to breathe life into the already antiquated idea of air piracy.

However, the real giant of *Science and Invention* was Clement Fezandié. Fezandié first appeared in the July 1920 issue of *The Electrical Experimenter* with 'My Message to Mars'. This was an ideal Gernsback story, or rather lecture in the theory of interplanetary communication. The approach was typical of all Fezandié's stories. His regular contributions began in the May 1921 *Science and Invention* with the first of his long-running series of 'Doctor Hackensaw's Secrets'. Like 'My Message to Mars', the episodes hardly qualify as stories, being more a series of discourses, just as you might imagine Fezandié lecturing. In the first, 'The Secret of Artificial Reproduction', Dr Hackensaw is visited by Silas Rockett, a newspaper reporter, for an interview about his latest discovery. Hackensaw proceeds to tell the reporter all the known facts about artificial reproduction, the processes of artificial insemination and genetic engineering, and then unveils some of his marvels, such as a half-dog/half-cat, perfect trick ponies, and a baby girl incubated inside the womb of a cow. The story concentrates solely on the possibilities generated by Hackensaw's inventions with total disregard for the human or humane consequences. The emphasis is on scientific advance, initially for profit, and secondarily for the various industrial or social advantages that might arise.

The series continued in the same vein for the next four years, with Hackensaw lecturing on suspended animation (October 1921), invisibility (May 1922), robots (June 1922), television (October 1922) and the secret of life (July 1922). Seldom was there any action, although, in a three-part sub-series, Hackensaw takes a trip to the moon (September–November 1923). There were also trips in time, to the year 2025 (December 1922) and then 3000 (January 1925), a journey 'Around the World in Eighty Hours' (June 1924), and into sub-microscopic worlds (October 1924). There were 40 stories in the series in *Science and Invention*, culminating in the only real adventure Hackensaw has, a four-part serial entitled 'Journey to the Center of the Earth' (June–September 1925).

Writing in 1961, Gernsback called Fezandié a 'titan of science fiction'.[14] That is hard to grasp by today's definition of science fiction, but we have to remember that Gernsback was talking about his own definition. These stories more than any others in *Science and Invention* epitomized Gernsback's model for scientific fiction. They extrapolated from existing known science to suggest future inventions and what they might achieve; and all for the sole purpose of stimulating the ordinary person with a penchant for experimenting with gadgets, into creating that future.

Once in a while Gernsback did like to over-stimulate, to really pump the imagination. Perhaps his own best example was an article in the February 1922 *Science and Invention*, '10,000 Years Hence'. Howard Brown provided a stunning illustration of floating health cities (like huge health farms) kept aloft in the upper atmosphere by power rays drawing their energy from the sun. Gernsback described how these cities could be directed to move around the Earth, a concept one might believe inspired two later noted works of science fiction, Edmond Hamilton's 'Cities in the Air' (1929) and James Blish's *Earthman, Come Home* (1955), were it not that neither author knew of the article. Gernsback also postulated how individuals would have personal power packs enabling them to jet through the atmosphere, propelled by power rays derived from electro-energy converted from static energy in the atmosphere.

Gernsback posed these more dramatic concepts clearly in the hope of inspiring writers to take that one extra leap of the imagination. Where his own writers could not provide the material, he chose to reprint stories by H.G. Wells. 'The New Accelerator' *(Science and Invention*, February 1923) is a straightforward invention story telling of a drug that speeds up the taker's metabolism so that to his perception time slows down. 'The Star' (March 1923) is on a more cosmic scale, as Earth is threatened by an errant star but is saved when the star is eclipsed by our own Moon. Whilst most of Gernsback's writers could have attempted something along the lines of 'The New Accelerator', although with moderately less success, a story such as 'The Star' would not have entered their minds, because it was not a gadget story. It was a story of cosmic consequences.

14. Hugo Gernsback, 'Guest Editorial', *Amazing Stories*, 35 (4) April 1961, p. 7.

Gernsback's use of these two stories and his own highly speculative articles suggest that he was trying to achieve more in *Science and Invention* than simply inspiring readers to create new inventions, although that was (and to a large extent always remained) his basic premise. He can only have been using them to provoke a response from readers as to their own feelings on having such stories in their magazine. He was probably already seriously considering the possibility of issuing a separate scientific-fiction magazine, but needed to know reader reaction and writer response. Further activities that year were also having an effect, which would make 1923 a significant year in the evolution of science fiction.

The Pulp Perspective

In the years between 1911 and 1923 we have seen how Gernsback had sought to develop scientific speculation in his magazines. No matter how he strove, it is evident that Gernsback's imagination was always more creative than his contributors' who, by and large, felt themselves bound by scientific convention. This was not helped by Gernsback's strict requirement for scientific accuracy. The result was fiction that might stimulate invention but held little enter-tainment value. This was a dilemma that Gernsback was forced to face in later years, because his rivals on the news-stands were the bright and bold pulp magazines that were equally able in stimu-lating the imagination but held little regard for scientific accuracy.

At the same time that Gernsback was serializing 'Ralph 124C 41+', Munsey's *Cavalier* had been serializing Garrett Serviss's 'The Second Deluge' and George Allan England's 'The Elixir of Hate'. By this time Serviss was 60 years old and had reached the peak of his career. But England, then just 34, was a rising star. Following 'The Elixir of Hate', *The Cavalier* began serialization of 'Darkness and Dawn' (6–27 January 1912), England's novel of a degenerate Earth in the distant future. Although now badly dated the story was im-mensely popular at the time and led to two sequels, 'Beyond the Great Oblivion' (*The Cavalier*, 4 January–8 February 1913) and 'The After Glow' (*The Cavalier*, 14 June–5 July 1913). England became one of the leading writers of scientific fiction of the period, contri-buting eight more stories and serials in the Munsey magazines during the decade, including the noted 'The Flying Legion' (*All-Story*, 15 November–20 December 1919), which took stories of air piracy and warfare to their pulp zenith.

However just as England's star was rising it was eclipsed by a more imaginative talent and the most influential writer in the field outside of Verne and Wells: Edgar Rice Burroughs.

Burroughs was only 18 months older than England, though far less experienced as a writer, but his imagination was even more creative. For his first novel, 'Under the Moons of Mars' (*All-Story*, February–July 1912), he thought the ideas were so wild that he submitted the story under the pen name of Normal Bean ('bean' being an old term for 'head' and therefore meaning he was really normal-minded), but a typesetter thought it an error and changed it to Norman Bean!

'Under the Moons of Mars' (later printed in book form as *A Princess of Mars*, McClurg, 1917) was the first of Burroughs's adventures featuring John Carter who, through an out-of-body experience, is able to travel to Mars. He finds himself in the midst of violent rivalry between the two main races of a dying Martian civilization. Due to the difference in gravity between Earth and Mars Carter has great strength and is regarded as a superman. Although the Martians are scientifically advanced their cultures are warrior-like, and due to their telepathic abilities some of their activities border on the supernatural. The Martian novels are thus early forms of what Robert E. Howard later developed into the sword-and-sorcery sub-genre of fantasy. Single-handedly Burroughs created a new form of fantastic scientific adventure, and influenced a whole generation of writers. The success of the novel demanded a sequel, 'The Gods of Mars' (*All-Story*, January–May 1913), and many more followed.

Burroughs had even greater success with his second appearance, 'Tarzan of the Apes' (*All-Story*, October 1912), which was to be more influential than his Martian novels. Tarzan must rival Sherlock Holmes and Peter Pan as the best-known character in fiction.

Burroughsian fiction would dominate pulp science fiction for the next 40 years. He created other memorable series and stories, not least the Pellucidar adventures which began with 'At the Earth's Core' (*All-Story*, 4–25 April 1914), his lost-race stories including 'The Cave Girl' (*All-Story*, July–September 1913) and those set on Caspak starting with 'The Land that Time Forgot' (*Blue Book*, August 1918). His presence created a transition in the pulps. Many of the old guard continued to contribute but their influence became less, whilst a new strain of writer developed, much more able to blend scientific concepts into thrilling adventures. In the same period that Gernsback was developing *The Electrical Experimenter* with contributions from a host of unknown and long-forgotten writers, the Munsey magazines, particularly *All-Story*, were publishing science fantasy by Victor Rousseau, Charles B. Stilson, J.U. Giesy, Perley Poore Sheehan and Philip M. Fisher, and new writers Austin Hall, Homer Eon Flint, Garret Smith, Ray Cummings and, above all, Abraham Merritt.

Merritt has to be the most influential early pulp writer after Burroughs. He first appeared with 'Through the Dragon Glass' (*All-Story*, 24 November 1917), which was followed by 'The People of the Pit' (*All-Story*, 5 January 1918), but the real impact was made with 'The Moon Pool' (*All-Story*, 22 June 1918). This and its sequel, 'The Conquest of the Moon Pool' (which started in the 15 February 1919 *All-Story*), shot Merritt to the front of the popularity ranks. The scientific content was virtually nil. The stories were written in a fantasy vein, brilliantly brought to life through Merritt's exotic and extravagant language, but there was always the hint that the strange worlds were governed by an alien science unknown to humans. Merritt's lost worlds were more fantastic than Burroughs's and between them the two had captured the public imagination. It would be ten years before the sf field started to pull away from their combined influences, and almost twenty years before their impact became regarded as old style.

Science fiction had a boom year in 1919. Over a hundred stories and serials featuring scientific or fantastic concepts would appear in the pulps, along with an abortive attempt to create a magazine devoted to fantastic fiction. This was *The Thrill Book*.

Hitherto most pulps had carried a general range of fiction and there had been limited specialization. As far back as 1906 *The Railroad Man's Magazine* had appeared, followed by *The Ocean* in 1907, but popular though these were neither had created a genre. The first major specialist magazine was *Detective Story Magazine* issued by Street & Smith on 5 October 1915. Street & Smith were, in fact, bringing the dime novel to the pulp field. This magazine was a direct development from *Nick Carter Stories* (it continued a serial started in the last issue of *Nick Carter Stories*) which was itself a direct descendant from the dime novel series *Nick Carter Library*, which began in 1891. The influence of the dime novel would remain with the pulps for many more years and would be particularly strong on the hero pulps that emerged in the 1930s.

With *Detective Story Magazine* established, other detective magazines quickly followed. *Mystery Magazine* came from Frank Tousey on 15 November 1917 under the editorship of Luis Senarens. Later would come *Detective Tales* (the elder sister to *Weird Tales*), *Flynn's* and the redoubtable *Black Mask*, all before there were any science-fiction magazines. Street & Smith decided to repeat the success of their detective transformation by converting a western dime-novel series, *New Buffalo Bill Weekly*, into *Western Story Magazine* on 5 September 1919, and the cowboy pulp was created. It is quite possible that had Street & Smith had a regular science-fiction dime-novel series it might have been converted into a science-fiction pulp, but even without that, in 1919 they began to explore the territory.

The Thrill Book was planned by editor Harold Hersey to feature stories of the 'strange, bizarre, occult, mysterious', which would have made it a precursor of *Weird Tales* and a development of the unusual story in *The Black Cat*. In the event, when the first issue appeared on 1 March 1919 in dime-novel format on a semi-monthly schedule, it had toned down that desire and it consisted primarily of adventure stories, albeit with an unusual twist. In later years Hersey himself had to admit that the magazine did not live up to its legend. Writing in his autobiography, he said:

> It seems that I enjoy a reputation as editor and publisher in the fantasy field far out of proportion to my just deserts. I failed miserably with *The Thrill Book* in 1919, a pulp that included many excellent pseudo-science yarns by Murray Leinster and others in its several issues, but which was not entirely devoted to this type of story.[15]

In fact only about a fifth of the stories in *The Thrill Book* would properly be classified as science fiction, though more than twice that are supernatural or fantastic. It may be that Hersey was unable to find sufficient good stories amongst the submissions. He was given free rein to reprint stories from the Street & Smith archives but still did not fill the magazine with stories fitting the original policy, suggesting a change in direction. The first issue is perhaps important for launching the writing career of Greye La Spina with her werewolf tale 'Wolf of the Steppes'. La Spina would go on to be a worthy contributor to *Weird Tales*. Amongst *The Thrill Book*'s more scientific offerings were 'The Man who Met Himself' by Donovan

---

15. Harold B. Hersey, *Pulpwood Editor* (New York: F.A. Stokes, 1937), p. 188.

Bayley (reprinted from the British *Red Magazine*, 1 February 1918), about a man who, following an accident, frees his inner self; 'In the Shadow of Race' by J. Hampton Bishop, a short lost-race serial set in Africa and featuring intelligent apes; and 'The Jeweled Ibis' by J.C. Kofoed, featuring a cult that worships the ancient Egyptian gods.

Probably the best remembered name from *The Thrill Book* and one of the more important writers of modern science fiction was Murray Leinster. Leinster, whose real name was William F. Jenkins, had been selling fiction and fillers to magazines such as *The Smart Set* and *Argosy* since 1915, including some fantasies, but his sf career is usually measured from 'The Runaway Skyscraper' (*Argosy*, 22 February 1919) in which the Metropolitan Tower in Manhattan is suddenly plunged back into the past. Leinster had three stories in *The Thrill Book* although only two are science fiction. 'A Thousand Degrees Below Zero' (15 July) is typical of much of Leinster's early sf. It features a scientist who has created a process (in this case freezing the Earth) and threatens to destroy all life unless he can rule the world. 'The Silver Menace' (1–15 September) is an ecological disaster novella about a new life-form that turns the sea to jelly.

By the time Leinster appeared in the magazine changes had been made. From 1 July Hersey was replaced as editor by Ronald Oliphant. As part of the continuing shift the magazine was reformatted from dime novel to pulp. The amount of fantastic fiction increased marginally. 'The Lost Empire' (15 July–1 August), a short serial by Frank Wall (possibly a pseudonym of Harold de Polo), tells of the discovery of a culture from colonial times living on a lost island in the Sargasso Sea. 'The Lost Days' by Trainor Lansing (1–15 August) is about a drug that distorts the time sense. 'The Ultimate Ingredient' by Greye La Spina (15 October) is about a mad scientist who learns how to control vibrations and thus turn the human body invisible. 'Tales of the Double Man' by Clyde Broadwell was a five-part series (15 July–15 September) about a man who discovers he shares his soul with another man half-way round the world. Probably the most important story in *The Thrill Book* was 'The Heads of Cerberus' by Francis Stevens (15 August–15 September). Set in Philadelphia in the year 2118 it is a disturbing study of a dystopian society. It is an imaginative and highly readable novel, if now somewhat dated, and is historically important as one of the first stories to suggest the possibility of alternative time tracks.

The Thrill Book survived for 16 issues, folding with the 15 October 1919 number. It featured a blend of the scientific and fantastic adventures prevalent in the Munsey magazines with the unusual and bizarre stories in *The Black Cat*. It was definitely a step towards a full-blown fantasy magazine, and in the right hands it might have established itself. It would be another 14 years before Street & Smith entered the sf world, but when they did, they did it in style.

During the period of *The Thrill Book*'s short life, Munsey's *All-Story* had published an equal amount of fantastic fiction and introduced us to a further new author who would dominate sf's early years: Ray Cummings. Cummings's debut was with 'The Girl in the Golden Atom' (15 March), the first of his many adventures into infinite smallness. Although the basic idea is derivative of O'Brien's 'The Diamond Lens', Cummings's work is more influenced by H.G. Wells. Unfortunately, each time he struck a popular vein he overmined it, with the result that he is today regarded as a one-idea hack. He was immensely prolific, as we shall see, but was also one of the most popular writers of sf during the twenties.

Austin Hall was another regular contributor with a vivid imagination whose ideas thankfully overcame his poor writing. 'Into the Infinite' (*All-Story*, 12 April–7 May 1919) builds upon his earlier novella 'The Rebel Soul' (*All-Story*, 30 June 1917), but rationalizes the supernatural content by considering the accelerated evolution of a future superman conditioned to hate. It is a remarkable story even by today's standards. Hall also wrote 'The Man who Saved the Earth' (*All-Story*, 13 December 1919), wherein the dying Martian civilization seeks to drain the Earth of its resources.

Austin Hall's occasional collaborator was Homer Eon Flint whom *All-Story*'s editor, Bob Davis, regarded as one of the most talented of his sf contributors. Flint had been a movie scenarist before turning to the pulps. His first sf had been 'The Planeteer' (*All-Story*, 9 March 1918), a remarkable work of interplanetary and future fiction which includes Saturn being converted into a second sun. Flint developed his concepts of interplanetary societies in a series featuring Dr Kinney, a scientist who, with his colleagues, sets out to explore outer space. 'The Lord of Death' (*All-Story*, 10 May 1919) studied society on Mercury whilst 'The Queen of Life' (*All-Story*, 16 August 1919) ventured to Venus. Flint had a good grasp of social concepts and endeavoured to create more than cardboard characters. He later wrote two more Dr Kinney adventures, 'The Devolutionist' (*Argosy/All-Story*, 23 July 1921) and 'The Emancipatrix' (*Argosy/All-Story*, 3 September 1921), which explored the Capellan and Arcturan systems.

With all of this wealth of talent it may seem surprising that no one took the initiative by 1920 to launch a science-fiction magazine, but in fact the stories we have been surveying, whilst popular, were still only a small proportion of the type of fiction being published. In 1920 the detective and western stories dominated the field.

The detective field attracted the interests of the Rural Publishing Corporation of Chicago, headed by Jacob C. Henneberger, then publishing *College Humor* and *Magazine of Fun*. With the issue dated 1 October 1922 Henneberger launched a large-size pulp called *Detective Tales* on a semi-monthly schedule. It was edited by Edwin Baird and featured the work mostly of local writers, of whom Vincent Starrett, Frederick C. Davis, Henry Leverage and Harold Ward are perhaps the best known. It was undistinguished and had a rocky start, almost folding after its fourth issue. Henneberger needed to do some refinancing and as part of the deal arranged to issue a companion magazine to help share the overheads. Henneberger was a fan of the work of Edgar Allan Poe and decided on a magazine focusing on horror stories. Thus *Weird Tales* was born.

Weird Tales became not so much a magazine as an institution, but it had an inauspicious start. Its first issue, dated March 1923, contained a mixture of horror and ghost stories with few items of significance. The cover story was 'Ooze' by Anthony M. Rud which deals with the creation of a giant amoeba that gets out of hand. Its creator is also described as a writer of pseudo-scientific stories which shows the extent to which the field was becoming recognized by 1923. The issue also saw the debut of Otis Adelbert Kline with a short serial, 'The Thing of a Thousand Shapes'.

Weird Tales was the first magazine to be devoted entirely to fantasy and occult fiction. The time seemed to have arrived for such a magazine but in fact Henneberger found it difficult to attract either the writers or the readers he wanted. He experimented with the magazine's format, switching to the large pulp size, but there was no denying that the magazine remained drab and uninspiring and its covers unattractive. Part of the problem was that Edwin Baird's heart was not in the magazine. He was a specialist in crime and mystery stories and held the supernatural field in low regard. He picked a few of the more creative writers from the Munsey magazines, though almost certainly with stories previously rejected. Francis Stevens, for instance, was present with a short serial, 'Sunfire' (July/August–September 1923), a somewhat Merrittesque story set amongst a lost civilization in Brazil. Austin Hall presented 'People of the Comet' (September–October 1923) with its discovery of survivors from a long-dead polar civilization.

Nevertheless the October 1923 issue is especially important as it introduced to readers three writers who would become closely associated with the magazine: H.P. Lovecraft, Seabury Quinn and Frank Owen. Only Lovecraft is of relevance to the development of science fiction, and his story, 'Dagon', has overtones of Munsey and Merritt in dealing with a previously submerged land mass (containing records of an ancient monster god) which is disturbed by wartime action.

A few other writers who emerged in *Weird Tales* at this time are worth noting briefly. John Martin Leahy is remembered primarily for his later story of Antarctic horror, 'In Amundsen's Tent' (*Weird Tales*, January 1928), but his earlier work, though poor by comparison, is fondly remembered by a few. 'Draconda', a serial starting in the November 1923 issue, is a close imitation of H. Rider Haggard's *She*, although the lost-race action is translated to Venus. Richard Tooker later established himself as a significant ghost-writer for other authors. His first sale was a poor Burroughsian-style interplanetary story set on Mars, 'Planet Paradise' (February 1924). 'The Abysmal Horror' (January–February 1924) was the first appearance in *Weird Tales* by B. Wallis, the Canadian cousin of George C. Wallis, with whom he occasionally collaborated. This story may owe something to Leinster's 'The Silver Menace' as it deals with an alien life-form that multiplies rapidly and clogs the sea and land.

By early 1924 *Weird Tales* was in deep financial trouble, but Henneberger kept faith with the magazine. *Detective Tales*, which was now retitled *Real Detective Tales*, had started to make a profit but, rather than keep it and fold *Weird Tales*, Henneberger decided to sell the detective title to his business partner, J.M. Lansinger, who took it over from its June 1924 issue. The money was ploughed into *Weird Tales*, which had been suspended after a bumper summer issue dated May/June/July 1924. It was reissued in November 1924 with new editor Farnsworth Wright. Wright was an erratic editor who admitted he was not over fond of science fiction, but there is no denying that he had more affinity with unusual and bizarre stories than Baird and, allowing for the occasional slip in quality, he developed a publication that lived up to its subtitle as 'the Unique Magazine'.

Nevertheless for a while science fiction made little advance in the magazine. It was all highly imitative and took one of three forms. Predominant was the lost-race novel in the style of Haggard or Merritt. Next came the monster-mutation story, featuring either an ape transformed to man (or vice versa) or amoeba-like laboratory monsters. Finally came the interplanetary story: either voyages to Mars or Venus for Burroughs-like adventures, or the invasion of Earth by hostile forces. Few authors succeeded in rising above the mediocrity of these plots, although a few had fun with them. Not least was the delightfully named Nictzin Dyalhis who established a reputation in *Weird Tales* out of proportion to either the quality or quantity of his contributions. In 'When the Green Star Waned' (April 1925) experiments on Earth to create gold weaken the Earth's atmosphere and enable amoeba-like aliens from the dark side of the Moon to invade. Almost all of the Earth people are destroyed, and scientists on Venus notice the sudden radio silence. They set out to explore and discover the Lunarian menace. The story is badly written and plotted, but is often cited as an early space opera.

A more genuine early space opera, though, is 'Invaders from Outside' by J. Schlossel (January 1925). Schlossel is virtually ignored in the sf field although his work in the twenties showed considerable originality. 'Invaders from Outside' may have drawn some inspiration from the work of Julian Hawthorne and Homer Eon Flint in *All-Story*, but it brought the concepts together into a seminal story. Set millions of years in the past, long before intelligent life developed on the Earth, our Moon and the outer planets form an interplanetary confederacy which joins forces to rebuff an alien invasion from beyond the solar system. It was the type of story that during the next 10 years would dominate sf.

The writer most associated with the development of space opera, Edmond Hamilton, also first appeared in *Weird Tales*. His first published story was 'The Monster God of Mamurth' (August 1926) about an invisible lost city in the Sahara and its invisible giant spider guardian, but the first story he actually sold was 'Across Space' (September–November 1926). Here it is revealed that Martians had colonized Earth long before mankind emerged and still survive in underground caverns. They decide to take over the Earth and, to help in this, try to move Mars from its orbit closer to Earth. The story was almost certainly influenced by Hamilton's reading of the Munsey magazines which he had enjoyed since his teens, but in a short space of time Hamilton was to become the main focus for this type of science fiction. It was not only in *Weird Tales* that he would develop this, for, a few months before Hamilton's first appearance, a new magazine had been launched in which he would excel: *Amazing Stories*.

We have at last reached the birth of the first science-fiction magazine and en route have demonstrated that its appearance was neither sudden nor a surprise, but the inevitable result of years of development of science fiction in the popular magazines. The person who took the decisive step and provided a focus for a whole new world of fiction was Hugo Gernsback.

CHAPTER TWO
An Amazing Experiment[1]

Scientifiction

Although Chapter One has shown that there was a profusion of science fiction in the magazines prior to 1926, it is questionable whether any person or persons believed they 'owned' it as a distinct field of fiction. By 'owned' I mean looking after and nurturing the field, seeking its positive development.

There was actually so much variety of fiction which has subsequently been classified as sf that it is arguable that no one could own it. One could put forward a case to say that Pierre Hetzel claimed some kind of ownership over the extraordinary voyage story when he took Jules Verne under his wing. One could perhaps make a similar case for H. Rider Haggard and the lost-race story, and possibly C. Arthur Pearson and the future war story. It is very doubtful whether Bob Davis as editor of *All-Story* claimed any guardianship over the fantastic fiction that he published, for all that he encouraged it for some years.

Yet the supposition that Hugo Gernsback 'owned' the gadget story would surprise no one and, through the development of such stories, he 'owned' his own embryonic version of science fiction. This is an important point to consider in the development of science fiction and is what lies behind the statement made by Sam Moskowitz and others that Hugo Gernsback was the 'father of science fiction'. With a field that had so many antecedents no one could really claim to be its father. What Gernsback did was become a foster father to a variety of homeless children, with his favourite being the invention story. He subsequently acknowledged other forms of science fiction, though, as we shall see, he soon lost control of the medium. It is only by 'owning' the field at this stage that Gernsback could subsequently 'disown' much that masqueraded as

---

1. Chapter Two contains some details also included in my more detailed study of the period 1926–1936, *The Gernsback Days* (Gillette, NJ: The Wildside Press, 2001).

science fiction. It is that rise and fall of Gernsbackian sf that is the subject of this section.

Whilst *Weird Tales* was struggling to make its mark, Hugo Gernsback was endeavouring to develop *Science and Invention* beyond the hobbyist base of *The Electrical Experimenter* to a magazine that broadened readers' minds about the wider possibilities of science and technology. His leading contributor was Clement Fezandié whose stories read like lectures and were far away from the wild adventures appearing in *Argosy*, *All-Story* and *Weird Tales*.

What Gernsback needed was somehow to blend the two. He was fortunate when a story came to him from George Allan England who, although he had arguably passed his peak in the Munsey magazines, was a considerably better writer than any of Gernsback's contributors and was still a close third to Burroughs and Merritt in sf popularity in the Munsey magazines. The story, 'The Thing from – Outside', appeared in the April 1923 *Science and Invention*. It may well have been a reject from the pulps but it was still one of the best stories *Science and Invention* published. It tells of a scientific expedition in northern Canada which is menaced by an invisible entity. The story has little scientific premise and was out of the norm for Gernsback, but if he was going to encourage more contributions to his magazine he needed more stories along those lines.

Gernsback continued to develop the magazine. He commissioned a story from Ray Cummings which he started to serialize in the July 1923 issue. 'Around the Universe' is poor, even by Cummings's standards, but it doubtless fitted Gernsback's requirements. It is little more than a tour of the universe, exploring planets and stars, finally reaching the limits of the universe and breaking through into the macrocosm. The story has no plot or characterization, but it does put across a wealth of ideas sufficient to stimulate the imagination, which is what Gernsback wanted.

The August 1923 issue was a special 'Scientific Fiction Number' and had an effective cover by Howard Brown of a spacesuited man. It was not, as some people have believed, an all science-fiction issue. The magazine retained all its usual features and departments but ran a special section devoted to six sf stories. These included the second instalment of Cummings's serial and a Dr Hackensaw episode by Fezandié, 'The Secret of the Super-Telescope'. All but one of the other stories are forgettable. Gernsback's own 'The

Electric Duel' is nothing more than a description of a dream and not a story, whilst 'Vanishing Movies' by Teddy Holman is a pointless story about a cinema where the screen goes blank when the building is full. 'Advanced Chemistry' by Jack G. Huekels is a humorous story about a professor who invents a serum capable of bringing the dead back to life. All goes well until the professor dies and a stranger administers the serum wrongly, with electrifying results.

The one story with merit in the issue is 'The Man from the Atom' by G. Peyton Wertenbaker. Wertenbaker was only 16 but was a member of a literary family. His story is emotionally strong and considers the fate of an explorer who travels through into the macrocosm only to discover he cannot return to Earth because, with time relative to mass, the Earth had grown old and died within minutes of his own subjective time. Wertenbaker was Gernsback's first important writing discovery.

There is no evidence within *Science and Invention* to show how popular this experiment had been but one presupposes from Gernsback's own actions that it must have elicited a welcome response. He later noted that:

> Several years ago when I first conceived the idea of publishing a scientifiction magazine a circular letter was sent to some 25,000 people informing them that a new magazine, by the name *Scientifiction* was shortly to be launched. The response was such that the idea was given up for two years.[2]

I believe Gernsback had misjudged his readership. He had expected a similar response to that he had received when he had used the same tactic to launch *Modern Electrics* in 1908, but it is a different type of person who responds to hobbyist and experimenter advertisements than to those for new fiction magazines. I suspect most of the readership would have preferred to see the magazine first rather than submit an advance subscription. Gernsback was not giving much away about his new magazine and, if the experimental issue of *Science and Invention* was anything to go by, the contents would not be all that exciting. Fans of science fiction could read much better work in *Weird Tales* and *Argosy*. Gernsback would have to produce his goods before readers would commit themselves.

2. From Hugo Gernsback's editorial, 'Editorially Speaking', *Amazing Stories*, 1 (6) September 1926.

So for two years Gernsback busied himself in other activities, not least launching his radio station WRNY. It was one of the first regular radio stations in New York. After some test transmissions it went live on 12 June 1925 and provided a mixture of music and talks. Gernsback gave a talk every Monday evening, often using the medium to experiment with his future editorials and articles.

Gernsback had probably been stockpiling stories for *Scientifiction* and these now appeared not only in *Science and Invention* but also in *Practical Electrics*, a magazine that Gernsback had started in 1921 to appeal to those hobbyist readers who were dissatisfied with the change from *The Electrical Experimenter* to *Science and Invention*. In fact *Science and Invention* now featured only serials, including new work by Ray Cummings and John Martin Leahy, whilst *Practical Electrics* ran the short fiction. Few of these showed any advance over earlier invention stories. Only 'The Man who Saw Beyond' by James Pevey (May 1924) rises above the mediocre. An inventor has perfected a ray which will disassociate the atoms in his body and free his soul. He demonstrates it to two doctors who are present to switch on a new ray to reform the atoms. The experiment is a success but what the inventor has witnessed in the world beyond is too vast for him to remain on Earth so he frees his soul again and this time destroys the invention.

With the November 1924 issue *Practical Electrics* changed its name to *The Experimenter* and dropped all short stories. It serialized Victor MacClure's novel 'The Ark of the Covenant', originally published in Britain as *Ultimatum* (Harrap, 1924). This is another master-of-the-world story, this time with a scientist having developed a super airship as well as a sleep gas with which he threatens the Earth unless all war is stopped.

Gernsback was still not attracting the more sensational stories that he needed. Nevertheless he increasingly felt the time was right to reconsider his magazine of scientifiction. Perhaps the title had been wrong, but that could be easily remedied. *Scientifiction* went. In came *Amazing Stories*, and with no prior consultation Gernsback issued the magazine on 10 March 1926, with the issue dated April 1926.

Amazing Stories

What Gernsback had done was discontinue *The Experimenter* and use that publishing schedule to accommodate *Amazing Stories*. What it also meant was that with the magazine came *The Experimenter*'s editor, the ageing but still remarkably bright Thomas O'Conor Sloane. Sloane was born in New York in 1851 and became Professor of Natural Sciences at Seton Hall College in South Orange, New Jersey in 1888. A string of inventions, mostly electrical, are connected with him. He was also the author of several books including *Electric Toy Making for Amateurs* (1892) and *Rapid Arithmetic* (1922). A benign, bearded old man, he was 74 when he found himself at the helm of *Amazing Stories*. Essentially, Sloane undertook the practical editorial duties. Whilst he read the fiction the final choice of content was left to Gernsback. Gernsback also enlisted the help of two consultants to recommend and seek out appropriate fiction. The first was Conrad A. Brandt, a chemist who had emigrated from Germany. He was one of the foremost collectors of science fiction of the day. Gernsback made him literary editor and much of the choice of reprints was down to him. He remained with *Amazing* for many years, later providing a regular book review column. Another consultant who also advised on selective reprints was Wilbur C. Whitehead, better known in his day as an expert on auction bridge.

The final part of the team was artist Frank R. Paul. Paul had trained as an architect and it was his technical skills that were utilized when Gernsback first employed him on *The Electrical Experimenter* in 1914. Paul had illustrated most of the stories since 1918 but had not painted any covers, although the cover for the August 1924 *Science and Invention* depicting Gernsback's feature 'Evolution on Mars', which was almost certainly by Brown, is sometimes credited to Paul. Nevertheless his covers for *Amazing Stories* would become one of the most striking features of the magazine and certainly a major sales attraction.

Gernsback was determined that *Amazing* would not be overlooked on the bookstalls. It kept the large format (8½ by 11 inches) of the technical magazines and the paper was of such heavy stock that its 96 pages were as thick as the 192-page standard pulps. Paul's bold cover showed some smiling ice-skaters on a frozen world, with the great orb of Saturn seemingly inches away. It depicted a scene from Jules Verne's 'Off on a Comet' which was serialized in two parts.

In his editorial Gernsback explained his intentions in publishing the magazine. First he defined science fiction: 'By "scientifiction" I mean the Jules Verne, H.G. Wells and Edgar Allan Poe type of story – a charming romance intermingled with scientific fact and prophetic vision.' Gernsback had high hopes for science fiction, as later in the editorial he explains:

> Not only do these amazing tales make tremendously inter-esting reading – they are also always instructive. They sup-ply knowledge that we might not otherwise obtain – and they supply it in a very palatable form. For the best of these modern writers of scientifiction have the knack of imparting knowledge and even inspiration without once making us aware that we are being taught.[3]

It was Gernsback's firm belief – and it always remained so – that readers would be instructed through science fiction. Unfortunately he found it difficult to back this up with quality fiction. The type of story he was publishing in *Science and Invention* might be instructive but it scarcely met what had now become Gernsback's prime requirement of being interesting or entertaining. Over the previous 15 years Gernsback had changed his emphasis on stories being first instructive and secondly entertaining, with the entertainment value now coming first. Perhaps this was partly the influence of Brandt and Whitehead, but it was more likely Gernsback thinking sound commercial sense. His experience was already showing that, whilst his fiction in *Science and Invention* had been well received, it was still part of a package. The lack of response to his earlier circular sug-gested that readers wanted more than instructive fiction. They wanted to be entertained, to escape, to experience that sense of awe and wonder that good visionary fiction brought. As a con-sequence Gernsback was prepared to sacrifice instruction and good science for entertainment and excitement. Ideally he wanted both, but opportunities for the two to come together were rare.

Initially most of the works in *Amazing Stories* were reprints, including all but one of the first 18 serials. With a wide choice of fiction to reprint (limited, one assumes, only by the financial wherewithal to acquire the reprint rights) one would think that Gernsback would be able to acquire the best stories to represent his policy.

With the first issue it was a reasonable mix. The choice of the Verne story was perhaps strange, though if any proof was needed that Gernsback was abandoning scientific accuracy in favor of adventure this was it. 'Off on a Comet, or Hector Servadec' was

3. From Gernsback's editorial, 'A New Sort of Magazine', *Amazing Stories* 1 (1) April 1926, p. 3.

arguably one of Verne's least scientifically plausible novels. Gernsback admits this in his introductory blurb: 'the author here abandons his usual scrupulously scientific attitude and gives his fancy freer rein'. After summarizing the novel's plot, Gernsback says, 'These events all belong to the realm of fairyland.' 'Off on a Comet' had much in common with Ray Cummings's 'Around the Universe' and 'The Man on the Meteor', which had proved popular in *Science and Invention*, as fascinating odysseys around the solar system, though they contained little scientific instruction.

The H.G. Wells selection was 'The New Accelerator', already tested in *Science and Invention*, and in many ways the ideal Gernsback story. It not only describes a new invention – a drug that speeds up the taker's perceptions – but fits it into a 'charming' story. Wells was, of course, the master at this, and it is not surprising that Gernsback selected a story by Wells for each of the first 29 issues.[4]

The Poe selection was 'The Facts in the Case of M. Valdemar'. Although today regarded as a horror story, it does have a scientific base: the possibility that a hypnotized mind may stay alive after the body has died. It is a testament to Poe's talent that this story, which was 80 years old, could stand as an example of scientific fiction in 1926.

For the remainder of the issue Gernsback chose three further reprints. Two were from *Science and Invention*, fortunately the two most effective: 'The Man from the Atom' by Wertenbaker and 'The Thing from – Outside' by England. The third was 'The Man who Saved the Earth' by Austin Hall from *All-Story Weekly*.

It was a sensible choice, with a good mixture of themes and authors. However, one would have to delve deep and long to find much scientific knowledge among the contents. But there is little doubt that the public enjoyed it. Within months *Amazing*'s circulation was exceeding 100,000.

Amazing was scheduled as a monthly but Gernsback asked his readers to vote on what would be the ideal schedule. The results, reported in his September 1926 editorial, were: monthly, 498; semi-monthly, 32,644. It is astounding that over 33 per cent of his readership responded, and it is possible the reported results contained a printing error (perhaps the final four was doubled), but either way it was still an overwhelming vote in favour of a more frequent schedule. Gernsback stated that he would try and attain

4 See my article 'Mr H. and Mr H.G.', *Fantasy Commentator* 6 (4) (No. 40) Winter 1989/90, pp. 263–74, for a detailed analysis of Gernsback's financial dealings with H.G. Wells.

that schedule but he never did. Instead he offered something much greater, of which more in a moment.

Gernsback realized the potential of his readership. In the June 1926 editorial he remarked on his surprise at learning of the hidden army of fans in the country, 'who seem to be pretty well orientated in this literature'. Obviously *Amazing Stories* had attracted ardent followers who had previously haunted the Munsey magazines for their favorite literature but who now found it ready packaged. The future of *Amazing* was assured when Gernsback decided to respond to this readership. This he did in two ways.

The first was by way of competitions. It soon became synonymous with Gernsback that not many months would pass without a contest of some kind (these had been common in his technical magazines). The first in *Amazing* was in the December 1926 issue and it was aimed at encouraging the submission of new short stories. Frank R. Paul produced a bizarre cover and readers were requested to submit stories based around the picture. An added enticement was the $250 first prize. The response was beyond even Gernsback's wildest dreams. In his March editorial he declared that over 360 manuscripts had been received. The winner was Cyril G. Wates from Edmonton, Canada, with 'The Visitation'. Wates sold four stories to Gernsback over the next three years but apart from 'Gold Dust and Star Dust' (*Amazing Stories*, September 1929), which seems to predict the video-recorder, his stories were unremarkable.

Gernsback printed seven stories from the competition but only two of these were by authors of lasting significance. The third prize went to 'The Fate of the Poseidonia' by Mrs F.C. Harris, who became better known as Clare Winger Harris. She had already made one earlier sale, 'A Runaway World', to *Weird Tales* (July 1926), but now went on to become a Gernsback regular and one of his most popular writers. Miles J. Breuer rated her story 'The Miracle of the Lily' (April 1928) as the best published in *Amazing* up to that date. She later went on to collaborate with Breuer on 'A Baby on Neptune' (December 1929). She was the first regular female writer of science fiction in the specialist magazines, though Francis Stevens (hiding behind a male pseudonym) had preceded her in the general pulps. Gernsback commented about her: 'as a rule, women do not make good scientifiction writers, because their education and general tendencies on scientific matters are usually limited'.[5] This

5. *Amazing Stories*, 2 (3) June 1927, p. 213.

may today seem a sexist comment, but it was almost certainly a
clinical observation of the day. As it happened Gernsback would
encourage women writers as much as men, and a number would
establish themselves in his magazines.

One of the honourable mentions in the competition was 'The
Voice from the Inner World' by A. Hyatt Verrill. Verrill was by profession a naturalist and explorer, having undertaken many expeditions to South America, about which he wrote profusely; but he
also produced some early fiction, primarily aimed at the boys'
market and usually featuring lost cities in the Amazonian jungle,
starting with *The Golden City* (1916). Gernsback's magazine thus
became a natural market for his lost-race adventures. The first was
'Beyond the Pole' (*Amazing*, October–November 1926), which was
also the first new serial in *Amazing*. Verrill's work became increasingly more fantastic and took on the Merritt touch. Verrill was a
capable writer and, because of his personal experiences, was able to
bring a degree of realism alongside the fantastic imagery. That
mixture of basic fact and fantastic extrapolation made Verrill an
ideal Gernsback author.

Gernsback's second response to his readership was to establish a
letter column, called 'Discussions', which became a regular feature
from the January 1927 issue. Letter columns were not new in
magazines, not even in specialist ones, but 'Discussions' became
something different, and this was due to the nature of the science-
fiction fan. Gernsback had been impressed at the degree of interest
and knowledge that his correspondents revealed both in scientific
matters and in the field of science fiction. Because Gernsback was
keen to have readers explore and discuss the concepts in the fiction,
he actively encouraged this both in the letter column and in a later
feature he added for scientific questions. What Gernsback may not
have realized, but which soon became apparent, was that most fans
of science fiction were relatively lonely children given more to
imaginative flights of fancy than to active adventures with friends.
Also, because of the expanse of the United States, the likelihood of
two of these encountering each other in any town or city was quite
remote. *Amazing Stories* thus rapidly became a close friend, and the
letter column the only avenue for these fans to talk about their wild
imaginings which were otherwise viewed as crackpot by friends or
family. This was the real secret of Gernsback's *Amazing Stories* and is
the cause of the popularity of science fiction. He had tapped into
the secret dreams of the nation, and mostly the young, and allowed

them a channel for expression. This was to lead to both an explosion in the interest in and writing of science fiction, and the birth of science-fiction fandom.

During the magazine's first year Gernsback published mostly reprints. In addition to Wells and Verne, there were stories from the Munsey pulps, from back issues of *Science and Invention*, and ones imported from abroad. These included, in the July 1926 issue, 'The Eggs from Lake Tanganyika' by Curt Siodmak, a writer who would later establish himself in the American film industry.

Gernsback soon became aware from his correspondents that the two most popular writers were not Verne and Wells but Burroughs and Merritt. This gave him something of a problem. Although Burroughs did include strong scientific concepts in his work, they were marginal to the adventure. Merritt's work was even more extreme. His stories were fantasies where any scientific elements were minimal and certainly not educational. When Gernsback began serialization of 'The Moon Pool' in the May 1927 *Amazing* he faced the dilemma of introducing a story that was, by his definition, a fairy tale and not science fiction. He sought to rationalize this by arguing that the story introduced a new science and one that might become possible some day when more was understood about radiation. Gernsback was looking for an excuse for including such fantastic fiction in his magazine when it did not fit in with his basic creed. It did, however, fit in with the readers. The story remained one of the most popular of the period. What we see, as *Amazing* entered its second year, was Gernsback wrestling with the problem of a readership with greater interest in scientific and fantastic adventures than in stories about science and inventions.

After the first year Gernsback planned a yearbook but became more ambitious as time passed and, in June 1927, he issued a double-sized *Amazing Stories Annual*. Originally he had planned only an additional normal-sized issue, but he became emboldened when he agreed with Burroughs to purchase a new Martian novel which saw print in the *Annual* as 'The Master Mind of Mars'. This novel alone would have guaranteed the success of the *Annual*, which, despite the double cover price of 50 cents, sold out. The rest of the *Annual* was all reprint, with two stories by Merritt, and items by Austin Hall, A. Hyatt Verrill, Jaque Morgan and H.G. Wells.

The success of the *Annual* and the growing circulation of the monthly, allowed Gernsback to experiment further and in January 1928 he issued the first number of *Amazing Stories Quarterly*. This was a real bonanza: 144 large-size pages for 50 cents, carrying two novels and several short stories. Although the first issue reprinted the novel, *When the Sleeper Wakes* by H.G. Wells, it also carried a new short novel by Earl L. Bell, 'The Moon of Doom', a disaster story about the Moon falling towards the Earth and the resultant catastrophes.

Bell's story was only the third original novel-length work that Gernsback had published in his fiction magazines. It is rather strange that he had continued to run serials in *Science and Invention*, including reprints of Merritt's novels, rather than include new serials in *Amazing*. He was clearly still feeling his way during 1927 but was becoming increasingly convinced that the magazine was right. He had two problems, though. One was obtaining sufficient good new material, of all lengths. The second was getting the balance right between quality scientific material that followed his desire to stimulate scientific study, and the more adventurous fiction that may have stimulated the imagination but not necessarily into scientific experimentation. This last matter was becoming serious because Paul's exciting covers, whilst clearly attracting readers at the bookstalls, were giving the wrong impressions to parents, suggesting that this was harmful literature for their children, the very people Gernsback wanted to encourage.

A further problem was Gernsback's payment policy. Gernsback was notorious for his poor payment which was both low and frequently late. This did not enamour him to the more able pulp writers. Murray Leinster, whose fiction Gernsback was reprinting from the Munsey magazines, was discouraged by his agent from submitting new material to Gernsback partly due to the poor payment but also because of the puerile image that science fiction was attracting.

Other writers who encountered Gernsback briefly soon noted his poor payment. One of these was H.P. Lovecraft, whose 'The Colour out of Space' was the best story in the September 1927 issue, and the only story from *Amazing* to receive an honourable mention in Edward J. O'Brien's prestigious series, *Best American Short Stories*. The minimal, late payment that Lovecraft received caused him to call Gernsback 'Hugo the Rat',[6] a phrase that has since gone down in legend. Gernsback eventually fell out of favour with H.G. Wells

---

6. H.P. Lovecraft, *Selected Letters IV* (Sauk City: Arkham House, 1976), p. 343, HPL to F. Lee Baldwin, 13 January 1934.

following a misunderstanding about payments, and it is certain that many writers and agents were aware of Gernsback's practices. As a consequence it was difficult to attract quality names other than by reprinting stories. Initially most of the stories by new writers were poor in quality, and some that Gernsback did publish were still along the lines of humorous invention stories. Typical of these was 'Hicks' Inventions with a Kick', a series of four stories by Henry Hugh Simmons about various fairly basic inventions that go wrong and cause havoc.

What Gernsback had to face was that the popular stories were the fantastic ones, not the mundane invention stories. Although they were the original inspiration for *Amazing*, the magazine had rapidly attracted a different audience, one which delighted in the fantastic adventure stories of the Munsey magazines. Unfortunately Gernsback's magazines did not have the same quality image as *Argosy* which, only occasionally, printed a lurid, monster cover for its sf stories. Usually the covers portrayed historical, detective or western stories which were rather more staid and artistically acceptable.

Paul's covers caused some readers to say that they felt embarrassed to buy the magazine. No lesser person than Raymond A. Palmer, who will feature heavily in our history (and who would be guilty of even more garish covers on later issues of *Amazing*), wrote in to say that: 'Several months ago I had the opportunity to induce a friend to read *Amazing Stories* but he was forced to discontinue it by reason of his parents' dislike of the cover illustrations. He thought it was "trash".'[7] Gernsback took note of these comments. The last thing he wanted to do was to repel the very readers he had hoped to stimulate. He experimented. In the April 1928 *Amazing* he ran a competition for a symbol to represent the concept of scientifiction. The winning design – a pen on a cog writing the word 'Scientifiction' moving between fact and theory – was portrayed in full on the cover of the September 1928 issue. To test the sales, Gernsback printed 30,000 more copies of that issue. He reported the matter in the April 1929 *Amazing*. It transpires that the September issue had three times as many unsold copies as the issues published before and after. Much though Gernsback recognized the problems of the lurid covers, it made commercial sense to retain them.

Of course the imagery projected by the covers did not have to reflect the quality of the fiction but, unfortunately, it usually did.

7. *Amazing Stories*, 3 (7) October 1928, p. 662.

Despite the quality fiction by Wells, Verne and Poe, and better-than-average work by Merritt and Burroughs, the bulk of the fiction was uninspired. This was a concern from the outset for the precocious youngster G. Peyton Wertenbaker whose sequels to 'The Man from the Atom' (May 1926) and 'The Coming of the Ice' (June 1926) had been the first new stories Gernsback had bought for *Amazing*. In a long letter to Gernsback, Wertenbaker made some eloquent statements on the nature of science fiction.

> Scientifiction is a branch of literature which requires more intelligence and even more aesthetic sense than is possessed by the sex-type reading public. It is designed to reach those qualities of the mind which are aroused only by things vast, things cataclysmic, and things unfathomably strange. It is designed to reach that portion of the imagination which grasps with its eager, feeble talons after the unknown. It should be an influence greater than the influence of any literature I know upon the restless ambition of man for further conquests, further understandings. Literature of the past and the present has made the mystery of man and his world more clear to us, and for that reason it has been less beautiful, for beauty lies only in the things that are mysterious. Beauty is a groping of the emotions towards realization of things which may be unknown only to the intellect. Scientifiction goes out into the remote vistas of the universe, where there is still mystery and so still beauty. For that reason scientifiction seems to me to be the true literature of the future.

Wertenbaker then added a word of warning: 'The danger that may lie before *Amazing Stories* is that of becoming too scientific and not sufficiently literary. It is yet too early to be sure, but not too early for a warning to be issued amicably and frankly'.[8]

Gernsback hardly needed reminding for it was a dilemma he readily recognized. The same message came across from Miles J. Breuer, Gernsback's next important writing discovery. In a letter published in the July 1928 *Amazing*, Breuer highlighted a general opinion that the stories lacked literary quality, to which he added:

> I don't care how much science you put in, if the stories conform to modern literary standards the above criticisms will not occur. Let your stories have plot and unity of impression

---

8. *Amazing Stories*, 1 (4) July 1926, p. 297.

and the general reader will like them, in spite of the science … Which is the better purpose for your magazine: to provide light entertainment for the scientific people; or to carry the message of science to the vast masses who prefer to read fiction?

Gernsback's answer summed up his views:

Our stories … are written to popularize science. Our efforts have led to the publication and production of a quantity of good literature seasoned with science – perhaps too far-fetched in the latter aspect. This last is a dangerous admission, however, for no one knows how far science will develop in the future. The last sixty years have seen the world revolutionized by the developments of science. The younger readers, we believe, will live through another generation of almost miracles, and they seem especially to enjoy these stories. We are, of course, always on the look-out for 'literary scientific fiction'.

Amazing may have shifted from the scientific lecture to the adventure story, but not necessarily with a corresponding growth in literary values. Although it was a change in intent, it was a confirmation of the image that the title and cover art already suggested. It was what had been feared by many of the scientific purists who came to *Amazing* from *Science and Invention*. The stories might be educational and contain strong scientific principles but they were packaged in such a way as to suggest a more juvenile content.

Within two years Gernsback had created a new market niche for a product which he had called scientifiction, but in doing so had identified that product with the more lurid end of the literary spectrum. As later critics of Gernsback (amongst them James Blish, Damon Knight, Harlan Ellison and Barry Malzberg) would term it, Gernsback had 'ghettoized' science fiction. It had certainly not been his intention, but there is no doubt that by creating *Amazing Stories*, and by not providing stronger editorial control, Gernsback had harmed the reputation of science fiction and forced it into a category from which it has ever since been struggling to escape.

As we shall see Gernsback did redeem himself to some extent briefly in the early thirties but not sufficiently for his act to be recognized. By then the damage was done and science fiction was at its lowest ebb. Yet the writers that Gernsback discovered would themselves develop the field beyond Gernsback's control. The field he had named and promoted had all too rapidly grown out of his control, and it was left to his writers to save it.

The Birth of Super-Science

By 1928 Gernsback was starting to attract some regular new writers. For the most part these were writers unknown outside *Amazing Stories* which by now had created its own identity and needed to develop its own writers. Most of them were responding to Gernsback's ideals for scientifiction and their imagination usually triumphed over their ability to write. Few of these would survive the Gernsback era. Others were more adaptable and would take science fiction into its next phase.

The more significant writers to whom Gernsback could lay claim as his discoveries were G. Peyton Wertenbaker, Miles J. Breuer, Bob Olsen, Francis Flagg, David H. Keller, Fletcher Pratt, Harl Vincent, Stanton Coblentz, R.F. Starzl, Edward E. Smith, Jack Williamson and S.P. Meek. All were popular in their day. Breuer, a doctor from Nebraska, was noted for his stories about other dimensions, including an interesting trilogy, 'The Appendix and the Spectacles', 'The Captured Cross-Section' and 'The Book of Worlds' (all *Amazing*, 1929), of which the last is an early exploration of multiple realities. His novel 'Paradise and Iron' (*Amazing Stories Quarterly*, Summer 1930) is a cautionary tale about the dangers of dependence upon machines.

David H. Keller was arguably the most popular Gernsback author. He was certainly the most prolific. He was a doctor who specialized in psychology, an interest that he brought to both his scientific fiction and his weird stories. Unlike most of his contemporaries Keller concentrated on the social implications of technology rather than on the invention. His first appearance was with 'The Revolt of the Pedestrians' (February 1928), which portrayed a future in which the automobile had taken over and the remaining pedestrians were treated like animals. 'The Psychophonic Nurse' (November 1928) predicts a time when mothers leave their children to robot nurses. Keller's fiction was a good test of the freedom of expression allowed by Gernsback's publications. For example, 'A Biological Experiment' (June 1928) explored a future in which the urge for parenthood still existed in a world where all men and women were sterile. 'The Menace' (*Quarterly*, Summer 1928) was a series of four connected stories dealing with the revolution of the American Negro after he has perfected a way of turning his skin pigmentation white. When Negro scientists succeed in extracting gold from sea-water their plans for world domination come to fruition. It is unlikely that these stories could ever have appeared in any conventional magazine or have been tolerated by readers other than those of a magazine exploring future trends.

There is no doubt that Jack Williamson was Gernsback's most enduring discovery. No one could have anticipated at the time that Williamson would go on to produce high quality science fiction for over seventy years. His early stories were heavily influenced by Abraham Merritt, especially his debut story 'The Metal Man' (*Amazing Stories*, December 1928) and his first serial 'The Alien Intelligence' (*Science Wonder Stories*, July–August 1929), but he would soon develop a voice of his own and within a few years he was rated as one of the leading writers in the field.

Perhaps the most influential writer to appear in Gernsback's *Amazing* was Edward Elmer Smith (or 'Doc' Smith as he became affectionately known). Smith, a food research chemist, had been toying with a galactic extravaganza since 1915. By the time he had finished the novel which became 'The Skylark of Space' in 1920, science fiction had fallen from favour at *Argosy* and Smith was unable to find another pulp willing to consider it. Why Smith did not submit it to *Weird Tales* is not recorded, but he had probably lost faith in the work until he encountered *Amazing Stories* and prepared to give it another go. 'The Skylark of Space' is undoubtedly the seminal space opera. It tells of the search by super-scientist Richard Seaton for his betrothed who has been kidnapped by the villainous Dr Marc 'Blackie' DuQuesne. As a backcloth Smith chose the entire universe and the awesome spaceship *Skylark*, which toured the cosmos encountering multifarious adventures with countless strange aliens.

As we have seen, other writers were already experimenting with fiction on a galactic stage, particularly Homer Eon Flint and J. Schlossel. Indeed, Schlossel had produced a remarkable story, 'The Second Swarm', for the Spring 1928 *Quarterly*. In the far future mankind had left the Earth in a 'first swarm' to colonize distant worlds. Some of the expeditions were destroyed by hostile aliens, so a second swarm is prepared as a punitive expedition. In *Weird Tales* Edmond Hamilton had been subjecting the Earth to invasion from the Moon, from subatomic worlds, and from other dimensions, but in 'Crashing Suns' (August–September 1928), which was almost certainly influenced by Schlossel's earlier 'Invaders from Outside', he entered the realms of space opera with a Solar System Confederation in the far future faced with invasion by a distant star system. Hamilton went on to produce a series featuring the Interstellar Patrol, a law-keeping force run by the Federation of the Stars, a galactic government centred in the system of Canopus. This started with 'The Sun-Stealers' (*Weird Tales*, February 1929).

It is evident that during the 1920s, and independent of Gernsback's magazines, an interest in mighty space adventures had evolved through the writings of Flint, Schlossel, Ray Cummings to a lesser degree, and Edmond Hamilton. It is important to consider what 'Doc' Smith added to this process because 'The Skylark of Space' is a pivotal work. Up until that stage science fiction had concentrated on inventions, lost civilizations, time travel, future societies and space travel within the solar system. After 'The Skylark of Space' the super-science extravaganza took over and drove the field for much of the next decade, and in so doing dragged science fiction down to its nadir. The question remains as to what role *Amazing Stories* had in this.

The evidence for an answer to this is not apparent in 1928, and we will have to move on a few years before it becomes clear. What is evident from the letter columns in *Amazing* is that Smith's work tapped in to a particular type of reader that was not fully shared with *Weird Tales*. Indeed, it is unlikely that at this time the readerships of the two magazines overlapped that much. Readers of *Weird Tales* were looking for thrills and chills and if that took the form of a scientific adventure, so be it, but it was a secondary level of interest to them. Readers of *Amazing*, however, were looking for that scientific basis. For them, 'The Skylark of Space' opened their eyes to the wonders of atomic-powered spaceships and the worlds beyond like nothing had before. Despite the works of Flint, Schlossel and Hamilton (which clearly had not influenced Smith, as he had worked on the story since 1915), Smith had developed the super-science extravaganza on a firm scientific basis. In so doing he had redefined the horizons of science fiction and took it once and for all out of the parochial 'gadget' story where it had had its Gernsbackian roots and placed it firmly in the 'cosmic' which had been developing through the Munsey magazines.

This sea change in Gernsbackian science fiction is further emphasized by a second story in the August 1928 *Amazing*,

'Armageddon – 2419 AD' by Philip Francis Nowlan. This story introduced us to the character of Anthony (later 'Buck') Rogers, who is transported into a super-scientific future, five centuries hence. In both this story and 'Skylark of Space' super-science and amazing weapons hold centre stage. Nowlan was a financial reporter on the *Philadelphia Public Ledger* and thus part of the newspaper world. His story was seen by John F. Dille, president of the National Newspaper Syndicate, who convinced Nowlan to convert it into a comic strip, with Nowlan writing the continuity and with illustrations by Dick Calkins. Nowlan reluctantly agreed and 'Buck Rogers in the 25th Century' was syndicated in scores of newspapers starting from 7 January 1929. It was the first American science-fiction comic strip, and though it was intended to have an adult story-line it clearly appealed strongly to the American youth. Before long Buck Rogers's adventures became equated with crazy ideas, so that even before the American nation had come to terms with the phrase 'science fiction' they were aware of 'that crazy Buck Rogers stuff', which became a synonym for low-grade science fiction.

Gernsback, quite unintentionally, had created a field of fiction which had considerable appeal but which, because it had no adequate direction or quality editorial control, rapidly degenerated. It would be a few years before that quality was imposed but in the meantime science fiction had discovered its popular common denominator and the success of *Amazing Stories* and of the Buck Rogers strip had been noticed by other publishers. The proliferation of science fiction was about to begin.

A Gathering of Science Fiction

From April 1926 to April 1929 Hugo Gernsback had the monopoly of science-fiction magazine publishing, though not the monopoly of science fiction. *Weird Tales* and *Argosy* remained his closest rivals and, although *Argosy* exceeded *Amazing Stories* in circulation, its science-fiction content was shrinking. *Weird Tales* had a smaller circulation, but sustained a steady content of science fiction throughout this period. *Weird Tales* did have some slight competiton from a short-lived magazine, *Tales of Magic and Mystery*, which survived for five issues from December 1927 to April 1928. This magazine was established on a basis of stage magic and the occult, building on the reputation of people such as Howard Thurston and Harry Houdini. It was edited by writer and magician Walter Gibson who emerged a few years later as the author of the pulp series *The Shadow*, but it carried no science fiction. The closest it came was with H.P. Lovecraft's 'Cool Air' (March 1928) about a man whose body survives after death by hypothermic temperatures.

Weird Tales had a greater rival in *Ghost Stories*, which had appeared two months after *Amazing* in June 1926 as a monthly publication. It was published by Bernarr Macfadden, the health faddist who had started *Physical Culture* in 1898. The researches of Sam Moskowitz have shown that Macfadden was interested in science fiction mostly from the angle of developing an ideal healthy body and society. Both *Physical Culture* and *True Story* carried science fiction, including the future society novels of nutritionist Milo Hastings. *True Story* was the seminal confessions magazine, presenting fiction as purportedly true stories. This feature spilled over into *Ghost Stories* which likewise sought to present its stories as genuine, but *Ghost Stories* carried no science fiction. Neither did *True Strange Stories*, a short-lived companion magazine which ran from March to November 1929 and was edited by Walter Gibson.

Nevertheless, Macfadden's interest in science fiction has provided a basis for the argument that Macfadden noticed the success of *Amazing Stories* and was keen to take it over. What is more likely is that Macfadden disliked Gernsback encroaching into the health field with a new magazine, *Your Body*, which Gernsback had issued in April 1928. Moreover Gernsback's payment practices were becoming a problem.

Gernsback was investing his money in his radio service which was also now developing television broadcasts. Gernsback's first transmission of visual images was on 12 August 1928. Thereafter he inaugurated a regular daily television broadcast, the first in New York. These experiments soaked up money. In addition Gernsback and his brother Sidney, who was treasurer of Gernsback's companies, were paying themselves highly inflated salaries. So although Gernsback's total assets made him solvent, the extent of his liquidity was limited. Nevertheless it was the image of his rich lifestyle and his increasing delays in paying his authors and creditors that began to incense people. Eventually his two largest creditors, his printer and his paper supplier, took action and filed for bankruptcy proceedings on 20 February 1929.

The Experimenter Publishing Company went into receivership.

Three days later at the first meeting of creditors it was agreed that the directors had to step down. The receivers, Irving Trust, refloated the company and managed to keep it going until the proceedings were resolved. For this reason *Amazing Stories* and its companion magazines, including *Science and Invention* and *Radio News*, kept going with most of the same staff in place, but the Gernsbacks went. Arthur H. Lynch, a radio expert and former editor of *Radio Broadcast*, became the new editor-in-chief, but he worked primarily on *Radio News*. Though his name appears on the masthead of *Amazing Stories* he was never in practice its editor. That role remained in the hands of T. O'Conor Sloane, supported by C.A. Brandt and Miriam Bourne.

Irving Trust quickly secured confidence in the company and refloated it. They now sought bids from prospective purchasers. One came from Bernarr Macfadden, but he was unsuccessful. The publishing company passed to B.A. Mackinnon, whilst the radio stations passed to another company. All this time *Amazing Stories* continued to appear. Even if it had ceased publication, as Gernsback clearly expected, science fiction would have continued in magazine form, for within days of the bankruptcy proceedings Gernsback was establishing a new publishing company with not just one, but three new science-fiction magazines, and a radio magazine, *Radio-Craft*. This time Gernsback gave preference to science fiction over his technical magazines. Evidently he was convinced of the future success of science fiction and was prepared to gamble most of his investment in that direction.

The new magazine, *Science Wonder Stories*, appeared on 3 May 1929, dated June 1929. It was followed six weeks later by *Air Wonder Stories* and two months after that by *Science Wonder Quarterly*. The magazines seemed almost identical to *Amazing Stories*. Frank R. Paul provided the covers. There were the same editorial features and most of the same authors. In some cases Gernsback had brought with him stories submitted to *Amazing* but not yet purchased. He checked with the authors as to whether they wanted them returned or considered for his new magazine. Since the future of *Amazing* was at that time uncertain it seemed a safer bet to keep the manuscript with Gernsback. Fairly soon, though, *Amazing* was also contacting its authors to keep faith with them and rapidly writers found they had two markets instead of one. More precisely, the number of issues per year had nearly trebled from 16 to 44.

At *Amazing*, Sloane had to cast around for a new cover artist.

Initially Hugh MacKay and Hans Wessolowski filled in, though their covers were less dramatic, but from February 1930 the mainstay of the magazine was Peruvian artist Leo Morey. Brickbats and roses have been cast at the work of both Paul and Morey although, in my opinion, neither was spectacular. Paul had to be admired for his versatility – it has been claimed that he never drew the same spaceship design twice – but his failing was with people and continual study of his work will soon invoke a disdain for his flat-chested, jodhpur-clad females. Morey on the other hand may not have had the imagination of Paul but was passably the more artistic.

Science Wonder Stories was monthly, large-size, 96 pages, and sold for 25 cents. Its first issue began a serial, 'The Reign of the Ray' by Fletcher Pratt and Irwin Lester. *Air Wonder Stories* followed the same format and led with a reprint of the serial 'Ark of the Covenant' by Victor MacClure. *Science Wonder Quarterly*, which cost 50 cents and ran to 144 pages, led with the German novel 'The Shot into Infinity' by Otto Willi Gail. Gernsback had always sought to acquire good material in translation from European writers, and he now pursued this with increased enthusiasm. Perhaps one of the most important developments was the translation by Francis M. Currier of 'The Problems of Space Flying' by Hermann Noordung (*Science Wonder Stories*, July–September 1929), which had appeared in Berlin in 1928. This was an astonishingly accurate and detailed consideration of the problems associated with humans living in space. The pioneering work being undertaken by German engineers into rocketry was feeding into German literature and Gernsback brought that expertise to America. In Gernsback's new magazines there was a much greater emphasis on the practicalities and possibilities of interplanetary travel, not solely on the super-science adventures.

Three new sf magazines were not enough for Gernsback. He also began a series of original chapbooks, the *Science Fiction Series*, with a special offer of 12 books for one dollar. The first batch of six booklets, which led with 'The Girl from Mars' by Jack Williamson and Miles J. Breuer, was issued in October 1929. Apart from this first volume, most of the stories were of poor quality, suggesting that Gernsback did not consider them fit for his magazines but, because of the interest in sf, felt there might still be a lucrative market. The length of time during which the series remained advertized in Gernsback's magazines suggests that readers did not necessarily agree.

To top everything, Gernsback experimented one stage further. In December 1929 he issued a fourth fiction magazine, *Scientific Detective Monthly*, with the first issue dated January 1930. Gernsback had a penchant for such stories, having reprinted many of the tales by Edwin Balmer and William MacHarg. Arthur B. Reeve, the author of the Craig Kennedy stories, was enrolled as editorial commissioner, though that was more a promotional post, as Gernsback remained the overall editor, and the donkey-work of compiling each issue fell to Hector Grey. Strictly speaking the magazine was only borderline science fiction and carried little of any significance. The magazine fell into the chasm between two worlds. Its contents were insufficient to attract either the sf readership or detective readers who already had plenty of other titles of their own. After five issues it was retitled *Amazing Detective Tales* and an effort made to increase the sf content, but that had little effect. Neither did replacing Grey with Gernsback's primary editor, David Lasser. The magazine was an anomaly and, after ten issues, it bowed out of the sf field. It was sold to publisher Wallace Bamber who kept it going for a few more issues as *Amazing Detective Stories*. Basically, though, this was Gernsback's first failure in the sf field, and it was the result of branching out too far from his sf base.

Within this base Gernsback was moving ahead solidly. Because of worries over the trademarked use of the phrase 'scientifiction' at *Amazing*, Gernsback decided to tread carefully and for *Science Wonder Stories* coined the new phrase 'science fiction'. He had started to use the phrase in his letters and in a circular he mailed to subscribers for a competition on 'What Science Fiction Means to Me' so that by the time *Science Wonder Stories* appeared the phrase was in common usage throughout. Interestingly Gernsback, or it may have been Sloane, had used the phrase earlier in *Amazing Stories*. A reader wrote in complaining about the use of Jules Verne's old stories, to which the editorial response was that 'Jules Verne was a sort of Shakespeare in science fiction'.[9] The phrase, which was so much easier to use than scientifiction, rapidly took hold and finally the genre had a name.

Gernsback had found a resourceful and reliable editor to help him. This was David Lasser, who is a much neglected revolutionary in science fiction. It was through Lasser's efforts that science fiction started to mature. Born in Baltimore, Maryland in March 1902

9. *Amazing Stories*, 1 (10) January 1927, p. 973.

Lasser had entered the army in July 1918 and was a member of the US expeditionary force. He was discharged as a sergeant in February 1919, still only 16. He became an engineer at Rosendale, Newark, and then moved on to be a technical writer. It was that skill and a solid engineering background that Lasser brought to Gernsback's aid. Unlike Sloane, whose science was firmly rooted in the Victorian era and who believed that humans would not conquer Everest let alone space, Lasser was a believer in human beings' power over the planet. In this regard, through the aegis of *Science Wonder Stories*, Lasser became a founder member and first president of the American Rocket Society which was formed in March 1930. Through the Society, Lasser wrote the first book on space travel in the English language, *The Conquest of Space* (Penguin Press, 1931), which he part financed himself.

Lasser's initial impact on *Science Wonder* and *Air Wonder* was minimal, as he was working with manuscripts that Gernsback had acquired. He thought the quality of most of them was poor, but it would be a year or two before his efforts saw fruit. Until then, science fiction continued to decline in quality. Some interesting new talents were emerging, most in the wake of the success of *Amazing*: 1929 and 1930 saw the first appearances of the writers Neil R. Jones, Lloyd A. Eshbach, P. Schuyler Miller, Charles R. Tanner, J. Harvey Haggard, Leslie F. Stone, Ed Earl Repp, Drury D. Sharp, Raymond Z. Gallun, Raymond A. Palmer, Nathan A. Schachner and John W. Campbell, Jr.

Some of these, especially Ed Earl Repp, would be responsible for reducing the quality of sf even further. Repp was a newspaper reporter who was acquainted with Edgar Rice Burroughs and Zane Grey. Both of these had suggested that Repp turn to writing fiction which he did with moderate success. He wrote mostly in the fields of sf and the western, and increasingly these two fields merged. Science fiction in its worst form of space opera has often been accused of being little more than cowboys in outer space. Repp was one of those writers who helped that degeneration. Having said that, his first published work, 'The Radium Pool' (*Science Wonder Stories*, August–September 1929), a Merrittesque fantasy based on a location near to where Repp lived, retains some of that excitement and wonder from the early days of pulp sf and can still be enjoyed.

Neil R. Jones was not a particularly good writer, and his later science fiction is very poor, but he did have some clever ideas. His first sale was 'The Death's Head Meteor' (*Air Wonder*, January

1930), noted as being the first sf story to use the word 'astronaut', but by the time that appeared he was already working on a much bigger canvas. His story 'The Jameson Satellite' was rejected in December 1929 by Gernsback, who gave him some very sound advice. Jones had taken too much space to cover the preliminary basics of his concept about a professor who arranges for his body to be buried in space. Jones planned to follow this with a story called 'After a Million Years' which would explore what happened when Jameson's space capsule was discovered by benign alien explorers and his body was revived. Gernsback suggested that the first story should form the prologue to the more exciting later events. Jones took this advice but, dissatisfied with the payments he had received from Gernsback (the old practice of little and late remained), sent the story to Sloane at *Amazing*. The story was accepted but Sloane, who worked at glacier speed, held on to it for over a year. It eventually surfaced in the July 1931 *Amazing* and was immensely popular.

The better quality writers to emerge from this period were Miller, Tanner, Sharp, Gallun, Schachner and Campbell. Most of these would not start to establish themselves until the mid-thirties, and we shall encounter them all in due course. The most important, however, is John W. Campbell.

Campbell made his debut as a master exponent of the super-science extravaganza. His first story, 'When the Atoms Failed' (*Amazing Stories*, January 1930), was a relatively straightforward piece about the discovery of atomic energy, but his subsequent stories developed on a cosmic scale. He began a series featuring the characters Arcot, Wade and Morey. In the first, 'Piracy Preferred' (*Amazing Stories*, June 1930), Wade was a super-scientist (*à la* Blackie DuQuesne) who has perfected a method of making his spaceship invisible. He enters on a life of crime as a space pirate until he is thwarted by physicist Richard Arcot, mathematician William Morey and design engineer John Fuller (Campbell's projection of himself). Wade repents and joins forces with the others in a series in which these mighty scientific brains pitch themselves against increasingly cosmic foes. 'The Black Star Passes' (*Amazing Stories Quarterly*, Fall 1930) sees them fighting an alien race who inhabit a planet circling a dead star and who seek to take over Earth. 'Islands of Space' (*Amazing Stories Quarterly*, Spring 1931) sees the team exploring space at faster-than-light speed and engaging in mighty alien wars. Here was true cosmic science fiction. In 'Invaders from the Infinite' (*Amazing Stories Quarterly*, Spring–Summer 1932) the team help an alien race against a universal menace. This novel, which has been called the apex of space opera, uses some clever ideas such as harnessing the emotions as a weapon.

Alongside Campbell, E.E. Smith was writing his super-science fiction. 'Skylark Three', the sequel to 'The Skylark of Space', was serialized in *Amazing Stories* from August to October 1930 and took the space opera to new heights.

There is no doubt that 1930 was the year of super-science, but to make the point more forcefully it saw the establishment of the first genuine rival to Hugo Gernsback. With a cover date of January 1930, the first issue of *Astounding Stories of Super Science* appeared from publisher William Clayton. Clayton's publishing empire had been established with *Snappy Stories*, a saucy men's magazine issued in 1912, though his more recent pulps had been in the western and detective fields. He had occasionally moved towards the strange or bizarre adventure field, such as with *Danger Trail*, but that was short lived. For a period one of his editors was Harold Hersey who had 'discussed plans with Clayton to launch a pseudo-science fantasy sheet'[10] in 1928, but Clayton remained cautious. The following year, however, with new editor Harry Bates, Clayton consented to a new title, and *Astounding Stories of Super Science* was born.

It is with *Astounding* that science fiction's fate became sealed. *Astounding* was first and always a straight adventure pulp magazine. It had no intention of educating through science and shared no ideals with Gernsback. Whilst both *Science Wonder Stories* and *Amazing Stories* were publishing their share of poor science fiction, their ideals in the field remained noble. *Astounding*'s never were. Its aim was to tap into the popularity of science fiction and make what profit was possible. Nevertheless the publisher, William Clayton, was well respected. He paid good rates and he paid them promptly. Writers and agents had no qualms about dealing with him as they did with Gernsback (and increasingly so with Sloane, who was so frustratingly slow over everything). Consequently, from the first issue *Astounding* was able to boast some of the big names from the Munsey magazines: Victor Rousseau, Ray Cummings and Murray Leinster. The cover, by 47-year-old Hans Wessolowski (better known as 'Wesso'), illustrated a scene from Rousseau's serial 'The Beetle Horde', showing 'our hero' having a fight with an oversized bug. Wesso's covers were bright and action-packed. He would be the Paul of the Clayton magazines.

10. Harold B. Hersey, *Pulpwood Editor* (New York: F.A. Stokes, 1937), p. 188.

Before long other popular pulpsters began to appear in *Astounding*, including Arthur J. Burks, Sewell Peaslee Wright and Hugh B. Cave, as well as many of Gernsback's own discoveries: Harl Vincent, Lilith Lorraine, R.F. Starzl, Edmond Hamilton and Miles J. Breuer. Here, the writers were able to give full vent to their imagination with less concern over the quality of the scientific content. Science fiction, already suffering at the hands of Gernsback, now began to plummet. Harry Bates, who tends to be remembered fondly in the field of science fiction, mostly for his excellent story 'Farewell to the Master' (*Astounding*, October 1940), was at this stage destroying the ideals of science fiction.

Once Clayton had entered the science-fiction field, the market started to take notice. Gernsback had always been an outsider, but now it was becoming serious. Writer R. Jere Black reviewed the field in the May 1930 *Author & Journalist* and concluded that it was now a profitable area for the aspiring writer and one relatively easy to enter because the fiction tended to be of such low quality. His judgement of an sf story was that it usually involved a hero rescuing a woman from aliens which came from either space, another time or another dimension. This was the basic formula for science fiction that Edgar Rice Burroughs had set in train in 1912 and had seen little development since. Gernsback's attempts to encourage the invention story can now be seen as only a small detour on the wider road to pulp ruin.

The nadir was reached in the Hawk Carse series of space adventures written for *Astounding* by Harry Bates and his assistant Desmond Hall under the pen name of Anthony Gilmore. They started with 'Hawk Carse' in the November 1931 issue. Carse was a super-space hero who chased the evil pirate Dr Ku Sui throughout the solar system. The series was popular at the time – but then so was anything with a hero, villain, damsel-in-distress, monster and ray-gun, and it had no redeeming qualities.

The changes in science fiction were perhaps most noticeable in the late spring of 1930. On impulse Gernsback decided to merge *Air Wonder Stories* and *Science Wonder Stories*. This was not because either magazine's sales was ailing. *Air Wonder Stories*, which had started as a rather earth-bound (or perhaps I should say stratosphere-bound) magazine, had started to run more interplanetary stories and consequently the contents of the two magazines were becoming increasingly similar. The sudden decision to merge the two probably came about because Gernsback planned to issue a new magazine, *Aviation Mechanics*, and needed the printing schedule. What is most significant though is that when the two magazines joined they were rechristened simply *Wonder Stories*. The word 'science' was dropped. In an announcement in the May 1930 *Science Wonder Stories* Gernsback said: 'It has been felt for some time that the word "Science" has tended to retard the progress of the magazine, because many people had the impression that it is a sort of scientific periodical rather than a fiction magazine.'[11]

Here was a statement that would have been anathema to Gernsback five years earlier. He was having to recognize that the very reference to the word 'science' was detrimental to the magazine. It also meant that the image the magazine was seeking to project was more in line with that of *Astounding*. This was further compounded when, with the November 1930 issue, Gernsback changed the format from large size to standard pulp size. Now the magazine was completely on a par with *Astounding*.

Further deterioration of the field was seen in 1931. Harold Hersey, who had left Clayton to join Bernarr Macfadden, had now established his own publishing company and planned to issue a magazine called *Astonishing Stories*. Following such gosh-wow titles as *Amazing*, *Wonder* and *Astounding*, *Astonishing* would be a fitting addition. In the end the magazine emerged as *Miracle Science and Fantasy Stories*, which had less impact. Its first issue was dated April–May 1931. It followed in imitation of *Astounding*, and included fiction by Ray Cummings, Victor Rousseau and Arthur J. Burks, but was of even lower quality. The stories featured either lost civilizations, invasions by monsters, or adventures on distant planets.

The magazine was nominally edited by Douglas M. Dold who had worked with Hersey at Clayton Magazines and was the initial consulting editor on *Astounding*. As a result of an accident in the First World War, he was blind and so worked with his brother Elliott on reading and judging manuscripts. This must be one of the rare cases of a blind editor. Elliott illustrated much of the magazine and it is primarily for that reason that *Miracle* remains collectible today, as Elliott emerged as one of the great artists in later issues of *Astounding*.

However, after the second equally dire issue Elliott became ill and Hersey discontinued the magazine. This leaves one imagining that the magazine had not been showing a healthy profit. Nevertheless

11. *Science Wonder Stories*, 1 (12) May 1930, p. 1099.

Miracle demonstrated the way the field was heading unless action was taken to improve the quality of science fiction. Bates was less concerned about this. All the time that *Astounding* turned in a profit he was content to issue the magazine, although the suffix '*of Super Science*' was dropped with the February 1931 issue. Indeed Clayton issued a further new magazine, *Strange Tales*, in September 1931, in imitation of *Weird Tales* and also featuring some weird science fiction. Most of it was of the monster-in-the-laboratory type, although one of its more memorable stories is Jack Williamson's 'Wolves of Darkness' (January 1932) with its fourth-dimensional treatment of werewolves.

The improvement of science fiction was left to Gernsback to engineer, and this he strove to do. David Lasser felt equally strongly about it, annoyed that the science fiction he was publishing was being termed 'wild west stories of the future'.

The drive for originality began in *Wonder Stories*. Lasser was fortunate in that although *Astounding* paid good rates promptly, Bates was less amenable to experimental fiction. He wanted straight formula work. In addition Sloane was so slow at *Amazing* that a submission there could languish for many months and the author had no idea whether the story was accepted, lost or forgotten. So, although *Wonder* paid low rates and often late, Lasser was quick in his response and encouragement to authors and, as an added bonus, the letter column was especially lively, giving authors good and lengthy feedback on their stories. By 1931, therefore, amidst the dross, it was *Wonder* that tended to publish the more original fiction.

One obvious writer in this regard was Clark Ashton Smith. Smith did not particularly like science fiction, but he liked exotic locales. By 1931 he was becoming so prolific that *Weird Tales* was overstocked, and Smith tried his hand at *Wonder*. Lasser encouraged his early works, which Smith regarded as hack work, but the formula gelled with 'The City of [the] Singing Flame' (*Wonder Stories*, July 1931), a Merrittesque tale about another dimensional world. A sequel, 'Beyond the Singing Flame' (November 1931), was written on demand. Smith became arguably the most original contributor to *Wonder Stories* in the early thirties and brought a particular depth of horror to some stories, especially 'Dweller in Martian Depths' (March 1933) which Lasser had to edit to remove some of the more excessive descriptions. This act annoyed Smith and thereafter the relationship with *Wonder* was marred.

Edmond Hamilton, who by now must have been tiring of the space opera theme which he had excessively exploited, also started to explore more original ideas. He had made one such venture with 'The Man who Saw the Future' (*Amazing Stories*, October 1930) and he developed this with 'The Man who Evolved' (*Wonder Stories*, April 1931). David Lasser continued to encourage his writers to explore new approaches to fiction. In a long letter of instruction mailed to his regular contributors on 11 May 1931, Lasser exhorted them to bring some realism to their fiction. In this important letter he outlawed space opera, the giant insect story and the hero-versus-monster story. The main part of his letter emphasized that:

> Science fiction should deal *realistically* with the effect upon people, individually and in groups, of a scientific invention or discovery. The flow of the story should be reasonable, although dramatic; the situation should be convincing, the atmosphere conveyed vividly and the characters should really be human. In other words, allow yourself one fundamental assumption – that a certain machine or discovery is possible – and then show what would be its logical and dramatic consequences upon the world; also, what would be the effect upon the group of characters that you pick to carry your theme. The 'modern' science story should not try to be a world-sweeping epic. It should rather try to portray *intensively* some particular phase of our future civilization.

Lasser was now revealing himself as an unbiased and entrepreneurial editor keen to encourage the discussion and development of realistic themes within science fiction. As a consequence not only did the letter column become a vehicle for the free expression of values and beliefs, but the stories began to consider and develop themes hitherto considered taboo, including sex, feminism and religion. The outcry that followed publication of 'The Scarlet Planet' by Don Mark Lemon (*Wonder Stories Quarterly*, Winter 1931) showed that not all readers were yet fully prepared for the storming of the barricades. In fact this story was intended as a spoof on male-dominated society, but the more vocal readers only noticed the sexual adventures of spacemen on a female-occupied planet. Nevertheless it was not long before other writers were exploring the role of men and women in future societies. On the one hand Richard Vaughan, in 'The Woman from Space' (*Wonder Stories Quarterly*, Spring 1932), looked at how men had all but destroyed themselves in an unrelenting war, and it is left to the women to establish a utopia. At the other extreme Thomas S. Gardner, in 'The Last Woman' (*Wonder Stories*, April 1932), considered how men evolve beyond the need to breed and keep the last woman as a museum exhibit. Love is not understood and is seen as an animalistic throwback.

Meanwhile religious themes were also being explored. In 'The Voice in the Void' (*Wonder Stories Quarterly*, Spring 1932), Clifford D. Simak considers the discovery of a sacred tomb on Mars believed to contain the relics of the Messiah, whilst in 'The Venus Adventure' (*Wonder Stories*, May 1932), John Beynon Harris portrays the loss of innocence on Venus when a puritanical space pioneer corrupts the planet's natives.

The most noticeable development, however, was the outlawing of the space opera and the introduction of realism to space exploration. This had started to emerge in an abortive series being developed by P. Schuyler Miller and Walter Dennis which featured a villain called Gulliver who, through his own endeavours, overcomes perils in space. Only two stories were published, 'The Red Spot of Jupiter' (*Wonder Stories*, July 1931) and 'The Duel on the Asteroid' (*Wonder Stories*, January 1932), but they were the first to rely predominantly on character for the development of the story, and in so doing brought some grim realism to space.

Edmond Hamilton took this one step further in 'A Conquest of Two Worlds' (*Wonder Stories*, February 1932) in which his hero, Mark Halkett, stands by his principles and seeks to stop the exploitation of the friendly child-like Jovians by greedy space explorers. P. Schuyler Miller followed this with 'The Forgotten Man of Space' (*Wonder Stories*, May 1933), one of the best stories of the year, and a fine example of self-sacrifice by a space explorer determined to protect the innocent inhabitants of Mars.

Others were now considering the perils and hardship of space exploration. In 'The Hell Planet' (*Wonder Stories*, June 1932), Leslie F. Stone portrayed the horrors of the planet Vulcan, once believed to circle the sun inside the orbit of Mercury. Henrik Dahl Juve showed a hostile and unfriendly Mars in 'In Martian Depths' (*Wonder Stories*, September 1932). Laurence Manning produced two of the best stories of the period in 'The Voyage of the *Asteroid*' (*Wonder Stories Quarterly*, Summer 1932) and its sequel 'The Wreck of the *Asteroid*' (*Wonder Stories*, December 1932–February 1933) which showed the grim reality of exploration on Venus and later on Mars.

The teenage writer Frank K. Kelly was perhaps the best exponent of this hard realism. Despite his youth, Kelly was not lured into the excitement of the super-science epic, but instead produced a number of stories that considered the real perils of space. Perhaps the most poignant was 'The Moon Tragedy' (*Wonder Stories*, October 1933) which looked back at the fate of the last explorers to the Moon.

There was a tremendous sea change in the quality of science fiction published in *Wonder Stories* during 1931 and 1932, which has generally been overlooked before. Almost all of this was due to the determined control of David Lasser who realized that science fiction had to survive by the strength of its characterization and realistic plotting. Only in that way would the field develop. Even Harry Bates sat up and took notice, issuing a letter to his writers in August 1932 asking them to place emphasis on the 'story values' rather than solely the scientific content. Had Lasser been able to develop his writers further, *Wonder Stories* might have remained the field leader and science fiction might have matured more rapidly, but events outside the field were about to make their mark.

Order from Chaos

Looking back at science fiction during the mid–1930s reveals a world in turmoil. At the time the field was still reeling from its romp with the super-science epic, and it was struggling to understand its real form and being. But the world about it would not allow it to settle. Science fiction could not escape the financial restraints of the economic Depression that had gripped the world during the past few years. Neither could it escape the desire of its fans to see science fiction take bold and exciting new steps. And neither could it avoid the inevitable market pressures that would see popular science fiction and hard-core science fiction start to move apart, something that would rend the field during the next decade. All of these pressures will be explored in this section, and I will try to make some order out of what was a most turbulent period.

The basic pressures of the Depression can be covered first, as they had a direct effect upon the survival of the magazines. The Depression had been making its effects known ever since the stock market crash in October 1929, although magazines (like the film industry) had tended to fare better than other luxury items because they provided escapist entertainment. However, the credit squeeze introduced in May 1931 began to have an immediate bite. With credit frozen, banks began to call in their debts and the normal three-month credit delay between printer and publisher began to make itself felt. By August 1931 there is a suggestion that Gernsback's companies were experiencing financial difficulties. It was possible that *Wonder Stories* might have folded with its October 1931 issue. However, Gernsback overcame the problem, probably through a new printing or distribution deal involving his newly revamped technical magazine *Everyday Science and Mechanics*, and this allowed him to continue *Wonder Stories*, even to the extent of restoring it to the larger pulp format and printing it on coated stock rather than pulp paper. The November 1931 issue was imposing and featured good-quality fiction. To the reader, unaware of the behind-the-scenes activities, there was all the appearance of a prosperous publishing company. However, any new arrangement that Gernsback had with his printers or distributors was bound to restrict him financially. Thus it was a hard blow when in December 1931 Gernsback's bank closed. Although the magazines continued to appear, from then on Gernsback found it harder to pay his writers and the arrears in payments began to accumulate rapidly.

William Clayton was experiencing the same financial problems. His solution was to alternate the publication of his magazines. *Astounding Stories* became a bi-monthly after the June 1932 issue. This is never a good sign for a magazine. The majority of sales are from news-stands where purchasers look for magazines at regular intervals. Once a magazine becomes irregular there's more likelihood that purchasers may overlook it or dealers cease to order it. Clayton's solution was to buy out his printer to avoid this being a major creditor, and also to prevent what had become the common practice of printers taking over magazines in exchange for debts owed to them. This was a disaster as Clayton then found he could not pay the final instalment of the sum due to the printer for the purchase. In October 1932 Clayton ceased publication of both *Strange Tales* and *Astounding Stories* (with effect from their January 1933 issues). He then found he had purchased enough stories and paper to publish one further issue of *Astounding* which appeared in January (dated March 1933).

Amazing Stories fared better, despite its low circulation. Its parent company had passed through a number of transformations culminating in Teck Publications, a subsidiary of Macfadden Publishing, which took over the magazine in August 1931. Therefore, just at the time when the Depression was taking hold, *Amazing* fell into the comparatively wealthy lap of Bernarr Macfadden. Nevertheless belts had to be tightened. Although *Amazing* continued on its monthly schedule, the *Quarterly* became irregular after its Winter 1932 issue (released in January) and it also started to reprint fiction. *Amazing Stories* was fortunate not only in the following it had established because of its name but because it continued to attract fiction from Edward E. Smith. 'Skylark Three', the sequel to 'The Skylark of Space', was serialized in three parts from August to October 1930, and the following year another serial, 'Spacehounds of IPC', ran in the July to September issues. However, Smith became disenchanted with Sloane who had made some unauthorized changes in the manuscript, probably to fit it into three equal parts. Smith was too important a name for *Amazing* to lose, but lose him it did. Smith offered his next novel, 'Triplanetary', to Harry Bates at *Astounding*. Unfortunately the magazine ceased publication before the serial could be used, although the cover Wesso had drawn illustrating a scene from the novel ran on the March 1933 issue. The manuscript was returned to Smith who reluctantly sent it to Sloane. It was serialized in the January to April 1934 issues of *Amazing*.

Other than Smith's novels, *Amazing* was uninspiring. Sloane provided boring editorials with no sense of wonder or imagination, and the magazine frequently reprinted ageing stories, some of which, like Edward Everett Hale's 'The Good-Natured Pendulum', had no science-fiction content at all. Its science fiction, on the whole, lacked sparkle. It has often been contended that *Amazing* owed its survival to the popularity of the Professor Jameson stories by Neil R. Jones, although these did not appear with sufficient regularity to sustain that argument. Nevertheless this series, which follows the travels of the resurrected professor and the robot-bodied Zoromes around the universe, whilst poorly written, did have a verve and excitement that led readers to demand more. The series, though, did not really start to come alive until 'Into the Hydrosphere' (October 1933), but its popularity may have contributed to the magazine surviving for as long as it did.

In the summer of 1932 the Eastern Distribution Company went bankrupt. This distributed many of the smaller independent pulps, including Gernsback's, and with that Gernsback lost additional income. A new distributor was found, but *Wonder Stories Quarterly* had to be sacrificed, folding with its Winter 1933 issue, published in late 1932.

By early 1933, therefore, fans were left with an ailing *Amazing Stories Quarterly* (which never seemed to know quite when to give up the ghost),[12] an increasingly languid *Amazing Stories*, and *Wonder Stories*, which, during the spring and summer of 1933, was the only quality magazine. We have already seen the strides it was making in bringing realism into science fiction, and Lasser continued to push for this. Inevitably the effects of the Depression began to surface in science fiction, predominantly through the emergence of technocracy.

Technocracy was a movement to involve science more in the socio-economic decision-making process. Gernsback gave it his whole-hearted support, even to the extent of launching a new (though short-lived) magazine called *Technocracy Review*. Technocracy also featured strongly in *Wonder Stories*, mostly in the work of Nathan Schachner where science was ultimately shown to triumph. Gernsback was concerned that there were many who would blame science for the Depression, especially those who had been made unemployed as a result of increasing automation. Schachner's stories, in particular 'The Robot Technocrat' (March 1933) and the short series 'The Revolt of the Scientists' (April–June 1933), looked at the shortcomings of manual labour, and argued for a balance between social and industrial reform. Laurence Manning also considered the consequences of over-industrialization in his series 'The Man Who Awoke' (March–August 1933). This includes a remarkably advanced passage about ecology and the rationing of fossil fuels. Men of the future look back on the twentieth century as a period of extravagance and waste. Again the message was that industrialists and scientists needed to plan the future together.

During 1933 Lasser found himself becoming increasingly involved in workers' rights to the extent that he was devoting less time to editing *Wonder Stories*. Gernsback used this as an opportunity to dispense with his services in July 1933. At the same time Gernsback dissolved Stellar Publications and launched a new company, Continental Publications. *Wonder Stories* missed a couple of summer issues during this process, and from the November 1933 issue

12. There never seemed to be a firm decision to fold *Amazing Stories Quarterly*; instead it just faded away. The last two issues, dated Winter 1933 and Fall 1934, were filled with reprints. In answer to a reader's enquiry in the May 1935 *Amazing Stories*, Sloane responded that 'The *Quarterly* will be somewhat irregular in dates of publication. We have sometimes felt like discontinuing it completely.' Obviously the feelings became insurmountable as no more issues appeared.

reverted to the standard pulp size. That issue had a new editor, the 17-year old Charles D. Hornig, who had none of the experience or strength of purpose of Lasser, but who had a belief in science fiction that would change the character of *Wonder Stories* yet again.

Despite his youth, Hornig had been a fan of science fiction and weird stories since 1930. He had come to Gernsback's notice when he sent Gernsback a copy of the first issue of his fan magazine, *The Fantasy Fan*. Gernsback, having just fired Lasser, was giving thought to a successor and called Hornig to his office. Although he was surprised at Hornig's age, he gave him a manuscript to proof-read and copy-edit, and satisfied at the results, hired him on a salary of less than a third of that he had been paying Lasser.

Gernsback had told Hornig that he was looking for an enthusiastic fan to edit *Wonder Stories*. This was a sign of Gernsback's continued interest in and encouragement of the fan or hobbyist movement, something he had been allied to ever since *Modern Electrics*. In fact it was wholly due to Gernsback, through the letter columns of his magazines, that the fan movement had started, which made the employment of Hornig seem like Gernsback was reaping the reward of earlier investment.

The science-fiction fan movement, though small, was immensely active and becoming increasingly influential within its limited sphere. Fan clubs, initially devoted to Gernsback's ideal of studying and promoting scientific achievement, had soon metamorphosed into clubs discussing the merits and problems of science fiction. The fans dominated the magazine letter columns, and Gernsback was keen to encourage them. As early as the Spring 1930 issue of *Science Wonder Quarterly*, he had set a competition to discover 'What I Have Done to Spread Science Fiction'. The first prize was won by Raymond A. Palmer for his fan activities with the Science Correspondence Club, which he had founded with Walter Dennis. Palmer would later become the *bête noir* of the science-fiction field, but in the early 1930s he was amongst the most active devotees.

The organization of fan clubs, especially the Science Correspondence Club and the Scienceers, brought with it club magazines. The first was *The Comet*, edited by Walter Dennis. Its first issue, dated May 1930, has the distinction of being the first science-fiction fan magazine. Other club magazines began to appear, but soon there was a movement by a core of fans to publish an independent fan magazine. This was *The Time Traveller* produced by a consortium of Raymond Palmer, Forrest Ackerman, Mort Weisinger and Julius

Schwartz, with Allen Glasser as editor and (from the third issue) Conrad H. Ruppert as printer. The first issue appeared in January 1932 and it survived for nine issues until January 1933.

Glasser soon fell out with the consortium which, now assisted by Maurice Ingher, started *Science Fiction Digest* in September 1932. This was professionally printed by Ruppert from the first issue and managed to maintain a monthly schedule for most of its life. As the core news magazine of fandom it helped bond fans together and provide an independent vehicle for the discussion of science fiction and the dissemination of information.

A notable achievement in *Science Fiction Digest* (retitled *Fantasy Magazine* from January 1934) was the publication of its round-robin serial 'Cosmos' which began in the July 1933 issue and ran for 17 instalments until December 1934. Ralph Milne Farley set the story going. All the big names of sf contributed, including David H. Keller, Francis Flagg, John W. Campbell, Otis Adelbert Kline, Abraham Merritt, Edward E. Smith, P. Schuyler Miller, and Lloyd A. Eshbach, with Edmond Hamilton writing the concluding episode. The novel was a remarkable achievement, with each episode being relatively self-contained although still moving the narrative forward. Although the entire serial lacks the cohesive quality of a single novel it remains a fascinating novelty. It was also evidence of how much professional writers were prepared to co-operate with fandom. The two sides of science fiction were closely bonded at this time.

It was not too surprising that before long fans would seek to produce their own fiction magazine. The earliest known fan magazine featuring fiction was *Cosmic Stories* produced by Jerome Siegel in Cleveland, Ohio, and issued some time in 1930. This was only a typewritten magazine with carbon copies circulated to no more than a handful of fans in the Cleveland area. Apart from Siegel's own stories it did contain new fiction by Walter Dennis and Clare Winger Harris. No copies are believed to survive.

One of Siegel's correspondents, Carl Swanson, from Washburn, North Dakota, circulated details of a proposed new magazine called *Galaxy* to be issued early in 1932. By all accounts Swanson's original intention was to produce a professionally printed magazine, with formal distribution. Although he garnered some submissions he was unable to raise the finances to issue the magazine. In the end he issued two of the stories he had received as small mimeographed booklets late in 1932. These included a reprinting of Edmond Hamilton's 'The Metal Giants'. Whilst this was the first fan publication of a professional story, it wasn't the first independent publication of fan fiction. Earlier in 1932 Conrad Ruppert and Julius Schwartz had set up their own Solar Publications and their first publication was *The Cavemen of Venus* by Allen Glasser. Professionally printed by Ruppert this is the first true independent fan publication of fiction.

Meanwhile Jerome Siegel had teamed up with local artist Joseph Schuster to publish a new fan fiction magazine, *Science Fiction*. The first issue was dated October 1932 and it survived for five issues into mid-1933, attracting fiction from David H. Keller, Raymond Palmer and Clare Winger Harris. Its significance, though, is more than that of being the first regular fan fiction magazine. Siegel's fiction was uninspired and drew upon the super-science extravaganzas of the early thirties. One of these stories, 'The Reign of the Superman' (January 1933), was the seed from which he and Schuster developed the Superman comic strip. It was not until 1938 that the two were able to sell the strip to DC Comics which first published Superman in the June 1938 *Action Comics*, but his roots were firmly planted in the emerging fan magazines of 1932.

Many of the fans were becoming increasingly dissatisfied with the quality of fiction in the professional magazines during this period. One of these was the Pennsylvania fan William Crawford. He made plans to issue a magazine that would strike through the editorial conventions of the professional magazines and publish taboo-breaking fiction. However, he had problems finding a cheap printer. In the end he acquired his own printing press and with the help of fan and writer Lloyd A. Eshbach managed to issue an advanced flyer for *Unusual Stories* in November 1933. Crawford claimed he was going to print only original and different stories, and as a sample printed the first page only of P. Schuyler Miller's 'The Titan', which had been rejected by all of the magazines because of its strong sexual theme.

Crawford's aim was exactly the same as Harlan Ellison's 30 years later when he would publish his own taboo-breaking anthology, *Dangerous Visions*, to resounding critical acclaim. Crawford, however, was dogged by lack of finances and his efforts never satisfactorily got off the ground. *Unusual Stories* never saw a complete issue, though three partial issues appeared at erratic intervals during 1934 and 1935. Instead Crawford began *Marvel Tales* which featured a mixture of weird tales and science fiction. This first appeared in May 1934, an issue perhaps more notable for David H. Keller's horror story 'Binding Deluxe' than for its sf content. The third issue, dated Winter 1934, at last saw the first instalment of 'The Titan' (though the serial was never finished). That issue is also notable for 'Lilies', the first appearance in print of Robert Bloch. The fourth issue, dated March/April 1935, is perhaps the best. Apart from Miller's serial, it also published the now acknowledged classic 'The Creator' by Clifford D. Simak, which had been rejected by all other magazines because of its religious theme. This issue also featured a strong horror story, 'The Cathedral Crypt' by John Beynon Harris.

Marvel Tales saw five issues in total, the last achieving news-stand distribution, and it goes down in history as the first fan-produced semi-professional sf magazine. Crawford could not secure the finances to sustain it and it folded in mid–1935. Nevertheless by then Crawford had made his point and the science-fiction field was rapidly adapting to encourage more creative science fiction.

The main driving force for this was, surprisingly, *Astounding Stories*. In April 1933 William Clayton had been forced into bankruptcy. He had auctioned his titles, which included the profitable detective magazine *Clues* and western magazine *Cowboy Stories*. These passed, via an interim purchaser, to Street & Smith, who as part of the package acquired *Astounding Stories*. *Strange Tales* was not revived, though this was briefly the intention. Some stories acquired for the aborted revival of *Strange Tales* were used instead in the first new issue of *Astounding Stories*, dated October 1933.

We have already seen that this period was the time when Charles D. Hornig became the new editor of *Wonder Stories*, and when *Wonder* reverted to pulp format. It was also the period when William Crawford issued *Marvel Tales* and when *Amazing Stories* converted to pulp format. With the revival of *Astounding Stories* this makes October/November 1933 a significant date in the history of early magazine sf.

It was very fortunate that *Astounding* had fallen into the hands of Street & Smith. Unlike 14 years earlier when the company had failed to make the most of an opportunity with *The Thrill Book*, Street & Smith were now more aware of the market potential of extravagant fiction. Henry Ralston, their circulation manager, always had a keen eye and ear for an opportunity. In 1931 they had had a remarkable success with *The Shadow*. This magazine had grown out of a radio series that had been used as a vehicle for promoting mystery stories from Street & Smith's *Detective Story Magazine*. It was introduced by a mysterious character known only as The Shadow, and after a while dealers found the public were asking for The

Shadow's magazine instead of *Detective Story*. Ralston had long believed the dime novel's day had not passed, and harboured a secret desire to revive Nick Carter. As we have seen, *Detective Story Magazine* had been created in 1915 out of the old Nick Carter dime-novel weekly. Now Ralston used the opportunity to re-create the medium, in conference with *Detective Story*'s editor Frank Blackwell and writer Walter Gibson. The three created the main character of *The Shadow* and the magazine was launched in April 1931. It was instantly successful, with a circulation rocketing to 300,000 copies. It was soon converted from a quarterly to a monthly, and later twice-monthly, becoming one of Street & Smith's best-selling magazines.

With *The Shadow* the old dime-novel hero re-emerged into the pulps, and the single-character magazine was created. These would become one of the mainstays of the pulps of the thirties, and Street & Smith led the way. In March 1933 they began a new magazine, *Doc Savage*, featuring 'The Man of Bronze' written by Lester Dent under the Kenneth Robeson name. Unlike *The Shadow* which concentrated on the mysterious and bizarre but only occasionally trespassed into science fiction, *Doc Savage* was much closer to that territory. Clark Savage, Jr. was a physical and mental superman who operated out of his headquarters at the top of a New York skyscraper. He was an adventurer and soldier of fortune who pitted his strength and wits against a legion of master criminals. The first novel, 'The Man of Bronze', takes him to a lost valley in Central America where he saves the Mayans from an evil villain, and discovers a supply of gold which finances all his future adventures. Many of these featured lost worlds, several including dinosaurs. Savage also had a retreat in the Arctic which is revealed in 'Fortress of Solitude' (October 1938). *Doc Savage* was not regarded by its publisher as a science-fiction magazine but as a mystery title. Editor John Nanovic held the office next door to F. Orlin Tremaine and later John W. Campbell, Jr., but when the subject of science fiction arose Nanovic maintained he had no idea what they were talking about.[13] Yet author Lester Dent utilized many science-fiction concepts and this may have encouraged its readers to explore Street & Smith's other magazines.

The first new issue of *Astounding* was not too shattering. It was a mixture of mediocre material, and contained no editorial or reader

---

13. See Albert Tonik, 'Interview with John Nanovic', *The Science-Fiction Collector*, 9, June 1980, p. 44.

departments, or any clue as to its editor. The only story of any merit was Donald Wandrei's 'A Race through Time', which traces a romantic struggle into far futurity. The November issue equally lacked any embellishments, though the stories were better, in particular Jack Williamson's 'Dead Star Station' and Wallace West's tale of a two-dimensional world, 'Plane People'.

It was with the December issue that the wind of change blasted through *Astounding*, and it also revealed the editor. It was F. Orlin Tremaine, an editor with over 13 years' experience. He had been involved with Macfadden's *True Story* in 1924, had edited *The Smart Set* until 1926, and *Everybody's Magazine* in 1930. He then worked for William Clayton as editor of *Clues*, with which title he came across to Street & Smith, along with assistant editor Desmond Hall. Because Tremaine was also editing *Clues* and *Top-Notch*, Hall undertook most of the basic editing of *Astounding*, although it was Tremaine who kept the editorial control. It was probably Tremaine and Hall in conference who decided that something needed to be done to inject life into science fiction. It was certainly evident that science fiction was maturing under Lasser's guidance at *Wonder Stories*, and if *Astounding* were to make its mark it was necessary to create something clearly identifiable. The old hero-versus-monster space opera had had its day, and the hero-versus-villain was being more than capably handled in the emerging hero pulps.

With the December 1933 issue Tremaine announced his new policy for stories of total originality and scope. He called them 'thought variants', and the first example was 'Ancestral Voices' by none other than *Wonder Stories'* leading writer Nathan Schachner. The plot was simple. A man travels back in time and kills a Hun who would otherwise have been a distant ancestor. As a result thousands of people in the modern day disappear. The twist Schachner added was that these people were amongst every race and creed. The story is not amongst Schachner's best, and did not create the stir that Tremaine expected, but it had some degree of originality. The next 'thought variant', 'Colossus' by Donald Wandrei (January 1934), was even less original. It concerns a spaceship that reaches such speeds that it breaks out of our universe into a macro-universe. Ray Cummings and G. Peyton Wertenbaker had done this effectively 10 years earlier. What Wandrei brought to it though was brash excitement. The story ripples with energy. The reader is conveyed into this world of wonder at break-neck pace. That same issue contained another Schachner story, 'Redmask of the Outlands', which proved very popular. It depicts a future America where society has divided between high-tech city states and primitive wildernesses called the Outlands. It was a society that the Depression, and the agricultural disasters of the mid-west Dust Bowl, made all too real. Redmask is an outlaw turned hero who, by using an invisible flying machine, is able to plunder the cities for food and essentials.

'Rebirth' by Thomas Calvert McClary (February–March 1934) was the next thought variant. Civilization suffers global amnesia and is forced to return to the caves and start life again. It was another image inspired by the Depression. Jack Williamson's 'Born of the Sun' (March 1934) was a startling idea. The planets turn out to be eggs which, suitably warmed by the sun, hatch and give birth to space monsters.

The April 1934 *Astounding* is one of the most memorable from this period. It featured the first instalment of Jack Williamson's new novel 'The Legion of Space'. This was a rousing space opera, but controlled and humanized. Williamson introduced a cast of characters out of *The Three Musketeers* of Alexandre Dumas, who struggle against menacing aliens to capture a super-weapon. The issue also contained 'A Matter of Size' by Harry Bates, who having lost his editorial position had turned to writing, and 'He From Procyon' by Schachner. The latter, which is a take-off of H.G. Wells's 'The Man who Could Work Miracles', shows what becomes of greedy humankind when they are given the power of wish fulfilment. The issue also began serialization of Charles Fort's collection of unusual phenomena, *Lo!* (1931), with the idea that it might stimulate authors into producing even more wild ideas. Curiously it didn't have that affect. Although a few subsequent stories use Fortean concepts it seemed that most writers were quite capable of creating original stories once they knew there was a market receptive to them.

This was Tremaine's strength. He had expanded *Astounding* to be a magazine with hardly any apparent editorial taboos. In addition Tremaine was a conscientious and skilled professional editor, and Street & Smith was one of the oldest and most venerable of all magazine publishers with a large distribution network and sound financial backing. Through its outlets, it was able to get *Astounding* to a wider public. At this stage *Astounding*'s circulation was probably about 50,000, about half that of *Amazing* in 1926. Gernsback's *Amazing* had been aimed initially at young experimenters and those with scientific and technological interests. Its early circulation peak had rapidly dwindled, and by 1934 it was not much more than 25,000.

Wonder's was about the same. But *Astounding* was not only now reaching a wider readership, it was reaching a better informed and more mature one. This was reflected in *Astounding's* presentation. Its covers, by Howard V. Brown, whilst colourful and effective, were less brash than Paul's at *Wonder Stories*, but more inspiring than Morey's at *Amazing*. The interior illustrations, especially those by Elliot Dold, were entrancing, giving hints of higher technology without ignoring the human element. By his techniques Dold brought the reader into his illustrations, unlike Paul, who always gave the impression of someone viewing from a distance.

The year 1934 was earth-shattering for *Astounding*. One has only to catalogue a few of the authors and their stories to demonstrate the depth and quality of fiction being published: 'Blinding Shadows' by Donald Wandrei (an ingenious invasion from another dimension), 'Sidewise in Time' by Murray Leinster (one of the first serious explorations of alternative time-streams), 'Rex' by Harl Vincent (featuring a robot surgeon), 'Before Earth Came' by John Russell Fearn (perhaps one of the most original contributors to *Astounding*), 'Dr Lu-Mie' by Clifton B. Kruse (in which a scientist becomes so empathic to termites that he experiences their lives), 'Inflexure' by Clyde Crane Campbell (an alias for H.L. Gold; the story builds on Leinster's concept and depicts all times existing simultaneously), 'The Bright Illusion' by C.L. Moore (a thoughtful alien love story), and 'The Living Equation' by Nat Schachner (in which a computer creates its own universe).

Before the end of the year, a new Edward E. Smith serial had started, 'The Skylark of Valeron' (August 1934–February 1935), and that was soon running alongside John W. Campbell's blockbuster, 'The Mightiest Machine' (December 1934–April 1935). These two serials plus Williamson's 'The Legion of Space' showed the maturing of the space opera. They might still contain super-scientific concepts, but now they were harnessed and under the control of humanity, rather than running amok as in earlier stories.

Perhaps of most importance was the publication of 'Twilight' by John W. Campbell under the alias Don A. Stuart in the November 1934 issue. This was a new Campbell, toning down the super-science, to depict a far future Earth where machines continue to run the cities long after humans have forgotten how they work or how to repair them. The story is more than a token nod to technocracy, since it emphasizes how humans may not only become reliant upon machinery, but be protected by it. This became a theme for several other Don A. Stuart stories. In 'The Machine' (February 1935), a super-computer realizes that its constant vigil over humankind will ultimately harm them, so it leaves Earth, forcing humans to rediscover themselves. 'Night' (October 1935) took a step beyond 'Twilight' and showed how machines continued to survive long after humans.

The new mood stories of Don A. Stuart were encouraged by Tremaine and thus began to surface in the work of others, especially Raymond Z. Gallun, whose 'Old Faithful' (December 1934) tells of one of the last Martians who attempts to cross space to Earth. It was so popular that it demanded a sequel, 'The Son of Old Faithful' (July 1935), which was the first time 'The Son of …' title-concept was used in a science-fiction magazine. (Nat Schachner followed almost immediately with 'The Son of Redmask' in the August issue.)

Within a year *Astounding* had established itself as the leading science-fiction magazine. Not only was it publishing top-quality and original fiction, but it was also larger than its rival pulps (it increased to 160 pages in March 1934 compared with *Amazing*'s 144 and *Wonder*'s 128) and it was cheaper (20 cents compared with 25 cents for the others, although *Wonder* would reduce to 15 cents in June 1935).

The development and success of *Astounding* must have delighted Charles Hornig as a reader and fan, but it must have frustrated him as a rival editor. In the January 1934 *Wonder Stories* he had introduced his own 'New Policy', which was to outlaw old-fashioned stories with time-worn plots and place the emphasis on new and original ideas. This wasn't any different from Tremaine's thought variants, although Hornig was a month later in announcing it. Also *Astounding* was becoming a far more attractive market. Street & Smith paid at least one cent a word on acceptance, whereas Hornig had trouble paying anything at all, even months after publication. As a consequence Hornig was unable to attract regular writers. His most likely contributors were new writers, or old faithfuls to the magazine who had alternative means of income. One of these new writers, Donald A. Wollheim, whose first sale 'The Man from Ariel' (January 1934) is a touching tale of a dying alien, would soon become so exasperated at the lack of payment that he teamed up with other writers to sue Gernsback.

By contrast with *Astounding*, therefore, *Wonder* was unable to publish much in the way of original fiction. Nevertheless there are a few examples of note. 'The Sublime Vigil' by Chester D. Cuthbert

(February 1934) was later acknowledged by Gernsback as his own favourite story. It's a mood love story about a man who has lost his girl to a cosmic force and he awaits its return so that he can join her. 'The Spoor Doom' by Eando Binder (February 1934) is a prediction of germ warfare with humankind seeking refuge underground. 'The Last Planet' by R.F. Starzl (April 1934) could almost have been the first-generation starship story but fell just short of that. It tells of the last survivors on Earth building a mighty spaceship to seek a new world.

Hornig did have one stroke of remarkable good fortune. He was the lucky recipient of Stanley G. Weinbaum's first story, 'A Martian Odyssey', which appeared in the July 1934 issue. This story has rightly gone down in the annals of sf history as one of the first modern science-fiction stories. It actually isn't much of a story. What it is is a delightful travelogue across Mars looking at the wonderful variety of alien life-forms. Up until that date few writers had treated aliens sympathetically, and even fewer had done it light-heartedly with just the right level of humour. Weinbaum did just that, and did it well. The success led to the demand for a sequel, 'Valley of Dreams' (November 1934). Readers realized that Weinbaum was a special talent. However, Hornig, sticking a little too rigidly to his new policy, rejected a third story from Weinbaum, 'Flight on Titan', on the grounds that it was not sufficiently original. Weinbaum was rapidly poached by Tremaine who published 'Flight on Titan' in the January 1935 *Astounding*. If Hornig had had the financial means he might have been able to keep Weinbaum, but *Astounding* paid better and promptly. Also Hornig's adherence to the new policy meant that he had now lost Weinbaum's first offer of material and in future only received his second-level fiction. Lasser would probably have developed Weinbaum considerably, but Hornig was blinded by his new policy. This caused him to lose another top-quality story from Edmond Hamilton. 'Colonists of Mars' was a further response to Lasser's demand for realism in depicting a hostile and near-fatal expedition to Mars. Hornig rejected it as unoriginal, even though the number of stories with such emotion and realism were still rare. The story did not fit into *Astounding*'s up-beat cosmic wonder and was too horrible for *Amazing* but would have been ideal for *Wonder*. Instead the manuscript remained in Hamilton's bottom drawer for almost twenty years before it resurfaced as 'What's it Like out There?' and appeared to much acclaim in the December 1952 *Thrilling Wonder Stories*.

Although Gernsback always had the final say on stories accepted for publication, he would not have looked at stories Hornig rejected, and so probably had no idea what gems Hornig was overlooking. The number of original stories appearing in *Wonder* was actually quite minimal, with Hornig, despite his editorial regimen, still publishing some mediocre and uninspiring material. In the latter half of 1934 Laurence Manning's 'The Living Galaxy', which depicts a galaxy as a single sentient entity, was probably the only significant original story.

In 1935 the story quality and interest dropped even further. There was a good satirical novel by Stanton A. Coblentz depicting an advanced subterranean society 'In Caverns Below' (March–May 1935), and British writer Benson Herbert produced an intriguing serial in 'The Perfect World' (October 1935–February 1936), where an invading planet turns out to be a massive spaceship. Laurence Manning continued to produce good stories, including his Stranger Club series of adventures, which culminated in 'Seeds from Space' (June 1935). Manning also wrote a good short novel, 'World of the Mist' (September–October 1935), exploring another dimension. Stanley G. Weinbaum may be congratulated for his prophetic treatment of virtual reality in 'Pygmalion's Spectacles' (June 1935) which allows the wearer to experience the world seen through the glasses. Perhaps the strangest story published in the magazine was 'Dream's End' (December 1935) by Australian writer Alan Connell. This is mystical fantasy rather than sf. It depicts the fragmentation of existence when we discover that the universe is simply the dream of a super-being who starts to awaken.

By this time Gernsback was having less involvement in *Wonder Stories*. It is possible he thought that having created science-fiction fandom there was enough support out there to sustain *Wonder Stories*, especially in the hands of a fellow fan. To further encourage this he introduced from the February 1934 issue the Science Fiction League, which was there to enhance the popularity of science fiction and develop fandom. The League sponsored the creation of local chapters in the same way as Gernsback had created his Radio League many years earlier. In effect *Wonder Stories* became a professional fan magazine. To many readers the fiction was secondary. As Robert Lowndes recalled: 'From the days of Charles D. Hornig in *Wonder Stories* … I've been a sucker for the personal magazine that presents a distinct personality. That was why I looked forward to the next issue of *Wonder* more regularly than *Astounding* in those days ...'[14] There is no doubt that *Wonder Stories* was a fun magazine, whereas *Astounding* took itself seriously. Although the latter also had a long and lively letter column, it discouraged some of the more fannish excesses and pranks that otherwise thrived in *Wonder Stories*. The Science Fiction League was a major force in developing fandom. Chapters sprang up all over America, and in Britain, Ireland and even Australia. The official League membership soon rose to nearly a thousand. It is difficult to know how many of those thousand introduced new fans and new readers to *Wonder Stories*. It is probably unlikely that many did. It is quite typical for the active and more vocal part of any magazine's readership to be in the region of 3 per cent, and this was about the same for *Wonder Stories*. It meant that Hornig was now pandering to only 3 per cent of his readership and the other 97 per cent were probably anxiously awaiting new and revolutionary stories. Since these were appearing with increasing regularity in *Astounding*, it is not too surprising that *Wonder*'s readership began to fall and *Astounding*'s increased.

Gernsback's belief that fandom would sustain *Wonder Stories* was naïve. If anything, fandom became like Gernsback's own Frankenstein's monster, because some fans used the League to turn on him. The 'ringleader' was Donald A. Wollheim who, with John B. Michel and William Sykora, began to disrupt League meetings. This led to their expulsion from the League. Wollheim created a rival movement, the International Scientific Association, which actively opposed the League. Wollheim was also suing Gernsback for non-payment.

Thus by 1935 the position at *Wonder Stories* was rapidly becoming unsettled. Gernsback, however, seemed to have lost interest. He had other irons in the fire. Most successful amongst these was *Sexology*, a new magazine that he had launched anonymously in June 1933 to encourage and foster a scientific approach to sex education. *Sexology* was an instant success, outselling Gernsback's main profitable title, *Radio-Craft*. Between them these two magazines provided Gernsback with sufficient income to weather the Depression, and determined not to lose out again as he had in 1929 when forced into bankruptcy, Gernsback devoted most of his time to developing and sustaining their readership.

14. From a letter by Lowndes in the 'Or So You Say' column in *Amazing Stories*, 46 (5) January 1973, p. 121.

It is true that he did experiment from time to time with new titles – Gernsback was ever the experimenter. He had recognized the growing specialist pulp market and hoped he might make a quick killing in certain areas. However, his two attempts at magazines of nautical adventure – *Pirate Stories* and *High-Seas Adventures*, launched in November and December 1934 – failed. The two magazines merged after four issues and survived only another two. Gernsback also planned to publish *Exploration Tales* and *True Supernatural Stories* but neither of these got beyond the dummy stage. It is probable that Gernsback at last became wise to the volatility of fiction titles, and decided that his future and fortune lay in *Radio-Craft* and *Sexology*. Moreover at this time Gernsback was receiving further income from Standard Magazines for editing their *Mechanics and Handicraft*, which had been launched in February 1934. There is little doubt that by early 1935 Gernsback was shifting away from science fiction and back to the more stable non-fiction market.

And he was right. *Wonder Stories* continued to fail. A cut in the cover price did not attract new readers, and in November 1935 it was forced to go bi-monthly. By the March 1936 issue Gernsback had decided to make one last plea.

In his editorial, 'Wonders of Distribution', Gernsback explained how racketeering in the magazine business had grown out of all proportion. Dealers were removing magazine covers, returning them to distributors as unsold copies and selling the imperfect copies at a cheaper rate. Gernsback decided to by-pass the dealers and sell *Wonder Stories* totally by subscription. His postal plan was that readers would receive an advance issue of *Wonder Stories* containing a coupon which they then returned with 15 cents for the next issue. The idea failed miserably; his appeal received little support. Although the May/June issue was already in production, Gernsback decided to cut his losses. On 21 February 1936 he came to a deal with Ned Pines of Standard Magazines for Pines to take over the magazine. Ten years almost to the month after Gernsback had launched *Amazing Stories* and created the whole genre of magazine science fiction, he was now out of it. The child was in the hand of new parents.

Technically you might argue that with that handover Gernsback had passed on his 'ownership' of science fiction to Ned Pines. In practice that was not the case. Pines had no specific interest in science fiction other than as a marketable commodity. He certainly had no interest in its further development. But a new foster father of science fiction was waiting in the wings – one who was capable of taking the young medium through adolescence into manhood. That was John W. Campbell.

CHAPTER THREE
Towards the Golden Age

Heroes and Villains

For a brief period in the late spring of 1936 there were only two science-fiction magazines on the stalls, *Amazing Stories* and *Astounding Stories*, and *Amazing* had slipped to a bi-monthly schedule with its October 1935 issue. It was the lowest ebb the science-fiction magazine had reached since Gernsback had launched the companion *Amazing Stories Quarterly* in 1928, and it would never again be that low.

With the sale of *Wonder Stories* to Standard Magazines in hand, its May/June 1935 issue was dropped, and with it the first magazine appearances of William F. Temple and David A. Kyle. Dedicated fans may have missed the issue, though they would have picked up news of the sale through the fan press as it was reported in *Fantasy Magazine*.

There had almost been a new magazine. The Philadelphia-based Shade Publishing Company was planning a string of new magazines. It had established a New York office for a subsidiary company, Associated Authors, and was having moderate success with its crime magazines, *Murder Mysteries* (launched in October 1934) and *True Gang Life* (launched in November 1934). It planned to issue a weird fiction magazine entitled *Strange Adventures* in February 1935. This was not the company's first experience in this territory. In 1931 it had published a short-lived occult fantasy magazine, *Mind Magic*, which had attracted several sf writers including Ralph Milne Farley, Manly Wade Wellman and Joseph W. Skidmore. The magazine lasted for only six issues but Farley remained in touch with the publishers and encouraged them to reconsider the field. Farley brought Raymond A. Palmer on board and everything looked about to bloom in January 1935 when, overnight, Shade pulled the plug. The main reason was the departure of editor G.R. Bay, who had the main interest in science fiction and the bizarre, but the decision may also have been coloured by the sale of *Wonder Stories* and the shakiness of *Amazing*, which suggested that the field was not yet ready for a new magazine. Instead Shade's new editor, J. Bruce Donahoe, decided to explore the sleazier side of crime and issued *Scarlet Adventuress* in July 1935, followed by *Scarlet Gang Stories*. The moment had passed, though Farley, who was acting as something of a literary scout for Shade, had already encouraged some sf writers to consider the market. It explains why Stanley G. Weinbaum, for instance, turns up in the February 1936 *True Gang Life*, as author, in collaboration with Farley, of 'Yellow Slaves'.

Nevertheless the bookstands were awash with other pulps, and it is worth pausing briefly just to consider the world of pulps in America at this time so as to see the imminent growth of science fiction in context.

Although at the time *Amazing Stories* first appeared in 1926 specialist pulps were relatively new, by 1936 they dominated the scene. The more general fiction pulps, such as *Argosy*, *Blue Book*, *Short Stories* and *Adventure*, still appeared and still had high circulations, but they were surrounded by a welter of specialist pulps pandering to whatever interests the public professed. At one time the western magazines had dominated the field, and their numbers were still great, but they were now equalled, if not exceeded, by the detective, romance and sports pulps. There were also those devoted to war stories, air and sea adventures, courtroom cases, jungle and tropical adventures and horror stories. Amongst these were others not professing to be science-fiction magazines, or even necessarily aimed at that readership, but still featuring science fiction or utilizing its concepts.

We have already encountered the single-character pulps *The Shadow* and *Doc Savage*, from Street & Smith, which led the hero-pulp field and which featured many science-fiction elements. Their success had inevitably led to many imitations. Most bizarre amongst them was *The Spider*. This was published by Henry Steeger's Popular Publications and had first appeared in October 1933. The lead novels were published under the pseudonym Grant Stockbridge which disguised R.T. Maitland Scott for the first two issues, but thereafter the stories were almost all the work of prolific pulpster Norvell W. Page. The Spider was wealthy crime-fighter Richard Wentworth whose character became increasingly grotesque and his cases increasingly macabre. Most saw him pitted against master criminals intent on taking over America – not that different from other hero pulps – although the character of the Spider was more bizarre, and the plots and incidents more violent. The science-fiction motifs included a virus that ate metal in 'The City Destroyer' (January 1935), Neanderthal men surviving to the modern-day in 'Hordes of the Red Butcher' (June 1935), and a disease that makes men invulnerable in 'The Grey Horde Creeps' (March 1938).

There were many other single-character pulps, all modelled on the premise of hero-combating-villains-intent-on-conquering-the-United-States. *Operator #5*, from Popular Publications, featured Jimmy Christopher of the Secret Service attempting to thwart the ever-present threat. The early novels, which began in April 1934, were the work of Frederick C. Davis. Emile C. Tepperman and Wayne Rogers later took on the task. All were masked under the house name of Curtis Steele. Davis's contributions included a death-ray like a laser in 'Scourge of the Invisible Death' (November 1935), but it is Tepperman's work that is closest to sf, particularly his Purple Invasion novel sequence which ran from June 1936 to June 1937 and chronicled the invasion of America by the Purple Empire. The magazine ran until November 1939. The last issue featured 'The Army from Underground' by Wayne Rogers, in which America is being invaded by Japan and is being destroyed by atomic bombs.

There were any number of air-war magazines, several of which featured science fiction regularly. Probably the most popular was *G-8 and his Battle Aces*, also from Popular Publications. It ran from October 1933 to June 1944 and was written almost entirely by Robert Hogan. As in all of these series, the characters were stereotyped and the plots thin, but there was occasional scope for invention. In *G-8*, the adventures were set in the First World War and the Germans threw everything against our hero, including rockets, giant bats, beast men and giant flying heads!

Bill Barnes, Air Adventurer was a similar pulp, launched in February 1934 by Street & Smith. Barnes was an ace flyer and the magazine plots his adventures and inventions during the thirties. Some of the inventions verged on science fiction, such as a submersible aeroplane, but generally the series had no fantastic elements. The stories appeared under the by-line of George L. Eaton. Most were written by Charles S. Verral, but the first five novels and the creation of the character were the work of Major Malcolm Wheeler-Nicholson, whom we shall encounter again in our history. *Bill Barnes* was retitled *Air Trails* in February 1937.

The closest of all these pulps to science fiction was *Dusty Ayres and his Battle Birds.* Although this was similar to *G-8,* the stories were set in the future and chronicled the battle against the Black Invaders, an Asiatic horde that had conquered the world except for the United States. The novels bristled with new inventions and, although they followed the hero-pulp formula, were amongst the most inventive. *Dusty Ayres* was a continuation of the air-war magazine *Battle Birds* which Popular Publications had launched in November 1932, but which was clearly not selling as well as its companion *G-8.* With the November 1934 issue the magazine was revamped as *Dusty Ayres.* The whole of the magazine was now written by Robert Sidney Bowen. Although it increased in popularity there was a limit to how long the series could keep reworking variations on a theme. In the final novel, 'The Telsa Raiders' (July 1935), Fire-Eyes, the leader of the Black Invaders, is killed and the world set free. With that the magazine folded.

The immediate success of *Dusty Ayres* was recognized by Dell Magazines, which revamped its ailing pulp *War Birds* into *Terence X. O'Leary's War Birds* in March 1935. The setting was shifted to the future with O'Leary fighting the Ageless Men, immortals from Atlantis who want to dominate the world. The novels were by Arthur Guy Empey, a veteran air-story writer but with limited imagination. The new title lasted only three monthly issues.

The invasion novel remained very popular. After *Dusty Ayres,* Popular Publications began to focus on the villain. *The Mysterious Wu-Fang* ran for seven issues from September 1935 to March 1936. This was a blatant imitation of Sax Rohmer's Fu Manchu novels with little attempt at originality. The series was written entirely by Robert J. Hogan, who was also writing a *G-8* novel a month and during this period was arguably the most prolific writer for the pulps (averaging 1.7 million words a year, or the average then of about 40 novels). After seven issues the magazine suddenly metamorphosed into *Dr Yen-Sin,* with a new oriental villain. This time the series was written by Donald Keyhoe. Yen-Sin's adversary, Michael Traile, is interesting in that he was the victim of an accident that meant he could no longer sleep. This made him eternally vigilant. The magazine, though, was less eternal, seeing only three issues, from May to September 1936.

Finally, there was *Doctor Death,* a Dell magazine. This featured a mad scientist, Dr Rance Mandarin, who was a master of the supernatural and used all the forces of the occult against the United States. The magazine belongs more to the field of weird fiction than sf, except that the author, Harold Ward, made some attempt, albeit feeble, to explain the supernatural powers by scientific means. Although this didn't necessarily make them any the more plausible, it did show that science fiction was starting to get the upper hand over fantasy. The magazine lasted three issues, February to April 1935.

The two science-fiction magazines were little influenced by the hero/villain trend. They had seen it all before, at its worst excesses in the space opera stories of the early thirties, especially the abysmal Hawk Carse series in *Astounding*. Its popularity, though, remained evident in the Durna Rangue series by Neil R. Jones, running in *Astounding*, starting with 'Little Hercules' (September 1936). The Durna Rangue were a religious cult exiled for centuries to deep space. However, once in league with space pirates and able to acquire advanced super-weapons, they conquer Earth and establish a tyrannical government. The series thus has much in common with *Dusty Ayres* and *Operator #5*.

Weird Tales did respond to the influence of the hero pulp. It probably accounted for the continued success of Seabury Quinn's occult detective series featuring Jules de Grandin which, at the time, were the most popular stories in the magazine, though they now appear implausible and over-written. De Grandin was a mixture of Sherlock Holmes and Hercule Poirot and, with his trusty colleague Dr Trowbridge, sought to fight off a variety of supernatural or menacing human foe. The de Grandin series ran for almost the whole life of the pulp but the stories became noticeably more violent and threatening during the mid-thirties. It was at this time that Paul Ernst wrote his series pitting Ascot Keane against the villainies of the immortal enemy Dr Satan. The series lasted for five stories from August 1935 to August 1936, which was the peak period of the hero/villain pulps. Ernst, who was also a prolific writer of science fiction, having contributed to *Astounding Stories* since its September 1930 issue, went on to write his own hero character, Richard Benson, who featured in *The Avenger*. Although Benson has the ability to change his features, the stories are more direct crime-busting than scientific or supernatural. The magazine ran from September 1939 to September 1942, at the end of the hero pulps' heyday.

It is perhaps surprising in hindsight, but indicative of the period, that one of the most popular hero characters in *Weird Tales*, Conan the Barbarian, created by Robert E. Howard, did not move into the

hero pulps. The hero pulps were essentially bizarre mystery magazines and were aimed at the crime/mystery market. Even though
they relied heavily on science fiction and fantasy motifs, that was
not their image. A Conan pulp magazine might have been marginally popular at the time, but it was not the natural evolutionary line
that was developing. The evidence for this is the borderline science-
fantasy magazine, *Ka-Zar*. It was a shameless imitation of Tarzan.
The lead novels were written by Bob Byrd, starting with 'King of
Fang and Claw'. Ka-Zar had been raised by lions and could con-
verse with the animals. As jungle fiction it was competent and his
adventures were very Conanesque. Though the magazine was
popular with those enjoying the Tarzan films of the mid-thirties, it
lasted only three issues from October 1936 to June 1937. What is
interesting is that it was published by the Goodman brothers,
Abraham and Martin, who a year later would launch their own
genuine science-fiction magazine, *Marvel Science Stories*, which would
trigger the sf boom of the late thirties.

The hero pulp is a significant link in the chain of popular fiction
and science fiction. It was a direct descendant of the dime novel – in
fact the immediate son – and in turn fathered not only the comic-
book heroes, but also the heroes of many popular film and
television series. The imagery depicted on the covers of many of the
hero pulps, especially George Rozen's for *The Shadow* and Walter
Baumhofer's for *Doc Savage*, was often more symbolic of science-
fiction elements than direct painting, but nevertheless had a
powerful impact on the browsers of the news-stands where scores
of these magazines were on display. The numbers of issues of hero-
pulp magazines rapidly exceeded those of sf magazines by 1933 but
started to fade by 1940 when they were well overtaken by both the
sf pulps and the hero comics.

The comic-strip heroes were only just starting to emerge in 1936,
and their relationship with the science-fiction pulps is only too
evident in the mid- to late thirties. We have already seen how it was
the science-fiction magazine itself that gave birth to the first comic
strip, *Buck Rogers in the 25th Century*, derived from Philip Francis
Nowlan's character in 'Armageddon – 2419 AD' (1928). Now the
reverse would happen. In 1934 Alex Raymond created Flash Gordon
in imitation of Buck Rogers. It was syndicated through the Sunday
and daily newspapers, and the series rapidly grew in popularity.
The film rights were licensed to Universal. The film, starring Buster
Crabbe, was released towards the end of 1936 as a 13-part serial. To

coincide with the film, Harold Hersey, who had acquired the magazine rights, issued *Flash Gordon Strange Adventure Magazine*. The first issue was dated December 1936. The lead novel, 'The Master of Mars', is credited to James Edison Northfield. What is significant about this magazine is that it was the first to include a full-colour comic strip. It also included two stories by Russ Winterbotham, a writer who had made his debut in *Astounding* the previous year with 'The Star that Would Not Behave' (August 1935).

One would have thought Hersey had captured a winner here. As we have seen in the past, he tended to be an opportunist publisher but with something of a death-touch. He was not especially successful over his handling of *The Thrill Book* in 1919. He took over *Ghost Stories* from Bernarr Macfadden in 1930 and it folded within a year. His first genuine sf magazine, *Miracle*, lasted only two issues. And surprisingly, *Flash Gordon Strange Adventure Magazine* lasted only one issue. Hersey usually had good ideas but never enough finance to support them. In the case of *Flash Gordon*, it may have been that Hersey's distribution outlet was unsuccessful but, more likely, the licensed rights were granted by King Features only for one-off experimental use. The magazine served as a pilot to explore the role the pulps had in the expansion of the comic-strip medium. King Features probably concluded the Hersey's publication was inadequate for its purposes and, similarly, Hersey would have found the cost of the colour production expensive, even though he spread it over two other comic-strip related pulps that he issued at this time.

The Flash Gordon strip had already been running regularly in King Features' own *King Comics* since April 1936, and it was evidently the comic book that was going to become the vehicle for these new super-hero adventures. *Flash Gordon Strange Adventure Magazine* became a minor but significant drop in the gathering sf magazine cascade. Although it was the first to include full interior colour, it wasn't the first to include a comic strip. For that, we must return to *Wonder Stories*, now reborn as *Thrilling Wonder Stories.*

Wonder Anew

Standard Magazines had appeared in 1932, although the company had previously existed as Metropolitan Magazines, founded in 1931. The publisher was Ned Pines. His right-hand man and editor-in-chief was Leo Margulies, the real power behind the magazines. Margulies was known as 'the little giant of the pulps'. He was a short man, not much over five feet tall, but had a dynamism and aggression that made him feared and respected throughout the pulp publishing world. Margulies had started out at Munsey Publications and for a period ran its Authors' Sales unit. He worked his way through other companies until Ned Pines employed him to develop his Thrilling line of magazines. These were so called because many of the magazines began with the word 'thrilling', starting with *Thrilling Detective* and *Thrilling Love Stories* in 1931. Standard's main success came with its own hero-pulp magazine, *The Phantom Detective*, which started in February 1933.

As the company grew, Margulies took on more editors to cope with the growing tide of manuscripts. Amongst them was Mort Weisinger, who went to work for him in 1935. Weisinger was one of the leading science-fiction fans of the day, working closely with Julius Schwartz both on the fan publication *Fantasy Magazine* and as literary agents. Thus when Pines acquired *Wonder Stories*, Standard already had an in-house science-fiction expert. Weisinger was not directly credited as editor, because that was not the way things worked at Standard Magazines. Leo Margulies was overall editor-in-chief and had the final say on selection. Otherwise the editors worked as a team, reading submissions and assembling issues. However, because science fiction was such a speciality, Margulies and the others began to leave the editing to Weisinger. Margulies directed that the fiction be aimed at a younger readership, which was potentially a bigger market, as *Astounding* already catered for adult readers.

The first *Thrilling Wonder Stories* was dated August 1936 but appeared on the stands in June. In format, little had changed from when it had existed as *Wonder Stories*. There were all the same reader departments, including 'Science Questions and Answers', 'Test Your Science Knowledge' and the Science Fiction League, though this last was more truncated than before. But the change in fiction was obvious. The emphasis had moved from science-led to action-led fiction. Its first cover depicted a scene from 'The Land Where Time Stood Still' by Arthur Leo Zagat, showing a bug-eyed creature helping a human fight warriors from the past. Such covers, especially in the hands of Earle K. Bergey, would later epitomize the magazine and bring in the phrase 'bug-eyed monsters', so closely associated with juvenile sf.

The lead novelette was by Ray Cummings, still a major name in science fiction, even if most of his work in the field by that time had become repetitive. He was still a popular writer for *Argosy*, as were other contributors Otis Adelbert Kline and Paul Ernst. In fact the only authors present in that first issue who had also been regular contributors to *Wonder Stories* were Eando Binder and Stanley G. Weinbaum. Eando Binder was the pen name of two brothers, Earl and Otto Binder, though by 1936 most of the writing was by Otto alone. The Binder name had appeared regularly in the sf magazines and *Weird Tales* since 1932 and could usually be relied upon to be at the better end of routine fiction. Weinbaum had died tragically of cancer in December 1935 at the height of his fame. His death would catapult him into legend, though he was one of the few early sf writers who deserved that status. Also in the first issue was Abraham Merritt. Weisinger had taken the opportunity to reprint his short story 'The Drone Man' from *Fantasy Magazine*.

This was a strong cast of names and must have been welcomed by readers, even though to the fan of *Astounding Stories* the fiction was less mature and less challenging. Historically, one of the most interesting features was 'Zarnak', a comic-strip serial set in the year 2936. It was credited to Max Plaisted, a pseudonym for Otto Binder working with his artist brother, Jack. The first episode revealed that much of the Earth's population had been destroyed following germ warfare. The survivors develop a feudal system, with the exception of the descendants of a certain scientist. One of these, Zarnak, learned that before the Final War, another scientist had mastered space flight and had left the Earth. Zarnak vows to track him down. Both the plotting and the artwork were way below the quality expected of the Binders. Also, if the letters were any measure, the readers did not appreciate the strip. I suspect that was more due to the quality of the story than to the presence of the strip itself. It ran for eight issues before stopping. It was further evidence that the comic strip was making its presence felt, but that its vehicle was the burgeoning comic book, not the pulp magazine.

At the outset, Standard had decided to issue *Thrilling Wonder* every other month. This denied it the opportunity to run serials, but allowed for the development of linked stories. The series characters had always been popular in sf, and it was at *Thrilling Wonder* that that popularity was milked to advantage. One of the first featured the planet-hopping fugitives, Penton and Blake, in a series by John W. Campbell, Jr. Because of his reputation in

Astounding, Campbell was one of the biggest names in sf in the thirties. The series, which started with 'Brain Stealers of Mars' (December 1936) and ran for five episodes, was very popular.

Equally popular was the Via series by Gordon Giles, another pseudonym of Otto Binder. This began with 'Via Etherline' (October 1937) and ran for nine episodes. It was another series of space adventures peopled with an interesting cast of characters and intriguing plot situations. It has been suggested that for a period Binder, writing as both Eando Binder and Gordon Giles, was the two most popular writers for the magazine. Binder had another series running at that time, featuring the immortal man Anton York, starting with 'Conquest of Life' (August 1937).

One of the most popular series in the magazine was by Arthur K. Barnes and featured Gerry Carlisle, a female planetary explorer who captured alien creatures for zoos. The series began with 'Green Hell' (June 1937) and ran for eight stories. Although Barnes had been writing for the magazines since 1931, and would until 1946, this was his only claim to fame. The stories were later collected in book form as *Interplanetary Hunter* (1956).

One of Ray Cummings's most popular characters was Tubby, the little man with the big ideas. The series had started in *Argosy* over 15 years previously. With 'The Space-Time-Size Machine' (October 1937) he was introduced to *Thrilling Wonder*. The series was mostly a rehash of Cummings's old idea of the micro- and macrocosm, and its novelty soon faded, but for a period, and certainly for new readers, its re-appearance was welcome.

Henry Kuttner, who hitherto had been more closely associated with *Weird Tales* and the horror pulps, had written science fiction only sparingly. But under Weisinger's urging he began to dabble with the medium more seriously. His first appearance in *Thrilling Wonder* was with 'When the Earth Lived' (November 1937) which used the Cummings-concept of the Earth as an atom. Scientists from the macrocosm bombard Earth with rays which cause inanimate objects to come to life. Kuttner's big break came with the Tony Quade series which explored the movie industry of the future. It began with 'Hollywood on the Moon' (April 1938).

These series sustained reader interest from issue to issue. The magazine was also attractively illustrated and featured cameo biographies of the authors with inset photographs. Although they demanded little of the reader, the stories were readable, and some can still be enjoyed today. Although the magazine remained bi-monthly for the next three years, it was with a profitable company that paid its contributors promptly, and its future was, for the time being, assured.

When Mort Weisinger moved to Standard Magazines he had less time to work with Julius Schwartz on *Fantasy Magazine* or with the Solar Sales Agency – indeed the roles were in conflict. Schwartz continued *Fantasy Magazine* on his own, but needing to earn a living and wanting to promote his literary agency, he folded it in January 1937. With its passing the core news and features magazine of fandom had gone and the field was left to find its own direction. The magazine was never properly replaced, although to some extent *The Phantagraph* helped fill the gap. *The Phantagraph* had started life in May 1934 as the *International Science Fiction Guild's Bulletin*, and under various names and editors had staggered through a couple of years before floundering. Then, in July 1936, it was revamped under Wollheim's editorship, and established a new identity with a mixture of news, stories and features, though now slanted more towards weird fiction. It was professionally printed, which with Wollheim's mature approach made it a quality product. Amongst its contributors were H.P. Lovecraft, Robert E. Howard and David H. Keller. Wollheim kept it going on an almost monthly schedule until August 1938. It was revived again in 1940, but only as a personal interest magazine and a shadow of its former self.

Wollheim also turned his hand to producing an all-fiction magazine. With Wilson Shepard, one of the co-founders of the International Scientific Association set up in opposition to the Science Fiction League, Wollheim issued *Fanciful Tales* in the autumn of 1936. It was a slim, 48-page booklet, professionally printed, sporting a cover by fan artist Clay Ferguson. The fiction was more weird than scientific, though there was a dark sf vignette by Wollheim, 'Umbriel', and a 'science-phantasy', 'The Electric World', by Kenneth B. Pritchard. The big names were H.P. Lovecraft, with 'The Nameless City', David H. Keller, with 'The Typewriter', and August W. Derleth, with 'The Man from Dark Valley'. There was also a poem, 'Solomon Kane's Homecoming', by Duane W. Rimel.

A second issue was clearly planned because Wollheim announced future stories by J. Harvey Haggard, Ralph Milne Farley and Robert Bloch. He even found ways of promoting it in the professional magazines. In the letter column of *Amazing Stories* for February 1937, Wollheim (writing under the pen name of Braxton Wells) took issue over the publication of a less than scientific story, 'Hoffman's Widow' by Floyd Oles.

> I am one of those who thought 'Hoffman's Widow' decidedly out of place. When we want *Amazing Stories* we want them Scientific! Not anything else! There are magazines like *Fanciful Tales* for weird-fantasy and that story probably wouldn't even fit there.[1]

Wollheim had expended so much money getting *Fanciful Tales* into print that he found it impossible to finance a second issue. He also parted company with Wilson Shepard, and with that the death of *Fanciful Tales* was assured. Nevertheless it gave Wollheim some valuable experience in the production and distribution of magazines. In 1977 the magazine was reproduced in a facsimile edition by Marc Michaud with a new introduction by Wollheim, in which he acknowledged the impetus the magazine had given him on the road toward professional editing and publishing. Wollheim will not be far from this history for the next four decades.

One other magazine is worth mentioning at this stage, and is equally as rare as the original *Fanciful Tales*, even though this was a professional production. Ever since May 1931 American radio listeners had been treated to the weekly radio programme of weird and supernatural stories, *The Witch's Tales* which, despite the late hour of its broadcast, had attracted a faithful cult following. Probably because of that it was felt that a magazine of the series might sell well, and it probably would have in the hands of a major publisher, but the project was taken on by The Carwood Publishing Company, a minor operation with a chequered history. Its most successful magazine had been *The Underworld*, started by publisher Tom Wood under his own name in 1927, and which ran for over 80 issues to July 1935. Wood's assistant and editor was Tom Chadburn, who also edited *The Witch's Tales*, although its nominal editor was Alonzo Deen Cole, the author of the radio series. The first issue was dated November 1936. Cole contributed the lead story, 'The Madman', about a mad scientist who lures people to his house to kill them whilst they sleep. The story was unexceptional. Strangely, most of the remaining stories were reprints from the American edition of *Pearson's Magazine* and amongst them were some science-fiction stories. These included 'The Fountain of Youth' by William Hamilton Osborne (*Pearson's*, May 1906), about a catastrophe that releases a gas from under the Earth which, when properly controlled, induces longevity. The second issue reprinted 'The Death-Trap' by

---

1. *Amazing Stories*, 11 (1) February 1937, p. 144.

George Daulton (*Pearson's*, March 1908) and 'The Monster of Lake LaMetrie' by Wardon Allan Curtis (*Pearson's*, September 1899). The first was an effective story of a monster in the Chicago sewers. The second is a remarkable tale of the discovery of a monster in a remote lake. It includes the ingenious concept (for 1899) of transplanting a man's brain into the brain cavity of the monster.

The Witch's Tales radio series was still broadcast weekly in 1936 and the magazine ought to have taken advantage of that exposure, just as Street & Smith had with *The Shadow*. But such is the difference between a major publisher and a minor one. Poor editing and production, under-financing and poor distribution saw *The Witch's Tales* fold after just two issues.

The Rise of Campbell

By the end of 1936, despite the face-lift given to *Wonder Stories*, *Astounding* was still the field leader. After the first momentous year of 1934 when the cosmic thought variants gave sf a new lease of life, *Astounding* had, perhaps, sat a little on its haunches. This is probably not too surprising considering the scale of Tremaine's other editorial duties. Moreover in 1934 Desmond Hall had moved on from being Tremaine's assistant to edit Street & Smith's first slick magazine, *Mademoiselle*. Hall's place at *Astounding* was taken by R.V. Happel who had sold one story, 'The Triple Ray', to Sloane, who published it in the Fall 1930 *Amazing Stories Quarterly*. Despite Happel's enthusiasm for the medium he had a much less constructive impact. Tremaine still insisted on reading all manuscript submissions. Frank Gruber described the way in which Tremaine worked:

> As the stories came in Tremaine piled them up on a stack. All the stories intended for *Clues* in this pile, all those for *Astounding* in that stack. Two days before press time of each magazine, Tremaine would start reading. He would start at the top of the pile and read stories until he had found enough to fill the issue. Now, to be perfectly fair, Tremaine would take the stack of remaining stories and turn it upside down, so next month he would start with the stories that has been on the bottom this month.
>
>   Nothing could be fairer than that. Except … What if your story was in the middle of the pile. That foot of stories that

did not get reached last month, this month or ...? Months would go by.[2]

Gruber knew of some writers who had waited 18 months or more for responses. This inevitably meant that *Astounding*'s contents were in danger of becoming erratic, and this had started to show by 1936. That is not to say that it was not printing good fiction, but the punch that had been there in 1934 was slackening.

During 1936 and 1937 *Astounding* could rely on good quality and original fiction by a small stable of authors including Jack Williamson, Nathan Schachner, Frank Belknap Long, Raymond Z. Gallun, Murray Leinster and P. Schuyler Miller. It had its occasional surprises, such as serializing H.P. Lovecraft's short novel 'At the Mountains of Madness' (February–April 1936) and printing his novella 'The Shadow out of Time' complete in the June 1936 issue. This brought some protests from sf purists, but was an example of the variety and scope that Tremaine liked to bring to the magazine.

At the other extreme Tremaine would publish some real howlers, and his worst excesses came with the work of Warner Van Lorne. These stories began with 'Liquid Power' in the July 1935 issue. All of the Van Lorne stories were poorly written and few had any clever ideas. It was later discovered that most of the stories were written by Tremaine's brother, Nelson, plus one by F. Orlin Tremaine himself.

Fewer new writers were establishing themselves at this time, perhaps because of Tremaine's reliance upon a core of regulars, but some managed to break through.

Ross Rocklynne began his professional career in the August 1935 *Astounding* with 'Man of Iron'. He was soon reaping much reader acclaim with his exciting series of scientific problem stories about Lieutenant Jack Colbie and his efforts to catch criminal Edward Deverel. The series began with 'At the Center of Gravity' (June 1936) and continued with 'Jupiter Trap' (August 1937) and 'The Men and the Mirror' (July 1938). British writer Eric Frank Russell began with several stories that showed the inspiration of Stanley G. Weinbaum. The first was 'The Saga of Pelican West' (February 1937), which tells of the adventures of Pelican West on Callisto along with a python called Alfred. The German writer and scientist, Willy Ley, who had now settled in America, began to contribute regular non-fiction items to the magazine, along with his first piece of fiction, 'At the Perihelion' (February 1937), which was typical of

---

2. Frank Gruber, *The Pulp Jungle* (Los Angeles: Sherbourne Press, 1967), pp. 90–91.

his approach to exploring scientific problems. For years Ley would share with Isaac Asimov the role of popularizer of science. Nelson S. Bond also made his first appearance in a science-fiction magazine in the April 1937 issue with 'Down the Dimensions', a lighthearted piece about dimensional aliens. Finally in the September 1937 issue L. Sprague de Camp, who had previously written a textbook on patent law, but had not published any fiction, first appeared with 'The Isolinguals'. All of these stories showed a greater maturity in writing and in the treatment of science than was evident in the other magazines.

The magazine developments at Street & Smith made it necessary to make changes. Tremaine was elevated to assistant editorial director and that meant someone new had to be brought in as editor. The man chosen was John W. Campbell, Jr. Campbell began at Street & Smith in October 1937, which meant that he started to have an editorial impact from the December issue, although he did not take over the full editorial reins until March 1938. Nevertheless his presence was rapidly noticeable in a variety of changes. In the January 1938 issue Campbell instigated 'In Times to Come', whetting readers' appetites for the next issue. With the March issue he began 'The Analytical Laboratory', reporting back on the popularity of stories in previous issues. As an incentive to writers he was allowed to pay an extra 25% bonus above the one-cent a word rate to writers whose stories were voted number one.

His main crusade was to change the magazine's image. He first attacked the covers. Howard V. Brown had been the regular cover artist since 1933. Campbell used Brown to draw what he called 'mutant' covers. The first, on the February 1938 issue, portrayed the sun as seen from Mercury in astronomically correct detail. It was a striking cover and the first of many that Campbell hoped would attract more mature readers, and allow them to openly purchase and read the magazine rather than smuggle it around as if it were something bought for their kid brother. Other artists were used, all to good effect. This included the return of Wesso, who had painted the covers for the Clayton *Astounding*, and, in May 1938, the first cover by Charles Schneeman. Schneeman had made his first sales to *Wonder Stories* in 1934, but moved to *Astounding* in 1935. Under Campbell he became one of the mainstay interior artists and provided the occasional effective cover. Soon, however, Campbell would introduce a major new cover artist: Hubert Rogers. His first cover was for the February 1939 issue, and from

September 1939 he was almost the resident cover artist. His work was sophisticated and muted, not garish and brash as on the other sf pulps. As Robert Weinberg has pointed out, 'Rogers brought the first touch of class to science fiction.'[3]

Campbell also introduced a regular scientific non-fiction article. Tremaine had done this to some extent, though the main contributor had been Campbell himself with an 18-part series, 'A Study of the Solar System'. Campbell wanted a solid scientific base not so much to educate people, as was Gernsback's intent, but to inspire them with ideas for stories. He therefore often sought radical and innovative articles. Before long a small team of Willy Ley, L. Sprague de Camp and Dr Robert S. Richardson were producing most of these. Campbell added to the opportunity for discussion with his own thought-provoking editorials which began with 'Mutation' in the January 1938 issue; this was his alternative to thought variants in taking science fiction into the next generation.

Most significantly, with the March 1938 issue, the title was changed. He believed *Astounding Stories* linked the magazine too closely to the pulp excesses of the past. The magazine published science fiction and should be proud of it. The title thus became *Astounding Science-Fiction*. In fact Campbell never liked the *Astounding* title, and for a while directed that it be painted faintly on the cover whilst the words 'Science-Fiction' were more boldly declared. Probably, if he could have had his way from the start, he would have changed the title directly to *Science Fiction*, but the new boy could not change the world overnight. He needed a few months to do that.

Ironically, no sooner had the change taken place than Street & Smith changed its policy of employing editors-in-chief and that meant Tremaine was redundant. On 1 May he left the company. In hindsight this looks like a plot to be rid of Tremaine, but it was just one of the inevitable consequences of restructuring. It left Campbell in full control of *Astounding*, and the powers at Street & Smith seemed satisfied to leave him.

This year, 1938, has been called the year that began the Golden Age of *Astounding*. It was a remarkable beginning. Campbell was appealing directly to a mature and sophisticated readership and as such determined that the stories he published would be similarly adult. There were enough other publications appealing to the reader who wanted nothing more than excitement and gosh-wow wonder. Campbell wanted to deliver some of that, but he really wanted the reader to experience the future, or experience the new worlds that science might offer. To do that the reader needed to live the story and that meant the stories had to be humanized. As Campbell expressed it frequently to his writers, he wanted the stories to read just as though they were contemporary stories in a future magazine. New scientific concepts to us would be everyday things to people of the future and wouldn't require lengthy descriptions. The writer had to find a way to introduce new inventions and yet make them well-known objects.

Followers who had discovered Gernsback's magazines in their teens were now in their mid- to late twenties. They had followed science fiction through its upheavals and excesses and now knew all the old hackneyed plots and over-zealous writing. Many of the writers, though, could not adapt, and some didn't need to because other markets would buy their material. Rather rapidly, as 1938 aged into 1939, Campbell began to develop a new stable of writers as well as take with him those writers of sufficient skill and adaptability who could deliver what he wanted. Those who couldn't make the change regarded Campbell as a bully, and maybe he was. But if Campbell hadn't taken 'ownership' of science fiction and dragged it into the adult world, it is possible no one else would have done. The pulp excesses would be only too evident for the next decade, but thanks to Campbell there was at least one haven of respectability. A look at *Astounding*'s first year under Campbell will give some idea of the radical changes that happened.

A good example of a pulp writer who could produce quality material for Campbell was Robert Moore Williams. Williams would become much maligned for the volume of hack work he turned out later in his career, but under Campbell's early guidance he produced two excellent stories. 'Flight of the Dawn Star' (March 1938) is about how a ship, lost in an unfamiliar part of the galaxy, finds its way home. 'Robot's Return' (September 1938) was a sympathetic treatment of robots. A shipful of them are looking for their creator, only to discover it was that frail non-machine, Man.

April 1938 saw the first story by Lester del Rey, whose letters had appeared under his real name of Ramon Alvarez del Rey since the March 1935 issue. Interestingly in later years del Rey would prove to be as bullish and cogent an editor as Campbell, and the two had a similar mental intransigence that would have made any debate between them spark with ideas. 'The Faithful' was a remarkably powerful story for a 22-year old, with its emotional portrayal of intelligent dogs and the last human survivor. Emotion, though, was one of del Rey's strengths and was present in abundance in his next sale, 'Helen O'Loy' (December 1938), featuring a 'female' robot and its effects upon its maker.

L. Sprague de Camp also found he was talking the same language as Campbell. A polymath of the first order, de Camp could write knowledgeably on most matters but, more importantly, he could also use that knowledge convincingly in his fiction. He could do it so convincingly that it looked easy, and allowed de Camp to bring a skein of humour to his work. This was exactly what Campbell wanted when he meant future contemporary fiction. This humour was present in de Camp's 'Hyperpilosity' (April 1938) about a virus that results in people growing their own coat of hair. He also produced an instructive article, 'Language for Time Travellers' (July 1938), which considered how the English language might evolve over the next few centuries. His popularity rose with a series about Johnny Black, a bear with enhanced intelligence. The first story, 'The Command' (October 1938), in which Johnny has to save a scientific team, came first in readers' ratings.

Jack Williamson was an author of 10 years' experience by the time he started writing for Campbell, but had no problems adapting, having already written his own youthful excesses out of his system. Campbell would later encourage Williamson to forget the sf of his youth and start anew, writing what he was capable of. But for the moment Williamson produced a fascinating time travel novel, 'The Legion of Time' (May–July 1938), which played upon those significant moments in history when new alternatives might begin. These are the 'Jonbar hinges' of time.

Clifford D. Simak now returned to science fiction. Although he had sold a handful of fine stories at the start of the decade he was unable to fit into a market that only focused on immature adventure. The rejection of his sensitive story 'The Creator' had been the final straw. However, he still followed the field, and recognized the changes in *Astounding* under Campbell. Here was an editor he felt he could work with. His first new submission, 'Rule 18' (which utilized time travel to establish the all-time best American football team), appeared in the July 1938 issue.

L. Ron Hubbard, who had been contributing regularly to the adventure and mystery pulps for the past five years now entered the science fiction fold. 'The Dangerous Dimension' (July 1938) caused some discussion amongst readers on the grounds that it was more fantasy than sf – just the type of controversy Campbell liked to stimulate. It was, in fact, one of the first psi-power stories that Campbell would buy, since it dealt with a professor who, through mentally using a mathematical equation, could translate himself through space. Hubbard developed this more in a short novel, 'The Tramp' (September–November 1938), about a hobo who develops superior telepathic and telekinetic powers.

The August 1938 issue, apart from presenting Malcolm Jameson's first story, 'Eviction by Isotherm', and introducing Henry Kuttner to *Astounding*'s readership with 'The Disinherited', featured one of Campbell's last stories, and a fitting finale. This was 'Who Goes There?', published under his Don A. Stuart pseudonym, still rated by many as one of the best of all science-fiction stories. It tells of an alien that takes on the forms of the various men and animals in an Antarctic camp. The uncertainty and menace in the story make it not only a classic of sf, but a classic of horror fiction.

Campbell's first year as editor had been remarkable, yet it was only a taster for the magic still to come. Looking back through the issues you can see the transition between the old and the new unfolding before your eyes, and it happens so fast that its effect was just as apparent at the time. During 1938 and the start of 1939 many of the old guard of writers were still around, but producing better quality fiction than before. Certainly Raymond Z. Gallun, Manly Wade Wellman, Edmond Hamilton, Nathan Schachner, Harl Vincent, even Paul Ernst and Arthur J. Burks, were producing fiction to be proud of. But bursting through them were the new names of de Camp, Russell, Rocklynne, Horace L. Gold, Hubbard, del Rey, and the reinvigorated Jack Williamson and Clifford Simak. Because of this rapid transition it is easier to say that the Golden Age dawned during 1938 and 1939 rather than to point at any single issue. Nevertheless, the July 1939 issue is the one usually highlighted as the start of the Golden Age, which I think only belittles what came before it. The chief significance of this issue is that it introduced A.E. van Vogt and Isaac Asimov to *Astounding*, with these being followed rapidly by Robert A. Heinlein in August, Theodore Sturgeon in September and the start of 'Grey Lensman' by E.E. Smith in October. This rapid upthrust of talent is what makes it impossible to define a single start to the Golden Age, as it serves to emphasize the richness of the period.

Of course, 1939 was a very significant year throughout the world, and I shall return to it in more detail later. But having seen *Astounding* established under Campbell, we need to step back a short way and see the other changes happening in the magazine world.

More Heroes and Villains

First let's revisit *Amazing*. We haven't paid much attention to *Amazing* during the 1930s because, frankly, there was little to pay attention to. *Amazing* had bumbled its way along during the eight years since Gernsback's departure with little drive or direction. Sloane was content to publish the type of material that appealed to him. Because he was steadfastly Victorian, his vision extended little beyond the light bulb, and he firmly believed humans would not even conquer Everest, let alone space. He thus regarded science fiction as little more than harmless entertainment and certainly did not see it as progressive or stimulating. He did, though, like Gernsback, appreciate its educational potential, so he remained keen to see stories containing pages of scientific expostulation. Teck Publications, with the financial backing of the Macfadden publishing empire, was happy to let Sloane continue, particularly all of the time *Amazing*'s companion, *Radio News*, was making a profit.

However, as the thirties lengthened it became clear that *Amazing* had become decidedly unprofitable. During the depths of the Depression, when fans may have been able to afford only one magazine, they began to favour *Astounding*, whilst the younger fans now turned to the newly revamped *Thrilling Wonder*. *Amazing* had little extra to offer other than to the die-hard traditionalists who stayed with it from the outset and were still keen to follow the works of Neil R. Jones, Bob Olsen, Ed Earl Repp, Edmond Hamilton, David H. Keller, plus less well-known writers who seemed to sell almost exclusively to *Amazing*. These included such forgotten names as Isaac R. Nathanson, Edwin K. Sloat, William K. Sonneman, Milton R. Peril, Henry J. Kostkos, and at the nadir, Joseph W. Skidmore, whom many classified at the time as producing the worst sf in the magazines with his Posi and Nega series about intelligent electrons.[4]

4. As we shall see in the fifties, stories not only could but *did* get far worse. Skidmore did start to produce some better material for *Wonder Stories* before his sudden and untimely death in 1936.

To be fair there were some acceptable stories in *Amazing*, though most of these were prior to the magazine going bi-monthly in October 1935. Before then *Amazing* still had an aura as the first sf magazine and writers felt it an honour to make their debut there. Moreoever, despite the excellent rates Bates was paying at *Astounding* prior to 1933, that magazine had not then conveyed sufficient image to lure all sf or potential sf writers. Howard Fast, remembered today more for his mainstream and historical works, especially *Spartacus* (1951), first broke into print in *Amazing* with 'Wrath of the Purple' (October 1932), about a protoplasmic blob, created in a laboratory, that gets out of control. Fast later recorded that, 'As a kid … I was utterly enthralled by the original *Amazing Stories*. It became a very unique part of my life. I never missed an issue, and to me it was absolutely the most wonderful manifestation of the late 1920s and the 1930s.'[5] That same issue saw the first story from the writing team of Earl and Otto Binder, who wrote as Eando Binder. 'The First Martian' was a calm and measured first contact story. John Russell Fearn was also another Sloane discovery, although it was some time before 'The Intelligence Gigantic' made it into print (June and July 1933 issues).

Two other well-remembered stories from this period were by Charles R. Tanner. 'Tumithak of the Corridors' (January 1932) and 'Tumithak in Shawm' (June 1933) looked at the survivors of an alien invasion of Earth and how humanity fought back. The stories remind me of the later popular television series *V*.

John Beynon Harris's touching tale of a robot stranded on earth, 'The Lost Machine', appeared in the April 1932 issue and remains amongst the best of his early work. Harris, a British writer, established a fair reputation for himself in the pulps in the 1930s, but would later become far better known under the alias John Wyndham.

David H. Keller's fiction had a certain timeless quality about it, and whilst his best stories were the psychological dramas he was exploring in *Weird Tales*, *Amazing* published some quiet but perfectly readable fiction which today can be viewed as period pieces. These included 'The White City' (May 1935), in which New York is brought to a standstill by an unprecedented fall of snow, and 'The Fireless Age' (August–October 1937), an interesting exploration of

---

5 Howard Fast, quoted in Robert Reginald, *Science Fiction and Fantasy Literature: Volume II* (Detroit: Gale Research, 1979), p. 896.

man reverted to the primitive. This was a topical theme during the latter days of the Depression as many believed civilization could be on its last legs. However, once Keller was employed by Gernsback to edit (and at times almost wholly write) *Sexology*, his ability to produce new material diminished, and in fact rapidly his reputation as one of the leading writers of science fiction faded. Within a decade his work was all but forgotten.

It was frustrating that Sloane held on to manuscripts for so long before publication. Sometimes they were lost, and at other times even Sloane recognized that the stories had become dated by the time he came to reconsider them for publication, and he then returned them. It did mean on occasion that stories written quite early in a writer's career, and of reasonable quality at that time, would appear late and might seem to be current yet anachronistic work. This happened with P. Schuyler Miller, whose highly Merritt-influenced 'The Pool of Life' did not appear until October 1934, although his more recent 'The People of the Arrow', influenced by his growing interest in archaeology, followed soon after in June 1935.

Edmond Hamilton provided a few good stories in *Amazing*, of which the best was 'Intelligence Undying' (April 1936) which follows the successive lives of a scientist who is able to transfer his memory and knowledge to a new-born baby repetitively down the generations. The idea of perpetuating knowledge by eternal brains in machines was popular in the 1930s. Hamilton twisted the plot somewhat with 'Devolution' (December 1936), wherein we learn that man did not evolve, but instead devolved from a super-intelligent protoplasmic alien team that visited Earth millennia ago.

In the last days of the Teck *Amazing* there is probably only one story worthy of classic status, namely Henry Hasse's first solo sale, 'He Who Shrank' (August 1936). The plot isn't particularly original, but Hasse's treatment of an individual's regression into miniaturization and infinite smallness was far more humane than had previously been attempted.

There were clearly several stories in *Amazing* better than Neil R. Jones's Professor Jameson series, which was fun at the time but has not weathered well. The claim that it kept *Amazing* going may have a grain of truth but is almost certainly exaggerated.

By 1938, however, Teck Publications was having financial problems. The parent company of Macfadden's was putting most of its finances into the slick magazine *Liberty* and was not looking to support its subsidiaries. *Radio News* was losing sales, and *Amazing*'s circulation was down to 15,000. Sloane was now 86 and would obviously not continue as editor for many more years. In fact he did not die until 7 August 1940, three months before his eighty-ninth birthday. He had remained alert and nimble to the end. An interesting portrait of him appears in Frederik Pohl's biography. Pohl used to visit the editorial offices to peddle his fiction and was eventually rewarded by selling Sloane a poem. He described Sloane as

> an old man, white bearded and infirm of gait. He was a marvel to me just on account of age – my own grandfather, who died around that time, was only in his sixties, and Sloane was at least a decade or two past that. But he was amiable and cordial enough; he would totter out to meet me, chat for a moment, and retire with that week's offering in his hand.[6]

The description almost fits *Amazing* as well: although only 12 years old it already seemed to be heading towards its dotage. It is this which makes the change that was about to hit it all the more marked. In January 1938 Teck arranged for the Chicago-based firm of Ziff-Davis to take over the magazine. The April 1938 issue had been assembled by Sloane and was published in February by Teck on Ziff-Davis's behalf. With the June issue, the magazine was handed over entirely to the new company.

William B. Ziff, a former First World War pilot, had founded the company in 1933, and in 1935 entered into partnership with Bernard G. Davis. Ziff ran the publishing and art side of the business, and Davis headed the editorial department. It was not a typical pulp publisher since its magazines, such as *Popular Photography* and *Popular Aviation*, were aimed at rich hobbyists. In fact the purchase of *Amazing Stories* was Davis's idea, in order to expand into the pulp fiction field (and because it brought with it *Radio News*). It always remained his own special delight.

Davis needed an assistant to directly manage the selection of manuscripts and compile the issues. Being based in the Chicago area, Davis turned to one of Milwaukee's most noted writers, Roger Sherman Hoar, who was best known under his pseudonym Ralph Milne Farley. Hoar declined, but suggested Raymond A. Palmer, the

6. Frederik Pohl, *The Way the Future Was* (New York: Ballantine Books, 1979), p. 43.

most active fan in the area. An interview was held in February 1938 and Palmer was accepted.

The differences between Palmer and Sloane couldn't be more extreme. Palmer was 60 years Sloane's junior, and an ardent fan of science fiction. Whilst Sloane was a staunch Victorian with no vision who did things by the book, Palmer was a no-holds-barred revolutionary. He believed anything and everything and was prepared to do almost anything to promote science fiction.

Palmer was born in Milwaukee in August 1910, and was only seven weeks younger than John W. Campbell. But the differences between them were marked. Campbell believed in developing science fiction so that it would become regarded as quality speculative fiction. Palmer was solely interested in science fiction for its own sake. He loved the infinite possibilities that it opened up and wanted to enjoy the fiction, not what it stood for.

Palmer was a diminutive man as a result of an accident when he was seven. He was hit by a van which broke his back and led to a marked spinal curvature and hump. Palmer was accident prone, which was not an asset in his former job as a roofer, but it only added to his determination to succeed. It is interesting to contrast Palmer and Campbell. Campbell was dour, brash and self-opinionated with a strong idea of what science fiction should be and what writers should be trying to achieve. Single-handedly he re-shaped science fiction and created modern sf as we know it. Palmer was a workaholic, but he enjoyed life and wanted constant fun. He wanted sf to be escapist and uncomplicated. This desire is probably best summarized in the instruction he gave writer Don Wilcox, which was simply 'Gimme Bang-Bang'. The result was that *Amazing* published much that was instantly readable and enjoyable but equally forgettable. *Amazing* was for nothing but unabashed light entertainment. If you wanted serious sf, turn to *Astounding*.

This policy cannot have been solely Palmer's, but must have been agreed and possibly even suggested by Davis. I have no reason to doubt that had Davis requested Palmer to produce a magazine to rival *Astounding* he would have given it his best shot. As we shall see in volume II of this history, in the fifties Palmer published some very respectable stories that Campbell would never have sanctioned, but which did take science fiction forward against new editorial taboos. In fact that probably says more about Palmer *vs* Campbell than anything else. Campbell wanted to break the old mould and establish a new one, but that new one had to be the model for all science fiction. He could not sanction anything outside it. Palmer couldn't have cared less. Taboos were there to be broken, and though he would stay within bounds set by Bernard Davis, he would publish anything that tested those boundaries if he felt it was enjoyable fiction.

This change was evident from Palmer's first issue. Apparently he took one look at the inventory of material acquired from Teck and disposed of it all bar one story. That story was probably Eando Binder's 'Space Pirate', as it was a genuine Earl and Otto collaboration, and Earl had bowed out from writing a few years earlier. Within a short space of time Palmer had acquired the type of fiction he wanted. He was able to tap into the local talent in the Chicago area. His first issue included fiction by local writers Robert Moore Williams, Ross Rocklynne, Charles R. Tanner and Ralph Milne Farley. Also through Julius Schwartz's agency he acquired two stories by John Russell Fearn. One of these, 'A Summons from Mars', was voted the most popular story in the issue. As a consequence, Palmer remarked:

> It seems almost everybody liked it. And it rather tickles us, because we considered it an ideal of our policy. It had good sound science, and a fine human problem, and plenty of human element. It stayed down to earth in imagination, and yet was full of interest.[7]

That quotation may have stated Davis's and Palmer's original intent, but it is worth bearing in mind when we encounter statements Palmer would make over the next 20 years.

'A Summons from Mars' was pure pulp, though Fearn had made an effort to humanize it. He had originally written it with Campbell in mind, but Schwartz sent the manuscript to Palmer. The story was about the aftermath of the first Earthman's trip to Mars. He succeeds in reaching the planet but dies in the attempt. Bacteria from his body then wipe out the Martian race, all but one young girl. Twenty-two years later she manages to contact Earth and pleads with the space pioneer's son to come to Mars to help perpetuate the race. Trite though that plot may seem, it was the best story in the issue, which gives some idea of the overall quality.

The transformation in the magazine was marked. Gone were Morey's covers, which many readers had started to find drab. In

7. *Amazing Stories*, 12 (4) August 1938, p. 4, from Raymond Palmer's editorial column, 'The Observatory'.

their place was a posed photograph. Though boasted of as a new breakthrough (and it was the first time a coloured photograph had been used on a science-fiction magazine's cover), it was more a result of expediency, using the facilities of *Popular Photography* in the absence of any commissioned artwork. The experiment was continued on the next issue, but thereafter standard cover paintings returned. The first regular artist was Joseph Tillotson who used the brush name of Robert Fuqua for his cover paintings. His work was always bold and colourful, and he enjoyed painting bizarre aliens. The covers look only a notch above comic book art today, but at the time were on a par with the work of Brown and Wesso. The interior illustrations were initially poor, but soon Tillotson and other staff artists Rod Ruth, Harold McCauley and Julian Krupa got into their stride and the illustrations became action-packed and exciting, if always rather crude.

The fiction was little better than boys' magazine material, and it was clearly aimed at the teenage audience. Palmer adapted the reader departments accordingly. His editorial, 'The Observatory', was highly personalized and chatty. Gone were the long boring editorials that Sloane had produced. Palmer's approach was more like Hornig's had been at *Wonder Stories*, to make the magazine like a club where everyone was pals together. In addition to the standard letter column, 'Discussions', Palmer introduced a 'Correspondence Corner' and 'Collector's Corner' for fans, and a 'Questions and Answers' column on scientific matters as well as a science quiz. There was also a 'Meet the Authors' feature in which authors spoke about themselves and their work. This last column was also one of the first examples we find of Palmer's penchant for tricks. After all, how did you 'meet the author' when that author was a pseudonym? That didn't bother Palmer. He would ask his author to invent something. Polton Cross, we learn, was born in London, although his alter ego, John Russell Fearn, was born in Manchester. Later Palmer enjoyed creating fake photographs to accompany these aliases. Readers had to learn early on that they could never quite know when Palmer was being serious and when he was having fun.

One of Palmer's (or more likely Ziff's) biggest innovations was an illustrated back cover. This was normally reserved for advertisements, but Palmer commissioned McCauley to provide a painting for 'This Amazing Universe', to accompany a short article which he then provided on the scale of the universe and how long it would take to reach the planets at the speeds of the day. The illustrated back cover became standard on *Amazing*, and soon Frank R. Paul became the featured artist.

One of Palmer's practices was to ask a writer to produce a story around a future cover painting. By this means he introduced Robert Bloch to the world of sf. Bloch had hitherto concentrated on horror fiction, mostly in *Weird Tales*, and he regarded this first venture, 'Secret of the Observatory' (August 1938), about a camera that could photograph through walls, as one of his worst stories, but he soon became a regular contributor to the Ziff-Davis magazines. The combination of psychological drama and sf for which Bloch became justly renowned surfaced early in *Amazing Stories* with 'The Strange Flight of Richard Clayton' (March 1939). It tells of a man sent to Mars in a sealed spaceship. The ship's chronometer fails and as time passes so the man ages and his hair turns white. When he finally believes he has landed he learns that the ship never took off and it has taken them a week to free him from the capsule!

The number of good stories in Palmer's first year is negligible compared with those for Campbell, but the few are worth recording. The January 1939 issue published Eando Binder's 'I, Robot', a touching story about a selflessly noble machine. It ushered in a series (that grew progressively worse) featuring the robot, Adam Link. The first story made an impression on the young Isaac Asimov, and it was in *Amazing* that he first appeared professionally with a space problem story, 'Marooned Off Vesta' (March 1939).

Nelson S. Bond, whom we shall return to later, was a better writer than history records, and he contributed a superior story about a future feudal society in 'The Priestess Who Rebelled' (October 1939). Palmer also acquired William F. Temple's 'The Four-Sided Triangle' (November 1939), which explores the implications of two men in love with the same woman and how the problem is made worse through the use of a matter duplicator.

The initial response to *Amazing* was favourable, perhaps not too surprising considering the tedium of Sloane's final issues, though in hindsight it may be seen as an over-reaction to change. Many of the letters published welcomed a return to the 'good old days' which, in the light of Campbell's developments at *Astounding*, was perhaps not altogether a good message. It suggested that, at least in 1938, readers enjoyed the slash-and-thunder of the space-opera days rather than the more sophisticated sf that Campbell was encouraging. *Amazing*'s sales rose, and from the November 1938 issue it was back on a monthly schedule. Palmer was firmly ensconced as editor.

It is remarkable that in the space of two years all three of the magazines had been revitalized with new editors, and each had its own adoring audience and was prospering. As sf historian Sam Moskowitz has pointed out, they proved useful stepping stones for the fan: *Amazing*'s more sensational adventures for the younger readers, *Thrilling Wonder*'s slightly more thoughtful stories for the older teenagers, and *Astounding*'s sensitive and mature approach for adults.

By the close of 1938 two further developments had happened which would strongly influence the future of science fiction. By chance both events happened in May 1938 and both would subsequently be linked.

Late May 1938 saw the appearance of *Marvel Science Stories*, the first new science-fiction magazine (excluding semi-professional or media-spawned publications) since *Miracle* in 1931. This was one of the Red Circle magazines put out by the brothers Abraham and Martin Goodman under various imprints, but chiefly Western Fiction. Martin Goodman had launched his company in partnership with Louis Silberkleit in 1932, when he was just 22, to publish cowboy magazines. His first magazine was *Complete Western Book*, and he added further western titles before branching into detective, mystery and sports magazines. By 1938 he had established a sizeable empire of over 25 titles, although many of them were ephemeral and irregular in lifespan, such as *Ka-Zar*, which we have already encountered.

Goodman had kept an eye on the lucrative horror market. This was not the supernatural field as exemplified by *Weird Tales*, but the sex-and-sadism market which had come to the fore with *Dime Mystery* in 1933 and included *Horror Stories* and *Terror Tales*, all from Popular Publications. These stories placed the emphasis on bizarre and dangerous events, sometimes suggesting the supernatural but usually with rationalized conclusions. The intent was to create the most bizarre dangers in which women could be placed to allow the author to explore all kinds of sexual and sadistic situations. By today's standards the stories are only mildly titillating, though they are sometimes unusual, but they also bowed to the prejudice and bigotry of the day, especially against blacks, orientals and the mentally handicapped.

Nevertheless the sexual overtones sold the magazines, and other companies soon added titles to the list. Major amongst these were *Spicy Adventure*, *Spicy Detective* and *Spicy Mystery*, launched by Culture

Publications in 1934, and *Thrilling Mystery* from Standard Magazines in 1935. This last was the mildest of the so-called weird-menace pulps and featured stories by many fantasy and science-fiction writers, including Frank Belknap Long, Arthur J. Burks, Robert E. Howard, Edmond Hamilton, Jack Williamson and Henry Kuttner. Ray Cummings had also become one of the most prolific writers for all of the weird-menace pulps.

By late 1937 the Goodmans had decided to test these waters. *Detective Short Stories* was issued in August 1937 featuring tantalizing covers and story-titles and soon became their most profitable and longest surviving title. It was followed by *Mystery Tales* in March 1938.

It was against this background that Martin Goodman, also seeing the profitability of science fiction at Street & Smith and Standard Magazines, plus Ziff-Davis entering the market, brought *Marvel Science Stories* into play.

At the outset *Marvel* sought to resemble the other sf magazines. Editor Robert O. Erisman studied the field and brought in some of the best artists and writers. Norman Saunders painted a striking cover, and Arthur J. Burks provided the lead novel 'Survival'. This was about a band of survivors in the United States who venture underground to escape marauding Mongol hordes. They stay underground for 39 generations and the story plots their fight for survival. The novel had much in common with themes in earlier stories, especially the American-invasion stories in the hero pulps, and such classic sf stories as Charles R. Tanner's Tumithak series. In fact readers' memories may have harked back to those when they hailed 'Survival' as the best story of the year – some said three years!

Apart from 'Survival', Goodman felt they should spice the stories up a little and try to market science fiction to the same readers who enjoyed his mystery-and-mayhem pulps. Goodman and Erisman encouraged their writers to include a little more sex and lust than was usually associated with science fiction. They first approached Henry Kuttner, who wrote for their companion titles and who was known in sf circles. His novelette, 'Avengers of Space', which included scenes of aliens lusting after unclothed Earth women, brought immediate reaction from sf purists who found the story disgusting. More blows fell on Kuttner with his story in the second issue, 'The Time Trap'. Fan and future editor, William Hamling, wrote to say: 'I was just about to write you a letter of complete

congratulations when my eyes fell upon Kuttner's "The Time Trap".
All I can say is: PLEASE, in the future, dislodge such trash from
your magazine.'[8] If the readers had known that Kuttner had also
authored two other similar stories in the first issue under pen names
his name would have become even more disgraced than it did.
Fortunately the second issue, apart from 'The Time Trap', showed a
little more restraint. Burks contributed a sequel to 'Survival' called
'Exodus'. It could not repeat the success of the first novel, but was
much welcomed none the less. Jack Williamson produced a fine
novelette of a sudden blight that strikes the world in 'The Dead
Spot'. There was even a fantasy by David H. Keller, 'The Thirty and
One', one of his much neglected 'Tales from Cornwall' series.
Williamson, Burks and Keller were highly praised, but Kuttner was
railroaded. He had a few supporters, but these seemed vastly
outnumbered by the die-hard sf fans.

Initially, Erisman seems to have taken note of the fans' requests
but by 1939 *Marvel*'s sales were starting to drop and, under pressure
from Martin Goodman, Erisman stepped up the sex content of the
magazine. With the sixth issue, dated December 1939, the 'science'
was dropped and the title changed to *Marvel Tales*. The covers
became more like those of the other weird-menace pulps, with girls
being lowered into all manner of torture devices, and the horror
writers took over. Jack Williamson recalls how Erisman got him to
include some spicy passages in his previously unsold story 'The
River of Terror' which was then published under the title 'Mistress of
Machine-Age Madness' (May 1940). Williamson feared having his
name linked with it, so it appeared under the house name Nils O.
Sonderlund. 'It looks more insipid than daring now,' Williamson
later recalled, 'but I didn't want my name on it then. For most of us
in those days science fiction had to be pure as snow.'[9]

It may seem surprising that Erisman was able to get purist sf
writers to spice up their fiction, even if a sale was a sale. Williamson
wouldn't have done it for Campbell, so why did he for Erisman? It
was probably quite simply because Erisman was a very pleasant
person. Frederik Pohl called him 'one of the friendliest of the
editors'.[10] He almost certainly had a charm and charisma that enticed
writers into losing their virtue, and in so doing he almost ruined
Henry Kuttner's burgeoning career.

8. *Marvel Science Stories*, 1 (3) February 1939, p. 128, from a letter by W. Lawrence Hamling.
9. Jack Williamson, *Wonder's Child* (New York: Bluejay Books, 1984), p. 72.
10. Frederik Pohl, *The Way the Future Was* (New York: Ballantine Books, 1979), p. 94.

By 1940 *Marvel* was pretty much lost to the sf field. Nevertheless, its appearance and the success of the first issue was a further indication to publishers that science fiction was a field worth exploring. *Marvel* triggered what became science fiction's first boom period when the field became flooded with new titles. I'll explore these in a later chapter. First there was another trend that would rapidly affect the future of science fiction.

May 1938 also saw the appearance of the first issue of *Action Comics* (cover dated June 1938). The comic strip, as we have seen, had been gathering pace during the thirties. The comic book was a more recent phenomenon. The first retail comic book (as distinct from those sold as part of in-store promotional offers) was *Famous Funnies*, 'the nation's comic monthly', which first appeared in February 1934 and went monthly in October of that year. With that same issue it began reprinting the Buck Rogers strip, so that science fiction was associated with the comic book at an early stage. It was the success of *Famous Funnies* that printed the name 'comic' book so indelibly on the public's minds, so that even when publishers turned to non-humorous subjects, including war and horror stories, they remained, rather inappropriately, 'comic' books.

The innovation of using new material rather than reprinted 'funnies' was developed by retired army Major Malcolm Wheeler-Nicholson, whom we have already encountered with the hero pulp *Bill Barnes*. Wheeler-Nicholson was not a particularly good writer but he was an astute businessman. In 1935 he had established the Nicholson Publishing Company, which became the National Publishing Company, soon after and then D.C. Comics, named after its leading title, *Detective Comics*, issued in March 1937.

Jerome Siegel and Joseph Schuster were a writer/artist team at D.C., and by 1938 they had succeeded in interesting the company in a comic strip featuring their invincible hero, Superman. He first appeared in the June 1938 *Action Comics*. The impact was immediate. Sales rocketed and within a year a separate character comic, *Superman*, appeared. The first issue, dated Summer 1939, was released on 18 May. That same month *Detective Comics* ran the first strip of a new superhero, then called The Batman, drawn by Bob Kane. That was equally successful and the first issue of *Batman* appeared in April (Spring) 1940. Other titles were soon added and with this growth, D.C. recruited a new editor for the superhero comics: Mort Weisinger.

The comic-book field, especially focusing on superheroes,

suddenly became immensely lucrative, and this ushered in what has been called the Golden Age of the comic book. It is interesting that this Golden Age coincides so closely with that of science fiction at *Astounding*, even though the two were appealing to opposite ends of the market. It's something we shall consider later.

Martin Goodman was convinced of the merits of the comic book by Frank Torpey, sales manager of a writers-and-artists consortium called Funnies, Inc. Goodman entered into an agreement with Torpey to provide him with sufficient material to launch a comic-book series. One of the consortium, Bill Everett, had created a character called the Submariner, who sought to protect his under-world kingdom from invaders. The character had first appeared in *Motion Picture Funnies Weekly*, a short-lived magazine issued in April 1939 as a giveaway at cinemas. Everett now worked the character up for Goodman along with Carl Burgos who created another character called the Human Torch. The two appeared in the new *Marvel Comics* issued in September 1939 (cover date November). The cover of that first issue was drawn by none other than Frank R. Paul. Today it is an immensely treasured issue amongst collectors, far more than most of the pulps put together, and a mint edition could raise over $100,000.

One effect of the success of the comic book was to lure Hugo Gernsback back to the field. In April 1940 he issued his own *Super-world Comics*, written by Charles Hornig and illustrated by Frank Paul. Gernsback claimed as ever that all of his stories would be instructive and also that 'no superhuman feat impossible of accom-plishment will ever be published'. However it did not succeed. Gernsback's version of the prodigal son had long escaped his clutches and did not want to return.

The impact of the superhero comic book is immeasurable. It was the next link in the chain from the hero pulp and the dime novel. It clearly began to have an impact upon the hero pulp, as we shall soon see, and it also gave science fiction the juvenile image from which it has never escaped. Mention science-fiction magazines to people today and they will instantly think of comics. Among the public, the pulps and later digests have been forgotten, but the comic book lives on. This harm, and the continued rivalry between maga-zines and comics, will continue to feature throughout this history.

The Golden Age and science-fiction boom was about to start, but before tracing those events we need to bring the rest of the world up to date in order to see the wider global impact of science fiction.

Other Shores

During the development of magazine science fiction in America it may seem surprising that no equivalent was emerging in Britain. Our last contact with the British Isles was in 1919 with the special issue of *Pear's Annual* but in the years that followed, science fiction remained a small and almost unnoticed part of British magazines.

The American magazines had, however, been imported ever since the first issue of *Amazing Stories*, in fact further back with *Weird Tales* and *The Thrill Book*, and British writers took every opportunity to contribute to the American pulps. In the forefront was George C. Wallis from Sheffield, who had been writing for the popular magazines since the 1890s. He occasionally collaborated with a Canadian cousin, B. Wallis, and his stories began to appear in *Amazing* from 1928. By 1931 a number of British writers were appearing regularly in American magazines, and these increased in number over the next few years. Amongst them were Benson Herbert, John Beynon Harris, Ralph Stranger, Festus Pragnell, Philip Cleator, W.P. Cockroft, and most prolific of them all, John Russell Fearn. There were other contributors from Australia and South Africa and in addition Gernsback purchased and had translated many stories and novels from France and Germany.

Clearly there was no shortage of writers in these countries, and yet few magazines would dedicate much space to science fiction. In Britain, if genuine science fiction appeared anywhere it tended to be relegated to the boys' adventure magazines, especially *Chums* which even reprinted some material from Gernsback's *Science Wonder* and *Air Wonder Stories*. Occasional sf stories surfaced in *Pearson's*, *The Strand*, *The Red Magazine* and *Passing Show*, but these were the exception rather than the rule. The only other regular markets for science fiction were in two anthology series. One was the Not at Night series edited by Christine Campbell Thomson for the publisher Selwyn & Blount, and the other was the Creeps Library edited by Charles Birkin for publisher Philip Allan.

The Not at Night series had started with an anthology called *Not at Night* in 1925, and appeared annually. It was initially primarily reprint, with stories coming mostly from *Weird Tales*. In fact it had a close agency arrangement with that magazine to the extent that the series was regarded as a British edition of the magazine. Later volumes included more new material, again most of it straight horror fiction, but some of it of the scientific-menace type. The last volume in the series, *Nightmare by Daylight* (1936) included 'The Horror of the Cavern' by Walter Rose, a South African writer who made a few sales to *Amazing Stories* at the same time. This story is about a cave where people become trapped and degenerate into sub-humans.

The Creeps series of anthologies began in 1932 with *Creeps*. Although this reprinted some American material, most of it was British and original. The stories were mainly straight horror, few unleavened even by supernatural elements, but they also allowed an opening for science fiction. William F. Temple, for instance, made his first professional appearance in *Thrills* (1935) with 'The Kosso', about a tree that is injected with a chemical and becomes intelligent. An earlier volume, *Horrors* (1933), had printed 'Doctor Fawcett's Experiment' by Raymond Ferrers Broad in which, through a series of diary extracts, we learn of a doctor who is seeking to create life. His obsession turns to madness and his experiments, at first on plants and animals, turn to humans. He creates a bizarre form of fungoid life which is intent on revenge.

Both of these series had ceased by 1936, and they had no magazine equivalents. It's not as if the British were against genre magazines. Walter Hutchinson had started *Adventure-Story* and *Mystery-Story* in 1922 and 1923, and *The Detective Magazine* appeared from Fleetway Press in 1923. It seems strange that in Britain, where H.G. Wells had all but fathered the genre just over 30 years earlier, most science adventure stories were becoming regarded as fit only for younger readers.

Thus it should have been no surprise, although it was disappointing, that when in 1934 Pearson's issued a science-fiction magazine it was aimed solely at young readers. This was *Scoops*. It was issued weekly, in tabloid newspaper form running to 32 pages and selling for twopence, then the equivalent of 8 cents. Its first issue was dated 10 February, and was anonymously edited by Haydn Dimmock, who also edited *The Scout*, the magazine of the Boy Scout movement. None of its contributors was credited, and the reader was lured instead by such titles as 'Master of the Moon', 'The Striding Terror', 'The Rebel Robots', 'Rocket of Doom', 'Voice from the Void' and 'The Soundless Hour'. Most of the contents were serials, planned to hook readers from week to week.

With its second issue a further serial began, and this was the only story to credit the author: Professor A.M. Low, a highly regarded scientist and inventor. His novel, 'Space', was later issued in hardback as *Adrift in the Stratosphere* (1937). I can still remember the thrill when I first read this novel in my youth. It tells of three intrepid lads who accidentally launch themselves into space and undergo many dangers on their way to Mars. In the same way I imagine it must have evoked considerable interest amongst the youth of 1934.

Alas, the other stories were not of that quality. They were by authors who wrote regularly for the boys' magazine market, including Bernard Buley, J.H. Stein, Reginald Thomas, George E. Rochester and Stuart Martin. They knew how to write an exciting adventure, but had little scientific knowledge to make plausible future forecasts. As a result stories tended to be about youngsters who acquired special powers or strength, or who were menaced by robots or monsters.

It was not until after the first month or two that British sf writers caught up with *Scoops*. Haydn Dimmock was surprised to discover that science fiction had an adult audience. He began receiving more mature stories from John Russell Fearn, W.P. Cockroft and Maurice Hugi. This left Dimmock in something of a dilemma, unsure of his market. Clearly he made changes, as the adverts now included cigarette holders and shaving mirrors in addition to pen-knives and mouth organs. However, this was Dimmock's worst move. There was no way the magazine could please both readerships. Either it should have stayed as a boys' magazine, or it should have switched to an adult one. But Dimmock had no idea there was adult interest in science fiction until it was too late.

Scoops lasted for 20 weekly issues before Pearson's decided sales had dropped too far. The final issue appeared on 23 June 1934. Its failure gave British publishers the impression that a native sf magazine could not support itself. In fact, not only British publishers. Nottingham sf fan James Dudley wrote to Charles Hornig at *Wonder Stories* in 1935 proclaiming that: 'for the man or men with courage and the capital to start with, this little land of ours would be a "verdant pasture" for science-fiction, and prove a gold-mine to him or them.' To this Hornig replied:

> You do not seem to be acquainted with the fact that a British science-fiction magazine was published for twenty weekly issues, after which it 'went under'. This proved to us and other British publishers that your country is not yet prepared to support a professional science-fiction magazine enough to make it pay for itself.[11]

11. *Wonder Stories*, 7 (8) March/April 1936, pp. 1017–18.

No small wonder that more than 30 years later, Walter Gillings would look back on *Scoops* and call it 'the biggest blunder that British science fiction ever made'.[12]

It would be three years before science fiction was able to rear its head again in British publishing circles. During that period British science-fiction fandom, which was becoming organized via Gernsback's Science Fiction League, started to influence the market. Maurice K. Hanson, of the Nuneaton Chapter of the League, had started his own amateur magazine, *Novae Terrae*, in March 1936. This magazine later became the official magazine of the Science Fiction Association and metamorphosed into *New Worlds*, the fannish precursor to Britain's later premier sf magazine. In January 1937 Walter Gillings began issuing his formally printed and studiously assembled *Scientifiction* from Ilford in Essex, and two months later Douglas Mayer began his own magazine, *Tomorrow*, from Leeds in Yorkshire. These three fan magazines were the key to bonding science fiction in Britain and provided the base from which Gillings could stage an assault on the publishing houses to consider an adult science-fiction magazine.

Walter Gillings was a young newspaper reporter. He had been born in Ilford in February 1912 and became hooked on sf from an early age. He was amongst the earliest of active British fans, forming the Ilford Literary Circle in 1931. He had a more mature attitude to sf than some of his American counterparts as evidenced in his magazine *Scientifiction*, which gave detailed news, analysis and coverage of writers and developments in the sf field. It was this mature approach that caused him to be treated seriously by the publishers he contacted.

Gillings first tested the waters with Newnes, the publisher of *The Strand Magazine*. Newnes was at one stage receptive to the idea. As early as 1935 it had issued two specialist fiction pulps, *Air Stories* and *War Stories*, under the editorship of T. Stanhope Sprigg, and had started to commission sf stories from British authors. But the company had second thoughts and the idea went into cold storage.

Gillings next approached The World's Work, a subsidiary of William Heinemann. The World's Work was much more receptive. The company was so named because it was established to publish the British edition of the American magazine, *The World's Work*, published by Doubleday. It also published the British editions of

12. Walter Gillings, 'Science Fiction Weakly', *Vision of Tomorrow*, 1 (4) January 1970, p. 30.

Doubleday's *Short Stories* and another of the early genre pulps to appear in Britain, *West*.

Generally, though, The World's Work avoided establishing other single-genre pulps. Instead it started The Master Thriller series which experimented in different genres and then built on the success of the more profitable. The first was *Tales of the Foreign Legion*, published in July 1933, which was sufficiently successful to see five more annual issues. Titles of some fantasy relevance included *Tales of Mystery and Detection* (March 1934), *Tales of the Uncanny* (September 1934), *Tales of the Jungle* (June 1935) and *Tales of Adventure* (Spring 1937). There was also a separate mystery magazine called *Mystery Stories*. The editor for most of this series, which reached more than 30 titles by 1939, was H. Norman Evans.

When Gillings approached the company to include a science-fiction title in the series, The World's Work welcomed the idea. The result was *Tales of Wonder* which appeared on the bookstalls in June 1937, priced just one shilling (about 20 cents). It was the standard pulp size with 128 pages. The cover, by John Nicolson, illustrated 'Superhuman' by Geoffrey Armstrong, which marked John Russell Fearn's first voyage into the realms of pseudonymity. The name was devised by Gillings because Fearn was also present under his real name with 'Seeds from Space'. Here too were other leading names in British sf. John Beynon (who had truncated his name from John Beynon Harris) appeared with 'The Perfect Creature' (which has often been reprinted under its alternative titles of 'Una' or 'Female of the Species'). Eric Frank Russell, just starting to make a name for himself in the States, presented one of his early Weinbaum imitations, 'The Prr-r-eet', which proved to be the most popular story in the issue. And ex-policeman, Festus Pragnell, had 'Man of the Future', plus 'Monsters of the Moon' under the alias Francis Parnell, a name which led to confusion in later years as there was a well-known British fan and collector of the same name.

Gillings had not attempted to emulate the more sophisticated sf emerging under Campbell in *Astounding*. Most British readers were not ready for this. John Carnell recognized the position in his own response to the first issue when he stated, 'super "thought-variant" themes ... would be alien to probably ninety-five percent of British readers'.[13] *Tales of Wonder* consequently read more like the early

13. Edward J. Carnell, in a letter published in 'Readers' Reactions', *Tales of Wonder*, 2, 1938, p. 125.

days of *Amazing* and *Wonder Stories*. This would allow British sf to develop and encourage new writers who might otherwise find science fiction too advanced.

The sales of *Tales of Wonder* were sufficient for The World's Work to try a second issue six months later, which was also successful. Gillings was then commissioned to produce it on a quarterly schedule. The second issue appeared in the spring of 1938. It included 'Sleepers of Mars' by John Beynon, the sequel to his popular 'Stowaway to Mars', about a race into space, which had been serialized in *The Passing Show* in 1936. William F. Temple made his sf magazine debut with 'Lunar Lilliput', in which the British Interplanetary Society organizes the first trip to the Moon. The issue also included David H. Keller's 'Stenographer's Hands', reprinted from *Amazing Stories*, ostensibly to provide a direction to new writers, though really because Gillings was finding it difficult to obtain enough good-quality British fiction.

Gillings is to be congratulated for beginning the first adult British science-fiction magazine. It is a measure of its success that it was the only title arising from The Master Thriller series to develop a significant life of its own. More importantly it was through *Tales of Wonder* that the first generation of British sf magazine writers could develop and establish themselves.

Although the leading British sf writers had made their first sales to the American pulps, they were now able to take advantage of their only British market. Stories by John Beynon Harris, Eric Frank Russell, William F. Temple, Festus Pragnell and George C. Wallis began to appear with some degree of regularity. Temple contributed one of the most talked about stories in *Tales of Wonder*, 'The Smile of the Sphinx' (Autumn 1938), which considers cats as aliens now ready to complete their invasion of Earth.

New names began to emerge. The most famous was that of Arthur C. Clarke, whose professional debut was with an article, 'Man's Empire of Tomorrow', in the fifth issue (Winter 1938). Clarke was, at that time, very active in British science-fiction fandom as well as in the British Interplanetary Society, along with fellow visionaries William F. Temple, John Carnell and Philip Cleator.

Other names, less well known today but at the time all showing a promise for the future, were Charles F. Hall, Leslie J. Johnson, Frank Edward Arnold, D.J. Foster and Charnock Walsby (pseudonym of Leslie V. Heald). A few of these we shall briefly encounter again. The letter column also bristled with the names of those who would be the next generation of writers: Sydney J. Bounds, John F. Burke, Henry K. Bulmer, David McIlwain (Charles Eric Maine) and C.S. Youd (John Christopher).

Gillings also introduced Australian writer Coutts Brisbane to the sf magazines. Under that alias and the name Reid Whitley he had been selling to the British general fiction pulps and boys' magazines for over 20 years. Without crediting their source Gillings reprinted some of Brisbane's early material and acquired a new story, 'The Big Cloud' (Summer 1939). Brisbane, whose real name was R. Coutts Armour, remains something of a mystery man in sf circles. A prolific writer with a vivid imagination, he should be recognized as one of the pioneers of light-hearted and inventive science fiction, but he is generally forgotten. Gillings was the only editor to include him in a science-fiction magazine.

With the appearance and success of *Tales of Wonder*, Newnes reconsidered its science-fiction title. Theodore Stanhope Sprigg was given the green light to issue *Fantasy*, a magazine he claims he had planned to issue as far back as 1935. Sprigg was one of a noted family of writers and journalists. His brother Christopher had been killed in the Spanish Civil War. Theodore had been editor of *Airways* before joining Newnes in 1934 to develop its specialist pulp fiction line. He had a long-standing interest in science fiction and was certain not only that such a magazine would be a viable publishing proposition but also that it would provide the stimulus and opportunity for British writers. Had Newnes issued *Fantasy* in 1935 when first mooted, the British sf scene might have been much richer, and certainly more advanced, before the Second World War. Instead *Fantasy* appeared in late July 1938.

The first issue of *Fantasy* is spoiled only by the rather crude Frankenstein-like cover by staff artist Serge Drigin. It illustrated 'Menace of the Metal Men' by A. Prestigiacomo, reprinted from the September 1933 issue of the British *Argosy*, where it had appeared under the more restrained title of 'Zed Eight'. The story had apparently been written in English at the suggestion of Compton Mackenzie. The plot, a simple case of robots in revolt, was not new, but it was mildly entertaining. The story reflected the stereotyped image of science fiction. Fortunately Sprigg had also acquired new stories by John Beynon, John Russell Fearn and Eric Frank Russell which were more in line with conventional science fiction. Newnes' regular writers J.E. Gurdon and Francis H. Sibson were also present, and P.E. Cleator provided an article on interplanetary travel, a continuation of the series he had in *Scoops*. Cleator, who had been the co-founder of the British Interplanetary Society with Leslie J. Johnson in October 1933, had the potential to become the British Willy Ley had not the war intervened. In later years he established a reputation with his books on underwater archaeology.

The gathering clouds of war were making themselves only too evident in the first issue of *Fantasy* where it was a constant theme amongst the writers. 'Menace of the Metal Men' had already placed the army on alert. Beynon's story, 'Beyond the Screen', concerns civilization's most terrible weapon, Judson's Annihilator (by which title the story later appeared in *Amazing*), and J.E. Gurdon's 'Leashed Lightning' concerned aerial warfare.

Two more issues of *Fantasy* appeared in March and June 1939. They were both competent, with good stories, especially by Eric Frank Russell. But the threat of war with Germany was now becoming a terrible reality. Sprigg, as a member of the Royal Air Force Reserve, was mobilized. His magazines, relying upon him as editor, ceased publication, with the exception of *Air Stories* which survived for a few more years until paper rationing caused it to fold.

Britain declared war on Germany on 3 September 1939. War-time restrictions did not immediately apply and many believed the war would soon be over. Apart from the mobilization of forces, there were few effects in Britain until the following year. Paper rationing came into force in April 1940 and it was from then on that the effects began to bite.

Tales of Wonder continued much as before, although it was not helped by the fact that Gillings was editing it from his army training locale. With the ninth issue, Winter 1939, the page count dropped to 96, and progressively down to 80 and 72 over the next few issues. In that ninth issue, the first after war had been declared, Gillings asked his readers to look ahead and predict the war of the future. The responses were gloomy, the overall view being that humans would ultimately be the cause of their own self-destruction. Some of the imagery, with battles fought between giant tanks and robot war-machines, are reminiscent of the opening scenes of the films *Terminator* and *Mad Max*. Interestingly, though, at that time few of the writers had experienced any direct effect of the war, and their predictions, whilst disturbing, still held that sense of wonder over the achievements of super-science. The late thirties saw the final golden glow of Britain's aspirations of future science. Within a few years, Britain would have a different outlook.

The war had an immediate effect on a French magazine. Gillings had been dealing with George H. Gallet, a French journalist and science commentator, to reprint stories from *Tales of Wonder* in a weekly magazine. Gallet wanted to produce a periodical that properly fused science fiction with studies of the wonder and development of science. The magazine was *Conquêtes*. Two advance issues were released in September 1939 before the war intervened and Gallet had to shelve his plans.

As British writers were called to the war effort Gillings found himself increasingly relying on reprinted material from America. Only Eric Frank Russell and John Beynon consistently provided new material. Russell's 'I, Spy' (Autumn 1940), about a shape-shifting alien, was probably the best story in *Tales of Wonder* during the war years. The magazine struggled to maintain a quarterly schedule, but by mid-1941 this was impossible and the final two issues appeared in October 1941 and April 1942. Even these last two issues were on borrowed time and appeared only by luck and good fortune. The final issue, dated Spring 1942, was overstamped after publication with the notice that the publishers had 'been obliged, owing to paper restrictions and war conditions generally, to discontinue this magazine while the war lasts. No further issue will appear until peace comes when we hope to resume publication as before.' Had the magazine continued the next issue would have published the first professional story by John F. Burke, 'Before the Flood', another of those promised stories long since consigned to limbo.

The years 1937 to 1942 had seen the first shoots of British magazine sf which was now forced into shelter. Only one other attempt had been made before the war to issue a new magazine. British author William J. Passingham, who was a regular writer for the boys' magazines including a number of sf adventures, had interested the publishers The World Says in producing a science-fiction magazine in 1939. He approached leading sf fan John Carnell, and meetings were held during the winter of 1939/40 with plans to issue the magazine soon after March 1940, despite financial and production restrictions. Since March 1939, Carnell had taken over editorship of the magazine of the Science Fiction Association, *Novae Terrae*, and had retitled it *New Worlds*. Four mimeographed issues had appeared in March, April, May and August 1939, and it was now Carnell's intent to convert it into a professional magazine.

Stories were acquired, including one by Robert A. Heinlein, but at the last moment foul play was discovered. The World Says went into voluntary liquidation and the publisher returned to his native Canada. *New Worlds* was stifled at birth and would have to wait another six years before it could re-emerge into the world.

British readers were not starved of science fiction. They were able to read a much-edited British edition of *Astounding*. Before the war this had been imported by the Atlas Distributing Company, but from August 1939 Atlas began printing its own British edition. This did not correspond totally with the concurrent US edition, and as issues continued the disparity grew. Usually Atlas omitted one or two stories and rearranged other material.

The most enterprising of these wartime publishers was Gerald G. Swan of Marylebone, in London. Swan had started with a market stall, and began his publishing venture in 1938. He had the street sense to stockpile paper before the war, anticipating its rationing. This meant that as restrictions tightened, Swan still had a warehouse full of paper. He used it to issue a variety of cheap magazines and booklets, many with the appearance of US titles, some even having a US cover price. One of his many series was the *Swan Yankee Magazine*. Each issue had various sub-titles, and issues 3, 11 and 21, published in 1942, were called *Yankee Science Fiction*. The first of these reprinted stories from the Summer 1940 *Science Fiction Quarterly*, but the two later issues contained new fiction. Of interest is the third, published in July 1942, which featured new stories by W.P. Cockroft, Gerald Evans and Paul Ashwell. Ashwell, whose name would sometimes appear as Pauline Ashwell, was in real life Pauline Whitby, who also produced love stories under various pen names. In later years she would establish a reasonable reputation for her stories in *Astounding* and *Analog*, but few know that her first sf was tucked away in an opportunist British wartime magazine.

By the end of 1942 wartime restrictions had stifled almost all British magazines, not just the science-fiction titles. All of the major popular fiction magazines except for *The Strand* and *Argosy* had folded at the outbreak of war. It seems ironic, therefore, that whilst Britain and Europe were at their darkest hour, American science fiction was enjoying a Golden Age.

CHAPTER FOUR
The Golden Age

Multiplication

David Hartwell has amusingly noted that 'the golden age of science fiction is twelve'.[1] He was really alluding to the fact that most fans discover science fiction at the age of 12 and that thrill of discovery remains locked in the memory, always to evoke a golden glow. No matter how good later sf may be, those early stories retain that magical memory. But Hartwell was right in a different way. By 1938, magazine science fiction was 12 years old and was about to enter its teens. It was about to mature. However, like many teenagers, it was also about to rebel. Science fiction by 1938 had all of those tensions of puberty, and it would take a world war and the release of atomic energy to push sf finally into adulthood.

The following year, 1939, was a boom year for science fiction in the United States. In that year alone nine new magazines appeared, nearly twice as many as already existed. Of that nine, six were companion titles to current magazines, which emphasized the satisfaction those publishers were having with their sf titles. Although science fiction would never prove as popular as the detective or the western pulps, it was rapidly becoming the third string to publishers' bows. But some publishers were unsure whether science fiction belonged in the pulps or in the comic books, and at times the fiction became indistinguishable.

We have already seen that in 1938 the first signs of this boom came with the appearance of *Marvel Science Stories* amongst the pulps and *Action Comics*, featuring Superman, amongst the comic books. The hero pulps may already have sensed their day had passed. Although the leading hero pulps, *The Shadow* and *Doc Savage*, still had plenty of life and would be around for another decade or more, others striving to enter the field were less successful. May 1938, for instance, had seen the sole appearance of

---

1. David Hartwell, *Age of Wonders* (New York: Walker, 1984), p. 3.

Captain Hazzard from publisher A.A. Wyn (later the publisher of Ace Books). The magazine was seeking to copy *Doc Savage*, although its hero had telepathic powers. The magazine could not make an impact, and although a few more superhero pulps would appear, their future was increasingly in the comic-book field.

The science-fiction pulp, however, was having a heyday. Red Circle Magazines, which had started the boom with *Marvel Science Stories*, was clearly satisfied with the development because it launched a companion magazine, *Dynamic Science Stories*, with the first issue dated February 1939. Its intention was to carry longer fiction. The first, 'The Lord of Tranerica' by Stanton A. Coblentz, is typical pulp sf story of a dashing hero versus dictatorial powers in the future. Eando Binder's novel in the second issue, 'Prison of Time' (April 1939), is very similar, though set in another dimension. What should have been the strength of the magazine was in fact its weakest point. The short stories fared only slightly better with the best material coming from L. Sprague de Camp, Nelson S. Bond and Manly Wade Wellman. *Dynamic* was the first casualty of the boom, folding after just two issues. This is probably more a reflection of the whim of the publisher than of the public's attitude to science fiction, although it is possible that *Dynamic*'s lack of exposure may have contributed to its demise.

In the February 1938 *Thrilling Wonder Stories*, editor Mort Weisinger had asked readers for their suggestions on a possible companion sf magazine. Since at that stage *Marvel* had yet to appear it was the first intimation of any new magazine. Readers were all but unanimous in their approval, many recommending that the new title be published in the old large-size format. Although the last wish was not met, in late November 1938 the first standard pulp-size, 132-page issue of *Startling Stories* appeared, dated January 1939.

Startling's policy was to publish a long lead novel supported by one or two short stories, including a classic 'Hall of Fame' reprint. *Startling* was the first magazine to make this two-pronged approach. For a start the lead novel was always a popular feature, but had been missing from the sf pulps since the passing of the old Quarterlies. Secondly, as Standard Magazines had the rights to reprints from *Wonder Stories* back to 1929 it might as well take advantage of those for the new generation of readers that the field had attracted during the thirties. In all likelihood Standard paid no further fees for the stories as Gernsback would have acquired all serial rights (at least, for those stories he had paid for!).

The first lead novel was 'The Black Flame' by Stanley G. Weinbaum. This was a revised version of an earlier Weinbaum novella, 'Dawn of Flame', which had received several rejections and had been published in a memorial collection only, printed in a limited edition of 250 copies in 1936. This wasn't Weinbaum's best work, but by 1939, following his untimely death in 1935, he was already heading for legendary status – science fiction's first cult author – and *Startling* had a scoop in publishing it. The novel's theme struck a chord, depicting the rise of technology out of the ruins of post-catastrophe America.

The first Hall of Fame reprint was a good choice, 'The Eternal Man' by D.D. Sharp, one of the best mood stories from the early *Science Wonder Stories* (August 1929). The uncredited cover (probably by Howard V. Brown) illustrated an action-packed scene from Eando Binder's routine 'Science Island' (where a robot utopia fails). Features included a pictorial article by Jack Binder on Albert Einstein, the first in a series 'They Changed the World', and Weisinger provided a set of thumb-nail sketches of great scientists in 'Thrills in Science'. Otis Adelbert Kline provided a guest editorial and Otto Binder a tribute to Weinbaum.

The issue was a good package and was well received by readers. *Startling* rapidly became one of the core sf magazines. Although it printed some good short stories in its early years its strength lay in its novels. These were initially aimed more at young readers and were mostly space operas of one kind or another by capable pulp authors Eando Binder, Manly Wade Wellman, Edmond Hamilton and others. Hamilton's 'The Three Planeteers' (January 1940) is the most typical of these, a no-holds-barred fun romp around the solar system wherein an Earthman, Martian and Venusian team up against the evil forces of the solar system.

Amongst these novels were some showing more originality. 'Giants from Eternity' by Manly Wade Wellman (July 1939) tells of Earth faced with being overwhelmed by a red slime that devours everything it touches, and which has already destroyed native life on Mars and Jupiter. A scientist discovers that a gas generated by the slime can revive the dead, and he uses this to bring back to life the great scientists from the past to pool their knowledge to fight the slime. 'The Fortress of Utopia' by Jack Williamson (November 1939) is a clever time-travel story. In an attempt to save the Earth from future collision with a comet, humankind is sent back into the far past, with their memories erased, in order to re-evolve to a sufficiently advanced state to combat the comet. Wellman's 'Twice in Time' (May 1940) is another time-travel story, in which the protagonist goes back in time only to find that he has become Leonardo da Vinci. 'The Gods Hate Kansas' by Joseph Millard (November 1941) is a neglected but important early work exploring the idea of aliens using the bodies of Earth people as hosts. The theme was later developed by Robert A. Heinlein in *The Puppet Masters* (1951), and perhaps most memorably by Jack Finney in *Invasion of the Body Snatchers* (1955).

One factor that soon emerged in *Startling Stories* was that writers tended to develop fantastic plots unrestrained by science. It was here that science fiction began to stray into science fantasy, into the realms of what Hugo Gernsback always regarded as 'fairy tales' and not true science fiction. The main perpetrators were Henry Kuttner and Manly Wade Wellman. Kuttner began the trend with his wildly fantastic 'When New York Vanished' (March 1940), in which super-beings seeking to save their civilization from giant mutated insects invade the dimension of Earth. Kuttner's imagery was vivid and exciting but gave no token to authentic science. It was cosmic on a scale that readers found fascinating. Wellman developed the planetary adventure in 'Sojarr of Titan' (March 1941), borrowing from Edgar Rice Burroughs. Sojarr is the only surviving child of two Earth scientists who die in their attempt to explore Titan, the moon of Saturn. Sojarr grows up amongst the wild beasts of Titan and develops immense strength. Sojarr was a superhero transplanted to another world. His adventures are little short of the fantastic, but the enjoyment was immense.

The fantastic would soon become an essential part of *Startling*'s appeal. It was a sign that whilst some devotees wanted the hard science of *Astounding* others wanted their science fiction a little less technical and a lot more fun. It was also a sign that fantasy and weird fiction were increasing in popularity.

Hitherto this had predominantly been the domain of *Weird Tales*. We haven't looked at *Weird Tales* for some time because, although its early issues featured a number of weird-science stories, its later issues had focused more on genuine bizarre and weird stories. The main exceptions to this had been the cosmic stories of H.P. Lovecraft, and the fantastic tales of Edmond Hamilton in stories such as 'Child of the Winds' (May 1936) and 'He That Hath Wings' (July 1938). This last is one of Hamilton's best stories and far from his world-saving space operas of the previous decade. One of *Weird Tales*'s main strengths was its artwork. Regardless of its fiction, which was always variable in quality, *Weird Tales* was an attractive magazine. Throughout the mid- and late thirties the covers had been dominated by the lurid and erotic art of Margaret Brundage, featuring nudes in a variety of *risqué* poses. These covers almost certainly sold *Weird Tales* more than did the fiction and remain one of the main reasons for the magazine's collectibility. The great adventure artist J. Allen St. John had also provided covers in addition to the distinctive title logo which rapidly became *Weird Tales*'s trademark. Starting in February 1937, the young Virgil Finlay started to provide covers as well as his beautifully stippled detailed internal illustrations. All of this gave *Weird Tales* its unique flavour.

By 1939 *Weird Tales* found its monopoly of the bizarre challenged. Having launched *Startling Stories*, Standard Magazines now issued *Strange Stories*. The first issue was dated February 1939 and featured all of *Weird Tales*'s popular authors: Robert Bloch, August Derleth, Mark Schorer, Otis Adelbert Kline, Henry Kuttner and Manly Wade Wellman. Bloch, Derleth and Kuttner in particular dominated the magazine under their own names and pseudonyms with stories in almost every issue.

Despite *Strange Stories* being an obvious imitation of *Weird Tales*, few of its stories have been as regularly reprinted. The magazine lacked the character and appeal of *Weird Tales* and like all imitations can only be seen as lacking originality. The most memorable stories are Henry Kuttner's two sword-and-sorcery adventures featuring Prince Raynor, 'Cursed be the City' (April 1939) and 'The Citadel of Darkness' (August 1939), which, at a time when that sub-genre was still relatively new, showed both ingenuity and humour. Few of the stories in the magazine were science fiction, although C.L. Moore's 'Miracle in Three Dimensions' and Ralph Milne Farley's 'The Bottomless Pool' (both April 1939) use multi-dimensional concepts to evoke a feeling of strangeness. Likewise, August Derleth's 'Ithaqua' (February 1941) uses a blend of the Wendigo and Cthulhu myths to create a cosmic awareness.

Strange Stories lasted for 13 issues, folding with the February 1941 issue when Mort Weisinger left to take over editorial duties at *Superman*. The magazine was Weisinger's own and Leo Margulies did not wish to continue it. Stories remaining in the inventory were used in *Thrilling Mystery*.

Ironically, even though *Strange Stories* was only an imitation of *Weird Tales*, it appeared at a time when it could have captured

Weird's special place. In January 1939 *Weird Tales* had been sold to Short Stories, Inc. in New York, and that meant the transfer of editorial offices from Chicago. Farnsworth Wright, who had edited *Weird Tales* since 1924, moved with the magazine, but his health was failing and he soon found it impossible to continue. He left after the March 1940 issue and died shortly thereafter, aged only 52. The departure of Wright brought the end of an era. Only a few years previously H.P. Lovecraft and Robert E. Howard had died, and another favourite, Clark Ashton Smith, had almost ceased writing. Other leading names from the early days were contributing less frequently, and the magazine was undergoing a significant transition. The new editor was Dorothy McIlwraith, already the editor of *Short Stories*. McIlwraith was a competent editor, but lacked the eccentricity that Wright had brought to the magazine. Rapidly the creativity that had given *Weird Tales* its uniqueness began fading as the magazine was brought into the standard pulp mode to accord with *Short Stories*. Although Finlay, Brundage and new artist Hannes Bok continued to provide some attractive covers, the style was toned down from their previous excesses and some of the later covers by Ray Quigley and Franklin Wittmack were drab.

Thankfully there were sufficient of the old guard contributors, especially Robert Bloch, Manly Wade Wellman, Edmond Hamilton and Henry Kuttner, to sustain an interest, but the magazine lacked the appeal of the previous decade. Fortunately McIlwraith soon had a new assistant, Lamont Buchanan, who had more of an affinity with weird fiction and who was able to reinstate some of the old sparkle. During the forties he was encouraged, aided and abetted by August Derleth, who, though he had no editorial connection with the magazine, nevertheless advised and assisted as much as he could.

It is an interesting observation that just at the time when science fiction was growing up, weird fiction was growing old.

Weird Tales was now vulnerable and could have been toppled from its unique throne by *Strange Stories*. But Mort Weisinger had got the formula wrong, being too imitative. The man who made the right choice was John W. Campbell, Jr. Two months after *Strange Stories* appeared (with a cover date of March 1939), Street & Smith issued a new magazine called *Unknown*. It would revolutionize fantasy.

What *Astounding* had accomplished for sf, *Unknown* was about to do for fantasy. The most obvious difference between *Unknown* and

Weird Tales was the approach. In nearly every case *Weird Tales* presented bizarre fiction with the intent to frighten or shock. Not so *Unknown*, which treated fantasy as an everyday occurrence, and although the occasional scary story appeared, it was the note of humour pervading *Unknown* that makes it memorable. Here was the type of fiction popularized by Thorne Smith in his *Topper* series. *Unknown*'s fiction was never complicated; indeed, the opposite, as authors merely suggested a basic premise – 'What if …?' – and developed their stories logically from there. That development might lead to a frightening and bizarre denouement, but it was as likely to lead to a clever and satisfying jolt from reality which made the reader view the world afresh. If anything, the *Unknown*-style fantasy which developed (and which has passed its name down to today) was one visibly thumbing its nose at traditional horror, and giving the genre a refreshing kick-in-the-pants.

Not that this happened over night. Campbell was feeling his way from the outset, confident that there was scope for the new magazine, but still not quite sure where it was going. What had happened was that Campbell was receiving well-written and entertaining stories for *Astounding* that lacked the requisite hard science to fit into the image he was creating for that magazine. He discussed this with Henry Ralston who gave him the opportunity to create his own magazine. The initial selections were stories submitted to *Astounding*, and thus technically science fiction. The one generally regarded by legend to have flipped the switch and lit the bulb of *Unknown* in Campbell's mind was 'Forbidden Acres' (retitled 'Sinister Barrier' for publication) by Eric Frank Russell. The story was a strange mixture of science fiction and occult fantasy. Set in the future, it required an sf-premise to allow scientists to discover the existence of hitherto invisible energy-beings who oversee Earth and feed off mankind's negative emotions. Once Campbell asked Russell to rewrite parts to strengthen the fantasy element it freed the shackles of scientific discipline but still required a logical development. A strong trademark of the *Unknown* story is that even though the story has a fantastic premise, it always has a hint of the possible. Campbell had thereby brought the science fiction rationale to fantasy.

The authors who probably did most to develop the character of *Unknown* and move it from its sf origins into free-fall fantasy were L. Ron Hubbard and L. Sprague de Camp, and both these writers are still strongly associated with the magazine in people's memories.

Hubbard wrote arguably his best novel, *Fear* (July 1940), for the magazine. This story of a man's psychological quest to discover what happened during four missing hours in his life whilst he is beset by horrors from the supernatural, has become regarded by some as one of the best works of modern fantasy. Hubbard later believed that *Unknown* had been created to accommodate his new style of fiction, and though this is not the case, it is true that the popularity of Hubbard's quasi-sf/fantasies in *Astounding* had made Campbell realize that not all fantasy was unpopular, only the type of fantasy being written.

De Camp's first appearance was with 'Divide and Rule' (April–May 1939), which was still primarily an sf story of an alien-dominated future Earth, but his contributions soon began to remould. 'The Gnarly Man' (June 1939), one of the most popular stories from the first year, is about a Neanderthal man made immortal when struck by lightning, who today is a side-show freak. In 'Lest Darkness Fall' (December 1939), which could be classified as historical sf, de Camp has his hero transported by a lighting bolt back to the end of the Roman era, where he must rely on his twentieth-century knowledge to survive. The best developed of the de Camp fantasies were his collaborations with Fletcher Pratt on the adventures of Harold Shea, starting with 'The Roaring Trumpet' (May 1940). Shea is the character used to explore other fantasy worlds of legend, starting in this story with the Norse myths. De Camp and Pratt went to great lengths to ensure that their mythical worlds operated by strict rules of magic which were not akin to the rules of our own world but which were nevertheless internally consistent. This was new to fantasy, and from it developed an approach used frequently today. The Xanth series by Piers Anthony, for instance, is a direct descendant of the de Camp *Unknown*-type fantasy, and the first novel in that series would have been totally at home in the magazine.[2]

Another name closely associated with *Unknown* is that of Edd Cartier. Cartier had been illustrating for Street & Smith's magazines, especially *The Shadow*, since 1936 and had developed a strong light action-packed tone. Responding to Campbell's request for artwork Cartier developed a series of illustrations typified by

2. Campbell would have enjoyed the humour and the ingenuity of Xanth, but would not have supported a series of such inordinate length which had soon exhausted its originality.

gnomes and slightly-distorted humans who could be at once amusing and sinister. This ambivalence was perfect for the light-hearted dark side of *Unknown* fantasy.

Unknown published the greatest collection of fantasy stories produced in one magazine and many authors produced their best work for it. In addition to Hubbard and de Camp there were Fritz Leiber (whose Grey Mouser heroic fantasies, rejected by *Weird Tales*, first saw the light of day here), Nelson Bond, Henry Kuttner, Theodore Sturgeon, Anthony Boucher, Frank Belknap Long, Horace L. Gold, Lester del Rey and Howard Wandrei. Surprises were also in store. Norvell W. Page, one of the top pulp writers capable of producing fiction at speed, and the author of the lead novels in *The Spider*, appeared with two fine novels based on the legend of Prester John, 'Flame Winds' (June 1939) and 'Sons of the Bear God' (November 1939). The first was written within four days when Campbell was in urgent need of a novel to fill a space arising from a failed commission. This means a writing pace of 12,000 words a day, including all plot development, and yet the story is ingeniously conceived and written: the mark of a true story-teller. Manly Wade Wellman, who had hitherto produced some good stories in *Weird Tales*, was nevertheless regarded more as a writer of space stories, but in 'When It Was Moonlight' (February 1940) he produced a memorable story centred around Edgar Allan Poe. There is even a story by Raymond Chandler, 'The Bronze Door' (November 1939), a rare fantasy told in his characteristic style. Mention must also be made of Jack Williamson's 'Darker Than You Think' (December 1940), one of his best stories, with a fascinating scientific rationale for lycanthropy.

Unknown remains one of the best pulp magazines ever published, and almost certainly the most important in the fantasy genre, despite the reputation of *Weird Tales*. Its importance lies in the fact that it made fantasy respectable, and gave authors a chance to produce some of their best work.

Hot on the heels of *Unknown* came *Fantastic Adventures* as a companion to *Amazing Stories*. The first issue, dated May 1939, appeared in March, so was in press at the time that *Unknown* appeared. Raymond A. Palmer may have known that Campbell was planning such a magazine but this is unlikely to have influenced him. It is more probably a case of synchronicity. In fact Palmer's aim with *Fantastic Adventures* was almost identical to Campbell's with *Unknown*: to raise fantastic fiction to the level of the quality magazines, although Palmer added, 'and yet retain the lusty appeal of the pulp field'.[3] It seems a little strange to equate pulp fiction with quality, especially when the idea came from Palmer, and it would be some years before Palmer could rightly claim any quality fiction.

Nevertheless *Fantastic Adventures* did have a certain appeal, although the early issues were clearly not seeking to emulate *Weird Tales* or even copy *Unknown*, but concentrated on the Burroughsian style other-world/lost-race adventure. At the start Palmer had the same problem as Campbell and didn't seem to know whether to publish sf or fantasy. In all likelihood he was using stories that were submitted to *Amazing* but which had stronger fantastic elements. Even so, the first issue was mediocre with second-rate fiction by Eando Binder, Harl Vincent, Ross Rocklynne and A. Hyatt Verrill. There was even a comic strip, 'Ray Holmes, Scientific Detective', which was dropped after the first issue, again emphasizing the conflict between the pulp and the comic book. The best aspect of the first issue was Frank R. Paul's back-cover artwork depicting 'The Man from Mars'. The illustration, which was aided by *Fantastic Adventures* being published in the old large-style pulp format, was accompanied by an explanatory article.

The second issue is perhaps more interesting (though of only marginally better quality). Palmer was able to boast the name of Edgar Rice Burroughs with the lead novel 'The Scientists Revolt'. This was a long, previously unsold story by Burroughs which Palmer apparently extensively rewrote. It remained a poor story of international intrigue updated to the future, but Burroughs's name on the cover must have attracted readers. Also in the issue was 'The Golden Amazon' by Thornton Ayre, a pseudonym of John Russell Fearn. Somewhat in imitation of Stanley Weinbaum's Margot, the Black Flame, the Golden Amazon is superwoman Violet Ray. Fearn wrote three other stories featuring Violet Ray before converting the series into a novel format for the Canadian *Toronto Star Weekly*, a series that he continued to write until his death in 1960. The original four stories were amongst the most popular published in the early years of *Fantastic Adventures*.

The best story in the second issue was Nelson S. Bond's 'The Monster from Nowhere', about a being from another dimension. Bond was a capable writer of science fiction and fantasy and was one of the few authors at home in either *Fantastic Adventures* or

3. Raymond A. Palmer, 'The Editor's Notebook', *Fantastic Adventures*, 1 (1) May 1939, p. 4.

Unknown, or for that matter outside the pulps. He had scored premature fame with 'Mr Mergenthwirker's Lobblies', about a man with invisible friends, which appeared in the November 1937 issue of *Scribner's Magazine*. He also produced a memorable series about Meg, who becomes the priestess of her clan in a future set after the fall of civilization. The first story, 'The Priestess Who Rebelled', appeared in *Amazing Stories* (October 1939), but its sequel, 'The Judging of the Priestess', appeared in *Fantastic Adventures* (April 1940). The excellence of the series was proved when the third and final story, 'Magic City', was purchased by Campbell for *Astounding* (February 1941). This diversity demonstrates not only the quality of Bond's writing but his adaptability.

It was Bond who brought his light-hearted whimsy to *Fantastic Adventures*. Starting in the September 1939 issue, Bond wrote the first of what would become an unconnected multi-author series of fantastic romps in which innocuous and often downright daft people would suddenly have some remarkable ability. All of these stories had silly titles. Bond's first was 'The Amazing Invention of Wilberforce Weems'. While baby-sitting, Weems gives his charge a foul concoction of medicines to keep it quiet only to find that the potion has the ability to endow its taker with instant knowledge from any book applied to the head. The fact that another story, 'The Unusual Romance of Ferdinand Pratt', turned up in *Weird Tales* (September 1940), and 'Cartwright's Camera' in *Unknown* (November 1940), suggests that the approach was Bond's not Palmer's, but that Palmer rapidly milked it for what it was worth.

Palmer encouraged his developing stable of writers to produce similar humorous fantasies, and the *Fantastic Adventures* school of slightly 'nutty' fiction was born. David Wright O'Brien was the earliest to respond, with 'The Strange Voyage of Hector Squinch' (August 1940), about a hen-pecked husband who finds himself on a planet of the Greek gods, where Jove is an insurance salesman! This was in the same issue as Bond's 'The Fertility of Dalrymple Todd', in which a man can grow any plant he wishes on his head! O'Brien shared an office with William P. McGivern, the two of them producing copy for Palmer at a phenomenal rate. After the war, McGivern would establish a reputation as a writer of hard-boiled detective fiction, but at the start of his career he joined Bond and O'Brien in producing madcap fiction. During 1941 McGivern produced such stories as 'The Masterful Mind of Mortimer Meek', 'The Quandary of Quantus Quaggle', 'Sidney, the Screwloose Robot' and 'Rewbarb's Remarkable Radio'. This laid the trail for Robert Bloch to follow. Bloch, renowned for his sense of humour, began his own series about layabout Lefty Feep with 'Time Wounds All Heels' (April 1942), and produced such later titles as 'The Weird Doom of Floyd Scrilch' (July 1942). Leroy Yerxa soon followed with his zany adventures of Freddie Funk, starting with 'Freddie Funk's Madcap Mermaid' (January 1943).

Throughout the early 1940s, particularly during the war years, *Fantastic Adventures* provided considerable light relief. The fiction may not have been as sophisticated as *Unknown*'s, but it was enjoyable. It may seem surprising but *Fantastic Adventures* scarcely survived its first year. Although it was placed on a monthly schedule from January 1940 it still lagged behind *Amazing* in sales. In June 1940 it reverted to bi-monthly and was converted to the standard pulp format, which saved production costs. There were plans to drop the magazine after the October 1940 issue. It was this issue that featured 'Jongor of Lost Land' by Robert Moore Williams, a Tarzanesque adventure set in a lost land in central Australia. Palmer had commissioned foremost Tarzan artist J. Allen St. John to paint the cover depicting Jongor, and the combination of these two led to a doubling in sales. *Fantastic Adventures* was reprieved. Palmer now finalized a deal with Edgar Rice Burroughs for a new Carson of Venus series. The first, 'Slaves of the Fish Men', ran in the March 1941 issue, which was also adorned with a St. John cover. The combined effect boosted *Fantastic Adventures*'s circulation. This mixture of Burroughsian adventures and madcap humour typified *Fantastic Adventures* for the rest of the war years.

In January 1939 a new publisher entered the field: Blue Ribbon Magazines, with editorial offices in Hudson Street, New York. The publisher was Martin Goodman's former partner, Louis Silberkleit, who had established his own Winford Publishing Company in 1934. Silberkleit had been associated with Hugo Gernsback at the very start of *Amazing Stories* – in fact he had suggested that the title be *Future Fiction* – and, as we shall see, he remained with the pulp field till the very end. He was the publisher of the last ever regular sf pulp, *Science Fiction Quarterly*.

It was some recognition that the phrase science fiction was now so well entrenched that Silberkleit called his first entry into the field simply by that name – *Science Fiction* – and in so doing stopped John W. Campbell from shifting to that title by fading *Astounding* from his covers.

Science Fiction brought Charles D. Hornig back as editor, at the seasoned age of 22. He had clearly learned little about editing in the interim period. The new magazine looked superficially good. Despite a mediocre cover by Frank R. Paul, names such as Edmond Hamilton and Amelia Reynolds Long momentarily transported readers back to the glory days of *Wonder Stories*. In hindsight it might have been better if such memories had been left in the past as the stories were of poor quality. Hornig was operating under as much a handicap as he had with Gernsback. Although Silberkleit paid promptly, he did not want to pay much, and was not investing too heavily in *Science Fiction* in case it failed. Whereas Palmer, Campbell and Weisinger were able to pay a cent a word, sometimes more to their top writers, Hornig was limited to only half-a-cent a word, no matter who the author. He had to pull strings with his contacts to acquire either rejected stories or stories from old-time writers whose work was no longer welcome at other magazines. Writers who were selling at a cent a word elsewhere were dubious about being seen to sell stories at a lower rate for fear they might find their rates cut in other markets. Hornig thus came to an agreement that writers would be paid the full cent a word for stories published under their own names, but others at the half-cent rate were disguised under a welter of pen names. This allowed him to buy en masse a lot of stories from a few writers. The leading contributor was John Russell Fearn who also appeared as Ephraim Winiki, Dennis Clive and Dom Passante as well as the house name John Cotton, which was also used to hide work by Manly Wade Wellman. Edmond Hamilton appeared as Robert Castle, Henry Kuttner as Paul Edmonds and Eando Binder as John Coleridge (these were older stories co-written with Earl and revised for Hornig).

The leading writers had not been prepared for this sudden upsurge in markets. Suddenly where there had been only three regular sf magazines there were now twice that, and the flow of manuscripts had not yet caught up with the demand. At the outset, therefore, editors were having to acquire lower-quality material from either new writers or old hacks. Because Hornig was paying the lowest he became the market of last resort. Although it gave some writers such as Ed Earl Repp, Harl Vincent, Stanton Coblentz and even Ray Cummings a further market, it did nothing to improve their fiction and Hornig only seemed grateful for what he could get.

Ray Bradbury, a close friend of Hornig who was still seeking to make his first sale, gave some advice:

> don't let the magazine degenerate to the kindergarten class – let it grow with the minds of the fans. If the other mags want to play up to children, let them forge blindly on – but they won't carve a place for themselves in the hall of science fiction like you certainly will if you keep plugging with the ideas you hold in mind for the future.

To which Hornig's response was: 'I'm trying to give the magazine an appeal to mature minds, and am therefore avoiding illogical fairy tales.'[4]

Hornig and Bradbury were obviously deriding Palmer's policy at *Amazing* and perhaps Weisinger's at *Thrilling Wonder*, although the other titles were emerging rapidly by the time that note appeared. Hornig certainly tried to publish serious fiction – there were no light-hearted romps in his magazines – but little of it was of any quality. Indeed Hornig soon recognized that he was only able to buy old-style space opera or old-hat ideas. A determined search is necessary to find any good fiction in the magazine at all. The only spark of originality came from none other than Nelson S. Bond, with 'Proxies on Venus' (June 1940) about robot explorers who acquire emotions.

The situation wasn't helped when Silberkleit, deciding he could spread his overheads over further titles, launched two more sf magazines. *Future Fiction* came next, with its November 1939 issue, followed by *Science Fiction Quarterly* in July 1940. *Future Fiction* was no better or worse than *Science Fiction*, although it may hold more interest for collectors because it carried two stories by Isaac Asimov: 'Ring Around the Sun' (March 1940) and 'The Magnificent Possession' (July 1940). Otherwise it was the same blend of lower-grade material by John Russell Fearn, Manly Wade Wellman and Edmond Hamilton. *Science Fiction Quarterly* looked the better option. Silberkleit had reached a deal with Hugo Gernsback to reprint some of the early lead novels from *Science Wonder Quarterly*: 'The Moon Conquerors' by R.H. Romans and 'The Shot into Infinity' by Otto Willi Gail. These stories, now dated, had sufficient scientific appeal to remain of interest, and were of a better quality than most other material Hornig was publishing.

---

4. Ray Bradbury and Charles Hornig in 'The Telepath' letter column, *Science Fiction*, 1 (2) June 1939, p. 126.

In October 1940 Hornig was called up for military service. As a pacifist he wished to register as a conscientious objector and felt he might be treated more leniently in California than New Jersey, so he moved to Los Angeles. Thereafter Hornig endeavoured to edit the magazines long distance, an arrangement that Silberkleit rapidly came to dislike. Changes were in order and it was decided that Hornig would retain *Science Fiction*, but *Future Fiction* and *Science Fiction Quarterly* were handed over to a new editor. Silberkleit first approached Sam Moskowitz to edit the magazines but he declined and recommended Robert W. Lowndes. In fact the arrangement with Hornig only lasted another year, at which time sales of *Science Fiction* caused Silberkleit to combine it with *Future* from its October 1941 issue. The merged *Future combined with Science Fiction Stories* was at last able to sustain a regular bi-monthly schedule for a period.

Under Lowndes's editorship *Future Fiction* and *Science Fiction Quarterly* were transformed. This was because Lowndes was able to rely upon his close colleagues in a fan organization known as the Futurians. The membership of this group varied but at its core were Donald A. Wollheim, Frederik Pohl, Cyril Kornbluth, Isaac Asimov, John B. Michel, Richard Wilson, Damon Knight and Harry Dockweiler (Dirk Wylie), most of whom would become leading lights in science fiction. Initially most of these writers, especially Lowndes, Pohl, Kornbluth and Dockweiler, wrote either singly or in different collaborative combinations under a bevy of pen names. *Future Fiction* thus became the home of such shape-changing aliases as Paul Dennis Lavond, Millard Verne Gordon, S.D. Gottesman and Wilfred Owen Morley. To the reading public, who were still trying to identify with Ephraim Winiki and others from Hornig's issues, the science-fiction world suddenly appeared to be taken over by scores of unknowns.

In fact the depth of talent in the Futurians provided a most welcome breath of fresh air to science fiction. Outside of the writers that Campbell was developing at *Astounding*, they were the most creative force in science fiction, and it is worth considering their output in total as they began to permeate the field over the next couple of years. I shall return to them shortly.

Two other aspects of *Future Fiction* are worth identifying. Firstly, Silberkleit made a deal with Ray Cummings to reprint his early material and this became a regular feature starting from the October 1941 issue. Although this early material was not of exceptional quality, Cummings still retained a cult status in sf circles and these stories had a naïve optimism about them that was enjoyable. Also sustaining this old-time flavour was the work of Hannes Bok. Bok is better remembered as an artist than a writer, though he was equally skilled at both. Most of his fiction shows the influence of Abraham Merritt and can be enjoyed almost as much. Bok provided not only several covers for *Future* but also a number of scientific fantasies, including 'The Alien Vibration' (February 1942), 'Web of Moons' (April 1942) and 'Beauty' (October 1942), all heavy on the Merritt imagery. The combination of Bok/Merritt and Cummings gave the magazine a distinct old-time comfort which was balanced by the pyrotechnic bursts of the Futurians.

The old-time comfort was something that a new magazine also decided to market. Up until now it was perhaps surprising that Frank Munsey's company had not entered the specialist sf market. After all, it could claim to have launched the pulp popularity of sf back in early issues of *Argosy* and more especially *All-Story*. *All-Story* had merged with *Argosy* in 1920 (though subsequently was revived as a romance magazine, *All-Story Love*), but *Argosy Weekly* continued, occasionally publishing some science fiction. Nevertheless the appeal of the early scientific and fantastic romances published by Munsey was recognized and in the summer of 1939 the Munsey Corporation launched *Famous Fantastic Mysteries*, first issue dated September 1939. The cover was rather bland, declaring only a list of titles, but that included 'The Moon Pool' by Abraham Merritt and Ray Cummings's 'The Girl in the Golden Atom', both titles and names assured to attract fans. In fact the editor, Mary Gnaedinger, had a vast storehouse of material to choose from and was able to reintroduce major names from the scientific romances of the past 30 years, the only exception being Edgar Rice Burroughs.

The first issue was an immediate success and the magazine was placed on a monthly schedule. At the urging of Merritt himself, Mary Gnaedinger commissioned Virgil Finlay to illustrate 'The Conquest of the Moon Pool', which started in the second issue, and thus began the long partnership of Finlay and *FFM* (as it is often known). Finlay was able to bring just the right feeling of otherworldliness to Merritt's work, combining the exotic and the erotic. It was a combination that has made *FFM* one of the most treasured, collected and attractive of all pulp magazines.

In fact Gnaedinger soon realized that to reprint all of the old material for which readers were deluging her with requests would take years, especially the novel-length material. The obvious solution was a companion magazine, *Fantastic Novels*, which appeared with the issue dated June 1940. In an unprecedented but shrewd gambit, Gnaedinger ceased serialization of 'The Blind Spot', another legendary novel by Austin Hall and Homer Eon Flint, from the May 1940 *FFM* and ran the novel complete in the first *Fantastic Novels*, thus assuring a captive audience.

Between them, *FFM* and *Fantastic Novels* were reprinting good, reliable stories from the old days. In addition to Merritt and Cummings, there were Garrett P. Serviss, George Allan England, J.U. Giesy, Tod Robbins, Ralph Milne Farley and Homer Eon Flint, names of writers who today may be obscure, but who were pioneers of fantastic fiction in the pulps. Some of their work has now dated, but much of it has retained the special quality that made it memorable when first published. From the third issue Frank R. Paul joined Finlay as one of the mainstay artists, and though his work was not on an artistic level with Finlay's, it was nevertheless welcomed by his legion of admirers.

By the end of 1939 the appeal of the old-time scientific romances and adventures was only too evident. Two further magazines appearing that Christmas underscored the point. These were *Planet Stories* and *Captain Future*.

Planet Stories brought yet another publisher into the fray. Fiction House was a long-established firm going back to the twenties. Amongst its best-remembered titles were *Action Stories* and *Wings*. The firm had suffered in the Depression and had gone into temporary suspension, but was relaunched in 1934, quickly establishing itself with detective and romance pulps. The romance pulps in particular proved successful so that a subsidiary company was established called Love Romance, Inc., which published the successful pulp *Love Romances*. The company had dipped a toe in the fantastic adventure market with *Jungle Stories*, launched with the Winter 1939 issue, and featuring the adventures of yet another Tarzan clone, Ki-Gor, the White Lord of the Jungle, authored by John M. Reynolds (though later stories bore the house name John Peter Drummond). The stories often used sf settings and motifs including dinosaurs, survivors from Atlantis, and intelligent gorillas.

The editor of *Planet Stories* was Malcolm Reiss, a genial, well-liked man. Clearly he had been instructed to launch the magazine with little, if any warning. With no stories in the inventory he relied heavily on Julius Schwartz and other agents to provide stories to hand. Schwartz was still handling most of the old-time writers and the first issue of *Planet*, dated Winter 1939, was singularly unimpressive, despite the welcome return of such names as Laurence Manning and Fletcher Pratt. *Planet Stories* maintained a policy of publishing only interplanetary fiction and was unquestionably slanted towards the juvenile market, so that most of the early issues focused on space opera. As issue followed issue the verve of editor Reiss began to take effect and the quality of material improved, even though Reiss would be found apologizing for the poor stories as being the best to hand at the time of going to press. Nevertheless the magazine soon attracted a loyal following which would sustain the magazine for longer than its early contents might have otherwise suggested and gave it a chance, in the late forties, to develop a distinctive character.

What is most interesting about *Planet Stories* is that it was the first magazine to be launched in conjunction with a comic-book equivalent, *Planet Comics*. But whereas *Planet Stories* was quarterly, *Planet Comics* was monthly. *Jungle Comics* was issued at the same time, followed shortly by *Wings Comics*. It is entirely likely that the income from the comic books supported the pulps. It is just possible that *Planet Comics* would have provided a link for young readers into the pulps but, in the absence of a survey of readers, I suspect that *Planet Stories* retained a number of old-time adult readers who still yearned for the early days of sf.

Captain Future only emphasized the links between the pulps and the comics. This was the latest magazine from Standard under the editorial control of Leo Margulies who, according to Sam Moskowitz, had the idea for the magazine when he attended the first World Science Fiction Convention held in New York in July 1939. If that was the case then he must have had a poor impression of the fans because the magazine was slanted entirely towards the juvenile readership, without a single nod towards the more sophisticated work Campbell was trying to develop. Moreover the magazine was only a quarterly, not a monthly, which suggests that Margulies may not have had that much confidence in its success. Margulies would have known the market and that the single-character hero pulp was nearing the end of its days. Still, it was an opportunity to take advantage of the boom in science fiction that was now dominating the market in both pulps and comics.

Captain Future appeared in January 1940 (first issue dated Winter 1940). It was dominated by its long lead novel, the work of Edmond Hamilton, featuring Captain Curt Newton, a superscientist who lived on the Moon with his three companions, Grag the robot, Otho the android, and Newton's mentor, Simon Wright, who now existed as a disembodied brain in a unit moved by a force field. Hamilton was the first to specifically distinguish between a mechanical robot and a synthetic android and that distinction has remained to this day. Because Hamilton was a competent writer he was able to produce enjoyable, if simplistic, space heroics. The formula was the same as all previous space operas: Newton, with his colleagues and other allies, fights various villains in order to save the solar system or, ultimately, in 'The Quest Beyond the Stars' (Winter 1942), the entire universe. The magazine also contained a number of features about Captain Future, plus a regular serial reprinting longer stories from the early *Wonder Stories* (usually edited to fit into the space available), and occasional short stories. It may come as a surprise to find that it was in *Captain Future* that Fredric Brown, who had been selling detective and mystery stories for the past three years, made his first science-fiction appearance with 'Not Yet the End' (Winter 1940), an amusing story about a failed alien invasion.

The character of Captain Future may have been launched in the pulps but it was clearly developed with the comics also in mind. In May 1940 Standard Magazines launched *Startling Comics* (cover date June) with the lead strip featuring Captain Future. This had come hot on the heels of *Thrilling Comics*, first issue dated February 1940, which featured another superhero called Dr Strange. It was almost certainly the appeal of the comic-book superhero that Margulies had detected at the World SF Convention, and by 1940 the whole of the sf and fantastic adventure field was pandering to this common denominator. The same applied at Street & Smith where *Shadow Comics* started in March 1940, *Doc Savage Comics* two months later and *Bill Barnes Comics* (soon retitled *Air Ace*) in July.

There Were Giants in Those Days

The science-fiction boom was far from over by 1940 – new titles would continue to appear for some while – but it is timely to pause and look at what was happening at *Astounding*. It is already evident that *Astounding* had become isolated. All other science-fiction magazines, bar none, were focusing on interplanetary adventures, space opera, alien invasion stories and other sensationalistic plots that had dominated sf in the early thirties. It would seem that few lessons had been learned in the intervening years and that the early efforts by John Campbell to develop science fiction were to be wasted. Science fiction seemed to be looking backwards, not forwards.

In fact, it played into Campbell's hands. The science-fiction magazine field was currently a battleground between the pulps and comics, as well as a battle between the new sf and the old. The old sf had already developed a squad of writers who were finding it impossible to sell to Campbell and were too fixed in their ways to change. As the market grew so there was less need to change, and for the next few years the old style sf dominated the field, with many old-style writers gravitating to the comics. During that period Campbell was forced to develop his own coterie of writers, but that was all to the good. They were not so conditioned by early sf and were prepared to develop under Campbell's direction. Because the market had expanded it also meant they could risk the change, because any stories Campbell rejected could be sold elsewhere. It was thus the ideal situation for Campbell to create his new sf. This was not initially liked by everyone at the time, but it was not long before many readers and writers tired of the ubiquitous old-style sf and came to Campbell in welcome relief for something new and challenging. It was in that cauldron of hyperactivity that the Golden Age was born.

We last saw *Astounding* in mid-1939 as the first of these new writers were emerging. Although a number of these would soon establish themselves as the leading writers in the field, in most cases their first stories were unremarkable. There was Isaac Asimov's 'Trends' (July 1939), Robert A. Heinlein's 'Life-line' (August 1939) and Theodore Sturgeon's 'Ether Breather' (September 1939). Only A.E. van Vogt's 'Black Destroyer' (July 1939) was a powerful debut. It was the first of several stories van Vogt would write featuring the crew of the spaceship *Beagle*, and it is the most memorable. Set on a dying world it traces the lone native survivor Coeurl as it pits its wits in a life-or-death struggle against the scientists.

After van Vogt, the real gem of 1939 was the serialization of Edward E. Smith's new novel, 'Grey Lensman' (October 1939–January 1940), the sequel to 'Galactic Patrol'. This novel was both the longest and the most popular of the Lensman series which was regarded as the zenith of the space opera. Despite the cosmic scale of the adventures, the quasi-superhuman Lensmen are fully developed characters, especially Kimball Kinnison, and his search for the source of galactic evil kept thousands of readers enthralled.

Heinlein came into full flower in 1940. The January 1940 *Astounding* printed 'Requiem', the poignant story of a man's desire to reach the Moon. February saw the first instalment of Heinlein's short novel 'If This Goes On –', looking at America dominated by a religious dictator. The novel may, in hindsight, seem similar to the many hero-pulp adventures where superheroes use their powers to forestall American conquest, but Heinlein took a very simple, human angle to portray the horrors of total dictatorship. 'The Roads Must Roll' (June 1940) was another view of power, this time over the nation's transport systems. 'Blowups Happen' (September 1940) was Heinlein's chilling portrayal of an accident in an atomic power plant.

Other highpoints of 1940 were L. Ron Hubbard's controversial novel about the future of the war in Europe and the breakdown of civilization, 'Final Blackout' (April–June) and A. E. van Vogt's classic about superhumans as outcasts, 'Slan' (September–December). 'Slan' was an example of a partnership between van Vogt and Campbell. Although it was entirely written by van Vogt, it grew from a series of discussions with Campbell laying down the challenge that you can't tell a superman story from the viewpoint of the superman.[5]

Heinlein continued to dominate *Astounding* during 1941 under both his own name and the alias Anson MacDonald. The pseudonym arose because the stories under Heinlein's real name were developing a consistent future history. Of particular significance were 'Universe' (May 1941), one of the first and most powerful generation starship stories, and the serial 'Methuselah's Children' (July–September 1941), which used a form of controlled breeding to develop longevity and first introduced us to Heinlein's character Lazarus Long. Possibly Heinlein's most satisfying story of the year was the MacDonald by-lined 'By his Bootstraps' (October 1941), the first logically constructed time-travel paradox story which knits together bewilderingly like a moebius strip. Heinlein regarded the story as clever but hack work, yet it remains one of the most ingenious of all such stories. Also memorable was another MacDonald story, 'Solution Unsatisfactory' (May 1941), which considered the

5. See *The John W. Campbell Letters, Volume 1*, edited by Perry A. Chapdelaine, Tony Chapdelaine and George Hay (Franklin, TN: AC Projects, 1985), p. 368.

nuclear stalemate. Atomic energy had long been a feature of sf, but it was now becoming more pertinent. Theodore Sturgeon revealed some basic facts in 'Artnan Process' (June 1941), in which Earthmen seek to discover the secret of how the Artnans, who have established a nuclear plant on Mars, extract uranium-235 from uranium-237. It was the type of story that within a year would have caused apoplexy amongst national security.

This year, 1941, was also a good one for Isaac Asimov. It saw the development of his robot stories, and the emergence of his three laws of robotics which took shape before the readers' eyes through the stories 'Reason' (April 1941), 'Liar!' (May 1941) and 'Runaround' (March 1942) – all three developed in discussion with Campbell. It was also the year of 'Nightfall' (September 1941), a story which has achieved a classic status perhaps more legendary than the story deserves. It is nevertheless a fascinating portrayal of the terror that befalls a planet that has never known night. Soon after appeared the first of Asimov's Foundation stories, itself entitled 'Foundation' (May 1942), followed immediately by 'Bridle and Saddle' (June 1942) which set the basis for what would become arguably the best-known series in science fiction.

During this dominance of Heinlein and Asimov there was no shortage of other writers, both new and established. Edward E. Smith continued his Lensman series with 'Second Stage Lensman' (November 1941–February 1942). Eric Frank Russell began to contribute on a more regular basis, including his delightful space exploration series that began with 'Jay Score' (May 1941) and followed on with 'Mechanistria' (January 1942) and 'Symbiotica' (October 1943), the last two being highly original considerations of alien cultures and biologies. A.E. van Vogt contributed only a few stories but these included the fascinating 'Recruiting Station' (March 1942) about an interplanetary war stretched through time, which served as an introduction to his Weapon Shop series. Jack Williamson put on new clothes as Will Stewart for his seetee series about contraterrene matter which started with 'Collision Orbit' (July 1942). Henry Kuttner (now writing predominantly in collaboration with his wife, C.L. Moore) likewise created a new persona, Lewis Padgett, who would become a favourite amongst *Astounding* readers for his humorously written and deftly plotted wry studies of life. His early stories as Padgett, 'Deadlock' (August 1942) and 'The Twonky' (September 1942), focused on the problems robots would create in the future.

It was also 1942 that saw the welcome return of Murray Leinster to sf. A doyen of the field, Leinster had been writing in other genres under his real name of Will F. Jenkins. Starting from the October 1942 *Astounding* he began to produce new and original sf far advanced from his earlier efforts. These included 'First Contact', 'The Power' and 'A Logic Named Joe' (which is about a robot that goes to the extreme in helping people). The October 1942 issue also introduced George O. Smith, a 31-year-old radio engineer who employed his knowledge on a series of stories about a radio-relay station in space starting with 'QRM – Interplanetary'.

Other new names included Raymond F. Jones, who had first appeared in the September 1941 issue with 'Test of the Gods', in which three men who crash on Venus have to pass the test of the title. Jones produced another gem in 'Fifty Million Monkeys' (October 1943). Hal Clement put in his first appearance with 'Proof' (June 1942), although it would be some years before he established his reputation.

Perhaps the most popular story of 1942, and one of the few ever to receive a perfect first-place score in Campbell's Analytical Laboratory, was 'Nerves' by Lester del Rey (September 1942) which explored the disaster of an explosion at an atomic products factory.

It is impossible in a short space to do justice to the number of powerful stories that appeared in *Astounding* during 1940–1942. In retrospect the type of science fiction that was appearing in *Astounding* stands out so much in quality that one might wonder why at the time so many were prepared to read other magazines and why so many authors wrote for them. The answer is an inevitable one of evolution. Campbell's science fiction was certainly aimed at a readership more mature than those attracted to the comic books and therefore to the majority of sensationalistic pulps. The public's appetite in the years just before and at the outset of the war was for excitement and adventure, and especially stories about America beating the rest of the world or thwarting invasions from space. Many readers did not want to be reminded of the more sinister aspects of science or the realism of nuclear war.

Campbell's fiction was a development of the realism that David Lasser attempted to bring to sf in the early thirties, which had lain dormant under the cosmic 'thought variants' of Tremaine until Campbell reintroduced it via his Don A. Stuart mood stories. This approach to science fiction needed an acquired taste and would not have appealed to most readers. It was only the maturing of tastes as the younger readers developed, plus the overall fashion for more thought-provoking stories as the world moved through the horrors of the war, that saw the greater readership shift towards *Astounding*. The evidence for this change in tastes takes some while to be seen, but we shall encounter it in due course, not only in the survival of the fittest as the magazines faced wartime restrictions, but also in the increased selection of stories from the magazine in the newly emerging science-fiction anthologies.

During this period *Astounding* had undergone two significant changes in format. First in January 1942 it shifted to large pulp size, which caused some stir amongst readers, and then in November 1943 to the smaller digest format. There was a corresponding increase in number of pages so that readers did not feel unduly cheated. *Astounding* was the first professional magazine to go digest, and it would be some years before the change hit the rest of the field. The magazine remained technically a pulp, but the digest form, pioneered by *Reader's Digest* in 1922, was not tainted by the pulp image and had a degree of respectability. Thus as *Astounding* began to emerge from the war years, it dominated the science-fiction scene in quality, status and image.

Boom and Bust

Meanwhile, as Campbell was reshaping science fiction, the science-fiction pulp boom continued alongside the comic-book boom, one almost inspired by the other, both wrestling for dominance. Early 1940 saw the leading pulp publisher enter the field at last. This was Popular Publications which had dominated the hero pulp and crime, mystery and weird menace fields during the thirties, but had not seriously explored science fiction. Now Popular's editor, Rogers Terrill, was approached by Frederik Pohl. Pohl walked away from the interview as editor of not one but two new sf magazines. The date was 25 October 1939. Pohl was one month away from his twentieth birthday, making him the youngest new editor after Hornig. However, Pohl was far more mature in his ideas than Hornig, though, like Hornig, he was going to find finances a problem. Popular, not convinced that science fiction would be a big money-spinner in the pulps, placed the magazines under its Fictioneers imprint, which had been developed to publish lower-quality detective and sensational magazines. Pohl, like Hornig, found he had a limited budget for each issue which allowed him only half a cent a word. To begin with Pohl had to rely on rejected or old-time material, most of it of the interplanetary adventure type. The first issue of *Astonishing Stories* (dated February 1940) led with John Russell Fearn's 'Chameleon Planet' and Frederic A. Kummer's 'White Land of Venus'. Asimov was present, with 'Half-Breed', and so too were Henry Kuttner and Manly Wade Wellman, though pseudonymously. *Super Science Stories* (first issue, March 1940) – the title betrayed its early-sf bias – led with 'World Reborn' by Thornton Ayre (John Russell Fearn) and also contained fiction by Raymond Gallun, Frank Belknap Long and Ross Rocklynne. If it is noted for anything it is for publishing the first story ('Emergency Refulling') by James Blish, then a bright 18-year-old. Blish would later contribute 'Sunken Universe', under the alias Arthur Merlyn (*Super Science Stories*, May 1942), which became the basis for his accomplished Pantropy series.

Pohl must have exceeded Terrill's expectations because *Astonishing* and *Super Science* sold well. Certainly they had the advantage of Popular's major distribution network and displays which dominated the bookstalls. It proved that if you could get a science-fiction pulp on display the chances were that it would sell. The reason for the failure of so many pulps (and even more so the digests during the boom of the early fifties) was poor distribution and lack of display. The sales allowed Pohl to have an increased budget which gave him the chance to offer bonuses on the most popular stories. In June 1941, however, Pohl had a disagreement with publisher Harry Steeger that resulted in Pohl being fired. No one replaced him and for seven months *Astonishing* and *Super Science* were handled by Popular's editor-in-chief, Alden H. Norton, before Pohl returned for a brief period. It is thus difficult to know whether some stories were acquired by Pohl or by Norton. It is known that Norton can lay claim to being the first to buy a story from Ray Bradbury, namely 'Pendulum' (*Super Science Stories*, November 1941).

Because payments were prompt and their dealings respectable, Pohl and Norton soon began to have first stab at rejects from *Astounding* and thus began to acquire some good material. They ran two interesting collaborations by L. Sprague de Camp, the first, 'Genus Homo' (*Super Science Stories*, March 1941) with P. Schuyler Miller (in which humans trapped by a cave-in reawaken in a future where intelligent apes rule), and 'The Last Drop' (*Astonishing*, November 1941) with L. Ron Hubbard, about an elixir that can transform a person into a giant or a midget. They also ran several stories by Robert A. Heinlein under the pseudonym Lyle Monroe, including the novel 'Lost Legion' (*Super Science Stories*, November 1941). They also published Isaac Asimov's variant robot story 'Victory Unintentional' (*Super Science Stories*, August 1942), and the delightful Darkness series by Ross Rocklynne. The first of these, 'Into the Darkness' (*Astonishing*, June 1940), had been planned for the last issue of Gernsback's *Wonder Stories* which was never published. Why Weisinger did not select the story for the revived *Thrilling Wonder* remains a mystery for it is a remarkable story of sentient star systems that generated a short and much-loved series.

It was *Astonishing* and *Super Science* that saw the start of the collaborations between Kornbluth and Pohl, mostly under the S.D. Gottesman name. Some of these, such as 'Trouble in Time' (*Astonishing*, December 1940) and 'Mars-Tube' (*Astonishing*, September 1941), retain some of their period charm without hiding their early promise.

It was also in the pages of these two magazines that book reviews, which had hitherto been a commentary upon new books, became genuine criticism. The pioneers were Frederik Pohl and Damon Knight.

As the two magazines alternated on a bi-monthly basis they could almost be regarded as one magazine but on balance *Super Science Stories* was the better, though both are a testament to what a good editor can do with a poor budget.

Still the new magazines appeared. At the end of 1940 fans welcomed F. Orlin Tremaine back to the field, editing *Comet* (first issue dated December 1940). Tremaine was working on commission to H-K Publications, a small-time New York outfit seeking to cash in on the science-fiction boom. Whilst Tremaine had worked miracles at *Astounding* with the formidable backing of Street & Smith, the situation was different at *Comet*. For a start the market was now awash with magazines, as Tremaine acknowledged in his first editorial, and good material was scarce – there were just not enough good writers around. Tremaine hoped to capture them, but could only offer one cent a word, and castigated writers who sold for less. Because of his reputation Tremaine did start to acquire some good material, though it only began to emerge in later issues. Ross Rocklynne, Robert Moore Williams and Manly Wade Wellman were tempted to produce better-quality work, and there were competent stories by Jack Williamson, Leigh Brackett, Frank

Belknap Long and P. Schuyler Miller. One of the more intriguing stories was 'The Street That Wasn't There' by Clifford D. Simak and Carl Jacobi (July 1941), in which reality begins to fragment as aliens take over the world. Tremaine also purchased the first fiction from Sam Moskowitz, 'The Way Back' (January 1941), and acquired a new series from Edward E. Smith featuring Storm Cloud, Vortex Blaster. The first story, 'The Vortex Blaster', appeared in what proved to be the last issue of *Comet*, and the series later appeared in *Astonishing Stories*.

One of the worthiest features of *Comet* was a 'Short-Short Stories' department that gave preference to authors' first published stories, and even offered the chance of a Silver Medal for the best first story of the year. Regrettably the department published little of merit. Its most noted author who made his debut in the magazine was Robert W. Lowndes with 'A Green Cloud Came' (January 1941). Like most first stories it is unexceptional, taking as its theme the threat of a poisonous cloud in space which is approaching the Earth. But Lowndes gave it a twist by introducing a dominant female character who uses the situation to win back her lover.

Tremaine had striven against increasing odds to produce a quality magazine, and the published letters suggest it was very well received by its readers, but it seems these were not enough. When initial sales proved poor (again mostly due to H-K's lack of distribution power), money became tight and Tremaine found he could not pay promptly as he had promised. A man of principle, he resigned and with him, after only five issues, went *Comet*.

The last serious magazines to enter the field before the war came from Albing Publications, an opportunist outfit trying to develop a run of cheap genre magazines. It had no financial backing and persuaded Donald A. Wollheim to acquire stories on the basis that they would be paid for once the magazines were successful. This would mean waiting for at least three months, possibly more, before returns came in from the distributors. Jerry Albing spread his costs over a string of magazines starting with *Stirring Detective and Western Stories, Stirring Romance* and later *Stirring Science Stories* and *Cosmic Stories*, all published on credit from the distributor.

The only way Wollheim could produce these magazines for next to nothing was to acquire stories from his fellow Futurians, and write many himself, on the basis that they might gain a financial return in the future. With all the other paying markets, including two now edited by other Futurians (Lowndes and Pohl), it seemed remarkable that anyone would write for Wollheim, but the Futurians were prolific and it was a gamble worth trying.

The most prolific Futurian and the one who dominated *Stirring* and *Cosmic* was Cyril Kornbluth. He made his first appearance in the April 1940 *Astonishing* with 'Stepsons of Mars', a Foreign Legion story relocated to Mars. It was written in alternate sections with Richard Wilson as a last-minute dash to fill out the issue of *Astonishing* and the story appeared under the alias Ivar Towers. Kornbluth's first solo appearance was the following month in the May 1940 *Super Science Stories* with 'King Cole of Pluto', though here the alias was S.D. Gottesman, a name he sometimes used jointly with Pohl. With the advent of *Stirring* and *Cosmic* Kornbluth created a new alias, Cecil Corwin, which he used for his more fantastic fiction. This included 'Thirteen O'Clock' (*Stirring*, February 1941) and 'The City in the Sofa' (*Cosmic*, July 1941), enjoyable tongue-in-cheek fantasies that, with a little polishing, would have gone down well in *Unknown*. It was difficult at that stage to get any really serious fiction out of Kornbluth, although 'The Golden Road' (*Stirring*, March 1942) was a more sobering mood piece about life after death.

Damon Knight made his first professional appearance in *Stirring* with 'Resilience' (February 1941). Knight was only a few months older than Kornbluth but did not make the same impact at the time. He would start to make his mark 10 years later.

Lowndes was another prolific writer, despite his editorial duties. The first professional appearance of his name was a mistake. 'The Outpost at Altark' was a story by Wollheim that Lowndes had agented and sold to Pohl for *Super Science Stories* (November 1940) where it had been mistakenly credited to Lowndes. Lowndes's best-known story, if the number of times it has been reprinted is any measure, is 'The Abyss' (*Stirring*, February 1941). It isn't one of his best, but it does have a certain shock appeal. Betraying a strong Lovecraftian influence, it tells of a group of occultists under the influence of an adept, one of whom hallucinates and witnesses something terrifying in the depths of a pattern in a carpet.

Lowndes produced a number of dislocation fantasies, the best being 'The Long Wall' (*Stirring*, March 1942, as Wilfred Owen Morley) and 'Highway' (for his own *Science Fiction Quarterly*, Fall 1942, also as Wilfred Owen Morley), both of which consider the nature of reality.

When not being an editor, Wollheim was a capable writer with clever ideas that were usually just long enough for a very short story. Some of them are deliberate extended jokes, like 'Bomb' (*Science Fiction Quarterly*, Winter 1942) where we discover that the far side of the Moon has a detonator, or 'Up There' (*Science Fiction Quarterly*, Summer 1942), which spoofs Fortean beliefs by having the first space pioneer tear a hole in the sky. But at times Wollheim could be deadly serious. 'Bones' (*Stirring*, February 1941) is about an Egyptian mummy that comes hideously to life; 'Storm Warning' (*Future Fantasy*, October 1942) is about something nasty that turns up in a storm; and 'Mimic' (*Astonishing*, December 1942, as by Martin Pearson), arguably Wollheim's best story, is a chilling account of a shape-changing alien.

Stirring was in fact two magazines in one. The first half was *Stirring Science-Fiction*, the second half *Stirring Fantasy-Fiction*. Either the latter allowed more flexibility amongst the fiction, or it attracted the better contributions, but it was certainly the more enjoyable part of the magazine and, because of its artwork by Hannes Bok and other contributions by Clark Ashton Smith and David H. Keller, it makes the magazine highly collectible.

In fact fantasy was starting to be seen as more marketable than science fiction by 1942, perhaps because sf was being taken over by the comic books. The success of *Unknown* had made fantasy respectable, hence the duality of *Stirring Science/Fantasy* and a shift in title at *Future Fiction* to *Future Fantasy* in October 1942. But these were short-lived variations in a field that was already struggling for identity.

Only one further new title appeared in the United States before America entered the war, and this was *Uncanny Stories*, dated April 1941. Its appearance brings us back full circle to the start of the boom, since it was another opportunist product from Martin Goodman's Manvis Publications, edited by Robert O. Erisman. Its lead story, featured on the cover by Norman Saunders, was 'Coming of the Giant Germs' by Ray Cummings, which is one of his most appalling stories. In fact the whole issue has little merit and was probably released to clear stories in Manvis's inventory. The company was moving wholesale into the comic-book field with a host of comics led by its biggest seller, *Captain America*, which had been issued in March 1941.

On 7 December 1941 the Japanese attacked Pearl Harbor, and with that the United States entered the Second World War. Almost immediately wartime restrictions were imposed. The subsequent rationing of paper, ink and metal type, was a disaster for the pulps more than the comics, added to which the number of writers able to meet the demand for material was drastically reduced as they were called to the war effort. Most of the magazines survived 1942 and a few survived 1943, but few made it right through the war. By 1945 there were only 7 magazines compared with the peak of 22 in 1941. These survivors were *Amazing Stories* and its companion *Fantastic Adventures*, *Astounding SF*, *Thrilling Wonder Stories* and its companion *Startling Stories*, *Famous Fantastic Mysteries* and *Planet Stories*. The world they would enter was one vastly changed from that of five years earlier and one that requires a whole new chapter.

CHAPTER FIVE
Unleashing the Atom

The War Effort

Before exploring the post-war surviving magazines it is important to consider the effect upon magazine sf of the war and in particular the unleashing of atomic power.

For decades scientists had dreamed of harnessing the power of the atom, and science-fiction writers had considered its potential both in peace and in war. Future war had also been a strong theme in science fiction. With technology advancing rapidly to support the war effort, science-fiction fans realized that they were witnessing their dreams becoming the nightmares of reality. The development of helicopters, jet planes, radar, guided missiles, rockets and ultimately the nuclear bomb was all accelerated during the war, and though much was kept secret, that only made it all the more amazing when these inventions were suddenly released upon humanity.

Hitherto most science fiction had tended to glorify war, marvelling at the wonders of science rather than the impact upon the human race. The most significant anti-war novel to appear in the sf magazines hitherto was 'The Final War' by Carl W. Spohr (*Wonder Stories*, March–April 1932), a former German artillery officer. Spohr wrote from the heart in decrying the futility of war and showing how, with advanced weaponry, the next war would be the suicide of mankind.

It was not until the rise of Hitler, particularly after he assumed the presidency of Germany in August 1934, that writers began to consider the inevitable consequences of fascism, but even then it was still treated as distant and something that might yet be avoided. Once war erupted, however, censorship barred writers from exploring scientific developments in detail, though they could consider their consequences. We have already seen the conclusions of all-out destruction in L. Ron Hubbard's 'Final Blackout' and the nuclear stalemate in Heinlein's 'Solution – Unsatisfactory'.

A prime purpose of science fiction during the war, therefore, was not to predict but to raise morale. Instead of looking at the doom and gloom of war, writers sought to find as many ways as possible of defeating Hitler. On one level you had the comic books where Captain America and other superheroes used their superpowers to give the enemy its come-uppance. At the next level you had the fantasy writers who had a ball-game using whatever supernatural agency they desired against the foe. In 'The Kraken' by Frederick Engelhardt (*Unknown*, August 1940), a German U-boat disturbs a giant squid that then does battle with the submarine. In 'The Goddess' Legacy' by Malcolm Jameson (*Unknown*, October 1942), the Greek legend of Medusa comes to life to take her petrifying revenge. In 'The Devil is Not Mocked' by Manly Wade Wellman (*Unknown*, June 1943), Dracula takes it out on the Germans. Robert Bloch pitted the Pied Piper against them in 'The Pied Piper Fights the Gestapo' (*Fantastic Adventures*, June 1942). It's the turn of the Norse gods in 'The Daughter of Thor' by Edmond Hamilton (*Fantastic Adventures*, August 1942), though here the gods are first on the side of the war-loving Nazis, until they discover the butchery and deceit of the Nazis at which point they switch sides. William P. McGivern resurrects the Three Musketeers to do their bit to save France in 'The Enchanted Bookshelf' (*Fantastic Adventures*, March 1943) and 'The Musketeers in Paris' (*Fantastic Adventures*, February 1944).

There were several stories not unlike the adventures of Indiana Jones with the Nazis or Japanese in search of lost treasures. In 'The Lost City of Burma' by Edmond Hamilton (*Fantastic Adventures*, December 1942), an American and a Japanese vie to discover the Flame of Life deep in the Burmese jungle, and although the Japanese succeeds he then finds himself harnessed to the Flame and unable to return. In 'Drummers of Daugavo' by Dwight V. Swain (*Fantastic Adventures*, March 1943), an American agent tracks a Nazi spy into the South American jungle to find a lost race of Amazons with a secret force ray.

Even in *Astounding*, the only magazine to consider the war seriously, stories endeavoured to be up-beat. In 'Secret Unattainable' by A.E. van Vogt (July 1942), Hitler's secret weapons are sabotaged by their inventors, resulting in catastrophe for the Führer, whilst van Vogt's wife, Edna Mayne Hull, showed in 'The Flight That Failed' (December 1942) how a Hitlerian future was avoided by an alternative deed in the past. Henry Kuttner brought his own form of whimsy in 'Nothing But Gingerbread Left' (January 1943) in which a professor develops a semantic rhythm that so intrudes upon the consciousness as to make cohesive thought impossible. Beamed to the Nazis it destroys their capacity for thought. Lester del Rey's 'Whom the Gods Love' (June 1943) has a fighter pilot who is shot down by the Japanese and has a bullet dead-centre in his forehead. Instead of killing him it gives him superhuman powers.

Most of these stories were little more than morale-boosting fun. Few authors were either prepared or allowed to explore scientific advances and so could only use known science or fantastic concepts against the enemy. The race to harness atomic power, whilst a standard feature in science fiction for over 20 years, was now under a code of silence in the United States ever since President Roosevelt had signed a secret order on 6 December 1941 to develop a nuclear fission bomb. This became known as the Manhattan Project. Enrico Fermi, who had won the Nobel Prize in 1938 for his work on neutron bombardment, was placed in charge. Almost a year to the day later (2 December 1942) Fermi induced the first self-sustaining nuclear chain reaction. The atomic age was born.

Campbell had earlier written in *Astounding* that it was *Astounding*'s patriotic duty not to provide scientific details in stories for the potential use of the enemy,[1] but in practice he was more than happy to print stories using state of the art concepts that were demonstrably available to the public. He often flew close to the wind on this, by having guided missiles in Murray Leinster's 'The Wabbler' (October 1942) and radar in George O. Smith's 'Calling the Empress' (June 1943).

The matter came to a head with the publication of 'Deadline' by Cleve Cartmill (March 1944). It is not an exceptional story – it tells of an agent's attempts to stop an atomic bomb's detonation – but during the course of the story Cartmill detailed just how an atomic bomb could be created. Military Intelligence descended on Campbell and Cartmill, charging them with violation of security. Cartmill proved that all his facts were drawn from public libraries and eventually the scare was over. Devotees have always remained proud of this moment when science fiction caused such a stir, as it seemed to move it one more rung up the ladder of respectability.

There are tales of other cases where censorship won. Philip Wylie wrote 'The Paradise Crater' early in 1945 about defeated

---

1. John W. Campbell, 'Too Good at Guessing', *Astounding SF*, 29 (2) April 1942, p. 6.

Nazis after the end of the war who seek to take revenge upon America with an atomic bomb. *The American Magazine* rejected the story, whilst the editor of *Blue Book* checked it out with security who advised it should not be used. Wylie was even placed under house arrest while the facts were investigated.[2] The story only saw publication after the war in the October 1945 *Blue Book*.

But at that time plenty of stories were featuring details about nuclear reaction. In 'The Great Engine' (*Astounding*, July 1943) A.E. van Vogt utilized the issue about secrecy by having scientists who have developed atomic power fear its misuse on Earth and thus remove themselves and their secret to Venus. In 'The Giant Atom' (*Startling Stories*, Winter 1944) Malcolm Jameson considered a nuclear reaction out of control. Henry Kuttner and C.L. Moore, writing as Lewis Padgett, launched their Baldy series starting with 'The Piper's Son' (*Astounding*, February 1945). The Baldies are mutants as a result of exposure to atomic radiation who have developed telepathic powers. The Baldies, noticeable because of their lack of hair, become ostracized from society and some of them, dubbed Paranoids, believe they are the next step in evolution and have the right to dominate the Earth. The Kuttners were taking their own shot at Hitler's belief in the Nordic superman.

All this secrecy, all this waiting, all this prediction would soon change. On 8 May 1945 Germany surrendered and the war in Europe was over. The war with Japan continued. On 16 July 1945 the first nuclear fission bomb, or atomic bomb, was tested in the New Mexico desert. Three weeks later, on 6 August 1945, an atomic bomb was dropped on the Japanese city of Hiroshima, followed three days later by another bomb on Nagasaki. Within a week the Japanese surrendered and the war ended on 2 September 1945. Gernsback's early banner had proved chillingly true: extravagant fiction had become cold fact.

Writing in 1949, Theodore Sturgeon said:

> There is good reason to believe that, outside of the top men in the Manhattan District [*sic*] and in the Armed Forces, the only people in the world who fully understood what had happened on 6 August 1945 were the afficianados of science fiction – the fans, the editors and the authors. Hiroshima had a tremendous effect on me. I was familiar with nuclear

2. See details in Sam Moskowitz, *Explorers of the Infinite* (Cleveland: The World Publishing Company, 1963), pp. 292–93.

phenomena; I sold a story in 1940 which dealt with a method of separating Isotope 235 from pure uranium. Years before the Project, and before the War, we had used up the gadgets and gimmicks of atomic power and were writing stories about the philosophical and sociological implications of this terrible new fact of life.[3]

This same feeling pervaded many writers. In his first editorial written after the dropping of the bomb, Campbell said: 'The science-fictioneers were suddenly recognized by their neighbors as not quite such wild-eyed dreamers as they had been thought, and in many soul-satisfying cases became the neighborhood experts.'[4]

Experts or not, the science-fiction fans were as stunned as the rest of the world, in awe of the power that had been unleashed. They may have understood how it worked better than others but that in no way prepared them for accepting its threat and its implications for the future.

What happened was that science fiction had now reached a crucial turning point, not necessarily perceived at the time but very evident in hindsight, and it takes some while to unravel the full implications.

We need to backtrack a little to consider other threads contributing to this so as to better understand the direction that science fiction would take after the war, rather than the immediate impact of nuclear-war fever that hit everybody, not just sf writers.

Most of this development took place in *Astounding*, but its effects were as noticeable in the other magazines, particularly *Thrilling Wonder* and *Startling Stories*. There was a different development in *Amazing Stories* which I shall consider separately in the next section.

First the *Astounding* thread. We have already seen that in the thirties science fiction entered a cosmic age with super-science at the fore. This resulted in stories of limitless horizons, exploring the vastness of space and time with little regard for the implications for mankind. In fact mankind was almost an irrelevance. It was the thrill of imagination unlimited that drove science fiction on to bigger and vaster concepts. Whilst at the top end this led to some of the best science fiction of all in *Astounding*, as exemplified by the works of E.E. Smith, Clifford Simak and Jack Williamson, at the

3. Theodore Sturgeon, from the Preface to his story 'Thunder and Roses' in Leo Margulies and Oscar J. Friend, ed., *My Best Science Fiction Story* (New York: Merlin Press, 1949).
4. John W. Campbell, 'Atomic Age', *Astounding SF*, 36 (3) November 1945, pp. 4–6.

other extreme it resulted in some of the worst space opera ever written. With the abundance of sf pulps in the period 1938–42, the poorer work proliferated. The super-science concepts were soon embraced by the comic books and became more the domain of younger readers. Consequently, when paper rationing took hold and the pulps faded, there was a purging of the field. The comic books were able to appeal to their particular audience but the lower quality pulps went, with the exception of *Amazing Stories* and *Fantastic Adventures* which were often poor-quality fiction but were undeniably escapist and enjoyable and clearly had their role to play.

This purging gave Campbell a clearer hand in developing science fiction, but restricted by wartime censorship it also meant that the exploration of scientific concepts was limited. Additionally many of the writers who had been exploring those new territories, particularly Isaac Asimov, Robert A. Heinlein and L. Ron Hubbard, were undertaking war work and their writing time was limited. Campbell therefore was forced to explore new territory with new writers. Only a few years after he had determined to establish one new direction for the field, he found he had to bring in new thinking.

To do this he relied heavily on writers who were less restrained by past developments in sf. Predominant amongst these was A.E. van Vogt, the indisputable top writer for *Astounding* during 1943–45. There was also Clifford D. Simak, who developed a unique pastoral approach to sf that had never previously been explored. And then there were the threesome of Henry Kuttner, his wife C.L. Moore, and Fritz Leiber whose background had been more in the worlds of fantasy and the macabre than sf. These five writers shaped sf in the mid-forties and because their background was less technological than Asimov's, Heinlein's or E.E. Smith's, they started to develop a softer, more human approach. Above all the incidents in their stories were not necessarily explicable in scientific terms so that whilst they hid beneath a veneer of technology, that veneer could very easily be removed to reveal not the whirring of gears but something darker and more sinister, either the product of our mind or the product of another's that we are not about to understand. Thus was created the form of a more mystical, or as Alexei Panshin has termed it, more transcendent science fiction.[5]

---

5. This theory is more completely explored by Alexei and Cory Panshin in *The World Beyond the Hill* (Los Angeles: Jeremy Tarcher, 1989).

A.E. van Vogt was the prime architect of this. Van Vogt was one of the few Canadian sf writers of the period. Although he had discovered sf in the first year of *Amazing Stories* he had lost interest in it after Gernsback lost control, and only rediscovered sf with *Astounding* in 1938, fortuitously the issue featuring 'Who Goes There?'. Thus van Vogt had avoided the cosmic age of science fiction and had moved from the early technophilic lectures and the first bursts of E.E. Smith, straight on to the darker psychological dramas that Campbell was developing. It was the psychological aspect that intrigued van Vogt. Although he was a very systematic writer – indeed his whole approach to life was ordered and pragmatic – his fiction would attack order with chaos so that somehow order had to prevail. By 1942 van Vogt was envisaging this on a four-dimensional scale, not just across the vastness of space but through the whole spectrum of time. To add to this complexity van Vogt would develop his stories based upon intuitive flashes in his dreams, giving the plot an occasional dream-like dislocation from reality. The consequence of this was a number of extremely complex stories that moved the plotting, characterization and narrative techniques of science fiction ahead considerably.

Van Vogt had already proved his abilities in this area with 'Slan', but now made his work even more complex with his Weapon Shop sequence, which began with 'The Weapon Shop' (December 1942) and the subsequent serial 'The Weapon Makers' (February–April 1943). This novel includes such concepts as telepathic rapport between twins, trained intuitionists who can construct the full facts instantly out of only partial knowledge, individuals who exist simultaneously at key moments of history, and a recognition that the mind has other powers beyond intelligence. None of these concepts had any clear basis in science, nor was this van Vogt's intention, but their appearance in *Astounding* made them so. Van Vogt rapidly took these concepts further. He wrote a short set of stories, 'Concealment' (September 1943), 'The Storm' (October 1943) and 'The Mixed Men' (January 1945), sometimes linked as the Dellian Robots series. Here he explored the difference between artificially constructed androids and human beings, recognizing that intellectually it was possible for the robots to be superior, regardless of intelligence. But his magnum opus was 'The World of Null-A' (August–October 1945). Here van Vogt developed the concept of semantics proposed by Alfred Korzybski in *Science and Sanity* (1933), which proposed a new way of looking at man's philosophical and analytical processes. Van Vogt was moving closer to the metaphysical by exploring how mankind may transcend its current physical-bound abilities through new processes of thought. The result was a form of mental superman. Within a few years we shall see L. Ron Hubbard take this same thinking towards the notorious concept of dianetics. What van Vogt did, more than any other writer, was to consider logically and systematically the totality of human beings and to conclude, through his fiction, that their abilities and future lay more through the powers of the brain than the powers of the body. Van Vogt's supermen, therefore, were cerebral, unlike the physical superheros who had dominated sf in the thirties. This approach to sf was to become even more dominant in the fifties, but it was the first move away from the hardcore technological sf toward psi-oriented sf.

Running alongside van Vogt's new fiction were the more fantastic concepts of Henry Kuttner. Neither Kuttner, nor his wife Catherine Moore (they married in 1940), had any scientific training. Kuttner, in particular, was a creature of the pulps, having delighted in the sf and weird fiction magazines since his early teens. He was strongly influenced by his reading and his early work had been imitative of H.P. Lovecraft, Abraham Merritt, Robert E. Howard, Stanley G. Weinbaum – in fact anyone he liked. It meant he could write stock fiction to order, and he was thus much in demand amongst the run-of-the-mill pulps, but he had no voice of his own. Catherine Moore, on the other hand, was an original talent. Like Kuttner, she had developed in *Weird Tales* with her strongly characterized stories about Northwest Smith and Jirel or Joiry, but she also appeared in *Astounding Stories* with original and visionary tales that were clearly from her own thinking. The fusion of the two meant that the writing talents had the mercurial polymorph of Kuttner controlled by the individualistic perspective of Moore. Both their writings were transformed, but it had the greatest effect upon Kuttner. Now he could find his voice, emulating his wife, and the two increasingly became one. That one had several names. The best-known and most influential was Lewis Padgett, but they were also Lawrence O'Donnell and C.H. Liddell. Although they continued to write individually it became increasingly difficult to distinguish Kuttner from Moore and vice versa.

Campbell wanted Kuttner and Moore to write the scientific equivalent of the *Unknown* story. Interestingly, whereas Campbell's logical approach to sf had influenced his approach to fantasy in developing *Unknown*, it was the freedom and derestriction that he now wished to see exploited in *Astounding*. No one could do this better than the Kuttners, and nowhere did they prove this more than with 'Mimsy Were the Borogoves' (February 1943), a brilliant story merging the wonders of the unknown with its horrors. Children receive a box of toys that appears out of nowhere. They can see marvels and wonders within whilst their parents see nothing. The children persist with the toys from which, the parents gradually realize, the children are forming some alternative method of learning beyond our Euclidean world. Just as in van Vogt's non-Aristotelian world, the Kuttners are encouraging us to take a different viewpoint.

This alternative viewpoint had emerged strongly in Kuttner's own light-hearted series featuring his inventor Galloway Gallagher. These started with 'Time Locker' (January 1943) and continued through 'The World is Mine' (June 1943), 'The Proud Robot' (October 1943) and 'Gallagher Plus' (November 1943). Gallagher, who was frequently drunk, somehow let the right side of his brain take over and through a bit of tinkering here and wire-twisting there would re-create wonders out of nothing. He had no idea how he did it, but his inventions were always unbelievable. Once again we are letting the mind do the creating. The subconscious was taking control of the conscious.

The titles of stories, the identity of their pseudonyms and the imagery within the stories strongly show the influence of Lewis Carroll and fairy tales. In fairy tales anything can happen, but it usually happens by some form of skewed logic. It was this skewing of our world-view that the Kuttners achieved wonderfully. Their approach knitted together beautifully in 'The Fairy Chessmen' (January–February 1946), written before the end of the war though published after its conclusion. The story is set during a long-protracted war when the enemy has created a bomb that can penetrate the protective force-field of the allies. Scientists seek to solve the special properties of the bomb but because it was developed by unorthodox science it initially proves impossible, and requires new lateral thinking to resolve. This story, one of the Kuttners' best, forced the reader to accept lateral ideas from its very first line, one of the most memorable in all sf: 'The doorknob opened a blue eye and looked at him.'

Fritz Leiber was also ringing the changes. His novel 'Gather, Darkness!' (May–July 1943), set in the year 2305, or 360 of the

Atomic Age, establishes conditions that reverse the days of the Inquisition. This time a powerful ruling priesthood controls the advanced science of the day whilst the rest of mankind remains ignorant and superstitious. Up through these masses emerges a satanic cult with its own magical powers. Leiber was not only emphasizing the problems of secrecy in an oppressive society (which became only too real in Communist countries) but was also exploring the blurred regions between science and magic. In 'The Mutant's Brother' (August 1943) Leiber explored telepathy and mind control, but he hit the abnormal head on in 'Sanity' (April 1944) which considered the reality of the world-view from those considered sane and those insane and questioned which is normality.

Against all this one might think Clifford Simak would have restored sanity. Simak's work of the 1950s was so down-to-Earth that it was comforting and reassuring. But this was less so in the 1940s. Take 'Hunch' (July 1943), where Simak explores the science of intuition, or his award-winning City series, which plots the future progress of the Earth as humans leave and only robots and intelligent dogs remain. This commenced in the May 1944 issue with 'City', which showed how automation in the future would break down the urban complexes and allow a return to a more rural existence. The extension of this thinking shows man increasingly trapped in his own existence, unable to face the real world. As the series developed so we find humans increasingly needing to lose their own identity, either on Earth, where robots and dogs are about to assume mastery, or on their new paradise world on Jupiter where they need to be transformed to enjoy the otherwise hostile environemt. In 'Desertion' (November 1944) man and dog, transformed into something new and wonderful on Jupiter, decide not to return to their former selves.

These writers transformed science fiction in the mid-forties from being technocentric to being psychocentric. Their work would influence the next generation who would dominate sf in the fifties.

The change happened predominantly in *Astounding*, and though its effects would become noticeable in other magazines, that was not until after the war. During the war the other magazines focused on super-science and the fantastic, and only published relatively sober fiction when they were able to acquire rejects from *Astounding*. The magazines, though, were folding fast. Some suffered deservedly. They were poor magazines from opportunist publishers and showed little if any merit. But others were creative and suffered only because the rationing of paper, ink and type-metal meant publishers had to justify continuance of their magazines on grounds of economic use of materials (which meant high circulation) or the magazines were forced to fold.

The wartime attrition rate was high. We had already lost during 1941 Tremaine's *Comet* and Wollheim's *Cosmic Stories* and *Stirring Science Stories*. The other magazines survived through 1942, but in 1943 the casualty rate was bad. In the first months *Astonishing Stories* and *Super Science Stories* folded at Popular. At Silberkleit's Blue Ribbon Magazines *Science Fiction Quarterly* folded, followed rapidly by *Future* which, for its last two issues, was confusingly retitled *Science Fiction Stories*. Perhaps the greatest loss was *Unknown*, which had been retitled *Unknown Worlds* since the October 1941 issue.[6] It folded with its thirty-ninth issue dated October 1943. No magazine has come close to repeating the *Unknown* style of fiction, although a few have tried. It has long since passed into pulp magazine legend. The final magazine to fold was *Captain Future* in May 1944. Quite how it had survived that long is surprising and suggests that its sales must have been buoyed along with its comic-book counterparts. (The title *Captain* —— prefixed scores of comics at this time.) All of the remaining magazines except *Astounding* had been forced on to quarterly schedules, partly to eek out rationed paper and partly to maximize display time for sales.

Of these the one most radically different to *Astounding* was *Amazing Stories* and its war years are worthy of further consideration, particularly because they culminated in the Shaver Phenomenon which was another manifestation of the public's desire for some form of rationalization in a world increasingly going mad. In this case, though, the Shaver rationalization was even more crazy.

The Shaver Mystery

Ray Palmer's *Amazing* was instantly distinguishable from the other sf magazines. Its covers (front and back) were always more garish, looking more like the comic books than the other pulps. It was generally bigger, almost doubling its page count to 240 in May 1941

6. This was apparently because market research had shown that readers believed the title *Unknown* suggested a non-fiction occult magazine. Quite why the addition of *Worlds* should suggest anything different is difficult to understand.

and to 272 in May 1942. Though it was forced to drop to 208 in June 1943 it sustained this till the end of the war when it dropped to 180, still more pages than any other sf pulp. And it tended to carry fiction by its own stable of writers, most of whom were not seen elsewhere.

One of the earliest of these was Don Wilcox. He was a capable writer, who for a period had taught creative writing, but he succumbed too soon to Palmer's sensationalistic demands. His first appearance was with 'The Pit of Death' (*Amazing*, July 1939), but his most notable story from these early days is 'The Voyage That Lasted 600 Years' (*Amazing*, October 1940), one of the earliest generation starship stories.

Another early contributor was David Vern. He was a sub-editor at Ziff-Davis's New York office who came to Chicago to check out (and later assist) Palmer. Vern wrote mostly under pen names, his best known being David V. Reed under which he first appeared with the memorable disappearance story 'Where is Roger Davis?' (*Amazing Stories*, May 1939).

Over the next few years other names became established: David Wright O'Brien, William P. McGivern, Berkeley Livingston, Chester S. Geier, William Hamling and Leroy Yerxa. These formed the core of Palmer's writing circle. They were all immensely prolific and in addition to writing under their own names and several personal pseudonyms, they also shared a clutch of 'house' pseudonyms. Most of these started as personal names for one or two editorial writers, especially Palmer and Vern, but as writers were called to the war effort, the pen names became used by others to such a confusing extent that the true identity behind them has yet to be fully unravelled. The most prolific of these house names was Alexander Blade, originally one of Vern's aliases, but later used on a mass of stories and features in every issue.

The most prolific contributors to *Amazing* were David Wright O'Brien and William P. McGivern. These two, both only just into their twenties, shared an office in Chicago, and wrote both individually and separately. They were the forties equivalent of the Robert Silverberg/Randall Garrett team of the fifties, but because so much of their work was hidden under pseudonyms and because it was concentrated solely in the Ziff-Davis magazines it never really received its due recognition. Early criticism of their fiction was that it was too frivolous and written to order, although a serious study of their work (which is long overdue) will reveal a scope for originality and diversity hitherto denied them. O'Brien was tragically killed while flying a bombing raid over Berlin in 1944. McGivern never really overcame the loss of his friend. He also soured on Palmer who continued to expect the same type of frothy material. When he had an opportunity to write hard-boiled detective stories for the new mystery magazines that Ziff-Davis launched under editor Howard Browne, McGivern virtually turned his back on science fiction.

Palmer was besotted with early pulp sf and encouraged writers to return to the field. He not only perpetuated writing careers in sf that might otherwise best have moved on, such as Eando Binder's and Ed Earl Repp's, but also sought to resurrect series that were now out of their time. His friend Ralph Milne Farley brought Myles Cabot back briefly in 'The Radio Man Returns' (March 1939). Harry Bates resurrected his galactic hero Hawk Carse in 'The Return of Hawk Carse' (July 1942), which proved even worse than the original series. The fact that it was not welcomed even by *Amazing*'s readers showed that the series was well past retirement.

Arguably Palmer's greatest success was to encourage Edgar Rice Burroughs to write for him. The Burroughs revival in *Amazing* began with 'John Carter and the Giant of Mars' (January 1941). Astute readers suspected this was not entirely the work of Burroughs, and later research showed that it was predominantly the work of Burroughs's son, John Coleman. The other stories though were all by E.R.B.: 12 novelettes written at a furious pace during 1940, split over three series. The Carson Napier adventures on Venus started in *Fantastic Adventures* with 'Slaves of the Fish Men' (March 1941); the John Carter of Mars series continued in *Amazing* with 'The City of Mummies' (March 1941); whilst Alan Innes in Pellucidar was featured in 'The Return to Pellucidar' (February 1942), also in *Amazing*.

The name of Edgar Rice Burroughs on the magazines plus the smooth action-filled covers by J. Allen St. John further rocketed *Amazing*'s sales and secured its continuing publication.

To Palmer's credit, if ever he received a good story from outside his team of writers he had the sense to publish it. Thus the occasional surprise turns up in the wartime *Amazing*. John Beynon Harris appeared with 'Phoney Meteor' (March 1941), a clever tale about visiting aliens destroyed by insecticide. Eric Frank Russell contributed the covert alien story 'Mr Wisel's Secret' (February 1942). Ray Bradbury, who was just starting to establish himself in

Planet Stories and *Thrilling Wonder*, also sold some stories to *Amazing* that were different to the norm. His first was 'I, Rocket' (May 1944) about a sentient spaceship, which had it been written less melo-dramatically would probably have interested Campbell. He also produced 'Undersea Guardians' (December 1944), a war-inspired story of an aquatic race that attempts to protect American sub-marines from the German U-boats.

Despite the occasional serious story, Palmer strove to make both *Amazing* and *Fantastic Adventures* fun. He was never above pulling the occasional practical joke. He would frequently include hoax photographs of pseudonymous writers, such as his own alter-ego Frank Patton, whom he fixed up in the September 1943 issue. This was not always obvious at the time, of course, but one learned to treat Palmer warily. By early 1944 it was evident that Palmer was increasing his trickery. In the February 1944 *Fantastic Adventures* Palmer published a spoof letter purporting to be from a scientist born in 1970, who learns from an invention that he will die in 1941 as a result of a trip in a time machine inspired by a story in *Fantastic Adventures*. The letter was signed Scott Feldman, the real name of later literary agent Scott Meredith, who had been an active sf fan since the mid-thirties. Palmer dressed the story up as a real letter and put out an appeal to trace the writer.

At that same time in *Amazing* the biggest 'hoax' of them all was about to burst. I put 'hoax' in quotes deliberately because, whilst Palmer played the Shaver Mystery for all that it was worth, Richard Shaver remained serious and earnest about his beliefs.

In September 1943 Palmer received a letter from Richard Sharpe Shaver who lived in Barto, Pennsylvania. It presented the key to an ancient alphabet which Shaver claimed was the mother tongue of all languages, *Mantong* (Man Tongue). Palmer published the letter in the January 1944 *Amazing* and it brought in a healthy response from readers. Palmer struck up a correspondence with Shaver, then a welder in a war plant. Shaver was unfit to be drafted because he had smashed his ankle in a fall on board ship and had been invalided out of the merchant navy.

Palmer asked Shaver to write for him and he responded with a novelette entitled 'Warning to Future Man'. The submission was apparently first seen by *Amazing*'s associate editor, Howard Browne, who took one look at it and threw it into the wastepaper basket, saying, 'What a crackpot that guy is!' Palmer decided to challenge Browne's opinion. Before even reading the manuscript he determined to print it and find the readership's opinion of Shaver. He also sought to demonstrate to Browne how a mixture of showmanship, marketing and bravado could sell almost anything.

In later years Shaver claimed the whole of this first story was his. Palmer however claimed that he rewrote it 'from more than one million words of further correspondence with Mr Shaver'.[7] Palmer began to give advance notice of the story in the May 1944 issue, noting that 'For the first time in its history, *Amazing Stories* is preparing to present a true story,' and adding, 'We aren't going to ask you to believe it. We are going to challenge you to disbelieve it.'[8] Palmer gave it further advance hype in the December 1944 issue. He declared Shaver's sincerity and belief in what he was writing, stating that he had genuinely received details about lost Lemuria and had interpolated these memories into a story deliberately written to be exciting and entertaining. What was fact and what was fiction was thus blurred from the outset.

Palmer retitled the story 'I Remember Lemuria' and published it in the March 1945 issue, released on 8 December 1944. The story is set long before the Flood in the first great civilization on Earth, which Shaver called Atlan. It was related by Mutan Mion, the last Earthman to leave this planet when the Titans migrated. The story involved a battle between two factions: an evil Titan named Zeit, and a good Titan goddess, Vanue. The Titans and the Atlans had been two immortal races who discovered that harmful cosmic rays from the sun were causing them to age and die. They first built vast subterranean cities but over time found that even here they were not safe. Eventually they abandoned the planet, leaving behind them not only their advanced machinery but the simple humans who had been their slaves. These 'abandonderos' subsequently devolved into an evil race, the 'deros' (detrimental robots), and a benign race, the 'teros' (integrative robots). The teros were the ancestors of human beings. The deros found their way into the underground cities. Unable to understand the ancient machinery they misused it and as a consequence wreaked havoc upon the Earth's surface. Through this equipment, especially the 'telaug' (telepathic augmentor) and the disintegrating ray, the deros are responsible for all the wrecks, crashes and accidents on Earth. They are themselves the basis for such legends as ghosts, demons and

7. Ray Palmer, in 'The Observatory' editorial, *Amazing Stories*, 18 (5) December 1944, p. 8.
8. Ray Palmer, in 'The Observatory' editorial, *Amazing Stories*, 18 (3) May 1944, p. 6.

gremlins. Furthermore, Shaver stated that the Titans have kept watch on Earth and on occasions return, kidnapping people and raiding the caves for equipment. This would account for many mysterious disappearances and for unidentified flying objects (UFOs).

To many of the war-weary readers of *Amazing Stories*, the Shaver claim was an answer to all their problems. They took it to their hearts. Whereas Palmer was used to receiving around 40 to 50 letters a month from readers, he was suddenly deluged by over 2,500. This had been aided by the fact that the March 1945 issue of *Amazing* had an enhanced circulation. Palmer claimed this was the idea of circulation manager Harold Strong, though it was probably as much at Palmer's prompting. In addition to *Amazing Stories* and *Fantastic Adventures* Ziff-Davis published two other fiction pulps, *Mammoth Detective* and the newly launched *Mammoth Mystery*. The first issue of the latter had been published only a month earlier (dated February 1945 but issued in November 1944). Its sales may have been disappointing, though it is more likely that Palmer convinced Strong to divert the paper for *Mammoth Mystery* to *Amazing Stories*. It may also have been that Ziff-Davis was criticized for using paper for a new magazine during wartime restrictions and was forced to suspend *Mammoth Mystery* after its first issue (it reappeared after the war). Whatever the reason, the March 1945 issue of *Amazing* had an additional 50,000 copies printed and these all sold out.

The Shaver phenomenon now dominated the magazine. A new Lemuria story appeared in every issue of *Amazing*, culminating in the special Shaver issue, given over entirely to the Mystery (as it had become known by then) in June 1947. As a result of the notoriety and interest, the magazine's circulation continued to rise. The Mystery rapidly alienated Palmer from the core of dedicated science-fiction fans, but with the boost in circulation Palmer received a salary increase and was hardly likely to worry about the opinion of a few fans. By the end of the war *Amazing* had the highest circulation of any sf magazine and rapidly resumed monthly publication.

When I corresponded with Shaver in 1975 he gave me his side of the story, which is worth repeating here and contrasting with Palmer's.

Richard Shaver was born in Berwick, Pennsylvania in October 1907. His father was a pressman; he pressed the first parts for the first steel passenger coach made in America. His mother was an ex-schoolmistress who wasted no time in giving her five children plenty of pre-school teaching. She was also a poet, selling verse to such leading publications as *Ladies Home Journal* and *Good House-keeping*. When Shaver was 11, the family moved to Bloomsburg where, for a while, his father owned a restaurant. Once his formal education was over, Shaver took a variety of jobs ranging from being a foreman in a landscaping company to being an art instructor.

The Mystery began one evening when he was reading Byron's poem 'Manfred', and came to the line, 'By a power to thee unknown, Thou canst never be alone.' Was he really not alone? Shaver thought. At that point he began to receive visions until the reception was suddenly cut off as if deliberately intercepted.

This incident continued to prey on Shaver's mind. A while later, after spending some time working in Illinois, he was picked up for vagrancy while thumbing a lift back to Pennsylvania, and was placed in gaol. He tried to make contact as before with the plea, 'Get me out of here.' Shaver takes up the story.

> What happened is a girl comes leading the turnkey who acts like he is walking in his sleep. He turns the key and lets me go. She leads us both down the hall to the outer door, which he again opens and we both walked out. I followed her with somewhat mixed and numb sensations for about a mile in the night outside of the town. Then we walked into a hill – a section of the hill closed down behind us very like 'Sesame, close!', and we were in. A lot of stairways and slopes and dim light, and all the time I knew 'she' was just a sort of transparent projection, but you had to get close to see the difference from real.
>
> And so I was in. I spent a day or so talking with them, and they filled me in on the whole complex situation inherited from our misguided forebears who kept the secret so well that today nobody knows anything about their past. Between us we decided something should be done about the situation of ignorance. I was there for only twenty-four hours or so, when I walked out and went on my way. Later I began to write fiction about it.[9]

Palmer had initially not known what to believe, and all the signs are that he did it as a publicity exercise. But the subsequent influx of letters supporting Shaver convinced Palmer there must be some

9. Richard Shaver in private correspondence with the author.

grain of truth in the matter. It certainly would have appealed to Palmer. His proneness to accidents and his deformed stature could now be blamed on something external. Palmer visited Shaver many times during 1945 and 1946 and even claimed to hear the voices himself. And yet how does one reconcile this with Palmer's exasperated statement in 1955: 'Lissen! [*sic*] I usually plotted Shaver's stories. Much of his "mystery" is right out of my head.'[10]

It is possible to trace a parallel between Shaver's Mystery and a number of early sf and fantasy stories. It has similarities with H.P. Lovecraft's own fictional Cthulhu Mythos. Lovecraft had the Earth once inhabited by the Ancient Ones, a hostile, supernatural species, who are overpowered and banished by a more benign race, the Elder Gods. Ignorant mortals, tampering with the restraints, sometimes open up the way for the Old Ones to return. Some of Shaver's work also bears comparison to the exotic fantasies of Abraham Merritt, especially *The Moon Pool*, with its underground caverns and civilization of energy-beings. There is also a link to the theosophical beliefs of Helena Blavatsky, especially the teachings of the Tibetan masters and the links to ancient Atlantis. Palmer was well read in pulp fiction and Shaver was probably also aware of these stories and beliefs. Yet Shaver remained adamant to his death that he was sincere. It is fascinating that when Erich von Daniken's books appeared in the early seventies there was another upsurge of interest in Shaver's theories. In *The Gold of the Gods* (1972), von Daniken discusses at length a vast series of underground caverns in South America seemingly constructed by an advanced race many hundreds of years ago. Could these be Shaver's caverns of the Titans?

Palmer encouraged other writers to add to the Shaver Mystery. The German writer and traveller, Heinrich Hauser, temporarily resident in Chicago, provided *Amazing* with one of its most popular novels, inspired by both the Shaver Mystery and the teachings of theosophy, 'Agharti' (June 1946). It tells of a vast underground city in central Asia ruled by 'the King of the World', an immortal who plans to emerge and establish a new world civilization when mankind is ready. This novel also seems to owe much inspiration to Talbot Mundy's popular serial in *Adventure*, 'King of the World' (1930), better known in book form as *Jimgrim* (Century, 1931).

Although the Shaver Mystery alienated fans and attracted the

10. Ray Palmer, Ray, editorial comment in response to a letter in *Other Worlds Science Stories*, 32, May 1955, p. 121.

'lunatic fringe' to *Amazing*, the resultant boost in the magazine's circulation did allow it to pay top rates to authors and it was thus able to plough something back into science fiction. Shaver also contributed stories outside the Mystery, and although he was never a particularly able writer he did have a good sense of excitement and imagery and his fantasies in *Fantastic Adventures* tend to have fared better.

Fortunately Palmer did not devote *Amazing* entirely to Shaver, apart from the special June 1947 issue. He continued to present other stories by well-known writers and to develop new writers. One of these was Roger P. Graham, better known by his most frequently used pen name Rog Phillips. Within a year of his first story, 'Let Freedom Ring' (*Amazing*, December 1945), he was appearing under some 20 pseudonyms with scores of stories. He would also be found supporting the Shaver Mystery and discovering a bizarre book, *Oahpse*, purported to have been written in 1882 by intelligent beings thousands of years old.

Then there was Chester S. Geier. He had first appeared in the December 1942 *Amazing* with 'The Sphere of Sleep' when he was just 21. Geier was totally deaf, but this was by no means detrimental to his writing. He was skilful and had polish, but unfortunately wasted his time on hackwork. Geier had written a particularly powerful story for Campbell's *Astounding*, 'Environment' (May 1944), which showed his potential as an author of near-mystical sf. It is about explorers on a planet who encounter a strange set of artefacts which they eventually discover are a series of tests that will allow them to develop spiritually and intellectually on to a higher plane. This suggests that Geier had an interest in mystical and occult fiction, and it is not surprising that he became heavily involved in the Shaver Mystery, which detracted from his more capable work. He organized the Shaver Mystery Club and became editor of *The Shaver Mystery Magazine*, which serialized Shaver's 'Mandark', a story set at the time of Christ, which even Palmer considered too taboo to publish. Geier collaborated with Shaver on some stories as he was quicker at assembling the final manuscript. He also completed a fantasy written by Shaver's elder brother, Taylor Victor Shaver, who had died of influenza before finishing it. That story, 'The Strange Disappearance of Guy Sylvester', appeared in the March 1949 *Amazing*.

The Shaver Mystery reached its height during 1947. By then William Ziff was becoming concerned at the complaints and criticism the magazine was receiving in the quality magazines. *Harper's Magazine*, for example, had carried an article in its September 1946 issue entitled 'Little Superman, What Now?' by William S. Baring-Gould, which derided the Shaver Mystery as the mouthings of crackpots. Ziff told Davis and Palmer to tone down the Shaver material, and the Mystery was dropped as a regular feature from the March 1948 issue. This marked the start of Palmer's separation from *Amazing* and his move towards the occult.

In the meantime Palmer sought to restore some of the old appeal of *Amazing*. In the September 1947 issue he published complete Edmond Hamilton's 75,000-word novel, *The Star Kings*. Here was space opera de-luxe. Hamilton, having by now written over a million words of space opera, had honed it to a fine art. Although it lacked the style and depth of the works of Smith and Williamson, *The Star Kings* was a rousing adventure in the style of Burroughs. It introduces Hamilton's character John Gordon, who is summoned from 200 millennia in the future to exchange bodies with Zarth Arn, prince of the Mid-Galactic Empire. It was well received by readers, but showed that under Palmer science fiction had scarcely advanced from the day he took over the magazine.

In fact by 1947 Palmer's interest in the borders of fantasy and reality had started to dominate his thinking. After the Shaver Mystery, Palmer became interested in UFOs, or what soon came to be called 'flying saucers'. Palmer had become acquainted with fire-equipment salesman Kenneth Arnold. On 24 June 1947 Arnold had been flying his own aircraft over Mount Baker in Washington when he saw a chain of nine mysterious saucer-shaped objects. Investigating, he became embroiled in a fantastic series of events that led eventually to a dead-end and suspicion of a cover-up.

Coming so soon after the Shaver Mystery, and indeed with Shaver supporting the sightings as evidence for his own theories, this material was ideal for Palmer. He felt there was a market for a magazine that explored the fringe areas of strange phenomena and the occult. In fact there had been a number of these magazines over the years, including Bernarr Macfadden's *True Strange Stories*, and more recently Sam Youd's *New Frontiers*. But these either appealed to a specialist audience and thus minimized their circulation, or did not treat the subject seriously and often faked the articles which were more in the 'confessions' format. Palmer wanted to treat the subject seriously (or as seriously as Palmer could ever treat anything) but at the same time ensure it reached as wide a readership as possible. With his promotional talents the latter should not be difficult, though it would require much initial capital.

In 1947 Palmer went into partnership with Chicago business-man Curtis Fuller and formed the Clark Publishing Company in North Clark Street, Chicago, with the express purpose of concentrating on publications dealing with the strange and unusual. In the spring of 1948 he launched the first issue of *Fate*, a magazine devoted to the unusual. A slim but striking digest-size magazine selling for 25 cents, the first issue was such a success that it soon shifted from its quarterly schedule to bi-monthly. Although Palmer kept his identity masked behind the alias Robert N. Webster, his connections with the magazine were obvious, not just because of its frequent use of UFO and Shaver material, but also because of the reliance upon Ziff-Davis authors and artists, many of whom contributed material that they had been developing at *Amazing*.

With *Fate* as a successful base, Palmer then sought to launch his own science-fiction magazine. This was *Other Worlds*, one of the first of the new digest-sized magazines which would rule the fifties and sixties. The contribution of *Other Worlds* to science fiction is told in the second volume in this series.

Once plans for *Other Worlds* were finalized, Palmer formally resigned from Ziff-Davis. He had really been editor in name only since late 1947, with William Hamling covering much of the work-load. With Palmer's resignation Howard Browne came back from leave of absence, during which he had been writing mystery novels, and took over editorial control. On that day in late 1949 he threw out over 300,000 words of material accumulated for *Amazing Stories* and decided to start afresh. Browne was determined to make sure that the lunatics were no longer in charge of the asylum.

Into the Nuclear Age

With the dropping of the atom bomb on Japan the world was witness to the power and devastation of harnessing the atom. The science-fiction writers rapidly began to exploit the subject while it was still vivid in people's minds.

One of the earliest stories to appear in print was 'Memorial' by Theodore Sturgeon (*Astounding*, April 1946). Sturgeon called for the establishment of a perpetual memorial to warn future genera-tions of the horrors of nuclear war. Soon after, he wrote 'Thunder and Roses' (*Astounding*, November 1947) which tells of a United States ravaged by nuclear attack and how one man prevents the firing of retaliatory missiles so that future generations can survive. In a two-sided atomic contest there could be no survivors. Heinlein's predicted stalemate would soon come into force, with the start of the Cold War.

To some extent realization of the full horror of the bomb was dampened by the overwhelming relief that the war had ended. Several writers took it upon themselves to shock readers into understanding the consequences of total nuclear war. The May 1946 *Amazing Stories* featured 'Atom War' by Rog Phillips. Here the United States is attacked by a mythical country which threatens to bomb major cities. Australia aids America, only to be bombed out of existence. Total war follows. It lasts only fifteen hours before the mythical foe is destroyed, but in that time 75 million Americans are killed. Phillips produced a sequel, 'So Shall Ye Reap!' (*Amazing*, August 1947), which explores the war's after-effects and describes how the radioactive fall-out had produced mutations, in this instance a new race of super-beings.

The mutative effect of atomic radiation became a popular theme in sf immediately after the war. It served as the background to Poul Anderson's first sale, 'Tomorrow's Children' (*Astounding*, March 1947), wherein a team of scientists are hunting down mutants, and its sequel, 'Logic' (*Astounding*, July 1947). Henry Kuttner took the theme to heart. 'Way of the Gods' (*Thrilling Wonder*, April 1947), wherein mutants sprout wings and are hunted down and exterminated as freaks, received much acclaim. 'Atomic!' (*Thrilling Wonder*, August 1947) tells of a Final War, lasting three hours, which leaves behind hundreds of deadly rings, shunned by the survivors and found to be housing bizarre forms of sentient life. Writing as Keith Hammond, Kuttner also produced 'Dark Dawn', in the same issue as 'Atomic!', wherein radiation threatens the life of a race of sea-beings.

Writing as Padgett, Kuttner and Moore also brought their thoughts on atomic stalemate to *Astounding* with 'Tomorrow and Tomorrow' (January–February 1947), set a century in the future after World War III when the world is controlled by the Global Peace Commission. In its mission to ensure peace the Commission has banned original scientific research and the world is stagnating. The Kuttners suggest it is almost better to release war upon mankind in order to ensure we continue to evolve.

The July 1947 *Astounding* carried 'The Figure' by Edward Grendon which, despite its brevity (barely 2,000 words), creates a strong impact. It follows on immediately from a discovery of the effects of radiation on insect life after the New Mexico and Japanese detonations. Giant insects begin to appear. When two scientists experimenting with time probes succeed in retrieving a statue from the future, they are horrified to discover it is a statue with obvious religious overtones and that it is the figure of a beetle. It was seven years before Hollywood realized the potential of such stories and made the film *Them!* (1954) about giant insects that appeared in the Mojave Desert.

L. Ron Hubbard, who had done so much to warn of the perils of all-out war in 'Final Blackout', at last returned to the sf field in 1947 with 'The End is Not Yet' (*Astounding*, August–October 1947), a more upbeat story about a group of nuclear scientists who manage to thwart a conspiracy to provoke a nuclear war between the superpowers.

There was now a scientific basis for the creation of mutants and monsters and sf writers would make the most of it over the next decade. The theme linked closely to the mental superman concepts that van Vogt and Kuttner had been creating in *Astounding* – in fact Kuttner had started on the telepathic mutant concept with his Baldy series before the Hiroshima bomb. It meant that the immediate post-war sf concentrated heavily on considering mutations, both physical and mental. It was from here that one can date the emergence of stories about scientifically-induced psi-powers, which would dominate the field in the fifties.

Science fiction was rapidly casting off its old clothes. Although *Amazing* remained a refuge of the super-science space opera for a little while, other magazines were changing and attempting to make their image more respectable in line with the sudden greater awareness accorded the field. *Astounding* led the field not only in the quality of its fiction, but in its overall appearance and ability to shape the genre. Close behind it was *Thrilling Wonder Stories*, for all that it retained its garish covers and gosh-wow name. The change was predominantly due to a new editor, Samuel Merwin, Jr. When Mort Weisinger had left Standard Magazines in 1941 he had been replaced as editor on *Thrilling Wonder* and *Startling Stories* by Oscar J. Friend. Friend was a pulp writer of long standing, though better known in the western field, and he tended to perpetuate the image of science fiction being little more than cowboys-and-Indians in outer space. His editorial demeanour, which he conducted under the alias Sergeant Saturn, was condescending. He rated stories in 'jugs of Xeno' and referred to his readers as 'kiwis'. Friend was probably responding to editorial director Leo Margulies's wish to pander to younger readers and emulate the style of Ray Palmer, but it was only irritating.

Merwin, who was the same age as Palmer and Campbell, took his editorial role more seriously and rapidly sought to upgrade the magazines. He dropped the Science Fiction League which had limped on in *Thrilling Wonder* with little significance since 1936 and he encouraged Earle K. Bergey to upgrade his covers. Bergey's work, probably more than any other artist's, had come to typify pulp sf during the war years. A highly capable and skilled artist he responded to editorial requirements under Friend to paint covers featuring monsters and voluptuous women in danger. The women were invariably wearing ridiculous spacesuits which left them half-naked, or were wearing brass-brassières. They took on the style of pin-up paintings and were almost certainly popular with young readers and the troops, but they gave a totally misleading image to science fiction. Under Merwin's guidance Bergey began to paint women in rather more diaphanous outfits, still attractive but more realistic.

Merwin began to acquire material from Campbell's stable of writers as well as developing new writers. He purchased Jack Vance's first story, 'The World Thinker' (Summer 1945), a novelette that echoed Campbell's work at *Astounding* in its consideration of an entity capable of creating worlds from dreams. *Startling Stories* would later publish Vance's series about Magnus Ridolph, an interstellar investigator who seeks to solve crimes and puzzles on other planets. The series began with 'Hard Luck Diggings' (April 1948) and helped establish Vance's name, even though it is conventional pulp fiction and far from the literary pyrotechnics we soon came to expect from Vance.

Merwin acquired stories regularly from Murray Leinster, George O. Smith and L. Ron Hubbard, all of whom wrote credible hard-science stories. Hubbard provided a series of connected stories plotting the colonization of space that began with 'When Shadows Fall' (*Startling Stories*, July 1948). This included 'Forbidden Voyage' (*Startling*, January 1949) under the alias Rene Lafayette, which was rather strange at the time for discouraging space flight and noting the first landing on the Moon as being shunned and unheralded. Later stories in the series were similarly downbeat. It is ironic that

at the time Hubbard was contributing more mature and provoca-
tive stories to *Thrilling Wonder*, he was writing his Doc Methuselah
stories for Campbell. The series, also written as Rene Lafayette,
started with 'Ole Doc Methuselah' (October 1947), and featured
Methuselah, a Soldier of Light, who dedicates himself to maintain-
ing physical, moral and spiritual standards throughout the colonized
galaxy. It was superior space opera with a dash of the old hero
pulps, and whilst of much higher quality than its pre-war equivalent, still seemed a step backwards for *Astounding*. In *Thrilling
Wonder*, *Astounding* had its first serious rival since 1933.

Thrilling Wonder is especially remembered for its stories by Ray
Bradbury. Some of his finest stories appeared here, including some
later incorporated in *The Martian Chronicles*: 'And the Moon Be Still
as Bright' (June 1948), 'The Naming of Names' (August 1949) and
'Payment in Full' (February 1950). *Thrilling Wonder* also published
Bradbury's poetic and poignant story 'Kaleidoscope' (October 1949)
which follows the final thoughts of the survivors of a spaceship
explosion as they either hurtle into deep space or return to Earth to
incinerate in the atmosphere. In 'The Man' (February 1949), Bradbury poses a daring religious idea. A spaceship lands on another
world only to discover that Christ had come just the day before.

Henry Kuttner was also one of Merwin's most prolific contributors. When Kuttner wasn't writing as Lewis Padgett, he was at
his best when enjoying himself in his Merrittesque mood for the
lead novels in *Startling Stories*. These stories were often more fantasies
than sf, and are as enjoyable today as they were then. 'Valley of the
Flame' (March 1946), written as Keith Hammond, is pure Merritt,
telling of a hidden valley in South America where people have
evolved from jaguars and are under the control of an alien energy-
being, the Flame. 'The Dark World' (Summer 1946) is another lost-
race adventure, not unlike Merritt's *Dwellers in the Mirage*. The story
may have been written predominantly by C.L. Moore under
Kuttner's name. 'Lands of the Earthquake' (May 1947) considered
a parallel world where a lost remnant of the Crusaders survives.
Kuttner had more lead novels in *Startling* than any other writer in
the late forties, but he still found time to produce the occasional
short story, including one of his best, 'Don't Look Now' (March
1948). This is in his Padgett vein. It assumes that Martians are all
about us, spying upon us, disguised as innocent humans who may
open their third eye at any moment.

Other major names from *Astounding* appeared. Theodore Sturgeon's

'The Sky was Full of Ships' (June 1947) was nominated by the readers as one of the best stories ever published in the magazine. Robert Heinlein contributed 'Jerry is a Man' (October 1947) about an ape with enhanced intelligence, and even A.E. van Vogt was present with 'The Weapon Shops of Isher' (February 1949), the final story in his Isher sequence.

Fredric Brown wrote some extravagant works for Merwin. Perhaps the best is 'What Mad Universe' (September 1948), a fascinating portrayal of a Munchhausen-like parallel world. Charles L. Harness produced an especially fine novel in 'Flight into Yesterday' (May 1949) which has been compared to van Vogt in its portrayal of a genetically engineered superman striving to save a world from self-inflicted immolation amidst a turbulence of time-travel paradoxes. The novel is perhaps better known under its book title of *The Paradox Men* (1953).

Thrilling Wonder and *Startling Stories* began to feature some of the best work by writers of the new generation, including John D. MacDonald, William Tenn, Margaret St. Clair as well as the rather delayed flowering of the talents of Arthur C. Clarke, Damon Knight and James Blish.

This all meant that in the late forties, *Thrilling Wonder* took on something of the mantle of *Astounding* in the late thirties. Side by side with extravagant but intelligent space operas and science fantasies, *Thrilling Wonder* and *Startling* were encouraging writers to develop a sense of wonder at a more human level and to discover the excitement of scientific achievement, even at the simplest level. Frequently this meant looking at the down side of science, an inevitable result of the unleashing of atomic power, but something that normally Campbell would not condone. His one fixed premise was that man could overcome all odds, whether through scientific achievement or, increasingly of late, through the development of his mental powers raising him to the next stage of evolution.

By 1946 it was clear that *Astounding* was losing its Golden Age sparkle, although it remained the main source for emerging new talents. One of these was William Tenn, the pen name of London-born American, Philip Klass, who made his *Astounding* debut with 'Alexander the Bait' (May 1946). This had been written just three months after the end of the war when Tenn was working as a technical editor for the US Army Air Force. The story uses that background as a basis for a concerted effort to the reach the Moon. Tenn followed it with 'Child's Play' (March 1947), which starts with the delivery of a Christmas present from AD 2153 to a present-day man with chilling consequences. The story clearly showed the influence of Lewis Padgett's 'Mimsy Were the Borogoves' as did 'The Toymaker' by Raymond F. Jones (September 1946), another memorable story of the period.

Another new talent to emerge at this time was H. Beam Piper with 'Time and Time Again' (April 1947), about a chemist who finds his inner consciousness projected back 30 years to occupy his teenage body but with all its future memories. This came as a result of a pain-killing drug administered after he was wounded in World War III. The story was voted into first place in the readers' poll, a rare occurrence for a first story. Piper secured his popularity with 'He Walked Around the Horses' (April 1948), which seeks to explain the mysterious historical disappearance of British diplomat Benjamin Bathurst in 1809. Piper postulates that Bathurst vanished into a parallel world.

A respected but rare contributor to the field was T.L. Sherred who appeared in the May 1947 *Astounding* with 'E For Effort'. The story involves a pair of scientists who make a fortune producing 3D historical films by recording direct from history via a time-viewer. It has become regarded as a minor classic of the field as has 'In Hiding' by Wilmar Shiras (November 1948), which tells of the problems of a psychiatrist confronted with a supranormal 10-year-old child. Shiras was one of a handful of female writers who were beginning to make their names in the field. Until now the leading female writers had been C.L. Moore and Leigh Brackett. The June 1948 *Astounding* carried 'That Only a Mother' by Judith Merril. This story, about a mutated child prodigy who the mother regards as perfectly normal, was one of the most chilling sf stories to be written at that time and admirably highlighted the post-war terror of atomic mutation. Another woman writer to make her debut then was Katherine MacLean with 'Defense Mechanism' (*Astounding*, October 1949).

A number of British writers, still devoid of a regular native market, were also making a mark in the States. These included Arthur C. Clarke, who made his debut with 'Loophole' (April 1946), and Peter Phillips. Phillips's story 'Dreams Are Sacred' (September 1948) is a highly original concept of a psychologist who has to project himself into a patient's dream-world in order to cure him. It presaged by more than 40 years the current development of virtual reality.

The February 1949 *Astounding* saw the name Christopher Youd in print for the first time with 'Christmas Tree', a poignant tale of Christmas spent away from Earth. Christopher, or Sam Youd as he was better known to his colleagues, was the real name of John Christopher, the writer soon to be internationally famous with *Death of Grass* (1956). For a period he was to rival Arthur C. Clarke and John Wyndham as Britain's major sf writer. He had sold a story, 'Monster', to Gillings for *Fantasy* in 1946, but the story had to wait until 1950 to be published.

Pre-war British writers were also re-establishing themselves. Eric Frank Russell had supplied a fascinating serial, 'Dreadful Sanctuary', which ran in *Astounding* during 1948. It starts with the failure of any moon rockets to leave Earth and goes on to reveal that the Earth is an insane asylum for the galaxy, which was not too surprising a concept after the war. The novel helped cement Russell's already high regard. He became one of the most respected sf writers of the fifties, and was reputedly Campbell's own favourite.

John Wyndham also made a return to the fold. Writing as John Beynon he produced 'Adaptation' (*Astounding*, July 1949) about a baby girl who is especially conditioned for survival on an alien world. Soon after this he re-emerged as John Wyndham with 'The Eternal Eve' (*Amazing Stories*, September 1950), establishing a new name for himself that would become one of the best known in Britain.

Other quality stories from this period by established writers included 'Vintage Season' by C.L. Moore (September 1946, as Lawrence O'Donnell), 'Mewhu's Jet' by Theodore Sturgeon (November 1946), 'Metamorphosite' by Eric Frank Russell (December 1946), and several by Jack Williamson including 'The Equalizer' (March 1947) and the ingenious stories of alien robots who become insufferable in their benign servitude to mankind, 'With Folded Hands …' (July 1947) and '… And Searching Mind' (March–May 1948). It would be fair to say, though, that these are all imitative of *Astounding*'s past, consolidating the thinking and not taking it forward. This is not too surprising. It is impossible for the development of science fiction to continue at the rate it had done in *Astounding*. One or two writers could take the lead, but they then had to wait for others to catch up, especially new writers and those returning from the war. It meant that, whilst *Astounding* continued to publish excellent stories, the sense of discovery it had once generated had faded. Nevertheless any magazine that could also run E.E. Smith's 'Children of the Lens' (November 1947–February 1948), the last in the Lensman series, and A.E. van Vogt's 'The Players of Null-A'

(October 1948–January 1949) could hardly claim to be slacking. It was, perhaps, resting on its laurels.

It is perhaps significant that 1947 marked the twenty-first birthday of magazine science fiction, which in the capable hands of John Campbell had survived adolescence and was entering maturity. Gernsback, Lasser and Campbell had been good foster fathers, but from here on science fiction was pretty much on its own, although it would have a few more avuncular guardians for the next few years.

Some of the evidence for this can be seen in a few of the once less mature pulps which were now girding their loins. We have seen how *Thrilling Wonder Stories* and *Startling Stories* had developed after the war, and so too did *Planet Stories*. This magazine, which had started as an outright space adventure pulp, and which always promoted extravagant adventure, nevertheless developed remarkably by the end of the war and came into full flower in the late forties. This was due primarily to two significant writers: Leigh Brackett and Ray Bradbury. Both had a fascination with Mars: not the real scientifically evaluated Mars, but the romantic Mars of Burroughs. Brackett had made her first sale to John Campbell in 1939 with 'Martian Quest', which appeared in the February 1940 *Astounding*, but this did not prove to be her main market. She soon moved to *Planet Stories* with a number of extravagant space adventures. The early ones were written to a pulp formula, but over the next few years she developed a style which paid homage to tradition yet was nevertheless more honest and mature than that of her fellow writers. This development blossomed into longer, more imaginative works reminiscent of Burroughs at his best, starting with 'The Jewel of Bas' (Spring 1944), though the peak was reached with the series featuring her equivalent of John Carter, Eric John Stark, who first appeared in 'Queen of the Martian Catacombs' (Summer 1949). In the mid- and late forties there is no doubt that Leigh Brackett was herself queen of the spaceways having raised the planetary romance to the highest standard it was likely to achieve. Even while she was writing for *Planet* her influence was seen on fellow contributors, especially Gardner F. Fox, and her work would have an indelible impact upon later writers Lin Carter and Marion Zimmer Bradley.

Ray Bradbury and Leigh Brackett came together once – one of his rare collaborations – on a story initiated by her, 'Lorelei of the Red Mist' (Summer 1946). The story was well received, except that the love interest was panned by those fearful of it corrupting the youth. Further echoes of Burroughs may be seen in the title of 'The Creatures That Time Forgot' (Fall 1946), but Bradbury was already developing his own unusual perception of space. 'Morgue Ship' (Summer 1944) and 'Lazarus Come Forth' (Winter 1944), for instance, consider the problem of retrieving bodies from space during an interminable war. Two of his *Martian Chronicles* appeared here, 'The Million Year Picnic' (Summer 1946) and 'Mars is Heaven' (Fall 1948), as well as the ingenious story in which aliens seek to invade Earth with the assistance of young children, 'Zero Hour' (Fall 1947).

Although Malcolm Reiss remained in overall control throughout *Planet*'s existence, after 1942 he had handed over the direct editorial management to a series of sub-editors while he concentrated on the whole Fiction House line, including *Planet Comics*. Wilbur S. Peacock was the first of these sub-editors during 1942 to 1945. Peacock enjoyed science fiction and loved being one of the crowd. Chester Whitehorn succeeded him for a few months and then Paul L. Payne, who was editor from Fall 1946 to Spring 1950. It was during Payne's tenure that the science fiction in *Planet* came of age. It is perhaps surprising to find that during the forties the magazine included contributions from Isaac Asimov, Clifford Simak, James Blish, Fredric Brown and Damon Knight, all with stories that were a notch above standard fare.

Few of these stories, with the possible exception of Bradbury's, did anything to advance science fiction, but there is no doubt that they popularized it immensely. Many long-time fans have fond memories of *Planet Stories* from their childhood. If it were ever possible to make a full assessment (and fans' and writers' recollections are all we have to go by) it's likely that *Planet Stories* introduced more fans to science fiction than most other magazines during the forties. For *Planet Stories* to be considered even half-way respectable showed that more publishers were now prepared to acknowledge science fiction as having some role to play.

Sf Becomes Respectable

The dream of most writers in the pulp magazines was to sell to the quality slick magazines, so called because they were published on glossy, high-quality coated stock, and were aimed at the professional classes (many of whom it is to be sure also read the pulps).

There were few who made that transition during the heyday of the pulps, although some succeeded after the pulps had gone. To appear regularly in both the pulps and the slicks was rare. There was a divide, mostly caused by publishing snobbery, that was like a gaping chasm.

In some cases publishing houses produced both pulps and slicks, and that sometimes made the transition easier. Thus in the thirties, Bernarr Macfadden not only published his many pulp confession magazines but also the prestigious *Liberty*, and many writers, most notably Edgar Rice Burroughs and Ray Cummings, were able to claim they had made it to the slicks. Likewise Street & Smith published both *Mademoiselle* and *Charm*, two quality magazines aimed chiefly at women readers. Henry Kuttner made it into *Charm* with 'Housing Problem' (November 1945) because Campbell could no longer use it after *Unknown* had folded, and passed it to *Charm*. Ray Bradbury was able to sell 'The Invisible Boy' directly to *Mademoiselle* where it appeared in November 1945.

The top-quality slick magazine was the *Saturday Evening Post* to which everyone aspired. Not only its reputation for quality fiction, but its venerable status (it had been published regularly since 1821) made it one of the most respected magazines, and it paid top-quality rates. The editors at the *Post* were not averse to genre fiction. They regularly published detective stories and had already published some fantasy and science fiction, most notably by Lord Dunsany, Stephen Vincent Benet, Aldous Huxley and Gerald Kersh. But to publish science fiction by pulp writers was another matter. When Ben Hibbs took over as editor in 1942 he placed greater emphasis on non-fiction and it seemed that the scope for fiction, outside the popular detective stories and sea stories, was limited. So when Robert A. Heinlein sold 'The Green Hills of Earth' to the *Post*, where it appeared in the 8 February 1947 issue, it caused quite a stir in sf circles.

Heinlein had taken the advice of Murray Leinster, a long-time respected writer, who had sold westerns and other non-sf fiction to the slicks on occasions, usually under his real name of Will F. Jenkins. Heinlein recalls: 'Several years ago Will F. Jenkins said to me, "I'll let you in on a secret, Bob. *Any* story – science fiction or otherwise – if it is well written, can be sold to the slicks."'[11]

11. Robert Heinlein, 'On the Writing of Speculative Fiction', in Lloyd Arthur Eshbach, ed., *Of Worlds Beyond*, 2nd edition (Chicago: Advent, 1964), p. 13.

Heinlein's story was science fiction only by convention. It focused squarely on the human element. It told of the sacrifice made by a blind poet to save a spaceship. What Heinlein had learned in the process was making an economy of words. He knew that the average *Post* story was about 6,000 words and that was what he aimed for. In paring down his text he was able to achieve a tighter and more polished story. Having cracked the *Post*, Heinlein's agent, Lurton Blassingame, was able to market Heinlein even wider. In quick succession he made sales to *Town and Country*, *The American Legion Magazine* and three more to the *Post*.

Hot on his heels came Ray Bradbury who was already selling non-fantasies to slick markets. He placed his Martian Chronicles stories, 'Dwellers in Silence' and 'The Silent Towns', in the Canadian *Maclean's* (15 September 1948) and *Charm* (March 1949), respectively.

Probably the best-known emergence from the pulps to the slicks was the case of John Wyndham, the new pen name for John Beynon Harris, who sold his novel 'The Revolt of the Triffids' to *Collier's Weekly* where it began serialization on 6 January 1951. This novel, better known in book form as *The Day of the Triffids*, is one of the best-known of all science-fiction novels, partly because of its appearance outside the pulps.

At last science fiction had broken down the pulp barriers. This was happening not only in the slick markets but also in book publishing. In just the same way, book publishers had not been averse to issuing science fiction provided it was well written, but it was unusual for science fiction first published in the pulps to make it into book form. The main exception to this was fiction published in the Munsey magazines, because Munsey had developed an excellent secondary-rights sales service and succeeded in placing many novels with book publishers. This way Edgar Rice Burroughs, Ray Cummings, A. Merritt and Ralph Milne Farley all appeared in book form. But others outside the Munsey magazines found it difficult, especially to reprint any short fiction. Most authors were more than happy to sell all rights to a publisher because they never expected their stories to be reprinted.

But during the thirties and more especially in the forties the specialist fiction anthologies began to appear. These included some which were a mixture of science fiction and weird fiction. T. Everett Harré, for instance, used several stories from *Weird Tales* in his 1929 anthology *Beware After Dark!*, including 'The Call of Cthulhu' by H.P. Lovecraft, 'The Sunken Land' by George W. Bayly and 'The

Monster-God of Mamurth' by Edmond Hamilton, all arguably
science fiction. But it was some time before a specialist anthology
selected stories from the science-fiction magazines. The first to do
so was *The Other Worlds*, edited by Philip D. Stong for Funk &
Wagnell's in 1941. This anthology is another mixture of weird
fiction and sf, selected chiefly from *Weird Tales*, but it included some
stories from *Astounding*, *Unknown* and *Amazing Stories*, plus one
from *Thrilling Wonder*. The first paperback anthology of sf was *The
Pocket Book of Science-Fiction*, edited by Donald Wollheim for Pocket
Books in 1943. Wollheim ranged far and wide in his selection of
material, and included one story from each of *Wonder Stories* and
Amazing and three from *Astounding*.

After the war the steady increase in the number of science-
fiction anthologies was a further sign of the interest in and credibility being placed on science fiction as a marketable product and not
just something for the young and weird. There were two major
publications in 1946. For Crown Publishers, Groff Conklin assembled
The Best of Science Fiction, a massive 785-page volume containing 40
stories and a preface by John W. Campbell. Not surprisingly, because
of public interest, the opening section covered 'The Atom' and
included 'Solution Unsatisfactory' and 'Blowups Happen' by
Heinlein and 'Deadline' by Cartmill. Of the 40 stories, 25 were from
Astounding. The second such anthology was *Adventures in Time and
Space*, edited by Raymond J. Healy and J. Francis McComas for
Random House. Just short of a thousand pages this has always
remained a landmark anthology. Of its 33 stories, all but four came
from *Astounding*, and one other was from *Unknown*.

These two anthologies were not only a vindication of what
Campbell had been seeking to achieve, they were able to bring
science fiction to a wider audience (through lending libraries) and a
wider selection of people, particularly those happy to acquire books
for themselves or their children when they would never have
sanctioned the low-grade pulps. It's quite possible that many who
read the stories in the anthologies had no idea they came from the
pulp magazines.

All of this interest in science fiction had one inevitable result.
Publishers regarded it as a profitable venture and once again
everyone started to get in on the act. The first boom, which had
been stifled by the war, now began to revive.

The usually acknowledged first sign was the appearance of the
Fantasy Reader from Avon Books, better known as the *Avon Fantasy*

Reader. This was intended as a regular paperback anthology series and not a magazine. It was all reprint (though some later volumes did include new material), and was issued in digest format in the same way as Avon's *Murder Mystery Monthly*. Because at that time sf devotees were not used to paperback anthologies, especially a regular quarterly series, the *Fantasy Reader* was immediately regarded as a new magazine and has tended to remain so in all bibliographies.

The *Fantasy Reader* was edited by Donald Wollheim. In 1946 he was working for A.A. Wyn's Ace pulp magazines, but he wrote to Avon Books to see if it was interested in adding a fantasy title to its existing mystery and western series. The editor, Herbert Williams, was most enthusiastic and contracted Wollheim to compile a *Fantasy Reader*. There was no set schedule; once the previous number had broken even the next was published. The first number appeared in February 1947. It was instantly successful and Wollheim accepted an invitation to join Avon's staff. Soon after this, Williams fell out with publisher Joseph Meyers and Wollheim found himself editor of all Avon's books.

Despite the title, *Fantasy Reader* published as much science fiction as it did fantasy, but Wollheim selected from the whole range of imaginative fiction. The sf emphasis was evident from the start with the first number leading with Murray Leinster's 1931 classic of space station intrigue, 'The Power Planet', but there were also stories by William Hope Hodgson, A. Merritt, H.G. Wells, August Derleth, Clark Ashton Smith, H. Russell Wakefield and Lord Dunsany. Wollheim's selection was always varied and inventive, often drawing upon lesser-known material. The *Fantasy Reader* was much respected in its day and has become highly collected since. It appealed to the same reader who had sustained *Famous Fantastic Mysteries* throughout the war and who welcomed the revival of *Fantastic Novels* in March 1948.

Over the next year or two a number of other magazines would come out of cold storage. Popular Publications resurrected *Super Science Stories* in January 1949; Louis Silberkleit revived first *Future combined with Science Fiction Stories* in May 1950, followed by *Science Fiction Quarterly* in May 1951; and Martin Goodman, sensing another opportunity, revived *Marvel Science Stories* in November 1950. But these revivals were nothing compared with the new magazines that would start to snowball from the autumn of 1949. The first was *Magazine of Fantasy*, followed rapidly by *Other Worlds*,

Imagination and *Galaxy*, all of which appeared in digest format, as well as the pulps *Captain Zero, A. Merritt's Fantasy, Fantastic Story Quarterly, Wonder Story Annual, Out of This World Adventures* and *2 Complete Science-Adventure Books*. All of these appeared (and some disappeared) before the end of 1950, and many more were to come.

Fans and Pros

After 20 years of the science-fiction magazines, fans who had discovered them in their youth were now mature adults, many of them hardened by years away at the war. Returning to a war-torn Britain or the United States, some of them hoped to make a living out of science fiction. It is notable that from 1946 the future of sf was increasingly in the hands of the fans rather than the professionals. This had been true to some extent since the late 1930s with Campbell, Palmer, Weisinger, Lowndes, Pohl and Wollheim all graduating from fandom into roles as magazine editors. But from 1946 on some fans started to take on the role of publisher.

This development happened in Britain as well as America, and it gives us an opportunity to catch up with what was happening in Europe.

Britain had not been starved of science fiction during the war because there were British reprint editions of several magazines, particularly *Astounding*, which sustained publication throughout the war, although it became increasingly irregular and dwindled in size to 64 pages. Other occasional publications appeared, most of them reprinting American material. These included an occasional series from Benson Herbert's Utopian Publications where Walter Gillings served briefly as editor. Wartime restrictions did not allow the registration (and therefore publication) of new magazines which would have committed paper for serial publication. One-off books were allowed. As a consequence individual booklets were published, some containing more than one story, making them more like anthologies or collections than magazines, though their exact designation has remained borderline. The contents of the Utopian series were selected from material Gillings had stockpiled for future issues of *Tales of Wonder* which languished when the magazine folded and, despite good intentions, never resurfaced. In a sense, therefore, the Utopian series publications are phantom copies of *Tales of Wonder*. The first was *Girl in Trouble* by E. Frank Parker, a new story issued in September 1944, followed in November by *Arctic Bride*, a title which contained two short stories by S.P. Meek. Of special interest in this series is *Sea-Kissed* by Robert Bloch, containing four short stories and thus technically his first collection, beating his first Arkham House volume into print by almost a year. Most of the booklets bore a story title, but the first release in 1946 was called *Thrilling Stories*, and this was followed by a first and second selection of *Strange Tales*. This last title has often been indexed as a magazine, and serves to emphasize, as with *Avon Fantasy Reader*, how the distinction between paperback anthology and magazine was blurred right at the outset.

The Utopian series was distinctive for its efforts to portray a female nude on the cover of every issue. This certainly helped sell the early releases but surprisingly, by the end of the war, there was such a glut of booklets on the market that Herbert had troubling shifting the remainder. The series ended in June 1946 with *Romance in Black* by Gans T. Field (Manly Wade Wellman). Towards the end of 1946 Herbert managed to publish two issues of a new magazine, *New Frontiers*, edited by fan Sam Youd. *New Frontiers* was a non-fiction magazine focusing on the occult and parapsychology, the direction that Benson Herbert would follow for the rest of his life. Although he never returned again to science fiction he remained intensely active in the psychic research field.

In Britain, 1946 saw an upsurge of interest in science-fiction publications, including a few magazines. The variation in quality was enormous. One of a handful of opportunist London publishers, Hamilton & Co. (Stafford) Ltd., issued two magazines a month apart, the first called *Strange Adventures* (September 1946) and the other *Futuristic Stories* (October 1946). Both were published in large-size pulp format, running to a slim 48 pages. Hamilton's had been founded in 1943 by Harry Assael and Joseph Pacey, publishing imitation American gangster books, but with a quick eye for anything likely to have public appeal. Science fiction looked a profitable new area so the editor Dennis Pratt commissioned writer N. Wesley Firth to put together two volumes of material. Firth had never written science fiction before, but by writing a few monsters into his gangster stories he was able to fit the bill. Slap them together with a cover painting of a monster attacking a woman, and there you were. The stories were dreadful with no literary merit, but that may not be too surprising since Firth was writing over a million words a year in all fields and he was still only 26. Mercifully only one further issue of each title appeared a couple of months later (each featuring a single Firth story), before Hamilton's decided the money was in gangster and western books and dropped science fiction for a few years. When it did return, the company came back with a vengeance and its legacy is still with us today, but that must wait for the next volume.

Hopefully true devotees of science fiction were not deterred by Hamilton's puerile magazines, and with luck they had spotted *New Worlds* first.

Edward J. Carnell had at last been lucky. As far back as 1940 he had been involved in negotiations to produce a professional sf magazine, but it never materialized. Then in January 1946, just out of the army, Carnell met his old friend Frank Arnold who had interested a small-time London publisher in issuing a series of sf titles. Arnold took Carnell to meet the publisher, taking along Carnell's prospectus for the still-born *New Worlds*. The publisher was Pendulum Publications and the man in charge was Stephen Frances, later better known as the original Hank Janson. Frances was most enthusiastic and overcame the problems involved with paper and printing. Carnell had soon assembled the first issue and *New Worlds*, subtitled 'Fiction of the Future', hit the stands in July 1946, priced 2 shillings.

It featured as its lead novelette 'The Mill of the Gods' by Maurice G. Hugi, about cheap merchandise flooding the Earth from an unknown source. Hugi was a friend of Eric Frank Russell, and Russell had helped Hugi with earlier stories. This tale was competent and read like something aimed at *Astounding* but not quite hitting the mark. Hugi would probably have developed into a good writer had he had the confidence, but he was robbed of the opportunity to develop as he died in 1947 aged only 43. The most popular story in the issue was 'The Three Pylons', an intriguing fantasy by William F. Temple, unlike anything else he wrote. The rest of the issue consisted of four stories by John Russell Fearn, which resulted in a certain sameness. Fearn was a competent writer who took too much advantage of easy markets both in America and Britain and never challenged himself to produce the quality material of which he was capable.

As a first issue it was average, though when compared with other material being published in Britain it was exceptionally good. Unfortunately the cover illustration by Bob Wilkin, showing a new

Earth rising from the ruins of a nuclear war, lacked vitality and seemingly did not inspire potential readers. His interior artwork was also uninspired. When sales of the first issue proved poor, 3,000 out of a print run of 15,000, Carnell suspected the cover and eventually had the remaining copies of the first issue bound with the cover of the second issue, a spaceship scene devised by Carnell and effected by Victor Caesari. This time the first issue sold out, as did the second, which was issued in October. The fiction in the second issue was also moderately better than the first, especially John Beynon's 'The Living Lies'. Britain was reaping the benefit of writers having been able to sell to US markets and Britain's *Tales of Wonder*. A grounding was there that would at last allow British sf writers to flourish.

There was further encouragement by the end of 1946 when two more magazines appeared. In October came a diminutive publication called *Outlands*, 'A Magazine for Adventurous Minds'. Its somewhat pastoral cover, all in blue with an inset river scene, was hardly set to trap the sf fan: it looked more like a church magazine. What might have caught their eye was the banner declaring 'Pre-Natal' by John Russell Fearn. Once again the ubiquitous Fearn was in print, this time nearer to home.

Outlands was edited by Leslie J. Johnson from his home in Liverpool. Johnson had been instrumental in forming the British Interplanetary Society with Philip E. Cleator in 1933. He had also worked on science-fiction stories with both Fearn and Eric Frank Russell, his highspot being the publication of 'Seeker of Tomorrow', a Wellsian story written with Russell which appeared in *Astounding* in July 1937. Johnson had used his RAF gratuity to establish *Outlands* with fellow fans Leslie V. Heald and Ernest Gabrielson. It was a mature magazine with readable fiction by George C. Wallis, a veteran now of 50 years' writing, Charnock Walsby (Leslie Heald) and Sydney J. Bounds, whose first sale, 'Strange Portrait' (a latter-day Dorian Gray), appeared here. The issue also contained an obituary of H.G. Wells who had died on 13 August 1946, a month before his eightieth birthday. The man who had almost single-handedly popularized science fiction in Britain, and had once dreamed of the wonder science might bring, had lived to see the horrors of the atom bomb. His passing was another sign that the old days of sf had gone and a new world was opening. A second issue of *Outlands*, advertized as forthcoming in December, never appeared as the main distribution channels declined to handle it.

Nevertheless that same month, December 1946, saw a new magazine, *Fantasy*. This was not the rebirth of Newnes's pre-war *Fantasy*, but a new, neat digest magazine edited by Walter Gillings and published by Temple Bar in London. Gillings had been preparing for the magazine since 1943 and had already collected enough material for nine issues, but Temple Bar kept stalling, unsure of the market. The success of the first two issues of *New Worlds* finally convinced them. Here again was John Russell Fearn with the lead story, 'Last Conflict', but more notably Arthur C. Clarke saw his first story publication in Britain with 'Technical Error'.

Clarke had previously had two science articles in *Tales of Wonder* before the war. Conscripted into the RAF in 1941, he became involved with the trial experiments for radar and later sold a short article to *Wireless World* entitled 'Extra-terrestrial Relays' which predicted three satellites in Earth's orbit being used for global television. Seventeen years later Telstar became a reality. When Clarke learned Gillings was requesting material for a new magazine he sent a batch of stories along, several of which Gillings bought. As time passed and *Fantasy* still had not appeared, Gillings returned several stories and suggested Clarke try selling them in the States. He did. John W. Campbell bought two for *Astounding*, 'Loophole', which appeared in April 1946, and the more famous 'Rescue Party' (May 1946), wherein aliens explore a vacated Earth hours before the sun goes nova.

A second *Fantasy* appeared in April 1947 leading with Eric Frank Russell's fascinating 'Relic', which tells of the landing on Earth of an ancient spaceship and the subsequent explorations by its robot occupant. Clarke was also present with 'Castaway' under the pen name Charles Willis. He used a second pen name, E.G. O'Brien, for 'The Fires Within' which appeared in the third *Fantasy* in August 1947. That was the last issue. Although each had sold out, the magazine was discontinued because the paper restrictions forced Temple Bar to concentrate on more lucrative publications.

Fantasy was a competent magazine and much of its fiction stands up well today. It is clear that by now the writers were much better acquainted with science fiction and they were also assuming their readers would know it better, not just from having had access to British editions of *Astounding* during the war but also because those interested, especially those inspired by the achievements of science and the threat of the atomic bomb, already had a grounding in science. This allowed writers to be bolder and more inventive in their ideas, and though much of the writing was clearly modelled on the work appearing in *Astounding*, that was no bad thing – learn from the best.

While *Outlands* and *Fantasy* came and went readers had waited patiently for the third issue of *New Worlds*. It eventually appeared a year late at the end of October 1947. Pendulum was experiencing financial problems and was now in receivership, and the third issue was the last. It was another good issue, though the fiction wasn't quite of the same standard as that in *Fantasy*. The best story was Arthur Clarke's 'Inheritance' under his Charles Willis alias. This story, about a son living out the future his father had foreseen, was also bought by Campbell for *Astounding*. Although that magazine had a no-reprint policy, 'Inheritance' appeared in the September 1948 issue, the only time *Astounding* ran a story that had seen earlier publication. Clarke was under way with an auspicious start.

Unfortunately, 1946 had proved something of a premature spring for British science fiction and by the end of 1947 things were again looking bleak. Two haphazardly compiled reprint issues of *Amazing Stories* had appeared during the winter of 1946/47. The slimmer British edition of *Astounding* continued to appear alongside the reprint *Unknown* which, because it only used selected stories, survived long after its American original folded. It eventually ceased in 1949. Atlas then began British reprint editions of *Thrilling Wonder Stories* and *Startling Stories*. Science fiction was thus available to the British reader, but what was needed were markets to allow British sf writing to develop.

It was a little ironic that just at the time of the demise of *New Worlds*, the London publisher Zodiac brought out a new hardcover edition of Aldous Huxley's 1932 novel *Brave New World*. Maybe it caused inspiration, because by 1948 it became apparent that Britain's own brave *New Worlds* was not dead but only sleeping.

After the war, British fans had taken to meeting weekly at the White Horse Tavern in Fetter Lane in London, meetings later immortalized in Arthur C. Clarke's *Tales from the White Hart* (1957). At one gathering someone asked, if Carnell couldn't interest a British publisher in *New Worlds*, why didn't they start their own publishing company? This idea was taken up by Frank Cooper, a retired RAF officer who had put his gratuity into a bookshop in Stoke Newington which had a specialist sf section. Within a short time Cooper had developed a company prospectus and was floating shares. Over 50 enthusiasts became shareholders which raised enough capital to launch the company: Nova Publications. The initial directors were John Beynon Harris, G. Ken Chapman, Frank Cooper, Walter Gillings, Eric Williams and John Carnell.

Cooper and his bookshop manager Leslie Flood handled the distribution, and issue four of *New Worlds* appeared in June 1949. Here was indication that at its heart British science fiction would never die. *New Worlds* would be the centre of sf in Britain for the next 20 years.

From this fourth issue *New Worlds* started to develop its own character. It was sufficiently different from its American counterparts to be distinctive. Although its size, format and policy echoed *Astounding*, there remained a typically British atmosphere about it. The covers were subdued, thus making them more appealing to the general reader rather than the more juvenile elements who were attracted by the brash action covers of most 1940s American pulps. It is almost certain that the average age of readers of *New Worlds*, as with *Astounding*, was older than that of readers of the other sf pulps. The stories also had a strong British flavour. Most British sf is permeated with a sense of the unhurried, reserved life that has been our heritage rather than the American frontier existence. Much American space opera was accused of being interplanetary wild west. That was not the British approach, although some authors imitated it.

Since the demise of *Fantasy*, Walter Gillings had been privately publishing his highly professional-looking critical magazine *Fantasy Review*, packed with news, reviews and information about the field. After its fifteenth number he retitled it *Science-Fantasy Review* and three more issues appeared until the spring of 1950. By then the next part of Nova's publication plan was put into operation: to produce a sister magazine for *New Worlds*, thereby sharing the overheads. This was *Science-Fantasy*, under the editorship of Gillings. Its first issue, incorporating *Science-Fantasy Review*, appeared in the summer of 1950. It was a smaller digest size than *New Worlds*, though its 96 pages also cost 1 shilling and sixpence. The lead story was 'The Belt' by J.M. Walsh. Walsh was a prominent character in the British sf scene, having sold a feature novel, 'Vandals of the Void', to Gernsback's *Wonder Stories Quarterly* in 1931. The lack of a British market meant that Walsh had to concentrate on mysteries and thrillers in order to earn a living, but he wrote sf whenever he could. 'The Belt', which tells how an errant piece of space flotsam knocks the Moon from its orbit, causing it to disintegrate and form a ring around the Earth, was a polished piece of writing and set a good standard for the magazine. It was followed by 'Time's Arrow' by Arthur C. Clarke, one of his short but neat O. Henry-like stories, which emphasizes the quality that *Science-Fantasy* had from the outset. It was, in fact, drawing upon the very best of the unpublished stories which Gillings had acquired for *Fantasy*.

Since Gillings was as much a scholar and collector of sf as he was an editor and reader, *Science-Fantasy* included a fine mix of articles and reviews. One such piece, 'The Jinn in the Test-Tube' by Herbert Hughes (one of Gillings's many journalistic pseudonyms), explored the views of those outside sf as to the gathering pace of sf in the USA and in particular the comments of the then much respected professor and philosopher, Dr Jacob Bronowski, who christened sf 'the folklore of the atomic age'. Although sf had been around for decades, it had been the dream of the atomic age that had inspired much of the development of sf in the twenties and thirties, and which fuelled it into the fifties and beyond. Bronowski's epithet would remain appropriate until the seventies when sf, or what most sf had evolved to, started to become the folklore of the 'space age'.

A second *Science-Fantasy* appeared in January 1951 and included Arthur C. Clarke's much reprinted 'History Lesson' which had previously appeared in the May 1949 *Startling Stories*. Import restrictions still applied at this stage, allowing authors to sell British and North American serial rights separately to UK and US magazines and thus get more mileage and money out of their fiction. This would happen increasingly throughout the fifties.

A full year elapsed before the third *Science-Fantasy* appeared, dated Winter 1951/52. Now 2 shillings in price it was a larger digest size, compatible with *New Worlds*, and it was not edited by Walter Gillings, although he did supply the editorial. Nova Publications had decided that it was uneconomical to have two editors and the vote had gone in favour of John Carnell, the decision being swayed to some extent by the fact that the design and make-up of *Science-Fantasy* were more expensive than those of *New Worlds*. In the process Gillings lost control of *Science-Fantasy Review* which disappeared from the magazine's pages in favour of an all-fiction line-up. This, coupled with a domestic tragedy, caused Gillings, the man who had been the main driving force for the establishment of a British science-fiction magazine since 1934, to withdraw into the background, and he would not take any further part in the professional sf scene for almost 25 years.

One other development in Britain in 1950 was a sign of some encouragement. There had been much opposition in Britain to the growing cult of American horror comics which many feared would have an adverse affect on their children's psychology. The enterprising Reverend Marcus Morris determined to ensure there was a more uplifting moral alternative. He approached the publishers Hulton and proposed the idea of a comic magazine that children could read which had a religious and educational slant. Hulton agreed, and Morris prepared *The Eagle* which was issued amidst great publicity on 14 April 1950. The lead character was Dan Dare, Pilot of the Future. Morris had originally envisaged him as the Reverend Dan Dare but thankfully Hulton modified it along more conventional lines. The Dan Dare strip was drawn and plotted by ex-RAF artist Frank Hampson who had acquired a special technique of clean-line realism which revolutionized comic-strip art. Printed on high-quality paper, *The Eagle* had a superb professional appearance and its advance publicity was such that parents readily bought it for their children. Its success was noted by John Carnell in his editorial for the Summer 1950 *New Worlds*, which said in part:

> it gave me a very warm feeling to know this national juvenile weekly is selling out everywhere. Edited by a clergyman, who devised and designed it prior to submitting it to Hulton Press, it carries a strip-cartoon adventure on Venus, and regular science-fiction stories with a strong juvenile appeal. Not without a little pride, author Clarke informs me that he has sold a story to the *Eagle*.[12]

If ever any juvenile publication served to recruit new readers to the adult sf magazines it was *The Eagle*. This was due in no small part to Hampson's thorough knowledge of sf, and the remarkable inspiration shown in his artwork. The adventures of Dan Dare against the all-green Venusian villain, the Mekon, thrilled children throughout the fifties.

By 1950, British sf was becoming firmly established in the magazines and there would be much more to come, for good and for ill, which will be studied in the next volume. This development had been thanks not to professional publishers but to fans. Gernsback's dream that scientific development would be advanced through science fiction might not quite have come true yet, but

12. John Carnell, 'Good Companions …', editorial in *New Worlds*, 3 (7) Summer 1950, p. 3.

there was no doubt that the fans had taken the future of sf into their own hands and were keen to ensure its survival and safe-keeping. That was as true in the States as it was in Britain.

After the war a number of American fans began to invest their savings and gratuities in various fan enterprises. The majority of these sought to publish books rather than magazines, their main intention being to rescue classics of science fiction from the pulps and reprint them between hardcovers for more enduring quality. The grandfather of all of these specialist publishers was Arkham House founded in 1939 by August Derleth and Donald Wandrei to collect the works of H.P. Lovecraft into hardcover. Arkham House was more of a weird-fiction than science-fiction specialist, though Derleth was not immune to the commercial benefit of sf. I shall return to Arkham House shortly.

The core of the first wave of post-war specialist publishers were Donald Grant, Thomas Hadley and Ken Krueger. None of these at the time published sf magazines, though Krueger did later produce a few issues of *Space Trails*. The first endeavours of Grant and Hadley were also linked to H.P. Lovecraft. Both came from Providence, Rhode Island, and felt that Lovecraft's home town should have some local tribute to the author. In 1945, before the end of the war, they produced a small paperbound booklet, *Rhode Island on Lovecraft*, which met with moderate success. Inspired, the two determined to publish further books, but Grant was drafted and unable to parti-cipate. Krueger, who was stationed near Providence, joined with Hadley and formed the Buffalo Book Company. Between them they published two sf books in hardcover: *The Time Stream* by John Taine, from *Wonder Stories*, 1931, and *The Skylark of Space* by E.E. Smith, from *Amazing Stories*, 1928. Both of these were crucial stories in the pulps for breaking previous barriers and setting new standards, and it is not too surprising that they were amongst the first pulp stories that fans wished to have perpetuated in hard-covers.

Krueger returned to Buffalo in 1946 and Hadley continued with his own Hadley Publishing Company. Between 1946 and 1948 he reprinted *The Skylark of Space*, and brought into hardcovers *The Weapon Makers* by A.E. van Vogt, *The Mightiest Machine* by John W. Campbell and *Final Blackout* by L. Ron Hubbard, all from *Astounding*.

By 1947 other small-press speciality fan publishers were emerg-ing. From Philadelphia came Prime Press which began in 1947 with *The Mislaid Charm* by Alexander M. Phillips, from *Unknown*. This

may seem a strange first choice until one understands that Phillips
was a local fan and president of the Philadelphia SF Society. Prime's
second volume was *Venus Equilaterial* by George O. Smith, from
Astounding.

In the same year Fantasy Press appeared, run by Lloyd Eshbach
from Reading, Pennsylvania, who took over the mailing lists from
Thomas Hadley. Eshbach's first book was *Spacehounds of IPC* by E.E.
Smith, from *Amazing Stories*, followed quickly by *The Legion of Space*
by Jack Williamson and *The Forbidden Garden* by John Taine.

These specialist publishers were selecting either novels which
had rapidly acquired a classic status since their magazine publication or authors who had developed an almost legendary status in
the field. E.E. Smith, A.E. van Vogt, A. Merritt, John W. Campbell
and Stanley G. Weinbaum enjoyed the majority of the early
publications which, most importantly, not only gave new fans a
chance to acquire these classics but also allowed an opportunity for
libraries to acquire them, thus spreading the message of science
fiction further afield.

Amongst these speciality publishers were a few who not only
undertook book publication but sought to issue magazines. These
were a step above basic fanzines or amateur magazines, but are not
fully professional magazines in the accepted sense. They tend to be
called semi-professional, or semi-prozines, an inadequate term
which can cover almost any attempt by a publisher to produce a
quality magazine usually on a subscription basis but sometimes
obtaining news-stand distribution. They are important to consider
because they are the forerunners of the many small-press
magazines which dominate the sf and fantasy fields today.

One of the first, towards the end of the war, was *Different*. This
was not really a fanzine, as it was sponsored by the Avalon Arts
Academy in Arkansas which was dedicated to the promotion of
poetry and literary achievement. It was what has been described,
somewhat patronizingly I always feel, as a 'little' magazine. Its first
issue, in letter-size format, was dated March/April 1945, and it
appeared on a bi-monthly schedule, dropping to quarterly. Its
editor was Lilith Lorraine, who had almost made a name for herself
in the sf pulps in the mid-thirties before domestic pressures
diverted her energies. The magazine soon took on the sub-title 'a
Voice of the Atomic Age' and, as its title suggested, it wanted to
publish material that was out of the ordinary. Although the
emphasis was on poetry, the magazine also published short stories

and prose narratives, most of it fantastic. For a period Stanton
Coblentz, who published his own poetry magazine called *Wings*,
served as fantasy story editor. *Different* published stories by
Coblentz, Francis Flagg and even Robert Silverberg, who earned 5
dollars for a short piece, making it his first professional sale.[13]
Lorraine also issued a separate magazine devoted entirely to sf and
fantasy poetry, called *Challenge*. It survived for only four quarterly
issues during 1950/51 before being absorbed into *Different*, which
in turn succumbed to the costs of printing with the Autumn 1951
issue. It was revived briefly as a quarterly literary digest in the
spring of 1953 before folding in the autumn of 1954. Although it
only published a limited amount of science fiction its freshness
attracted interest throughout the sf world and helped encourage a
new generation of writers.

The first post-war fan-produced semi-prozine came from two
relatively unknown fans and was not part of a book publishing
enterprise. This was *The Vortex*, a highly professional-looking
magazine published and edited out of San Francisco by Gordon M.
Kull and George R. Cowie. How much money they sank into the
publication is not known but it must have been considerable, for
the magazine was printed on high-quality coated stock and every
page carried a coloured whorl as the symbol of *The Vortex*. What's
more the first issue, released in early 1947, was distributed free. A
leaflet enclosed requested that if any reader felt so inclined a
donation of 20 cents would be gratefully received. Eighty digest-
sized pages carried five stories, a poem and two articles, though
none of the authors was known, and the items were rather bland.
The enterprise must have drained the duo's resources considerably
as only one further issue appeared, towards the end of 1947.
Although this was a much cheaper-looking production its contents
were more varied, including stories by E.E. Evans, Forrest J.
Ackerman, David H. Keller and a poem by Clark Ashton Smith,
thus making the issue rather more collectable than the first. It also
demonstrates that at the end of the day it is the quality of the
content that is important, not the quality of the product, especially
when seeking to distribute primarily by subscription.

Stanley Mullen, from Denver, Colorado, who had a story in that
second issue of *The Vortex*, had professional aspirations of his own.

---

13. Robert Silverberg, in Brian W. Aldiss and Harry Harrison, ed., *Hell's Cartographers*
(London: Weidenfeld & Nicolson, 1975), p. 5.

In March 1947 he had started his own amateur magazine, *The Gorgon*. The first few issues were hectographed and of little significance, featuring mostly articles and stories by Mullen himself. Of minor interest is the fact that in the third and fourth issues Mullen reprinted 'The Vanguard of Venus' by Landell Bartlett, a novelette that Hugo Gernsback had published as a separate booklet for promotional purposes in 1928, and technically one of the first specialist sf books. Some more significant names began to appear from the fourth issue, including Lloyd Eshbach, Marion Zimmer and David H. Keller. With the seventh issue in March 1948, *The Gorgon* became printed and started to look moderately professional. At this time Mullen, who was operating under the guise of the Gorgon Press, had also encountered Paul O'Connor who had founded the New Collector's Group and had recently moved to Denver. The New Collector's Group had published *The Fox Woman & the Blue Pagoda* by Abraham Merritt and Hannes Bok in 1946, and *The Black Wheel* by Merritt and Bok in 1947. By then Bok had become increasingly disenchanted with O'Connor, and O'Connor was squeezed from the picture as Bok started to work more closely with Mullen. The result was that a short story by Mullen, *The Sphinx-Child*, was published by the New Collector's Group in mid-1948 with illustrations by Bok, which make the item more collectible than the hasty production standards might otherwise suggest.

Mullen produced one more book for the New Collector's Group, a reprint of Frank Belknap Long's poetry volume *The Goblin Tower* (1949), but placed most of his efforts in his own Gorgon Press. He succeeded in issuing a volume of his own stories, *Moonfoam and Sorceries*, in late 1948. Containing stories and poems in the style of Merritt and Bok, and with a cover and illustrations by Roy Hunt also imitating Bok, the book was well received and has some interest amongst collectors. At the time, though, the book consumed more of Mullen's finances than he was prepared to invest. A further volume which he had announced, his novel *Kinsmen of the Dragon*, was instead sold to another speciality fan press, Shasta, and published in 1951. *The Gorgon* ceased publication in May 1949 with its eleventh issue soon after Mullen had made his first professional sale to *Planet Stories*. He went on to appear regularly in the sf magazines during the 1950s before fading from the scene.

Meanwhile, in Los Angeles, William L. Crawford was endeavouring to relaunch his own publishing activities. Crawford, who had started speciality publishing in the early thirties, including the magazines *Unusual Stories* and *Marvel Tales*, had moved to Los Angeles during the war years. In 1945, he issued a small booklet of stories from *Marvel Tales*, *The Garden of Fear*, plus a booklet of Clifford D. Simak's novella *The Creator*, before launching FPCI in 1947. The booklets sold moderately well and having secured a distributor Crawford decided to take advantage of the situation and issue a magazine. Unfortunately before the first issue of *Fantasy Book* was ready the distributor ceased business, leaving Crawford stranded. He had arranged for the printing of a thousand copies and was forced to seek distribution through specialist dealers and subscription.

The first issue appeared in the summer of 1947. Crawford was still using some of the stories he had acquired for *Marvel Tales* 12 years earlier. Thus the first issue led with 'People of the Crater' by Andrew North, the pen name of Andre Norton. Norton had delivered the manuscript to Crawford in 1935 along with a sequel 'Garan of Yu-Lac'. This last had to wait until 1969 to see print, and even then it was incomplete.

Fantasy Book was never a quality production. Crawford used whatever paper he was able to acquire, which was often cheap. His printing techniques were poor, and he was seldom able to pay for quality artwork. Of interest in the first issue is artwork by Charles McNutt, who would become better known as the writer Charles Beaumont.

Crawford was therefore reliant on having good-quality fiction, and this was variable. Robert Bloch and A.E. van Vogt were amongst his better contributors in the early issues. The second issue, which featured van Vogt's 'The Ship of Darkness', is also a good example of the vicissitudes of Crawford's publishing. Crawford produced a special book-paper edition which was priced at 35 cents, had good-quality paper, but an appalling cover illustration by Lora Crozetti. A less-circulated news-stand edition, priced at 25 cents, but on poor-quality paper, carried a superior cover by Roy Hunt.

Determined to publish regularly, Crawford ambitiously commenced a serial in the second issue, 'The Machine-God Laughs' by British writer Festus Pragnell. Its minor plot, involving a super-robot and Chinese agents, was barely sufficient to support reader interest through its three instalments spread over ten months.

With its third issue *Fantasy Book* became digest-sized, but the cover and interior art, mostly by Crozetti, were appalling. Still printed on pulp paper, nothing was done to elevate its shabby appearance. By issue four, Crawford had wisely abandoned interior illustrations and reprinted a pleasant Neil Austin sketch for the cover. Presentation improved steadily thereafter, reaching a high spot with the sixth issue in January 1950. A smaller digest size with a cover by Jack Gaughan (his professional magazine debut), it ran to 112 pages and featured 'Scanners Live in Vain', a novelette which marked the start of the short but stunning sf career of Cordwainer Smith. A harsh story, it relates the grim existence of the Scanners, whose lives are devoted to the safety of mankind. The story left an indelible impression on the minds of readers, all the more so as the enigmatic Cordwainer Smith did not reappear in the magazines until 1955. Smith was the pen name of American professor of Asiatic politics and military advisor, Paul M. Linebarger. The story reflected Smith's interest in brainwashing and other military techniques, some of which had featured in his early reference work *Psychological Warfare* (1948). The story had been rejected by the more prestigious pulps, including *Astounding*, during the war years, probably because it was too bleak to publish at a time when sf was seeking to raise morale. Nevertheless its eventual appearance in *Fantasy Book* was a further example of how the small-press magazines could be a refuge for the more extreme stories of the day which might otherwise never have been published (just as Crawford had earlier saved Simak's 'The Creator' and Miller's 'The Titan'). In due course their true merit would be recognized.

Crawford deserved more success with *Fantasy Book* than it ever achieved, not because of the quality of the magazine, which was variable, but because of his determined efforts to produce something of value. Crawford's story is always one of 'what might have been', and we shall see the formula repeated with further mixed success in the fifties, sixties and seventies!

August Derleth had declared in the thirties that he was not a fan of science fiction, preferring weird fiction when not otherwise engaged in regional writing. However the change in sf during the war years and its increased commerciality attracted Derleth's attention. Arkham House, which had originally been created to bring Lovecraft's work into hardcovers, and then extended to other writers from *Weird Tales*, had started to expand its publishing in 1946, and in that year published its first science-fiction novel, A. E. van Vogt's *Slan* from *Astounding*. For a period Derleth invested much time in Arkham House, overreaching himself financially, almost to the point of bankruptcy and certainly endangering his health through overwork, but in the process producing some excellent volumes.

In January 1948 Derleth decided to issue a literary quarterly companion as part of his book publishing: *The Arkham Sampler*. The magazine was primarily intended to feature news about Arkham House, and to print new and rare weird and scientific fiction. It became a showcase of rare fiction and poetry by luminaries of *Weird Tales*, especially Lovecraft and Clark Ashton Smith. Although its amount of first-run fiction was small, the stories were all of interest. The first issue, for instance, carried a previously unpublished story, 'Messrs Turkes and Talbot', by H. Russell Wakefield, who was finding it difficult to place new stories in Britain. Wakefield had two other stories in the *Sampler*. There was also new fiction by Robert Bloch, John Beynon Harris, A.E. van Vogt, Ray Bradbury and David H. Keller, as well as some rare reprints by Lovecraft, Jules Verne and Lord Dunsany. The fifth issue, dated Winter 1949, was dedicated to a survey and discussion of science fiction. It was one of the first serious academic studies of the field. Derleth found the cost of sustaining the *Sampler* prohibitive, however, and ceased publication after eight quarterly issues.

It was these and other activities by British and American fans that further signalled to book publishers that science fiction had commercial potential. Particularly in America, publishers began to feature sf as a regular part of their output, and this included the increasing appearance of anthologies. We have already seen the seminal work carried out by Groff Conklin and Healey and McComas. By 1949 the sf field was seen as sufficiently lucrative and respectable to sustain an annual selection of the best stories. This was the work of fans and collectors Thaddeus ('Ted') E. Dikty and Everett F. Bleiler. Bleiler had just established his reputation amongst devotees with his tremendous bibliographic work, *The Checklist of Fantastic Literature* (1948), listing over five thousand works of fantasy and sf. This had been published by the Chicago specialist small press Shasta which was then run by Erle Korshak, Mark Reinsberg and Ted Dikty. Bleiler and Dikty's first selection of best sf was originally planned for Shasta, but Korshak suggested they try it with a New York publisher in the hope that any profit could be ploughed back into Shasta. Thus their first volume, *The Best Science Fiction Stories: 1949*, issued in September 1949, came from publisher Frederick Fell. It included 12 stories, 10 of which originally appeared in the sf magazines. They ran from Ray Bradbury's

'Mars is Heaven!' (*Planet Stories*, Fall 1948) to Fredric Brown's 'Knock' (*Thrilling Wonder*, December 1948). In summary, six were from *Astounding*, three from *Thrilling Wonder*, one from *Planet Stories* and two from outside the sf magazines. A second volume appeared in August 1950 with 13 stories selected from 1949. This time *Astounding* and *Thrilling Wonder* had three stories each, plus one from each of *Startling Stories, Planet Stories* and *Fantastic Adventures*, and three from outside the field, two of these from the same issue of *Saturday Evening Post*.

The sf field was now firmly becoming respectable, with as much credit to the fans and devotees as to the writers. In 1949 the New York publisher, Doubleday, decided to inaugurate a regular science-fiction line of books, the first such speciality line from a major publisher. The series began in January 1950 with *Pebble in the Sky* by Isaac Asimov. A quarter of a century after science fiction had first been identified as a separate publishing genre it had graduated from the pulps into the slick magazines and to major hardcover publishers. From 1950, sf would never be the same. It had moved from its own microcosm into the world at large.

Exports and imports

During the immediate post-war period there was a significant show of interest in science fiction in several countries around the world. Appendix 1 covers the development of magazines in languages other than English. This section looks at the emergence of other English-language magazines outside the United States and Britain.

The most interesting developments were in Canada. Most American publishers had publishing outlets in Canada so that magazines were published there simultaneously. However, with the onset of war, import restrictions and paper rationing caused problems. One answer was to publish an indigenous magazine. This was *Uncanny Tales*, first issue dated November 1940, which came from the Toronto firm Adam Publishing, and was edited by a Canadian journalist, Melvin Colby. It was originally issued in a large-digest format but soon became a standard pulp. It managed to maintain a monthly schedule for most of its life with only minor hiccups towards the end. Initially it relied heavily on Thomas P. Kelley for material. Kelley was one of only a few Canadian pulp writers and was at that time appearing in *Weird Tales*. (There were other notable Canadian writers and it is perhaps surprising that Colby did not acquire material from Laurence Manning or A.E. van Vogt.) Kelley probably wrote most of the contents under pseudonyms, though other Canadian fans, Leslie A. Croutch, John Hollis Mason and Dennis Plimmer, also started to appear. During 1941 Colby attended a New York gathering of fans where he met Donald A. Wollheim and Sam Moskowitz. Both of these agreed to provide him with material. Thus for a period *Uncanny Tales* became almost a reprint edition of *Cosmic Stories* and *Stirring Science Stories*, though it also published some material which Wollheim had considered too *risqué*. Best known amongst these is Robert Lowndes's 'Lure of the Lily' (January 1942). *Uncanny Tales* began to falter towards the end of 1942 and nine months elapsed between its December 1942 issue and the final issue, number 21, released in September 1943. Although it had little impact outside Canada it did have some impact within the country, encouraging new writers and acting as a regular focus for Canadian fandom which had hitherto lain hidden in the shadow of its American neighbour.[14]

Uncanny Tales briefly had a companion magazine, *Eerie Tales*, issued in July 1941. Although it came from a different publisher, C.K. Publishing in Toronto, and no editor is cited, its format and content were so similar to *Uncanny* as to suggest that Melvin Colby also compiled this issue. As further evidence, albeit circumstantial, Thomas P. Kelley contributed a story, 'The Man Who Killed Mussolini', that was a companion piece to 'The Man Who Killed Hitler' in the concurrent issue of *Uncanny*. For whatever reason, *Eerie Tales* only saw the one issue.

When the United States entered the war, Canadian publication of American titles became even more complicated. Popular Publications began to issue special Canadian editions of its magazines through its Toronto offices. The main difference was that the Canadian editions featured local artwork, some of it rather crude. The first of Popular's sf magazines to have a special Canadian edition was *Astonishing Stories*, although that title hides a more complicated story. Its first issue, January 1942, was a reprint of the November 1941 *Astonishing*, but the next issue, dated March 1942, reprinted the November 1941 *Super Science Stories*. The third and

14. In 1952 a slim pocketbook anthology (or magazine) was issued in Toronto called *Brief Fantastic Tales*. Most of its stories were reprinted from *Uncanny Tales*, and though it was issued by Studio Publications, it is likely that it was produced by the same editors and publisher as *Uncanny Tales*, taking advantage of stories in their inventory.

final issue, dated May 1942, reprinted the March 1942 *Astonishing*.

A few months later, in August 1942, the first Canadian *Super Science Stories* appeared. This magazine soon acquired a life of its own, outlasting its American original. It originally reprinted material from alternate issues of *Super Science Stories* and *Astonishing* but then began to draw in material from *Famous Fantastic Mysteries*, and to reflect that change the title was amended from the December 1944 issue to *Super Science and Fantastic Stories*. What is especially interesting about this magazine was that it gave first printing to stories left in the inventory after the American *Astonishing* and *Super Science* folded. Although these stories were later used when *Super Science Stories* was revived in America in 1949, their first publication was in Canada. The earliest of these were Cleve Cartmill's 'Cabal' and Manly Wade Wellman's 'The Sky Will Be Ours', both published in the January 1949 American *Super Science Stories* but originally published in the April 1944 Canadian issue. Others worthy of mention are 'The Black Sun Rises' by Henry Kuttner (June 1944), 'And Then – the Silence' by Ray Bradbury (October 1944) and 'The Bounding Crown' by James Blish (December 1944). The later issues drew stories mostly from *Famous Fantastic Mysteries*, which were in themselves reprints from the Munsey magazines, and thus saw further but little known reprints of 'The Derelict' by William Hope Hodgson (April 1945), 'The Girl in the Golden Atom' by Ray Cummings (October 1945) and 'The Moon Pool' by Abraham Merritt (December 1945). With the end of the war the Canadian edition ceased separate publication in December 1945.

It is perhaps surprising that at that time Popular Publications did not immediately relaunch the American original, but instead waited until December 1948 (issue dated January 1949). That first issue was made up almost entirely of reprints from the Canadian edition. The revived American *Super Science Stories* was edited by Ejler Jakobssen, a Finn who had come to the United States in 1926 when only 14. He and his wife Edith had become prolific writers for the pulps during the thirties, especially the horror and weird-menace magazines, before he joined Popular Publications as an editor in 1942. Jakobssen had helped Alden H. Norton produce the final issues of *Astonishing Stories* and *Super Science Stories* after Frederik Pohl had been drafted. By 1948 Jakobssen was a department head, which included control of *Famous Fantastic Mysteries*. In the summer of 1948 Jakobssen was on holiday. He recalls,

I was five miles from the nearest phone, floating on my back in a lake, on an unbearably hot day, when a boy on a bicycle showed on shore and shouted, 'Call your office.' I followed him the requisite five miles to a farmhouse, called, and Al Norton told me that *Super Science Stories* had been revived and added to my department.

His department included Damon Knight who was an uncredited assistant editor.

Super Science Stories has tended to be overlooked by collectors, yet for its period it was a highly competent magazine and carried a variety of readable and enjoyable stories by all the leading writers. Ray Bradbury was regularly featured with stories that included his classics 'I, Mars' (April 1949), which deals with the psychology of a man alone on the Red Planet, and 'Changeling' (July 1949), wherein a man has several android duplicates of himself made in order to satisfy his various lovers. Arthur C. Clarke appeared with his Möbius-strip puzzle story, 'The Wall of Darkness' (July 1949). *Super Science Stories* was the first magazine to feature a story by Chad Oliver, 'The Land of Lost Content' (November 1950). It also ran a number of excellent stories by Poul Anderson, William F. Temple and John D. Macdonald. Although *Super Science Stories* was never a top-rate magazine, it was a good second-level publication which was an excellent proving ground for developing writers.

It was also a proving ground for Damon Knight who was frustrated at being only an assistant editor and wanted a magazine of his own. That happened when Frederik Pohl directed him to Hillman Publications and Knight talked publisher Alex Hillman into issuing a science-fiction and fantasy magazine, *Worlds Beyond*, first issue dated December 1950. Knight is an excellent editor and *Worlds Beyond* is one of the best unknown magazines in sf. It was a blend of new and reprint fiction, the selection mirroring to some extent Wollheim's solid but eclectic taste at *Avon Fantasy Reader*. For instance, Knight unearthed a lost fantasy by Philip Wylie, 'An Epistle to the Thessalonians', and gave William F. Temple's 'The Smile of the Sphinx' its first American publication. The magazine has been rifled by anthologists for stories, amongst them 'Null-P' by William Tenn, 'The Acolytes' by Poul Anderson, and 'Like a Bird, Like a Fish' by H.B. Hickey. Space was also given to promote Jack Vance's novel *The Dying Earth*, which had just been published by Hillman, by including an excerpt about Liane the Wayfarer called

'The Loom of Darkness'. Sales of the first issue were poor, not because of quality but because of poor distribution, and Hillman rapidly lost interest. Although sales improved on the next two issues Hillman had already made up his mind and after three issues the magazine folded. It robbed the field of a potentially fascinating publication, but as Damon Knight returned to writing it gave the field back one of the best writers of the fifties.

The above digression demonstrates part of the significance of Canadian sf during the forties. There was more to come. In 1949 the first French Canadian sf magazine, *Les Adventures Futuristes*, was published in Montreal. It was originally twice monthly, the first issue dated 1 March 1949, but after the sixth issue it became monthly and folded in September 1949 after 10 issues. It was really a belated superhero magazine, featuring the adventures of two scientists encountering bizarre scientific and alien mutations. The magazine probably had little, if any, effect and copies today are extremely rare.

The only other country to enter the world of the science-fiction magazine at this stage was Australia. Australia could claim a number of early sf writers, including Coutts Brisbane, Erle Cox, J.M. Walsh and Alan Connell, but there was little publishing activity before the war. The only exception was a short-lived magazine called *Flame*, issued during 1936, that ran a number of sf stories, mostly predicting a future in which Australia was invaded by Japan or suffered strife of some kind. In a land of eternal optimism, the magazine must have met with limited appeal. It was not until March 1950 that another Australian sf magazine appeared, and this was the juvenile and crude *Thrills, Inc.* Editor Alister Innes was unacquainted with sf but clearly felt that it was simply stories of the present day rewritten to be set in the future or outer space. Mostly by Australian writers, the stories were either crudely written space operas, or blatantly plagiarized from American magazines. Innes attempted to recover the position after a number of issues and began to officially reprint American material as well as some minor original stories. The most competent work was by Norma K. Hemming who was English, having been born in Ilford, Essex, and emigrated to Australia in 1949. *Thrills, Inc.* staggered through 23 undated issues, folding in June 1952, and was best forgotten. Australia's more significant contributions to sf were still some years away. Even more embarrassing was that *Thrills, Inc.* had a short-lived British edition called *Amazing Science Stories*, issued as a large-size slim pulp by Pemberton's of Manchester in March and April 1951. Surprisingly intermingled amongst the Australian dross were stories from the American *Super Science Stories*, which brings us back to where we started.

The Passing of the Pulps

The period 1950 to 1954 marked a turning point in magazine publication. It saw the end of the dominance of the pulp format magazine and the start of the digest magazine, now setting up in rivalry to the burgeoning pocketbook field. The new pulps that had appeared added little to the development of sf, but they should not be dispensed with out of hand without at least some consideration of their existence.

The omens had been around since the war that the future of the pulps might be limited. Wartime rationing had one significant effect in encouraging the more limited use of paper for small pocketbooks. The pocketbooks were so convenient for all concerned, but especially the troops, that they rapidly caught on in popularity, and noticeably fewer people turned back to the pulps. The same was true when publishers sought to develop the digest format or pursue the more profitable slick magazines.

The major change came in 1949 with Street & Smith. This company was one of the most respected and revered in the field. In that year the company closed down all of its remaining pulp magazines, including *The Shadow*[15] and *Doc Savage*, folding with their Summer 1949 issues. Quentin Reynolds, in writing a history of Street & Smith, considered this moment:

> In 1949 the surviving pulp magazines had all been put to rest. *Detective Story, The Shadow, Doc Savage* and *Western Story* all followed *Love Story* into oblivion. Each had been a money-maker, but each was weighted down with years. They could not compete with the entertainment offered by radio, movies and something new called television. Only *The Shadow* and *Nick Carter* had been adaptable for use in these new media. It was increasingly evident to Gerald Smith and

15. By now *The Shadow* was literally a shadow of its former self and had become little more than a standard mystery magazine with none of the sinister or menacing overtones that had made the original series so popular.

his associates that the public wanted a lot for its twenty-five or thirty-five cents. It wanted a good-looking package, fine art work, interesting articles, entertainment and service.[16]

In one swoop Street & Smith wiped out its pulp past and concentrated on its slick magazines, *Charm, Seventeen* and *Mademoiselle*. Of its former pulps only *Astounding* remained, sufficiently profitable and established in its digest form to survive. Unlike the other pulps, *Astounding* looked forward and had market credibility.

In 1950 Henry Ralston retired after 52 years with Street & Smith. His career paralleled the history of the pulps and he was a key figure in their development. After his retirement, Gerald Smith, the president of Street & Smith, announced that the day of the pulps had ended. Rival publisher Henry Steeger remembered the moment:

> In New York this was printed on the front page of the second section of the *New York Times* and it was like the President of the United States issuing a stern edict to be believed and followed by everyone, because from that point on the pulps literally died.[17]

Steeger's Popular Publications was the biggest publisher in the pulp field and in cornering the remaining market it managed to sustain the pulps for a few more years. It even acquired the title to Street & Smith's *Detective Story Magazine*, the first of the specialist fiction pulps, which was given a new lease of life in November 1952 and survived for another year. But it was clear that the death-knell had tolled and the days were limited.

Of the new pulps launched into the sf field few made any mark. *Captain Zero* was the last dying twitch of the hero pulp. Steeger must have felt he could capture readers still reeling from the loss of *Doc Savage*, but Lee Allyn, the character behind Captain Zero, was not up to this, nor was the writing by pulp veteran G.T. Fleming-Roberts. Allyn undergoes radiation therapy as a human guinea pig. A mixture of extreme radiation and drugs results in Allyn's body going transparent during the hours of night, at which time he turns crime fighter. Apart from the new twist of invisibility, we had been here before, and so had the readers. *Captain Zero* lasted for three issues from November 1949 to March 1950 and like Lee Allyn, faded away.

16. Quentin Reynolds, *The Fiction Factory* (New York: Random House, 1955), p. 232.
17. Henry Steeger, in interview with Nils Hardin in *Xenophile*, 3 (9) July 1977, p. 14.

A. Merritt's Fantasy was a new companion to *Famous Fantastic Mysteries*,[18] but unlike its elder brother it was not able to capture the full appeal. Merritt's work was being released in abundance by Avon Books in paperback, and the magazine added nothing that was not already available in *FFM* and *Fantastic Novels*. It lasted just five issues from December 1949 to November 1950. *Fantastic Novels* folded soon afterwards in June 1951. *Famous Fantastic Mysteries* lasted somewhat longer. During 1951, Popular Publications flirted with converting it into a digest magazine, but it met with enormous opposition from the readers. Somehow this magazine, appealing as it did to the nostalgia market, had to be pulp, which allowed for full appreciation of the magnificent artwork by Virgil Finlay and Lawrence Stevens. It reverted to the pulp format and went out with all guns blazing, its final issue dated June 1953. It was always one of the most attractive of pulp magazines, and is remembered with extreme fondness. It may have done nothing to advance science fiction during its 14 years and 81 issues but that didn't stop it being one of the most popular of all fantasy pulps.

This nostalgia aspect also inspired the launch of *Fantastic Story Quarterly* in April 1950. Ned Pines at Standard Magazines anticipated that, whilst readers might be turning to pocketbooks and digest magazines for their new fiction, the old material was suited only to pulps, and to some extent he was right. Early pulp fiction somehow never reads right in book form. You need the crumbling paper, the smell of woodpulp, and the mixture of advertisments, illustrations and old pulp-style text to create the right atmosphere. *Fantastic Story Quarterly* (which soon changed its name to *Fantastic Story Magazine*) concentrated on reprints from the early days of *Wonder Stories* but also included an occasional new story of which the best was 'Lazarus II' by Richard Matheson (July 1953). But its reputation rested mostly on nostalgia appeal and it succeeded moderately well, lasting for 23 issues until the spring of 1955 when it merged with *Startling Stories*.

The same principle fuelled *Wonder Story Annual*. This concentrated on reprinting longer works from the publisher's archives. Its first issue was a tempting 196 pages selling for 25 cents, and was issued in May 1950.

Standard Magazines issued one other new pulp, *Space Stories*, in

18. Popular Publications had in 1942 taken over the Munsey chain of pulps, which included *The Argosy* and *Famous Fantastic Mysteries*.

October 1952. This was another space-opera magazine aimed at a younger readership than *Thrilling Wonder* or *Startling*. It might have succeeded a few years earlier, but distributors were no longer interested in new pulps, and were only prepared to take the older ones with guaranteed sales. The magazine contained nothing memorable and folded after five issues.

Out of this World Adventures was a rather half-hearted effort from Avon Books to try and capture the comic-book market with a pulp. This had already been tried and failed over 10 years earlier, and by 1950 even the science-fiction comics were past their heyday. The fiction was clearly aimed at a young readership and much of it read like the weaker offerings in the early *Planet Stories*. Wollheim, always a conscientious editor, sought to acquire a few quality stories. He attracted a contribution from A.E. van Vogt, 'Letter From the Stars' (July 1950), about a man with an alien pen pal who deduces that the alien is seeking to invade the Earth. The best story in either of the two issues was 'The Puzzle of Priipiirii' by William Tenn (July 1950), an outrageous title for an intriguing story about trying to unravel the mystery of a Martian labyrinth. The comic strips in each issue were unremarkable and perhaps only worth noting for the inclusion of a Conan pastiche, 'Crom the Barbarian', scripted by Gardner Fox and drawn by John Giunta. A second issue appeared in December 1950 before publisher Joseph Meyers lost interest and the magazine folded. One last attempt was made with *Ten Story Fantasy* when Meyers made another deal with his printer for a cheap supply of pulp paper. *Ten Story Fantasy* is a better magazine, for all that it survived only the one issue, dated Spring 1951. Meyers insisted that the magazine be pepped up and sexy, hence the cover of our hero seeking to rescue a voluptuous maiden from a whip-wielding villain. The story titles were also pepped up so that John Beynon's innocent-sounding 'No Place Like Earth' became 'Tyrant and Slave-Girl on the Planet Venus'. The issue contains some clever stories, such as Cyril Kornbluth's 'Friend of Man', in which a murderer, dying on Mars, is saved by a large insect-like alien and nursed back to health. He vows to live a better life, little knowing that the alien is actually fattening him up for food! But the issue is memorable because it saw the first publication of Arthur C. Clarke's 'The Sentinel', which subsequently formed the basis for Clarke's novel and film *2001: A Space Odyssey*. The magazine was a good mixture of sf and weird fiction, and a good example of Wollheim's editorial talents, but again Meyers's whim resulted in the magazine meeting a premature demise. A couple of months later Meyers agreed that Wollheim could issue a science-fiction companion to the *Fantasy Reader*, namely the *Avon Science-Fiction Reader*, which was the same digest format but now seemed far more a magazine than an anthology. It again reprinted from the early days of sf, but had less appeal than the *Fantasy Reader*. By 1952, though, Wollheim had taken all he could stand of the antics of Joseph Meyers and took the first opportunity to return to A.A. Wyn to develop his line of Ace paperbacks. Meyers combined the two *Reader*s into the *Avon Science Fiction and Fantasy Reader* which saw just two issues in January and April 1953. It was edited by Sol Cohen, who edited Meyers's Avon comic books, and who we shall meet again 12 years hence. *Avon Science Fiction and Fantasy Reader* was a good magazine with some sharp stories, particularly Alfred Coppel's 'For Humans Only', which considers racial prejudice against robots, and Arthur C. Clarke's 'The Forgotten Enemy' with the return of a new Ice Age. Both of these were in the first issue. The magazine had the potential to develop, but the whims and caprices of Meyers extinguished it after two issues. Thereafter Avon never again entered the magazine field.

The last new pulp to appear was a reprint magazine, *Tops in Science Fiction*, which sought to recycle some of the popular fiction from *Planet Stories*. The old stories were accompanied by new illustrations, some by Kelly Freas, which made the magazine attractive. Its fate is symptomatic of the period. After the first pulp issue in the spring of 1953, Malcolm Reiss found he was having problems securing distribution and his distributor advised him to convert it to digest size. The second issue, dated Fall 1953, thus appeared in the smaller format, but it was too late to do anything and no more issues appeared.

Of the existing pulp magazines the one that most needed to change its image was *Amazing Stories*. By 1950 it was still marked with the lunatic-fringe element that had pandered to the Shaver Mystery, and whilst this had been siphoned away into Palmer's new magazine, *Fate*, it was going to take a major change to alter the public's perception of the magazine. New editor Howard Browne hoped to make that change. Browne was convinced there was a market for an all-slick magazine, paying top rates and seeking to appeal to the same readers who were enjoying the sf in the *Saturday Evening Post, Collier's* and other leading slicks. The change announced by Street & Smith was further evidence of the need to go up-market, and Browne used this to convince Ziff and Davis of the need for a change. They agreed, backing him sufficiently to be able to offer up to 5 cents a word instead of the customary 1 cent. In early 1950 Browne made the rounds of the leading literary agents, seeking quality stories. He secured promises from Isaac Asimov, Theodore Sturgeon, Fritz Leiber, Clifford Simak and other major names. By April 1950 he had compiled a dummy issue (which has since become a major collector's item), with a view to launching the new slick on *Amazing*'s twenty-fifth anniversary, in April 1951. But before he had the chance, the axe fell.

In June 1950 the North Koreans invaded South Korea. The North American economy was redirected towards combating the invasion. Budgets were cut and the gamble of a new, slick *Amazing* was dropped as too risky. Had it not been for the Korean War, Browne's new *Amazing* might have revolutionized the field. No one will really know, because when Browne had a second chance three years later the field had changed (as we shall see in the next volume) and the opportunity afforded in 1950 had gone.

The stories Browne had purchased made their way into the pulp pages of *Amazing*, among them 'Operation RSVP' by H. Beam Piper and 'Satisfaction Guaranteed' by Isaac Asimov. Fortunately, the news of Browne's plans had caused other agents and writers to reconsider *Amazing* as a market and this brought in stories from other respectable writers – Fritz Leiber, William F. Temple, Fredric Brown and Clifford Simak – so that as 1950 progressed there was a restoration of quality in *Amazing* and *Fantastic Adventures* that had not been evident for many years. In addition new writers started to nudge aside Palmer's old regular stable; Rog Phillips, Berkeley Livingston, Don Wilcox and Chester Geier found themselves being gradually replaced by new names. John W. Jakes, who would later establish himself with a series of best-selling civil-war novels, made his first sale to Browne with 'The Dreaming Trees' (*Fantastic Adventures*, November 1950). Mack Reynolds made his first appearance in *Amazing* with 'United We Stand' (May 1950). Milton Lesser (known today as historical writer Stephen Marlowe), made his debut in November 1950 with 'All Heroes are Hated!'. Charles Beaumont and Walter M. Miller both made their debuts in the January 1951 issue. All of these writers would establish themselves during the 1950s.

A final break with the old era came at the close of 1950 when Ziff-Davis moved its editorial offices to New York. Browne was happy with the move, as was associate editor Lila Shaffer, but William Hamling, who had been the primary associate editor since 1948, was less enthusiastic. He had too many connections in Chicago. He left Ziff-Davis and followed in Palmer's footsteps by establishing his own publishing company called Greenleaf. He took over publishing *Imagination*, an sf and fantasy magazine that had been started on his behalf by Ray Palmer in October 1950.

It is rather uncanny how many events focus on 1950 as a clear turning point in science fiction's fortunes. This was further emphasized in the film industry with the release of *Destination Moon*, a George Pal production with a screenplay by Robert Heinlein based on his novel *Rocket Ship Galileo* (Scribner's, 1947). The success of the film, the first serious sf film made for over a decade, ushered in the science-fiction film boom of the fifties, which in hindsight probably hurt sf more than it helped. But at the time it was a further sign of sf's growing acceptance and respectability.

The most bizarre event of 1950, however, was the one that would signal decisively the end of *Astounding*'s golden reign. Coming hot on the heels of the Shaver Mystery, another fringe science was almost too much for fans, but that's what they had with the emergence of dianetics.

During the 1940s, L. Ron Hubbard was one of the field's most exciting writers. His works were always borderline science fiction but were written with a brash excitement and a sense of logic and vision that was compulsive. Hubbard had followed his Doc Methuselah series, which ended in the January 1950 *Astounding*, with a short and controversial serial, 'To the Stars', which depicted the sacrifices humans must make in order to explore space. Hubbard's presence always brought controversy to the magazine, and it was thus with mounting interest that fans awaited the May 1950 *Astounding* as Campbell had announced it would feature a major article by Hubbard heralding a new science: dianetics. In conjunction with the publication of the article, the New York publisher Hermitage House was issuing a hardcover book by Hubbard, *Dianetics: The Modern Science of Mental Health*.

What was dianetics? Was it a science or another crazy concept? It is evident from the development of sf in *Astounding* that during the forties Campbell had become increasingly interested in the power of the mind, and Hubbard had been one of his most inventive writers in that area. Between them Campbell and Hubbard had given much thought to the possibilities not only in fiction but in fact. In his article 'Dianetics' (May 1950), Hubbard postulated that the mind is divided. The Analytical Mind is that part which is fully aware, which stores and records everyday events and thoughts, the part with which you are considering this now. But there is also the Reactive Mind, which continues to store information even when the Analytical Mind is focused on some significant event. If that Reactive Mind has to be used to assess problems which should be solved by the Analytical Mind then it is likely that the wrong solution will result, and might be disastrous to that individual. This is analogous to a computer having two memories, of one of which it is not aware, but which nevertheless feeds back information. Hubbard claimed that through hypnosis these false memory banks, which could cause harm, could be erased with the result that the person becomes a 'clear', one who is perfectly sane and who can think clearly in solving a problem without the necessity of relying on some past solution which could probably be wrong.

Hubbard maintained that this method would cure all mental diseases. Campbell believed Hubbard was on to something. 'What have the psychologists been doing for the past fifty years?' he asked.[19] He also believed that 'Freud is finished',[20] and that dianetics 'contradicts most of Freud'.[21]

It is evident that Campbell had helped Hubbard develop some of his thinking about dianetics in the same way he challenged and postulated ideas with all his writers. It seems though that this idea captured his imagination more than any other and it dominated his editing of *Astounding* for a while. He promoted it unstintingly in his editorials in *Astounding* leading up to the article's publication. This advance publicity generated so much interest that in April 1950 Hubbard and Campbell, along with others who had become interested through Campbell and Hubbard's promotion, established the Hubbard Dianetic Research Foundation. It was at this stage, just before the book's publication, that the seed of future problems was planted. Dianetics had overnight moved from theory into practice before anyone, least of all Hubbard, had fully considered the

19. John W. Campbell in a letter to A.E. van Vogt, 16 November 1949, reprinted in Perry A. Chapdelaine, Sr., Tony Chapdelaine and George Hay, eds., *The John W. Campbell Letters, Volume II* (Franklin, TN: AC Projects, 1993), p. 631.
20. Alfred Bester, 'My Affair with Science Fiction' in Brian W. Aldiss and Harry Harrison, ed., *Hell's Cartographers* (London: Weidenfeld & Nicolson, 1975), p. 58.
21. John W. Campbell in a letter to A.E. van Vogt, 22 December 1949, reprinted in Perry A. Chapdelaine, Sr., Tony Chapdelaine and George Hay, eds., *The John W. Campbell Letters, Volume II* (Franklin, TN: AC Projects, 1993), p. 632.

consequences. Thus when the book was published and became a bestseller within months, the Foundation was besieged by queries and visitors, and Hubbard found it an expensive and all-consuming task running the operation. Staff included top sf writer A.E. van Vogt, who became an 'auditor' (one who listens to the patient as he pours out his life under hypnosis). Van Vogt's fiction had featured much of the same material as was now emerging in dianetics – not too surprising considering the common link with Campbell – and van Vogt now found himself fully committed to the new science. Katherine Maclean was another writer who, for a period, became ensnared.

The medical profession rapidly ridiculed Hubbard's 'science' as quackery. As Hubbard's financial problems rose with the Foundation over the next year, he began to alienate himself from others, not least his wife, Sara, who sued him for divorce on the grounds that he was insane. Hubbard also alienated Campbell on the basis that he was no longer qualified to write upon the subject. Once Campbell had disavowed dianetics in 1951 the sf field was able to settle down again. But in its various incarnations dianetics flourished. Although it was bringing in considerable income from patients, the Foundation's expenditure was also high. The potential of the science was huge, however, and Hubbard encountered problems with others who claimed control over the Foundation. In 1952 Hubbard moved to Arizona to establish a new doctrine, an extension of dianetics called scientology. Whereas dianetics dealt with the mind, scientology dealt with the soul. Hubbard was thus able to proclaim the new doctrine a religion, with its consequent financial benefits, and from then on Hubbard was established.

Scientology has become a forbidden religion in many countries, and was banned in Britain. Hubbard's name became notorious, the religion a scandal, and it still evokes hostile reaction amongst many when the name is mentioned. Hubbard had abandoned science fiction and would not return to it for 30 years until he reappeared with *Battlefield Earth* in 1982. Even then few realized that this same L. Ron Hubbard had been one of the most popular and influential sf writers of the pulps.

It is significant however that 1950, at the height of the dianetics fever, saw Campbell and *Astounding* at their most fanatical and many readers did not like it. Some linked it to the similar fervour at *Amazing* over Shaver's theories and began to feel that science fiction was being overrun by crackpots. How ironic that at the very time that science fiction was becoming respectable outside the pulps, the field itself seemed to be moving beyond the fringes of recognized science and into the realms of fantasy. At the very moment when Campbell and *Astounding* were at their most vulnerable, along came two new magazines, *The Magazine of Fantasy and Science Fiction* and *Galaxy*, which would revitalize science fiction and lead it into the new decade. Their story is part of science fiction's next major step forward.

Epilogue

The remaining pulps would survive until 1954/55 and would have something new to contribute to the development of science fiction, especially *Thrilling Wonder* and *Startling Stories*. As such they are considered in the second volume of this history. A few magazines would flirt with pulp formats throughout the fifties, but the last regular sf pulp magazine was *Science Fiction Quarterly* which folded in 1957.

The passing of the pulps and the dawn of the nuclear age is an appropriate moment to pause in our history of the science-fiction magazines. After the war, and particularly from 1950 with the appearance of the *Magazine of Fantasy* (called *Magazine of Fantasy and Science Fiction* from the second issue) and *Galaxy*, science fiction matured and gathered a veneer of respectability that, at least for a period, allowed it to reach out and be part of a wider, interested audience. As we shall see that respectability did not last long, and it required another revolution in the mid-sixties to again place science fiction on the map. But, for the moment, it was holding its own.

So, what had the science-fiction pulp magazine contributed to science fiction? There is no doubt that in the 25 years from 1926 to 1950 science-fiction editors left their mark on the development of sf in a far stronger way than if the sf magazine had not come into existence, though not always for the better. It is impossible to know whether science fiction would have become a sustainable genre on its own without the hand of Hugo Gernsback, though it is more than likely that, even had Gernsback not established *Amazing Stories* in 1926, someone else would have started a science-fiction publication at some time. In establishing *Amazing Stories* Gernsback gave sf an identity and one which writers could therefore develop and with which readers could identify.

Gernsback's role though was clear. He wanted sf to be educational. As a consequence it did not need to be particularly cosmic in scale. In fact the narrower the focus the better. Gernsback wanted fiction that instructed and inspired. The inspiration was intended to make the reader creative or inventive. However, fiction that only inspired someone to invent a few new uses for the radio was limiting, and science fiction would not survive long with that as its ambition. We can call this, though, Phase 1 of magazine sf – gadget sf.

The readers soon demanded something more exciting, and they urged Gernsback to develop the type of science fiction that had been appearing in the Munsey pulps. It was the Burroughsian planetary adventure that won through, tempered slightly by the Merrittesque exotic lost world, so that within two years, Gernsbackian sf gave way to space opera, Phase 2 of its evolution. This was developed by E.E. Smith and Edmond Hamilton, and then rapidly ruined by scores of opportunist writers. Space opera was already the common denominator of sf, and in fact always remains so. It has never gone away, but in capable hands can develop into quality sf. It dominated sf throughout the thirties and did much to give it a bad image. It was typified by the hero-rescues-heroine-from-monster school, and because it gave rise to the hero-pulp style of fiction is best typified as hero sf.

The third phase came in at the urging of David Lasser. Had Gernsback's magazines not been around, therefore, it is quite possible that science fiction would have degraded itself out of existence. Lasser forced realism into science fiction and, for a brief period around 1932 and 1933, at the depths of the Depression, encouraged writers to consider the logical results of scientific achievement and its effects upon all aspects of society, including economical and environmental. This brief but important interlude is best described as realist sf. Its influence never went away and it permeated sf over the next decade, particularly under Campbell, but another strand entered the field first.

Under F. Orlin Tremaine and Desmond Hall the 'thought variant' and no-holds-barred policy at *Astounding* led to science fiction breaking all barriers. True cosmic sf exploded. This took the space opera to its better extremes, considering not just the exploration of space but the nature of time, space and the universe. It was arguably the most exciting period in sf when writers explored and flaunted themes and plots with total abandon. Such a time could never happen again, because sf would increasingly become controlled, but for a period in the mid-thirties we had the thrill of Phase 4 – cosmic sf.

Cosmic sf of course had two effects. It encouraged again the ever-present demand for space opera which came back to dominance in the late thirties and into the war years, but it was not the leading edge. That developed under Campbell in *Astounding* and brought a true rational approach to technological progress. It thus took Lasser's realistic sf forward in the way he had originally intended, but with a force and conviction that probably no previous editor could have achieved. It also explored the cosmic nature of sf, but in a controlled and mechanistic fashion. Thus under Campbell sf entered the true machine age and became technological sf – Phase 5.

This takes us almost to the end of the war, but at that stage sf was clearly seeking new boundaries. Campbell led the way with van Vogt and Kuttner, but those pressures were emerging elsewhere. Writers were now exploring not what humans could achieve with machines but what humans could achieve with their minds. Thus Phase 6 emerges (in a phrase used by Alexei Panshin that I cannot better) as transcendental sf.

No sooner was this developing than the nuclear bomb took us into the atomic age, and sf, post-1945 and up to 1950 and beyond, was exploring what that would mean. But it opened sf up to world and blew away its pulp confines. There is thus no better way to describe Phase 7 than as nuclear sf.

Seven phases, spread over 25 years, gives some indication of the volatility of the field. But that is no different from any infant growing into adulthood, and science fiction does so closely parallel the life of human being. From babe to infant to juvenile to adolescent to teenager to young person to maturity. And then what? Would the next 25 years bring another seven stages, and the next 25 another seven? No, science fiction would continue to evolve, but it now had seven clear strands running through it, each one from time to time seeking mastery, and each of them gradually bonding and developing. Only a few more strands needed to develop, but they were significant ones and will be explored in the next volume.

APPENDIX 1
Non-English-Language Science-Fiction Magazines

Although the earliest proto-science-fiction magazines may be traced to Europe as already discussed in Chapter One, these were always one-off cases and a genre of magazines did not emerge outside the United States until after the Second World War. Even then it was powered by the US publishers. Most of these non-US magazines emerged in Europe and in the Latin American countries, and most contained reprints from American and British magazines, and thus did little to develop science fiction. Even those magazines which sought to encourage writers from within their countries had negligible influence beyond their borders and it would not be until the sixties that the depth of sf around the world would be justifiably recognized and considered by English-language publishers.

In the late forties American pulp publishers were quick to recoup income from sales of stories to foreign magazines, seeking to secure those sales officially before stories were pirated in places where copyright regulations were not enforced. The quickest sales were to Mexico and Argentina.

Argentina

Argentina's *Narraciones Terrorificas* (*Terror Tales*) had been reprinting material from the horror and terror pulps since before the Second World War. Most of its stories came from pre-war pulps issued by Popular Publications and thus contained little sf, but those published from 1945 onwards (when for a period it sustained a monthly schedule) carried increasingly more sf, particularly from *Astonishing Stories*, *Super Science Stories* and *Famous Fantastic Mysteries*. By the end of 1946, however, the magazine had become irregular again, its last eight issues being spread over four years until it folded in January 1950. During this period Argentina had another but much shorter lived magazine, *Hombres del Futuro* (*Men of the Future*) which had three monthly issues published between August and October 1947. It also reprinted from American magazines and little is known of its content.

Mexico

Mexico's leading pulp magazine of the period was *Los Cuentos Fantasticos* (*Fantastic Tales*) which published 44 issues between July 1948 and May 1953. It is an important if overlooked magazine. Not only did it reprint stories legitimately from a variety of sources, it also published new material, some by Latin American writers and some by British and American writers courtesy of Forrest Ackerman's literary agency. The magazine used some original covers but reprinted most from the various Popular Publications pulps, especially *Famous Fantastic Mysteries*, on which it seems to have been modelled, but also *Astounding* and *Marvel Science Stories*. The same magazines provided most of the story reprints. It was published by Editorial Enigmas in Mexico City, originally on a twice-monthly schedule though this soon slipped to monthly and later became more irregular. Its original publisher and editor was Antonio Mejia, though from mid-1950 he was assisted by José Sotres who guided the magazine through its final days. Because it reprinted works by Lovecraft, Burroughs and Merritt (admittedly in Spanish) and covers by Finlay and Paul, the magazine will be of interest to specialist collectors. As it also printed some original Spanish material it almost certainly encouraged and inspired writers and fans within Mexico, though the extent of that influence is difficult to measure.

Sweden

In Europe a number of countries were developing sf magazines. One of the first had been Sweden which surprisingly had succeeded in producing the first sustainable weekly sf magazine, *Jules Verne Magasinet*. This had started with the issue dated 16 October 1940. It was an attractive digest-sized magazine reprinting covers and stories from American pulps, mostly those published by Standard Magazines and Ziff-Davis. It thus regularly reprinted writers Robert

Moore Williams, John Russell Fearn, Jack Williamson and Edmond Hamilton, including all of the Captain Future series. The links to the comic books were made at the same time, as the magazine also reprinted a number of comic strips, including Batman, Superman and Jungle Jim. It carried some original stories and illustrations, most of them very crude, but much of the original work was non-fiction features which tended to be more about sports than science. Quite rapidly editor Rolf Ahlgren began to interweave sf stories with detective and western stories, again reprinted from American pulps, and the magazine also grew to pulp size and format. Gradually the sub-title 'Veckans Aventyr' ('Adventures of the Week') supplanted the main title until by July 1941 the magazine was effectively retitled *Veckans Aventyr* and had ceased to be an sf publication. It survived until February 1947 with a total of 332 issues.

Belgium

After the war, Belgium was the first European country to issue a science-fiction magazine. Its title, *Anticipations*, instantly conveyed both the hopes and fears of those emerging from the horrors of war. Its first issue was dated 25 September 1945. It was a slim magazine with its contents reprinted from *Tales of Wonder* and translated into French. This meant it featured both British and American material, though for some reason the by-lines were so distorted as to make identification difficult. The magazine managed to maintain a twice-monthly schedule until the end, when it missed a month and then published a double issue before its final issue in May 1946. There are thus 15 numbered issues but only 14 actual volumes.

Holland

Belgium's neighbour, Holland, soon followed with the first known Dutch sf magazine, *Fantasie en Wetenschap*. It was edited by Ben Abbas and reprinted some material, but apparently published mostly stories by its publisher, Lo Hartog van Banda, under various pseudonyms. It survived only four issues from December 1948 to March 1949.

Spain

There is some evidence that a Spanish magazine existed in the late forties called *Fantastica*. It apparently ran for about 19 issues around 1948, and is supposed to have featured mostly original Spanish stories, though it is as likely to have been a reprint or pirated edition of *Los Cuentos Fantasticos*.

Japan

Outside Europe the only other non-English speaking country to have a magazine was Japan. In 1950 publisher Seibundo Shinkosha in Tokyo arranged to publish a science-fiction anthology series, reprinting from *Amazing Stories* and *Fantastic Adventures*. It ran for only seven volumes during April and July 1950. Technically it was not a magazine, but it represents the first signs of Asian interest in the sf magazines.

European sf would not really start to establish itself until economies had settled and the cultures had themselves recovered from the war. The 1950s, though, would see a blossoming of European sf, as we shall explore in the next volume.

APPENDIX 2
Summary of Science-Fiction Magazines

This appendix lists all the science-fiction magazines covered by this volume together with issue and editorial details. It also covers strongly associational titles. Magazine titles are listed in alphabetical order of first issue. Individual issues are listed for each year together with a cumulative total at the end of each column (in brackets). Dates shown are cover dates. The cut-off date for this volume is December 1950, though magazines which folded in 1951 are shown to their final issue. Magazines continuing beyond that date are covered in Volume II. Combined months are shown thus: May/Jun means a single issue with the cover date May/June. Months are abbreviated to their first three characters. Seasonal dates are shown thus: Spr = Spring; Sum = Summer; Aut or Fall = Autumn or Fall; Win = Winter. Seasonal issues and undated issues are shown in the column corresponding to the month of sale. Reprint editions are not listed unless their contents vary significantly.

Air Wonder Stories
Publisher: Stellar Publishing, New York.
Editor-in-Chief: Hugo Gernsback, all issues.
Managing Editor: David Lasser, all issues.
1929:   Jul   Aug Sep   Oct   Nov Dec (6)
1930: Jan   Feb   Mar   Apr   May   (11)

Amazing Adventures see *Strange Adventures*

Amazing Detective Tales see *Scientific Detective Monthly*

Amazing Stories
Publisher: Experimenter Publishing, New York, April 1926–October 1930; Radio-Science Publications, New York, November 1930–September 1931; Teck Publishing Corporation, New York, October 1931–February 1938; Ziff-Davis, Chicago, April 1938–February 1951.
Editor-in-Chief: Hugo Gernsback, April 1926–April 1929; Arthur H. Lynch, May–October 1929; T. O'Conor Sloane, November 1929–April 1938; Bernard G. Davis, June 1938–February 1947; Raymond A. Palmer, March 1947–December 1949; Howard Browne, January 1950–August 1956.

Managing Editor: T. O'Conor Sloane, April 1926–October 1929; Miriam Bourne, November 1929–November 1932; T. O'Conor Sloane, December 1932–April 1938; Raymond A. Palmer, June 1938–February 1947; William L. Hamling, March 1947–February 1951.

Year	Jan	Feb	Mar	Apr	May	Jun	Jul	Aug	Sep	Oct	Nov	Dec	
1926:				Apr	May	Jun	Jul	Aug	Sep	Oct	Nov	Dec	(9)
1927:	Jan	Feb	Mar	Apr	May	Jun	Jul	Aug	Sep	Oct	Nov	Dec	(21)
1928:	Jan	Feb	Mar	Apr	May	Jun	Jul	Aug	Sep	Oct	Nov	Dec	(33)
1929:	Jan	Feb	Mar	Apr	May	Jun	Jul	Aug	Sep	Oct	Nov	Dec	(45)
1930:	Jan	Feb	Mar	Apr	May	Jun	Jul	Aug	Sep	Oct	Nov	Dec	(57)
1931:	Jan	Feb	Mar	Apr	May	Jun	Jul	Aug	Sep	Oct	Nov	Dec	(69)
1932:	Jan	Feb	Mar	Apr	May	Jun	Jul	Aug	Sep	Oct	Nov	Dec	(81)
1933:	Jan	Feb	Mar	Apr	May	Jun	Jul	Aug/Sep		Oct	Nov	Dec	(92)
1934:	Jan	Feb	Mar	Apr	May	Jun	Jul	Aug	Sep	Oct	Nov	Dec	(104)
1935:	Jan	Feb	Mar	Apr	May	Jun	Jul	Aug		Oct		Dec	(114)
1936:		Feb		Apr		Jun		Aug		Oct		Dec	(120)
1937:		Feb		Apr		Jun		Aug		Oct		Dec	(126)
1938:		Feb		Apr		Jun		Aug		Oct	Nov	Dec	(133)
1939:	Jan	Feb	Mar	Apr	May	Jun	Jul	Aug	Sep	Oct	Nov	Dec	(145)
1940:	Jan	Feb	Mar	Apr	May	Jun	Jul	Aug	Sep	Oct	Nov	Dec	(157)
1941:	Jan	Feb	Mar	Apr	May	Jun	Jul	Aug	Sep	Oct	Nov	Dec	(169)
1942:	Jan	Feb	Mar	Apr	May	Jun	Jul	Aug	Sep	Oct	Nov	Dec	(181)
1943:	Jan	Feb	Mar	Apr	May	Jun	Jul	Aug	Sep		Nov		(191)
1944:	Jan		Mar		May				Sep			Dec	(196)
1945:			Mar			Jun			Sep			Dec	(200)
1946:		Feb			May	Jun	Jul	Aug	Sep	Oct	Nov	Dec	(209)
1947:	Jan	Feb	Mar	Apr	May	Jun	Jul	Aug	Sep	Oct	Nov	Dec	(221)
1948:	Jan	Feb	Mar	Apr	May	Jun	Jul	Aug	Sep	Oct	Nov	Dec	(233)
1949:	Jan	Feb	Mar	Apr	May	Jun	Jul	Aug	Sep	Oct	Nov	Dec	(245)
1950:	Jan	Feb	Mar	Apr	May	Jun	Jul	Aug	Sep	Oct	Nov	Dec	(257)

[continues in Volume II]

Amazing Stories Annual

Publisher: Experimenter Publishing, New York.
Editor-in-Chief: Hugo Gernsback.
Managing Editor: T. O'Conor Sloane.

1927:	#1	(1)

Amazing Stories Quarterly

Publisher: Experimenter Publishing, New York, Winter 1928–Summer 1930; Radio-Science Publications, New York, Fall 1930–Summer 1931; Teck Publishing Corporation, New York, Fall 1931–Fall 1934.
Editor-in-Chief: Hugo Gernsback, Winter 1928–Spring 1929; Arthur H. Lynch, Summer–Fall 1929; T. O'Conor Sloane, Winter 1930–Fall 1934.
Managing Editor: T. O'Conor Sloane, all issues.

Year	Win	Spr	Sum	Fall	
1928:	Win	Spr	Sum	Fall	(4)
1929:	Win	Spr	Sum	Fall	(8)
1930:	Win*	Spr	Sum	Fall	(12)
1931:	Win*	Spr	Sum	Fall	(16)
1932:	Win	Spr/Sum		Fall/Win	(19)
1933:	Spr/Sum			Win	(21)
1934:			Fall		(22)

* both issues were dated Winter 1930

A. Merritt's Fantasy Magazine

Publisher: Recreational Reading, Inc., an affiliate of Popular Publications, New York.
Editor-in-Chief: Alden H. Norton, all issues.
Editor: uncredited; probably Harry Widmer, all issues.

1949:				Dec	(1)
1950:	Feb	Apr	Jul	Oct.	(5)

The Arkham Sampler

Publisher: Arkham House, Sauk City, Wisconsin.
Editor: August Derleth.

1948:	Win	Spr	Sum	Aut	(4)
1949:	Win	Spr	Sum	Aut	(8)

Astonishing Stories

Publisher: Fictioneers, Inc., a subsidiary of Popular Publications, New York.
Editor-in-Chief: Rogers Terrill, all issues.
Editor: Frederik Pohl, February 1940–September 1941; Alden H. Norton, November 1941–April 1943.

1940:	Feb	Apr	Jun	Aug	Oct	Dec	(6)
1941:	Feb	Apr		Sep	Nov	(10)
1942:		Mar	Jun		Oct	Dec	(14)
1943:	Feb	Apr				(16)

Astonishing Stories [Canadian edition]

Publisher: Popular Publications, Toronto.
Editor-in-Chief: Rogers Terrill, all issues.
Editor: uncredited, but probably Alden H. Norton.

1942:	Jan	Mar	May	(3)

Astounding Science-Fiction

Publisher: Clayton Magazines, New York, January 1930–March 1933; Street & Smith Publications, October 1933–January 1961.
Editor: Harry Bates, January 1930–March 1933; F. Orlin Tremaine, October 1933–November 1937; John W. Campbell, Jr., December 1937–December 1971.
Note: magazine entitled *Astounding Stories* until February 1938.

	Jan	Feb	Mar	Apr	May	Jun	Jul	Aug	Sep	Oct	Nov	Dec	
1930:	Jan	Feb	Mar	Apr	May	Jun	Jul	Aug	Sep	Oct	Nov	Dec	(12)
1931:	Jan	Feb	Mar	Apr	May	Jun	Jul	Aug	Sep	Oct	Nov	Dec	(24)
1932:	Jan	Feb	Mar	Apr	May	Jun			Sep		Nov		(32)
1933:	Jan		Mar							Oct	Nov	Dec	(37)
1934:	Jan	Feb	Mar	Apr	May	Jun	Jul	Aug	Sep	Oct	Nov	Dec	(49)
1935:	Jan	Feb	Mar	Apr	May	Jun	Jul	Aug	Sep	Oct	Nov	Dec	(61)
1936:	Jan	Feb	Mar	Apr	May	Jun	Jul	Aug	Sep	Oct	Nov	Dec	(73)
1937:	Jan	Feb	Mar	Apr	May	Jun	Jul	Aug	Sep	Oct	Nov	Dec	(85)
1938:	Jan	Feb	Mar	Apr	May	Jun	Jul	Aug	Sep	Oct	Nov	Dec	(97)
1939:	Jan	Feb	Mar	Apr	May	Jun	Jul	Aug	Sep	Oct	Nov	Dec	(109)
1940:	Jan	Feb	Mar	Apr	May	Jun	Jul	Aug	Sep	Oct	Nov	Dec	(121)
1941:	Jan	Feb	Mar	Apr	May	Jun	Jul	Aug	Sep	Oct	Nov	Dec	(133)
1942:	Jan	Feb	Mar	Apr	May	Jun	Jul	Aug	Sep	Oct	Nov	Dec	(145)
1943:	Jan	Feb	Mar	Apr	May	Jun	Jul	Aug	Sep	Oct	Nov	Dec	(157)
1944:	Jan	Feb	Mar	Apr	May	Jun	Jul	Aug	Sep	Oct	Nov	Dec	(169)
1945:	Jan	Feb	Mar	Apr	May	Jun	Jul	Aug	Sep	Oct	Nov	Dec	(181)

1946:	Jan	Feb	Mar	Apr	May	Jun	Jul	Aug	Sep	Oct	Nov	Dec	(193)
1947:	Jan	Feb	Mar	Apr	May	Jun	Jul	Aug	Sep	Oct	Nov	Dec	(205)
1948:	Jan	Feb	Mar	Apr	May	Jun	Jul	Aug	Sep	Oct	Nov	Dec	(217)
1949:	Jan	Feb	Mar	Apr	May	Jun	Jul	Aug	Sep	Oct	Nov	Dec	(229)
1950:	Jan	Feb	Mar	Apr	May	Jun	Jul	Aug	Sep	Oct	Nov	Dec	(241)

[continues in Volume II]

Astounding Stories (of Super Science) see *Astounding Science-Fiction*

Avon Fantasy Reader
Publisher: Avon Publishing, New York.
Editor: Donald A. Wollheim, all issues.

1947:	#1		#2	#3	#4	#5	(5)
1948:	#6			#7		#8	(8)
1949:	#9			#10		#11	(11)
1950:	#12			#13		#14	(14)

[continues in Volume II]

Captain Future
Publisher: Better Publications, New York.
Editorial Director: Leo Margulies, all issues.
Editor: Mort Weisinger, Winter 1940–Summer 1941; Oscar J. Friend, Fall 1941–Spring 1944.

1940:	Win	Spr	Sum	Fall	(4)
1941:	Win	Spr	Sum	Fall	(8)
1942:	Win	Spr	Sum	Fall	(12)
1943:	Win	Spr	Sum	Fall	(15)
1944:	Win	Spr	Sum	Fall	(17)

Captain Hazzard
Publisher: Ace Magazines, New York.
Editor-in-Chief: Aaron Wyn.
Editor: Rose Wyn.

| 1938: | May | (1) |

Captain Zero
Publisher: Recreational Reading, an affiliate of Popular Publications, New York.
Editor-in-Chief: Alden H. Norton, all issues.
Editor: uncredited; probably Harry Widmer, all issues.

| 1949: | | | Nov | (1) |
| 1950: | Jan | Mar | | (3) |

Comet
Publisher: H-K Publications, New York.
Editor: F. Orlin Tremaine, all issues.

| 1940: | | | | Dec | (1) |
| 1941: | Jan | Mar | May | Jul | (5) |

Cosmic Science-Fiction see *Cosmic Stories*

Cosmic Science Stories
This was a British reprint edition of the September 1949 Super Science Stories.
Publisher: Popular Press, London.

Editor: uncredited; possibly Tom V. Boardman.
1950:   (#1)   (1)

Cosmic Stories (retitled *Cosmic Science-Fiction* on cover only of last two issues)
Publisher: Albing Publications.
Editor: Donald A. Wollheim.
1941:   Mar   May   Jul   (3)

Doc Savage
Publisher: Street & Smith, New York.
Editor: John Nanovic, March 1933–November 1943; Charles Moran, December 1943–May 1944; Babette Rosmond, June 1944–May/June 1948; William DeGrouchy, July/August–September/October 1948; Daisy Bacon, Winter–Summer 1949.

Year	Jan	Feb	Mar	Apr	May	Jun	Jul	Aug	Sep	Oct	Nov	Dec	
1933:			Mar	Apr	May	Jun	Jul	Aug	Sep	Oct	Nov	Dec	(10)
1934:	Jan	Feb	Mar	Apr	May	Jun	Jul	Aug	Sep	Oct	Nov	Dec	(22)
1935:	Jan	Feb	Mar	Apr	May	Jun	Jul	Aug	Sep	Oct	Nov	Dec	(34)
1936:	Jan	Feb	Mar	Apr	May	Jun	Jul	Aug	Sep	Oct	Nov	Dec	(46)
1937:	Jan	Feb	Mar	Apr	May	Jun	Jul	Aug	Sep	Oct	Nov	Dec	(58)
1938:	Jan	Feb	Mar	Apr	May	Jun	Jul	Aug	Sep	Oct	Nov	Dec	(70)
1939:	Jan	Feb	Mar	Apr	May	Jun	Jul	Aug	Sep	Oct	Nov	Dec	(82)
1940:	Jan	Feb	Mar	Apr	May	Jun	Jul	Aug	Sep	Oct	Nov	Dec	(94)
1941:	Jan	Feb	Mar	Apr	May	Jun	Jul	Aug	Sep	Oct	Nov	Dec	(106)
1942:	Jan	Feb	Mar	Apr	May	Jun	Jul	Aug	Sep	Oct	Nov	Dec	(118)
1943:	Jan	Feb	Mar	Apr	May	Jun	Jul	Aug	Sep	Oct	Nov	Dec	(130)
1944:	Jan	Feb	Mar	Apr	May	Jun	Jul	Aug	Sep	Oct	Nov	Dec	(142)
1945:	Jan	Feb	Mar	Apr	May	Jun	Jul	Aug	Sep	Oct	Nov	Dec	(154)
1946:	Jan	Feb	Mar	Apr	May	Jun	Jul	Aug	Sep	Oct	Nov	Dec	(166)
1947:	Jan	Feb	Mar/Apr		May/Jun		Jul/Aug		Sep/Oct		Nov/Dec		(173)
1948:	Jan/Feb		Mar/Apr		May/Jun		Jul/Aug		Sep/Oct		Win*		(179)
1949:			Spr				Sum						(181)

* *issue dated Winter 1949.*

Doctor Death
Publisher: Dell Publishing, New York.
Editor: Carson Mowre.
1935:   Feb   Mar   Apr   (3)

Dr Yen Sin
Publisher: Popular Publications, New York.
Editor-in-Chief: Rogers Terrill.
Editor: Edythe Seims.
1936:   May/Jun   Jul/Aug   Sep/Oct   (3)

Dusty Ayres and his Battle Birds
This was a continuation of the non-fantasy air-war pulp Battle Birds.
Publisher: Popular Publications, New York.
Editor-in-Chief: Rogers Terrill.
1934:   Jul   Aug   Sep   Oct   Nov   Dec   (6)
1935:   Jan   Feb   Mar   Apr   May/Jun   Jul/Aug   (12)

Dynamic Science Stories
Publisher: Western Fiction, New York.

Editor: Robert O. Erisman.

| 1939: | | Feb | | Apr/May | | | | | | | | (2) |

Eerie Tales
Publisher: C.K. Publishing, Toronto.
Editor: uncredited but probably Melvin Colby.

| 1941: | | | | | | Jul | | | | | | (1) |

Famous Fantastic Mysteries
Publisher: Frank A. Munsey, New York, September/October 1939–December 1942; All Fiction Field, a subsidiary of Popular Publications, New York, March 1943–June 1953.
Editor: Mary Gnaedinger.

1939:								Sep/Oct		Nov	Dec	(3)
1940:	Jan	Feb	Mar	Apr	May/Jun		Aug		Oct		Dec	(11)
1941:		Feb		Apr		Jun	Aug		Oct		Dec	(17)
1942:		Feb		Apr		Jun	Jul	Aug	Sep	Oct	Nov	Dec	(26)
1943:			Mar					Sep			Dec	(29)
1944:			Mar			Jun		Sep			Dec	(33)
1945:			Mar			Jun		Sep			Dec	(37)
1946:		Feb		Apr		Jun	Aug		Oct		Dec	(43)
1947:		Feb		Apr		Jun	Aug		Oct		Dec	(49)
1948:		Feb		Apr		Jun	Aug		Oct		Dec	(55)
1949:		Feb		Apr		Jun	Aug		Oct		Dec	(61)
1950:		Feb		Apr		Jun	Aug		Oct			(66)

[continues in Volume II]

Fanciful Tales of Time and Space
Amateur magazine.
Publisher: Donald A. Wollheim and Wilson Shepard, Oakman, Alabama.
Editor: Donald A. Wollheim.

| 1936: | | | | | | | | Fall | | | | (1) |

Fantastic Adventures
Publisher: Ziff-Davis, Chicago, May 1939–February 1951.
Editor-in-Chief: Bernard G. Davis, May 1939–January 1947; Raymond A. Palmer, March 1947–December 1949; Howard Browne, January 1950–March 1953.
Managing Editor: Raymond A. Palmer, May 1939–January 1947; Howard Browne, March–October 1947; William L. Hamling, November 1947–February 1951.

1939:					May		Jul		Sep		Nov		(4)
1940:	Jan	Feb	Mar	Apr	May	Jun		Aug		Oct			(12)
1941:	Jan		Mar		May	Jun	Jul	Aug	Sep	Oct	Nov	Dec	(22)
1942:	Jan	Feb	Mar	Apr	May	Jun	Jul	Aug	Sep	Oct	Nov	Dec	(34)
1943:	Jan	Feb	Mar	Apr	May	Jun	Jul	Aug		Oct		Dec	(44)
1944:		Feb		Apr		Jun				Oct			(48)
1945:	Jan			Apr			Jul			Oct		Dec	(53)
1946:		Feb			May		Jul		Sep		Nov		(58)
1947:	Jan		Mar		May		Jul		Sep	Oct	Nov	Dec	(66)
1948:	Jan	Feb	Mar	Apr	May	Jun	Jul	Aug	Sep	Oct	Nov	Dec	(78)
1949:	Jan	Feb	Mar	Apr	May	Jun	Jul	Aug	Sep	Oct	Nov	Dec	(90)
1950:	Jan	Feb	Mar	Apr	May	Jun	Jul	Aug	Sep	Oct	Nov	Dec	102)

[continues in Volume II]

Fantastic Novels
Publisher: Frank A. Munsey, New York, July 1940–April 1941; New Publications, a
subsidiary of Popular Publications, New York, March 1948–June 1951.
Editor: Mary Gnaedinger.

1940:			Jul	Sep	Nov	(3)
1941:	Jan		Apr *(publication suspended)*			(5)
1948:		Mar	May	Jul	Sep	Nov	(10)
1949:	Jan	Ma	May	Jul	Sep	Nov	(16)
1950:	Jan	Mar	May	Jul	Sep	Nov	(22)
1951:	Jan		Apr	Jun			(25)

Fantastic Story Quarterly (retitled *Fantastic Story Magazine* from Spring 1951)
Publisher: Best Books, a subsidiary of Standard Magazines, New York.
Editor: Sam Merwin, Spring 1950–Fall 1951.

1950:	Spr	Sum	Fall	(3)

[continues in Volume II]

Fantasy
Pulp magazine, not to be confused with the later digest.
Publisher: George Newnes, London.
Editor: T. Stanhope Sprigg.

1939:		#1		(1)
1940:	#2	#3		(3)

Fantasy
Digest magazine; not to be confused with the earlier pulp.
Publisher: Temple Bar, London.
Editor: Walter Gillings.

1946:			Dec	(1)
1947:	Apr	Aug		(3)

Fantasy and Science Fiction see *Magazine of Fantasy and Science Fiction*

Fantasy Book
Not to be confused with the semi-professional magazine issued in 1981.
Publisher: Fantasy Publishing Company, Los Angeles, California.
Editor: 'Garret Ford' (alias for William and Margaret Crawford).

1947:		#1		(1)
1948:	#2	#3	#4	(4)
1949:		#5		(5)
1950:	#6		#7	(7)
1951:	#8			(8)

Fantasy Fiction
Entitled Fantasy Stories *for second issue.*
Publisher: Magabook, New York.
Editor: Curtis Mitchell.

1950:	May	Nov	(2)

Flash Gordon Strange Adventure Magazine
Publisher: C.J.H. Publishing, New York.
Editor: uncredited; may have been publisher Harold Hersey.

1936:		Dec	(1)

Future Fiction

Magazine retitled Future Combined with Science Fiction *from October 1941; retitled* Future Fantasy and Science Fiction *from October 1942, and* Science Fiction *from April 1943. Magazine was revived as* Future Combined with Science Fiction Stories *in May/June 1950.*

Publisher: Columbia Publications, New York.

Editor: Charles D. Hornig, November 1939–November 1940; Robert W. Lowndes, April 1941–April 1960.

Year							No.
1939:					Nov		(1)
1940:	Mar		Jul		Nov		(4)
1941:		Apr		Aug	Oct	Dec	(8)
1942:	Feb	Apr	Jun	Aug	Oct	Dec	(14)
1943:	Feb	Apr	Jul *(title suspended)*				(17)
1950:			May/Jun	Jul/Aug	Sep/Oct	Nov/Dec	(21)

[continues in Volume II]

Futuristic Science Stories

Publisher: John Spencer & Co., London.

Editor: Samuel Assael.

Year					No.
1950:		#1	#2	#3	(3)

[continues in Volume II]

Futuristic Stories

Publisher: Hamilton & Co., London.

Editor: Dennis H. Pratt.

Year			No.
1946:	#1	#2	(2)

Galaxy Science Fiction

Publisher: World Editions, New York, October 1950–September 1951.

Editor: Horace L. Gold, October 1950–October 1961.

Year				No.
1950:	Oct	Nov	Dec	(3)

[continues in Volume II]

Imagination

Publisher: Clark Publishing, Evanston, Illinois, October–December 1950.

Editor: William L. Hamling.

Year			No.
1950:	Oct	Dec	(2)

[continues in Volume II]

Jungle Stories

Publisher: Fiction House, New York.

Editor: Malcolm Reiss, Winter 1939–Winter 1949; Jerome Bixby, Spring 1949–Spring 1954.

Year						No.
1938:					Win*	(1)
1939:			Sum	Fall	Win*	(4)
1940:		Spr	Sum	Fall	Win*	(8)
1941:		Spr	Sum	Fall	Win*	(12)
1942:		Spr	Sum	Fall	Win*	(16)
1943:	Feb	Apr	Sum	Fall	Win*	(21)
1944:		Spr	Sum	Fall	Win*	(25)
1945:		Spr	Sum	Fall	Win*	(29)
1946:		Spr	Sum	Fall	Win*	(33)

1947:	Spr	Sum	Fall	Win* (37)
1948:	Spr	Sum	Fall	Win* (41)
1949:	Spr	Sum	Fall	Win* (45)
1950:	Spr	Sum	Fall	Win* (49)

*all Winter issues appeared in December but are dated the following year, e.g. Winter 1939
appeared in December 1938.

[continues in Volume II]

Ka-Zar
Final issue retitled Ka-Zar the Great.
Publisher: Manvis Publications, New York.
Editor: Charles Goodman.

1936:			Oct	(1)
1937: Jan		Jun		(3)

Magazine of Fantasy see *Magazine of Fantasy and Science Fiction*

The Magazine of Fantasy and Science Fiction
First issue only entitled Magazine of Fantasy.
Publisher: Fantasy House, a subsidiary of Mercury Press, New York, Fall 1949–
February 1958.
Editors: Anthony Boucher and J. Francis McComas, Fall 1949–August 1954.

1949:			Fall		(1)
1950:	Win/Spr	Sum	Fall	Dec	(5)

[continues in Volume II]

The Magic Carpet Magazine see *Oriental Stories*

Marvel Science Stories
Retitled Marvel Tales *from December 1939 and* Marvel Stories *from November 1940.*
Publisher: Western Publishing, New York.
Editor: Robert O. Erisman.

1938:			Aug	Nov	(2)
1939:	Feb	Apr/May	Aug	Dec	(6)
1940:		May		Nov	(8)
1941:		Apr *(publication suspended)*			(9)
1950:			*(publication revived)* Nov		(10)

[continues in Volume II]

Marvel Stories see *Marvel Science Stories*

Marvel Tales
Semi-professional magazine; not to be confused with the later retitling of Marvel Science
Stories.
Publisher: Fantasy Publications, Everett, Pennsylvania.
Editor: William L. Crawford.

1934:		May	Jul	Win	(3)
1935:	Mar	Sum			(5)

Marvel Tales see *Marvel Science Stories*

Mind Magic
Retitled My Self *for final two issues.*

Publisher: Shade Publishing, Philadelphia.
Editor: G.R. Bay.

1931:   Jun Jul Aug Sep/Oct Nov Dec (6)

Miracle Science and Fantasy Stories
Publisher: Good Story Magazine, New York.
Editors: Elliott and Douglas Dold.

1931:   Apr/May Jun/Jul   (2)

My Self see *Mind Magic*

The Mysterious Wu Fang
Publisher: Popular Publications, New York.
Editor-in-Chief: Rogers Terrill.
Editor: Edythe Seims.

1935:   Sep   Oct Nov Dec. (4)
1936: Jan Feb Mar   (7)

New Worlds
Publisher: Pendulum Publications, London, first three issues; Nova Publications, London, #4–April 1964.
Editor: John Carnell, #1–April 1964.

1946:   #1   #2   (2)
1947:   #3   (3)
1948:   (3)
1949:   #4   #5   (5)
1950:   Spr   Sum   Win   (8)

[continues in Volume II]

The Octopus
This was a continuation of the non-fantasy Western Raider. *See also* The Scorpion.
Publisher: Popular Publications.
Editor-in-Chief: Rogers Terrill
Editors: Ejler and Edith Jakobsson.

1939:   Feb/Mar   (1)

Operator #5
Publisher: Popular Publications, New York.
Editor-in-Chief: Rogers Terrill.
Editor: Henry Sperry.

1934:   Apr May Jun Jul Aug Sep Oct Nov Dec (9)
1935: Jan Feb Mar Apr May Jun Jul Aug Sep Oct Nov Dec (21)
1936: Jan Feb Mar Apr   Jun   Aug   Oct   Dec (29)
1937: Jan Feb Mar/Apr May/Jun Jul/Aug Sep/Oct Nov/Dec (36)
1938: Jan/Feb Mar/Apr May/Jun Jul/Aug Sep/Oct Nov/Dec (42)
1939: Jan/Feb Mar/Apr May/Jun Jul/Aug Sep/Oct Nov/Dec (48)

Oriental Stories
Retitled The Magic Carpet Magazine *from January 1933.*
Publisher: Popular Fiction Company, Chicago.
Editor: Farnsworth Wright.

1930:   Oct/Nov Dec/Jan (2)
1931:   Feb/Mar Apr/May/Jun Sum   Aut   (6)

1932:	Win	Spr	Sum				(9)
1933:	Jan	Apr	Jul	Oct			(13)
1934:	Jan						(14)

Other Worlds Science Stories
Publisher: Clark Publishing, Evanston, Illinois, November 1949–July 1953.
Editor-in-Chief: Raymond A. Palmer, all issues.
Editor: Bea Mahaffey, May 1950–November 1955.

1949:						Nov	(1)
1950:	Jan	Mar	May	Jul	Sep Oct Nov		(8)

[continues in Volume II]

Out of this World Adventures
Publisher: Avon Periodicals, New York.
Editor: Donald A. Wollheim.

1950:		Jul		Dec	(2)

Outlands
Publisher: Outlands Publications, Liverpool.
Editor: Leslie J. Johnson.

1946:		Win		(1)

Planet Stories
Publisher: Love Romances, New York.
Editor-in-Chief: Malcolm Reiss, all issues.
Editor: Wilbur S. Peacock, Fall 1942–Fall 1945; Chester Whitehorn, Winter 1945–Summer 1946; Paul L. Payne, Fall 1946–Spring 1950; Jerome Bixby, Summer 1950–July 1951.

1939:				Win	(1)
1940:	Spr	Sum	Fall	Win	(5)
1941:	Spr	Sum	Fall	Win	(9)
1942:	Spr	Sum	Fall	Win	(13)
1943:	Spr	Sum	Fall	Win	(17)
1944:	Spr	Sum	Fall	Win	(21)
1945:	Spr	Sum	Fall	Win	(25)
1946:	Spr	Sum	Fall	Win	(29)
1947:	Spr	Sum	Fall	Win	(33)
1948:	Spr	Sum	Fall	Win	(37)
1949:	Spr	Sum	Fall	Win	(41)
1950:	Spr	Sum	Fall	Nov	(45)

[continues in Volume II]

Science-Fantasy
Publisher: Nova Publications, Summer 1950–April 1964.
Editor: Walter Gillings, Summer–Winter 1950.

1950:		Sum	Win	(2)

[continues in Volume II]

Science Fiction
The first series of this magazine was merged with Future Fiction *in October 1941. That magazine was retitled* Science Fiction Stories *in April 1943 but those issues are really a continuation of Future and not this magazine.*

Publisher: Columbia Publications, New York.
Editor: Charles D. Hornig.

1939:		Mar	Jun	Aug	Oct	Dec	(5)
1940:		Mar	Jun		Oct		(8)
1941:	Jan	Mar	Jun	Sep			(12)

[continues in Volume II]

Science Fiction [Canadian edition]

Consists of reprints from the American Science Fiction, Future Fiction and Science Fiction Quarterly.
Publisher: Superior Magazines, Toronto, October–November 1941; Duchess Printing and Publishing, Toronto, January–June 1942.
Editor: William Brown-Forbes.

1941:					Oct	Nov	(2)
1942:	Jan Feb	Mar		Jun			(6)

Science Fiction Quarterly

Publisher: Columbia Publications, New York.
Editor: Charles D. Hornig, Summer 1940–Winter 1941; Robert W. Lowndes, Spring 1941–Spring 1943.

1940:			Sum		(1)
1941:	Win	Spr	Sum	Win	(5)
1942:		Spr	Sum	Fall	Win	(9)
1943:		Spr			(10)

[continues in Volume II]

Science Wonder Quarterly see *Wonder Stories Quarterly*

Science Wonder Stories see *Wonder Stories*

Scientific Detective Monthly

Retitled Amazing Detective Tales *from June 1930. Revived in May 1931 as* Amazing Detective Stories *but this was a non-sf/fantasy magazine.*
Publisher: Techni-Craft Publishing, a subsidiary of Stellar Publishing, New York.
Editor-in-Chief: Hugo Gernsback, all issues.
Managing Editor: Hector Grey, January–June 1930; David Lasser, July–October 1930.

1930:	Jan Feb Mar Apr May Jun Jul Aug Sep Oct	(10)

Scoops

A weekly magazine with 20 issues from 10 February to 23 June 1934.
Publisher: C.A. Pearson, London.
Editor: Haydn Dimmock.

The Scorpion

A continuation of The Octopus.
Publisher: Popular Publications.
Editor-in-Chief: Rogers Terrill
Editors: Ejler and Edith Jakobsson.

1939:		Apr/May		(1)

The Shadow

Really a crime mystery magazine and only borderline sf in some issues, but it was the first hero pulp and as such highly influential. From October 1932–February 1943 (issues marked*) the magazine appeared twice-monthly, dated 1st and 15th.

Publisher: Street and Smith, New York.

Editor: Frank Blackwell, April 1931–March 1932 (with main editorial duties handled by Lon Murray); John Nanovic, April 1932–November 1943; Charles Moran, December 1943–May 1944; Babette Rosmond, June 1944–June/July 1948; William DeGrouchy, August/September 1948; Daisy Bacon, Fall 1948–Summer 1949.

1931:			Apr			Jul/Sep			Oct	Nov	Dec	(5)
1932:	Jan	Feb	Mar	Apr	May	Jun	Jul	Aug	Sep	Oct*	Nov*	Dec* (20)
1933:	Jan*	Feb*	Mar*	Apr*	May*	Jun*	Jul*	Aug*	Sep*	Oct*	Nov*	Dec* (44)
1934:	Jan*	Feb*	Mar*	Apr*	May*	Jun*	Jul*	Aug*	Sep*	Oct*	Nov*	Dec* (68)
1935:	Jan*	Feb*	Mar*	Apr*	May*	Jun*	Jul*	Aug*	Sep*	Oct*	Nov*	Dec* (92)
1936:	Jan*	Feb*	Mar*	Apr*	May*	Jun*	Jul*	Aug*	Sep*	Oct*	Nov*	Dec* (116)
1937:	Jan*	Feb*	Mar*	Apr*	May*	Jun*	Jul*	Aug*	Sep*	Oct*	Nov*	Dec* (140)
1938:	Jan*	Feb*	Mar*	Apr*	May*	Jun*	Jul*	Aug*	Sep*	Oct*	Nov*	Dec* (164)
1939:	Jan*	Feb*	Mar*	Apr*	May*	Jun*	Jul*	Aug*	Sep*	Oct*	Nov*	Dec* (188)
1940:	Jan*	Feb*	Mar*	Apr*	May*	Jun*	Jul*	Aug*	Sep*	Oct*	Nov*	Dec* (212)
1941:	Jan*	Feb*	Mar*	Apr*	May*	Jun*	Jul*	Aug*	Sep*	Oct*	Nov*	Dec* (236)
1942:	Jan*	Feb*	Mar*	Apr*	May*	Jun*	Jul*	Aug*	Sep*	Oct*	Nov*	Dec* (260)
1943:	Jan*	Feb*	Mar	Apr	May	Jun	Jul	Aug	Sep	Oct	Nov	Dec (274)
1944:	Jan	Feb	Mar	Apr	May	Jun	Jul	Aug	Sep	Oct	Nov	Dec (286)
1945:	Jan	Feb	Mar	Apr	May	Jun	Jul	Aug	Sep	Oct	Nov	Dec (298)
1946:	Jan	Feb	Mar	Apr	May	Jun	Jul	Aug	Sep	Oct	Nov	Dec (310)
1947:	Jan	Feb/Mar		Apr/May		Jun/Jul		Aug/Sep		Oct/Nov	Dec/Jan	(317)
1948:	Feb/Mar			Apr/May		Jun/Jul		Aug/Sep		Fall		(322)
1949:	Win		Spr			Sum						(325)

The Spider

A hero-pulp magazine that was sufficiently grotesque to be considered borderline sf.

Publisher: Popular Publications, New York.

Editor-in-Chief: Rogers Terrill.

1933:										Oct	Nov	Dec (3)
1934:	Jan	Feb	Mar	Apr	May	Jun	Jul	Aug	Sep	Oct	Nov	Dec (15)
1935:	Jan	Feb	Mar	Apr	May	Jun	Jul	Aug	Sep	Oct	Nov	Dec (27)
1936:	Jan	Feb	Mar	Apr	May	Jun	Jul	Aug	Sep	Oct	Nov	Dec (39)
1937:	Jan	Feb	Mar	Apr	May	Jun	Jul	Aug	Sep	Oct	Nov	Dec (51)
1938:	Jan	Feb	Mar	Apr	May	Jun	Jul	Aug	Sep	Oct	Nov	Dec (63)
1939:	Jan	Feb	Mar	Apr	May	Jun	Jul	Aug	Sep	Oct	Nov	Dec (75)
1940:	Jan	Feb	Mar	Apr	May	Jun	Jul	Aug	Sep	Oct	Nov	Dec (87)
1941:	Jan	Feb	Mar	Apr	May	Jun	Jul	Aug	Sep	Oct	Nov	Dec (99)
1942:	Jan	Feb	Mar	Apr	May	Jun	Jul	Aug	Sep	Oct	Nov	Dec (111)
1943:	Jan	Feb	Mar			Jun		Aug		Oct		Dec (118)

Stardust

Semi-professional magazine.

Publisher and editor: William L. Hamling, Chicago.

1940:		Mar	May		Aug	Sep	Nov	(5)

Startling Stories
Publisher: Better Publications, a subsidiary of Standard Magazines, January 1939–Fall 1955.
Editor: Mort Weisinger, January 1939–May 1941; Oscar J. Friend, July 1941–Fall 1944; Samuel Merwin, Winter 1945–September 1951.

1939:	Jan	Mar	May	Jul	Sep	Nov		(6)
1940:	Jan	Mar	May	Jul	Sep	Nov		(12)
1941:	Jan	Mar	May	Jul	Sep	Nov		(18)
1942:	Jan	Mar	May	Jul	Sep	Nov		(24)
1943:	Jan	Mar		Jun		Fall		Win	(29)
1944:		Spr		Sum		Fall		Win	(33)
1945:		Spr		Sum		Fall		Win	(37)
1946:		Mar	Spr	Sum		Fall		(41)
1947:	Jan	Mar	May	Jul	Sep	Nov		(47)
1948:	Jan	Mar	May	Jul	Sep	Nov		(53)
1949:	Jan	Mar	May	Jul	Sep	Nov		(59)
1950:	Jan	Mar	May	Jul	Sep	Nov		(65)

[continues in Volume II]

Stirring Science Stories
Publisher: Albing Publications, New York, February–June 1941; Manhattan Fiction Publications, March 1942.
Editor: Donald A. Wollheim.

1941:	Feb	Apr	Jun	(3)
1942:	Mar			(4)

Strange Adventures
First issue entitled Amazing Adventures *on the contents page.*
Publisher: Hamilton & Co., London.
Editor: Dennis H. Pratt.

1946:	#1	(1)
1947: #2		(2)

Strange Love Stories
A hybrid reprint unnumbered booklet/magazine.
Publisher: Utopian Publications, London.
Editors: Benson Herbert and Walter Gillings.

1946:	(#1)	(1)

Strange Stories
Publisher: Better Publications, a subsidiary of Standard Magazines, New York.
Editor-in-Chief: Leo Margulies.
Editor: Mort Weisinger.

1939:	Feb	Apr	Jun	Aug	Oct	Dec	(6)
1940:	Feb	Apr	Jun	Aug	Oct	Dec	(12)
1941:	Feb						(13)

Strange Tales
Sometimes referred to in full as Strange Tales of Mystery and Terror.
Publisher: Clayton Magazines, New York.
Editor: Harry Bates.

1931:				Sep	Nov		(2)
1932:	Jan	Mar	Jun		Oct		(6)
1933:	Jan						(7)

Strange Tales
A hybrid reprint unnumbered magazine/booklet.
Publisher: Utopian Publications, London.
Editor: Walter Gillings.

1946:	#1	#2	(2)

Super Science and Fantastic Stories see *Super Science Stories* [Canadian]

Super Science Novels Magazine see *Super Science Stories*

Super Science Stories
Retitled Super Science Novels Magazine *from March 1941 to August 1941 then reverted to* Super Science Stories.
Publisher: Fictioneers, Inc., a subsidiary of Popular Publications, New York, March 1940–May 1943; Popular Publications, New York, January 1949–August 1951.
Editor-in-Chief: Rogers Terrill March 1940–May 1943; Alden H. Norton, January 1949–August 1951.
Editor: Frederik Pohl, March 1940–August 1941; Alden H. Norton, November 1941–May 1943; Ejler Jakobsson, January 1949–August 1951.

1940:		Mar	May	Jul	Sep	Nov	(5)
1941:	Jan	Mar	May		Aug	Nov	(10)
1942:		Feb		May		Aug	Nov	(14)
1943:		Feb		May *(publication suspended)*			(16)
1949:	Jan		Apr		Jul	Sep	Nov	(21)
1950:	Jan		Mar	May	Jul	Sep	Nov	(27)
1951:	Jan		Apr		Jun	Aug		(31)

Super Science Stories [Canadian]
A Canadian continuation of the US Super Science Stories *printing several original stories and reprinting from other Popular Publications magazines. Retitled* Super Science and Fantastic Stories *from December 1944.*
Publisher: Popular Publications, Toronto.
Editor: Alden H. Norton.

1942:				Aug	Oct	Dec	(3)
1943:	Feb	Apr	Jun	Aug	Oct	Dec	(9)
1944:	Feb	Apr	Jun	Aug	Oct	Dec	(15)
1945:	Feb	Apr	Jun	Aug	Oct	Dec	(21)

Tales of Magic and Mystery
Publisher: Personal Arts Company, Philadelphia.
Editor: Walter Gibson.

1927:				Dec	(1)
1928:	Jan Feb	Mar Apr			(5)

Tales of Tomorrow
Publisher: John Spencer & Co., London.
Editor: Samuel Assael.

1950:		#1	(1)

[continues in Volume II]

Tales of Wonder
Publisher: The World's Work, Kingswood, Surrey.
Editor: Walter Gillings.

1937:			#1			#2	(2)
1938:			Sum	Aut		Win	(5)
1939:	Spr		Sum	Aut		Win	(9)
1940:	Spr		Sum	Aut			(12)
1941: Win		Spr		Aut			(15)
1942:	Spr						(16)

Terence X. O'Leary's War Birds
This was a continuation of the non-fantasy air-war pulp War Birds.
Publisher: Dell Publishing, New York.
Editor: Carson Mowre.

1935:	Mar Apr May/Jun	(3)

The Thrill Book
Publisher: Street & Smith, New York.
Editor: Harold Hersey, 1 March–15 June 1919; Ronald Oliphant, 1 July–15 October 1919.

1919:	Mar Apr May Jun Jul Aug Sep Oct	(16)
	published on 1st and 15th of each month	

Thrilling Stories
A hybrid reprint unnumbered magazine/booklet.
Publisher: Utopian Publications, London.
Editor: Walter Gillings.

1946: (#1)	(1)

Thrilling Wonder Stories see *Wonder Stories*

Thrills Incorporated
Publisher: Associated General Publications (later Transport Publishing), Sydney.
Editor: uncredited, but probably Alister Innes.

1950:	#1 #2 #3 #4 #5 #6 #7 #8 #9	(9)
		[continues in Volume II]

Two Complete Science-Adventure Books
Publisher: Wings Publishing, a subsidiary of Fiction House, New York.
Editor: Jerome Bixby, Winter 1950–Summer 1951.

1950:	Win	(1)
	[continues in Volume II]	

Uncanny Stories
Publisher: Manvis Publications, New York.
Editor: Robert O. Erisman.

1941:	Apr	(1)

Uncanny Tales [Canadian]
Not to be confused with the American weird-menace pulp of the same name which ran from April/May 1939 to March 1940.
Publisher: Adam Publishing, Toronto, November 1940–May 1942; Norman Book Company, Toronto, July 1942–September/October 1943.

Editor: uncredited, but Melvin R. Colby.

	Jan	Feb	Mar	Apr	May	Jun	Jul	Aug	Sep	Oct	Nov	Dec	
1940:											Nov	Dec	(2)
1941:	Jan		Mar		May	Jun	Jul	Aug	Sep	Oct	Nov	Dec	(12)
1942:	Jan	Feb	Mar	Apr	May		Jul		Sep			Dec	(20)
1943:									Sep/Oct				(21)

Unknown

Retitled Unknown Worlds *from October 1941.*
Publisher: Street & Smith, New York.
Editor: John W. Campbell, Jr.

	Jan	Feb	Mar	Apr	May	Jun	Jul	Aug	Sep	Oct	Nov	Dec	
1939:			Mar	Apr	May	Jun	Jul	Aug	Sep	Oct	Nov	Dec	(10)
1940:	Jan	Feb	Mar	Apr	May	Jun	Jul	Aug	Sep	Oct	Nov	Dec	(22)
1941:		Feb		Apr		Jun		Aug		Oct		Dec	(28)
1942:		Feb		Apr		Jun		Aug		Oct		Dec	(34)
1943:		Feb		Apr		Jun		Aug		Oct			(39)

Unusual Stories

Semi-professional magazine companion to Marvel Tales.
Publisher: Fantasy Publications, Everett, Pennsylvania.
Editor: William L. Crawford.

	Mar	May/Jun	Win	
1934:	Mar (*advance flyer*)			(1)
1935:		May/Jun	Win	(3)

The Vortex

Semi-professional magazine.
Publisher: Fansci Pubafi, San Francisco.
Editors: Gordon M. Kull and George R. Cowie.

	#1	#2	
1947:	#1	#2	(2)

Weird Tales

Publisher: Rural Publications, Chicago, March 1923–May/June/July 1924; Popular Fiction Publishing, Chicago, November 1924–October 1938; Weird Tales, Inc., a subsidiary of Short Stories, Inc., New York, November 1938–September 1954.
Editor: Edwin Baird, March 1923–April 1924; Jacob Henneberger and Otis Adelbert Kline, May/June/July 1924; Farnsworth Wright, November 1924–March 1940; Dorothy McIlwraith, May 1940–September 1954 (assisted by Lamont Buchanan, November 1942–September 1949).

	Jan	Feb	Mar	Apr	May	Jun	Jul	Aug	Sep	Oct	Nov	Dec	
1923:			Mar	Apr	May	Jun	Jul/Aug		Sep	Oct	Nov		(8)
1924:	Jan	Feb	Mar	Apr	May/Jun/Jul						Nov	Dec	(15)
1925:	Jan	Feb	Mar	Apr	May	Jun	Jul	Aug	Sep	Oct	Nov	Dec	(27)
1926:	Jan	Feb	Mar	Apr	May	Jun	Jul	Aug	Sep	Oct	Nov	Dec	(39)
1927:	Jan	Feb	Mar	Apr	May	Jun	Jul	Aug	Sep	Oct	Nov	Dec	(51)
1928:	Jan	Feb	Mar	Apr	May	Jun	Jul	Aug	Sep	Oct	Nov	Dec	(63)
1929:	Jan	Feb	Mar	Apr	May	Jun	Jul	Aug	Sep	Oct	Nov	Dec	(75)
1930:	Jan	Feb	Mar	Apr	May	Jun	Jul	Aug	Sep	Oct	Nov	Dec	(87)
1931:	Jan	Feb/Mar		Apr/May		Jun/Jul		Aug	Sep	Oct	Nov	Dec	(96)
1932:	Jan	Feb	Mar	Apr	May	Jun	Jul	Aug	Sep	Oct	Nov	Dec	(108)
1933:	Jan	Feb	Mar	Apr	May	Jun	Jul	Aug	Sep	Oct	Nov	Dec	(120)
1934:	Jan	Feb	Mar	Apr	May	Jun	Jul	Aug	Sep	Oct	Nov	Dec	(132)
1935:	Jan	Feb	Mar	Apr	May	Jun	Jul	Aug	Sep	Oct	Nov	Dec	(144)
1936:	Jan	Feb	Mar	Apr	May	Jun	Jul	Aug/Sep		Oct	Nov	Dec	(155)

Year	Jan	Feb	Mar	Apr	May	Jun	Jul	Aug	Sep	Oct	Nov	Dec	
1937:	Jan	Feb	Mar	Apr	May	Jun	Jul	Aug	Sep	Oct	Nov	Dec	(167)
1938:	Jan	Feb	Mar	Apr	May	Jun	Jul	Aug	Sep	Oct	Nov	Dec	(179)
1939:	Jan	Feb	Mar	Apr	May	Jun/Jul		Aug	Sep	Oct	Nov	Dec	(190)
1940:	Jan		Mar		May		Jul		Sep		Nov		(196)
1941:	Jan		Mar		May		Jul		Sep		Nov		(202)
1942:	Jan		Mar		May		Jul		Sep		Nov		(208)
1943:	Jan		Mar		May		Jul		Sep		Nov		(214)
1944:	Jan		Mar		May		Jul		Sep		Nov		(220)
1945:	Jan		Mar		May		Jul		Sep		Nov		(226)
1946:	Jan		Mar		May		Jul		Sep		Nov		(232)
1947:	Jan		Mar		May		Jul		Sep		Nov		(238)
1948:	Jan		Mar		May		Jul		Sep		Nov		(244)
1949:	Jan		Mar		May		Jul		Sep		Nov		(250)
1950:	Jan		Mar		May		Jul		Sep		Nov		(256)

[continues in Volume II]

The Witch's Tales

Publisher: Carwood Publishing, New York.
Editor: Tom Chadburn.

Year	Nov	Dec	
1936:	Nov	Dec	(2)

Wonder Stories

Began as Science Wonder Stories, *June 1929–May 1930; retitled* Thrilling Wonder Stories, *August 1936–Winter 1955.*
Publisher: Stellar Publishing Corporation, New York, June 1929–October 1933; Continental Publications, New York, November 1933–March/April 1936; Standard Magazines, New York, August 1936–Winter 1955.
Editor-in-Chief: Hugo Gernsback, June 1929–March/April 1936; Leo Margulies, August 1936–Fall 1944.
Editor: David Lasser, June 1929–October 1933; Charles D. Hornig, November 1933–March/April 1936; Mort Weisinger, August 1936–June 1941; Oscar J. Friend, August 1941–Fall 1944; Samuel Merwin, Winter 1945–October 1951.

Year	Jan	Feb	Mar	Apr	May	Jun	Jul	Aug	Sep	Oct	Nov	Dec	
1929:						Jun	Jul	Aug	Sep	Oct	Nov	Dec	(7)
1930:	Jan	Feb	Mar	Apr	May	Jun	Jul	Aug	Sep	Oct	Nov	Dec	(19)
1931:	Jan	Feb	Mar	Apr	May	Jun	Jul	Aug	Sep	Oct	Nov	Dec	(31)
1932:	Jan	Feb	Mar	Apr	May	Jun	Jul	Aug	Sep	Oct	Nov	Dec	(43)
1933:	Jan	Feb	Mar	Apr	May	Jun		Aug		Oct	Nov	Dec	(53)
1934:	Jan	Feb	Mar	Apr	May	Jun	Jul	Aug	Sep	Oct	Nov	Dec	(65)
1935:	Jan	Feb	Mar	Apr	May	Jun	Jul	Aug	Sep	Oct	Nov/Dec		(76)
1936:	Jan/Feb		Mar/Apr					Aug		Oct		Dec	(81)
1937:		Feb		Apr		Jun		Aug		Oct		Dec	(87)
1938:		Feb		Apr		Jun		Aug		Oct		Dec	(93)
1939:		Feb		Apr		Jun		Aug		Oct		Dec	(99)
1940:	Jan	Feb	Mar	Apr	May	Jun	Jul	Aug	Sep	Oct	Nov	Dec	(111)
1941:	Jan	Feb	Mar	Apr		Jun		Aug		Oct		Dec	(119)
1942:		Feb		Apr		Jun		Aug		Oct		Dec	(125)
1943:		Feb		Apr		Jun		Aug			Fall		(130)
1944:		Win			Spr			Sum			Fall		(134)
1945:		Win			Spr			Sum			Fall		(138)
1946:		Win		Spr			Sum			Fall		Dec	(143)

1947:	Feb	Apr	Jun	Aug	Oct	Dec (149)
1948:	Feb	Apr	Jun	Aug	Oct	Dec (155)
1949:	Feb	Apr	Jun	Aug	Oct	Dec (161)
1950:	Feb	Apr	Jun	Aug	Oct	Dec (167)
						[continues in Volume II]

Wonder Stories Quarterly

First three issues entitled Science Wonder Quarterly.
Publisher: Stellar Publishing Corporation, New York.
Editor-in-Chief: Hugo Gernsback.
Editor: David Lasser.

1929:				Fall	(1)
1930:	Win	Spr	Sum	Fall	(5)
1931:	Win	Spr	Sum	Fall	(9)
1932:	Win	Spr	Sum	Fall	(13)
1933:	Win				(14)

Wonder Story Annual

Publisher: Better Publications, a subsidiary of Standard Magazines, New York.
Editor: Sam Merwin, 1950–51.

| 1950: | #1 | (1) |
| | | *[continues in Volume II]* |

Worlds Beyond

Publisher: Hillman Periodicals, New York.
Editor: Damond Knight.

| 1950: | | Dec | (1) |
| 1951: | Jan Feb | | (3) |

Worlds of Fantasy

Not to be confused with the subsequent fantasy magazine issued in 1968.
Publisher: John Spencer & Co., London.
Editor: Samuel Assael.

| 1950: | #1 | #2 | (2) |
| | | | *[continues in Volume II]* |

Yankee Science Fiction

Science fiction issues of Swan Yankee Magazine.
Publisher and Editor: Gerald G. Swan, London.

| 1942: | #3 | #11 | #21 | (3) |

APPENDIX 3
Directory of Magazine Editors and Publishers

This appendix lists all the editors and publishers of the science-fiction magazines covered by this volume. The cut-off date is December 1950, though where magazines continue beyond that date the last issue of the individual's tenure is given.

Albing, Jerry
Publisher: *Cosmic Stories*, March–July 1941 (3 issues); *Stirring Science Stories*, February 1941–March 1942 (4 issues).

Assael, Harry
Publisher of Hamilton & Co., responsible for *Futuristic Stories* and *Strange Adventures*, 1946–47.

Assael, Samuel
Co-publisher and editor: *Futuristic Science Stories*, 1950–58 (16 issues); *Worlds of Fantasy*, 1950–54 (14 issues); *Tales of Tomorrow*, 1950–54 (11 issues).

Bacon, Daisy
Editor: *The Shadow*, Fall 1948–Summer 1949 (4 issues); *Doc Savage*, Winter–Summer 1949 (3 issues).

Baird, Edwin
Editor: *Weird Tales*, March 1923–April 1924 (12 issues).

Bates, Harry
Editor: *Astounding Stories*, January 1930–March 1933 (34 issues); *Strange Tales*, September 1931–January 1933 (7 issues).

Bay, G.R.
Editor: *Mind Magic/My Self*, June–December 1931 (6 issues).

Bixby, Jerome
Editor: *Jungle Stories*, Spring 1949–Spring 1954 (18 issues); *Planet Stories*, Summer 1950–July 1951 (7 issues); *Two Complete Science-Adventure Books*, Winter 1950–Summer 1951 (2 issues).

Blackwell, Frank
Editor-in-Chief: *The Shadow*, April 1931–March 1932 (8 issues).

Boardman, Tom V.
Probable editor of the British reprint *Cosmic Science Stories*, 1950 (1 issue).

Boucher, Anthony
Editor: *Magazine of Fantasy and Science Fiction*, Fall 1949–August 1958 (87 issues – joint with J. Francis McComas till August 1954).

Bourne, Miriam
Assistant/Managing Editor: *Amazing Stories*, November 1929–November 1932 (37 issues); *Amazing Stories Quarterly*, Winter 1930–Spring/Summer 1933 (12 issues).

Brown-Forbes, William
Editor: *Science Fiction* (Canadian), October 1941–June 1942 (6 issues).

Browne, Howard
Associate Editor: *Amazing Stories*, January 1943–October 1947 (38 issues); *Fantastic Adventures*, December 1942–January 1947 (26 issues). Managing Editor/Editor-in-Chief: *Amazing Stories*, January 1950–August 1956 (76 issues); *Fantastic Adventures*, March–October 1947; January 1950–March 1953 (44 issues).

Buchanan, Lamont
Associate Editor: *Weird Tales*, November 1942–September 1949 (42 issues).

Campbell, Jr., John W.
Editor: *Astounding Stories* (later *Astounding SF* and then *Analog*), December 1937–December 1971 (409 issues); *Unknown/Unknown Worlds*, March 1939–October 1943 (39 issues).

Carnell, John
Editor: *New Worlds*, 1946–April 1964 (141 issues).

Cerutti, Vera
Editor-in-Chief: *Galaxy*, October 1950–November 1951 (14 issues).

Chadburn, Tom
Editor: *The Witch's Tales*, November–December 1936 (2 issues).

Clayton, William M.
Publisher of Clayton Magazines, including: *Astounding Stories*, January 1930–March 1933 (34 issues); *Strange Tales*, September 1931–January 1933 (7 issues).

Colby, Melvin
Editor: *Uncanny Tales* [Canadian], November 1940–September/ October 1943 (21 issues); *Eerie Tales*, July 1941 (1 issue).

Cowie, George R.
Co-editor: *The Vortex*, 1947 (2 issues).

Crawford, William L.
Editor: *Unusual Stories*, March 1934–Winter 1935 (3 issues); *Marvel Tales*, May 1934–Summer 1935 (5 issues); *Fantasy Book*, 1947–51 (8 issues).

Davis, Bernard G.
Editor-in-Chief: *Amazing Stories*, June 1938–February 1947 (83 issues); *Fantastic Adventures*, May 1939–January 1947 (59 issues).

DeGrouchy, William
Editor: *Doc Savage*, July/August–September/October 1948 (92 issues); *The Shadow*, August/September 1948 (1 issue).

Derleth, August W.
Editor: *The Arkham Sampler*, Winter 1948–Autumn 1949 (8 issues).

Dimmock, Haydn
Editor: *Scoops*, 10 February–23 June 1934.

Dold, Elliot and Douglas
Editors: *Miracle Science and Fantasy Stories*, April/May–June/July 1931 (2 issues).

Erisman, Robert O.
Editor: *Marvel Science Stories*, August 1938–May 1952 (15 issues); *Dynamic Science Stories*, February–April/May 1939 (2 issues); *Uncanny Stories*, April 1941 (1 issue).

Ferman, Joseph W.
General Manager: *Magazine of Fantasy and Science Fiction*, Fall 1949–July 1954 (38 issues).

Friend, Oscar J.
Editor: *Thrilling Wonder Stories*, August 1941-Fall 1944 (18 issues); *Startling Stories*, July 1941–Fall 1944 (17 issues); *Captain Future*, Fall 1941–Spring 1944 (10 issues).

Gernsback, Hugo
Publisher and Editor-in-Chief: *Amazing Stories*, April 1926–April 1929 (37 issues); *Amazing Stories Annual*, 1927 (1 issue); *Amazing*

Stories Quarterly, Winter 1928–Spring 1929 (6 issues); *(Science) Wonder Stories*, June 1929–March/April 1936 (78 issues); *Air Wonder Stories*, July 1929–May 1930 (11 issues); *Science Wonder Quarterly/ Wonder Stories Quarterly*, Fall 1929–Winter 1933 (14 issues); *Scientific Detective Monthly/Amazing Detective Tales*, January–October 1930 (10 issues).

Gibson, Walter
Editor: *Tales of Magic and Mystery*, December 1927–April 1928 (5 issues).

Gillings, Walter H.
Editor: *Tales of Wonder*, (Summer) 1937–Spring 1942 (16 issues); *Thrilling Stories*, 1946 (1 issue); *Strange Tales*, 1946 (2 issues); *Strange Love Stories*, 1946 (1 issue); *Fantasy*, December 1946–August 1947 (3 issues); *Science-Fantasy*, Summer–Winter 1950 (2 issues).

Gnaedinger, Mary
Editor: *Famous Fantastic Mysteries*, September/October 1939–June 1953 (81 issues); *Fantastic Novels*, July 1940–June 1951 (25 issues).

Gold, Horace L.
Editor: *Galaxy*, October 1950–October 1961 (115 issues).

Goodman, Abraham and Martin
Publishers of Manvis Publications and Western Publishing whose titles included *Ka-Zar*, *Marvel Science Stories*, *Dynamic Science Stories*, *Uncanny Stories*,

Goodman, Charles
Editor: *Ka-Zar*, October 1936–June 1937 (3 issues).

Grey, Hector
Editor: *Scientific Detective Monthly*, January–June 1930 (6 issues).

Hamling, William Lawrence
Publisher and editor: *Stardust*, March–November 1950 (5 issues); *Imagination*, October 1950–October 1958 (63 issues).
Assistant/Managing Editor: *Amazing Stories*, March 1947–February 1951 (48 issues); *Fantastic Adventures*, November 1947–February 1951 (40 issues).

Henneberger, Jacob Clark
Publisher: *Weird Tales*, March 1923–October 1938 (177 issues); *Oriental Stories/Magic Carpet Magazine*, October/November 1930– January 1934 (14 issues).

Herbert, Benson
Publisher of Utopian Publications, including *Thrilling Stories*, 1946 (1 issue); *Strange Tales*, 1946 (2 issues); *Strange Love Stories*, 1946 (1 issue).

Hersey, Harold
Editor: *The Thrill Book*, 1 March–15 June 1919 (8 issues).
Publisher: *Miracle Science and Fantasy Stories*, April/May–June/July 1931 (2 issues); *Flash Gordon Strange Adventure Magazine*, December 1936 (1 issue).

Hornig, Charles D.
Editor: *Wonder Stories*, November 1933–March/April 1936 (27 issues); *Science Fiction*, March 1939–September 1941 (12 issues); *Future Fiction*, November 1939–November 1940 (4 issues).

Innes, Alister
Editor: *Thrills Incorporated*, 1950–52 (23 issues).

Jakobsson, Ejler
Editor: *The Octopus*, February/March 1939 (1 issue); *The Scorpion*, April 1939 (1); *Super Science Stories*, January 1949–August 1951 (15 issues).

Johnson, Leslie J.
Editor: *Outlands*, Winter 1946 (1 issue).

Kline, Otis Adlebert
Assisted in the compilation of the May/June/July 1924 *Weird Tales*.

Knight, Damon
Editor: *Worlds Beyond*, December 1950–February 1951 (3 issues).

Kull, Gordon M.
Co-editor: *The Vortex*, 1947 (2 issues).

Lasser, David
Editor: (*Science*) *Wonder Stories*, June 1929–October 1933 (51 issues); *Air Wonder Stories*, July 1929–May 1930 (11 issues); *Science Wonder Quarterly/Wonder Stories Quarterly*, Fall 1929–Winter 1933 (14 issues); *Amazing Detective Tales*, July–October 1930 (4 issues).

Lowndes, Robert W.
Editor: *Future Fiction*, April 1941–July 1943 (13 issues); *Science Fiction Quarterly*, Spring 1941–Spring 1943 (8 issues); *Future (combined with) Science Fiction*, May/June 1950–April 1960 (48 issues).

Lynch, Arthur H.
Nominally editor-in-chief of *Amazing Stories*, May–October 1929 (6 issues) and *Amazing Stories Quarterly*, Summer-Fall 1929 (2 issues).

McComas, J. Francis
Co-editor: *Magazine of Fantasy and Science Fiction*, Fall 1949–August 1954 (39 issues).

McIlwraith, Dorothy
Editor: *Weird Tales*, May 1940–September 1954 (87 issues).

Mahaffey, Bea
Editor: *Other Worlds Science Stories*, May 1950–November 1955 (32 issues).

Margulies, Leo
Editorial Director at Standard Magazines, 1932–51, with overall responsibility for *Thrilling Wonder Stories*, *Startling Stories*, *Strange Stories*, *Captain Future*, *Fantastic Story Quarterly*, *Wonder Story Annual*.

Merwin, Samuel
Editor: *Startling Stories*, Winter 1945–September 1951 (33 issues); *Thrilling Wonder Stories*, Winter 1945–October 1951 (38 issues); *Fantastic Story Quarterly*, Spring 1950–Fall 1951 (7 issues); *Wonder Story Annual*, 1950–1951 (2 issues).

Mills, Robert P.
Managing Editor: *Magazine of Fantasy and Science Fiction*, Fall 1949–August 1958 (87 issues).

Mitchell, Curtis
Publisher and Editor: *Fantasy Fiction*, May–November 1950 (2 issues).

Moran, Charles
Editor: *Doc Savage* and *The Shadow*, December 1943–May 1944 (6 issues each)

Mowre, Carson
Editor: *Doctor Death*, February–April 1935 (3 issues); *Terence X. O'Leary's War Birds*, March–May/June 1935 (3 issues).

Munsey, Frank A.
President of the Munsey Corporation that published such pioneering pulp magazines as *The Argosy*, *All-Story* and *Cavalier* and latterly the science-fiction pulps *Famous Fantastic Mysteries* and *Fantastic Novels*.

Murray, Lon
Editor: *The Shadow*, April 1931–March 1932 (8 issues).

Nanovic, John L.
Editor: *The Shadow*, April 1932–November 1943 (265 issues); *Doc Savage*, March 1933–November 1943 (129 issues).

Norton, Alden H.
Supervisory Editor of all Popular Publications magazines, 1944–1955, including *Super Science Stories*, January 1949–August 1951 (15 issues); *Captain Zero*, November 1949–March 1950 (3 issues); *A. Merritt's Fantasy Magazine*, December 1949–October 1950 (5 issues). Editor: *Astonishing Stories*, November 1941–April 1943 (7 issues); *Super Science Stories*, November 1941–May 1943 (7 issues); *Astonishing Stories* [Canadian], January–May 1942 (3 issues); *Super Science Stories* [Canadian], August 1942–December 1945 (21 issues).

Oliphant, Ronald
Editor: *The Thrill Book*, 1 July–15 October 1919 (8 issues).

Palmer, Raymond A.
Managing Editor/Editor-in-Chief: *Amazing Stories*, June 1938–December 1949 (117 issues); *Fantastic Adventures*, May 1939–December 1949 (90 issues); *Other Worlds Science Stories*, November 1949–September/October 1957 (45 issues).

Payne, Paul L.
Editor: *Planet Stories*, Fall 1946–Spring 1950 (14 issues).

Peacock, Wilbur S.
Editor: *Planet Stories*, Fall 1942-Fall 1945 (13 issues).

Pines, Ned
Publisher of Standard Magazines, 1931–1955, including *Thrilling Wonder Stories, Startling Stories, Strange Stories, Captain Future, Fantastic Story Quarterly, Wonder Story Annual*.

Pohl, Frederik
Editor: *Astonishing Stories*, February 1940–September 1941 (9 issues); *Super Science Stories*, March 1940–August 1941 (9 issues).

Pratt, Dennis H.
Editor: *Futuristic Stories*, 1946 (2 issues); *Strange Adventures*, 1946–1947 (2 issues).

Reiss, Malcolm
Editor-in-Chief (later General Manager) at Fiction House, including

editing: *Jungle Stories*, Winter 1939–Winter 1949 (45 issues); *Planet Stories*, Winter 1939–Summer 1955 (71 issues); *Two Complete Science-Adventure Books*, Winter 1950–Spring 1954 (11 issues).

Rosmond, Babette
Editor: *Doc Savage* and *The Shadow*, June 1944–June 1948 (35 issues each).

Seims, Edythe
Editor: *The Mysterious Wu Fang*, September 1935–March 1936 (7 issues); *Dr Yen Sin*, May/June–September/October 1936 (3 issues).

Shepard, Wilson
Co-publisher of *Fanciful Tales*, Fall 1936 (1 issue).

Silberkleit, Louis H.
Publisher of Columbia Publications (and subsidiaries Blue Ribbon Magazines and Double Action Magazines) including magazines *Science Fiction, Future Fiction, Science Fiction Quarterly*.

Sloane, T. O'Conor
(Associate/Managing) Editor: *Amazing Stories,* April 1926–April 1938 (128 issues); *Amazing Stories Annual*, 1927 (1 issue); *Amazing Stories Quarterly*, Winter 1928–Fall 1934 (22 issues). Total issues edited: 151.

Smith, Ormond
President of Street & Smith from 1887 to 1933 and responsible for inaugurating *The Thrill Book* in 1919, launching *The Shadow* in 1931, and the purchase of *Astounding Stories* in 1933.

Sperry, Henry
Editor: *Operator #5*, April 1934–November/December 1939 (48 issues).

Spivak, Lawrence E.
Publisher: *Magazine of Fantasy and Science Fiction*, Fall 1949–July 1954 (38 issues).

Sprigg, T. Stanhope
Editor: *Fantasy*, 1939–1940 (3 issues).

Steeger, Harry
Publisher of Popular Publications magazines from 1930 to 1955. Titles include: *A. Merritt's Fantasy Magazine, Astonishing Stories, Dr Yen Sin, Dusty Ayres and his Battle Birds, Famous Fantastic Mysteries, Fantastic Novels*.

Swan, Gerald G.
Publisher of many British reprint magazines including *Yankee Science Fiction*, 1942 (3 issues).

Terrill, Rogers
Editor-in-Chief of all Popular Publications magazines from 1932 to 1946, including: *The Spider*, October 1933–December 1943 (118 issues); *Operator #5*, April 1934–November/December 1939 (48 issues); *Dusty Ayres and his Battle Birds*, July 1934–July/August 1935 (12 issues); *The Mysterious Wu Fang*, September 1935–March 1936 (7 issues); *Dr Yen Sin*, May/June–September/October 1936 (3 issues); *The Octopus*, February/March 1939 (1 issue); *The Scorpion*, April 1939 (1 issue); *Astonishing Stories*, February 1940–April 1943 (16 issues); *Super Science Stories*, March 1940–May 1943 (16 issues).

Tremaine, Frederick Orlin
Editor: *Astounding Stories*, October 1933–November 1937 (50 issues); *Comet*, December 1940–July 1941 (5 issues).

Weisinger, Mortimer
Editor: *Thrilling Wonder Stories*, August 1936–June 1941 (38 issues); *Startling Stories*, January 1939–May 1941 (15 issues); *Strange Stories*, February 1939–February 1941 (13 issues); *Captain Future*, Winter 1940–Summer 1941 (7 issues).

Whitehorn, Chester
Editor: *Planet Stories*, Winter 1945–Summer 1946 (3 issues).

Widmer, Harry
Editor of Popular Publications' subsidiary company Recreational Reading, including: *Captain Zero*, November 1949–March 1950 (3 issues); *A. Merritt's Fantasy Magazine*, December 1949–October 1950 (5 issues).

Wollheim, Donald A.
Editor: *Fanciful Tales*, Fall 1936 (1 issue); *Cosmic Stories*, March–July 1941 (3 issues); *Stirring Science Stories*, February 1941–March 1942 (4 issues); *Avon Fantasy Reader*, 1947–1952 (18 issues); *Out of this World Adventures*, July–December 1950 (2 issues).

Wright, Farnsworth
Editor: *Weird Tales*, November 1924–March 1940 (179 issues); *Oriental Stories/Magic Carpet Magazine*, October/November 1930–January 1934 (14 issues).

Wyn, Aaron
Publisher of Ace Magazines, including *Captain Hazzard*.

Wyn, Rose
Editor: *Captain Hazzard*, May 1938 (1 issue).

APPENDIX 4
Directory of Magazine Cover Artists

The cover artists are the unsung heroes of the sf magazines for it was their covers that attracted the reader in the first place and their work that often became symbolic of the nature and style of science fiction. Frequently their work was not credited. The following seeks to identify so far as possible all cover artists for the magazines listed in Appendix 2. If an attribution is uncertain it is followed by (?). Where artists collaborate the cover is noted as (joint).

Ainsworth, K.P.
Uncanny Tales (Canadian)
    1942: Mar, Apr, Sep, Dec;
    1943: Sep/Oct.

Alejandro *see* Canedo, Alejandro

Anderson, Allen
Planet Stories
    1942: Win;
    1947: Spr, Sum, Fall, Win;
    1948: Spr, Sum, Fall, Win;
    1949: Spr, Sum, Fall, Win;
    1950: Spr, Sum, Fall, Nov.
Two Complete Science-Adventure Books
    1950: Win.

Austin, Neil
Fantasy Book
1948: #4.

Baumhofer, Walter M.
Doc Savage
    1933: Mar, Apr, May, Jun,
    Jul, Aug, Sep, Oct, Nov, Dec;
    1934: Jan, Feb, Mar, Apr,
    May, Jun, Jul, Aug, Sep, Oct,

Nov, Dec;
    1935: Jan, Feb, Mar, Apr,
    May, Jun, Jul, Aug, Sep, Oct,
    Nov, Dec;
    1936: Jan, Feb, Mar, Apr,
    May, Jun, Jul, Aug, Sep.
The Spider
1933: Oct.

Belarski, Rudolph
Captain Future
    1942: Sum, Fall.
Startling Stories
    1941: May, Jul, Sep, Nov;
    1942: Jan, Sep;
    1943: Jan;
    1947: Mar.
Strange Stories
    1939: Feb, Apr, Jun(?);
    1940: Apr.
Terence X. O'Leary's War Birds
    1935: Mar, Apr, May/Jun.
Thrilling Wonder Stories
    1941: Aug;
    1942: Feb, Aug, Dec;
    1944: Win, Fall.

Bennett, Richard
Weird Tales
  1942: Nov.

Bensen, Andrew
Weird Tales
  1926: May.

Bergey, Earle K.
Captain Future
  1940: Sum, Fall;
  1941: Win, Spr, Sum;
  1942: Win, Spr;
  1943: Win, Spr, Sum;
  1944: Win, Spr.
Fantastic Story Quarterly
  1950: Spr, Sum, Fall.
*Future combined with Science
  Fiction Stories*
  1950: May/Jun, Jul/Aug.
Startling Stories
  1940: Jul, Sep, Nov;
  1941: Jan, Mar.
  1942: Mar, May, Jul, Nov;
  1943: Mar, Jun, Fall;
  1944: Win, Spr, Sum, Fall;
  1945: Win, Spr, Sum, Fall;
  1946: Win, Mar, Spr, Sum,
  Fall;
  1947: Jan, May, Jul, Sep,
  Nov;
  1948: Jan, Mar, May, Jul,
  Sep, Nov;
  1949: Jan, Mar, May, Jul,
  Sep, Nov;
  1950: Jan, Mar, May, Jul,
  Sep, Nov.
Strange Stories
  1939: Aug, Oct, Dec;
  1940: Feb, Jun, Aug(?),
  Oct(?), Dec;
  1941: Feb.
Tales of Magic and Mystery
  1927: Dec(?);
  1928: Jan, Feb, Mar, Apr.
Thrilling Wonder Stories

  1940: Sep, Oct, Nov, Dec;
  1941: Feb, Mar, Apr, Dec;
  1942: Apr, Jun, Oct;
  1943: Feb, Apr, Jun, Aug, Fall;
  1944: Spr, Sum;
  1945: Win, Spr, Sum, Fall;
  1946: Win, Spr, Sum, Fall,
  Dec;
  1947: Feb, Apr, Jun, Aug,
  Oct, Dec;
  1948: Feb, Apr, Jun, Aug,
  Oct, Dec;
  1949: Feb, Apr, Jun, Aug,
  Oct, Dec;
  1950: Feb, Apr, Jun, Aug,
  Oct, Dec.

Bick
Uncanny Tales (Canadian)
  1942: Jan.

Binder, Jack
Astonishing Stories
  1940: Feb, Apr.
Science Fiction Quarterly
  1940: Sum.
Super Science Stories
  1940: Mar.

Blakeslee, Frederick M.
Dusty Ayres and his Battle Birds
  1934: Jul, Aug, Sep, Oct,
  Nov, Dec;
  1935: Jan, Feb, Mar, Apr,
  May/Jun, Jul/Aug.

Blumenfeld, H.J.
Fantastic Adventures
  1950: May.

Bok, Hannes
Cosmic Stories
  1941: May.
Future Fantasy and Science Fiction
  1942: Oct.
Imagination
  1950: Oct.

Other Worlds Science Stories
    1950: Nov.
Planet Stories
    1941: Win.
Science Fiction Quarterly
    1942: Win, Spr, Fall.
Stirring Science Stories
    1941: Apr, Jun;
    1942: Mar.
Weird Tales
    1939: Dec;
    1940: Mar, May;
    1941: May, Jul, Nov;
    1942: Mar.

Bonestell, Chesley

Astounding SF
    1947: Oct;
    1948: Apr, Jul, Sep;
    1949: Jun;
    1950: Jan.
*Magazine of Fantasy and Science
    Fiction*
    1950: Dec.

Brand, T.

Thrills Incorporated
1950: #1–#9 inclusive.

Brosnatch, Andrew

Weird Tales
    1924: Nov, Dec;
    1925: Jan, Feb, Mar, Apr,
    May, Jun, Jul, Aug, Sep, Oct,
    Nov;
    1926: Jan, Mar.

Brown, Howard V.

Astounding Stories/SF
    1933: Oct, Nov, Dec;
    1934: Jan, Feb, Mar, Apr, May,
    Jun, Jul, Aug, Sep, Oct, Nov,
    Dec;
    1935: Jan, Feb, Mar, Apr, May,
    Jun, Jul, Aug, Sep, Oct, Nov, Dec;
    1936: Jan, Feb, Mar, Apr, May,
    Jun, Jul, Aug, Sep, Oct, Nov,

Dec;
    1937: Jan, Feb, Mar, Apr,
    May, Jul, Aug, Oct, Dec;
    1938: Feb, Apr, Jul, Oct, Nov.
Startling Stories
    1939: Jan, Mar(?), May, Jul;
    1940: Jan, Mar, May.
Thrilling Wonder Stories
    1936: Aug, Oct, Dec;
    1937: Feb, Apr, Jun, Oct, Dec;
    1938: Feb(?), Apr, Jun, Aug,
    Oct, Dec;
    1939: Feb, Apr, Jun, Aug,
    Oct, Dec;
    1940: Jan, Feb, Mar, Apr,
    May, Jun, Jul, Aug.

Brundage, Margaret

Oriental Stories
    1932: Spr, Sum.
The Magic Carpet Magazine
    1933: Jan, Apr, Oct.
    1934: Jan.
Weird Tales
    1932: Sep, Oct;
    1933: Mar, Jun, Jul, Aug,
    Sep, Oct, Nov, Dec;
    1934: Jan, Feb, Mar, Apr, May,
    Jun, Jul, Aug, Sep, Oct, Nov,
    Dec;
    1935: Jan, Feb, Mar, Apr, May,
    Jun, Jul, Aug, Sep, Oct, Nov,
    Dec;
    1936: Jan, Feb, Mar, Apr,
    May, Jun, Jul, Aug/Sep, Nov;
    1937: Jan, Mar, May, Jun,
    Aug, Sep, Oct, Nov;
    1938: Jan, Mar, May, Jun,
    Aug, Sep, Oct.
    1940: Jul, Nov;
    1941: Mar, Sep;
    1942: Jul;
    1943: May;
    1944: May;
    1945: Jan.

Brush
Astounding SF
1950: May.

Caesari, Victor
New Worlds
1946: #2 (*and rebound on #1*)

Calle, Paul
Worlds Beyond
1950: Dec.

Canedo, Alejandro
Astounding SF
1946: Dec;
1947: Sep, Dec;
1948: Feb, May, Aug;
1949: Mar, Oct.

Caney
Tales of Wonder
1939: Win.

Cartier, Edd
Astounding SF
1950: Oct.
Doc Savage
1948: Mar/Apr.
Unknown
1939: Dec;
1940: Feb, Apr, Jun.

Clarke, Emery
Doc Savage
1937: Sep;
1938: Jan, Mar, Apr, May,
Jun, Jul, Aug, Sep, Oct, Nov,
Dec;
1939: Jan, Feb, Mar, Apr,
May, Jun, Jul, Aug, Sep, Oct,
Nov, Dec;
1940: Jan, Feb, Mar, Apr,
May, Jun, Jul, Aug, Sep, Oct,
Nov, Dec;
1941: Jan, Feb, Mar, Apr,
May, Jun, Jul, Aug, Sep, Oct,
Nov, Dec;
1942: Jan, Feb, Mar, Apr,
May, Jun, Aug, Sep, Oct,
Nov, Dec;
1943: Jan, Feb, Mar, Apr,
May, Jun, Jul, Aug.

Clothier, Robert
New Worlds
1949: #5;
1950: Spr, Sum, Win.

Clyne, Ronald
Weird Tales
1946: May.

Coye, Lee Brown
Weird Tales
1945: Jul, Nov;
1946: Mar;
1947: Jul;
1948: Mar, Sep;
1949: Jan;
1950: Mar.

Crozetti, Lora
Fantasy Book
1948: #2, #3.

de Feo, Charles
Astounding SF
1942: Jul(?).
Doc Savage
1942: Jul.

DeLay, Harold S.
Weird Tales
1939: May, Oct;
1941: Jan;
1944: Jan.

de Soto, Rafael
Captain Zero
1949: Nov;
1950: Jan, Mar.
Famous Fantastic Mysteries
1950: Oct.
Fantastic Novels
1950: Nov.
The Spider

1939: Oct, Nov, Dec;
1940: Jan, Feb, Mar, Apr,
May, Jun, Jul, Aug, Sep, Oct,
Nov, Dec;
1941: Jan, Feb, Mar, Apr,
May, Jun, Jul, Aug, Sep, Oct,
Nov, Dec;
1942: Jan, Feb, Mar, Apr,
May, Jun, Jul, Aug, Sep, Oct,
Nov, Dec;
1943: Jan, Feb, Mar, Jun,
Aug, Oct, Dec.

Dold, Elliott
Cosmic Stories
1941: Jul.
Miracle Science and Fantasy Stories
1931: Apr/May, Jun/Jul.

Dolgov, Boris
Weird Tales
1946: Nov;
1947: Mar, Sep;
1948: Jan;
1950: May.

Doolin, Joseph
Weird Tales
1925: Dec;
1926: Dec.

Drake, Albert
Planet Stories
1939: Win;
1940: Spr, Sum, Fall, Win;
1941: Spr.

Drigin, Serge R.
Fantasy
1938: #1;
1939: #2, #3.
Scoops
1934: 10 Feb–23 Jun (all
covers).

Durant, Charles
The Thrill Book
1919: 15 Jul, 15 Sep.

Epperley, Richard R.
Fantastic Adventures
1945: Apr.
Weird Tales
1923: Mar.

Eshbach, Lloyd Arthur
Marvel Tales
1934: May, Jul/Aug.

Facey, Gerald
Futuristic Science Stories
1950: #1, #3.
Tales of Tomorrow
1950: #1.
Worlds of Fantasy
1950: #1, #2.

Ferguson, Jr., Clay,
Fanciful Tales
1936: Fall.
Marvel Tales
1935: Mar/Apr, Sum.

Finlay, Virgil
Astonishing Stories
1942: Jun.
Astounding SF
1939: Aug.
Famous Fantastic Mysteries
1940: Mar, Aug, Oct;
1941: Feb, Apr, Jun, Aug,
Oct, Dec;
1942: Feb, Apr, Jun, Jul,
Aug, Sep, Oct, Nov, Dec;
1943: Mar, Sep;
1946: Dec;
1947: Feb, Jun, Aug, Dec;
1948: Feb, Jun.
Fantastic Novels
1940: Jul, Nov;
1941: Jan, Apr;
1948: Nov;
1949: Mar, Nov.
Planet Stories
1941: Sum.

Super Science Stories
1942: May;
1943: Feb, May.
Weird Tales
1937: Feb, Apr, Jul, Dec;
1938: Feb, Apr, Jul;
1939: Jan, Feb, Mar, Apr,
Jun/Jul, Aug, Sep, Nov;
1940: Jan.

Forte, Jr., John R.
Future Fiction
1941: Aug.
Future combined with Science Fiction
1942: Apr, Jun, Aug.

Fox, Matt
Weird Tales
1944: Nov;
1946: Jul;
1947: May, Nov;
1948: May, Jul;
1949: Mar, Jul, Nov;
1950: Jan, Jul.

Freas, Frank Kelly
Weird Tales
1950: Nov.

Frew, John
Astounding SF
1939: Jan.

Fuqua, Robert
(brush name of Joseph W. Tillotson)
Amazing Stories
1938: Oct, Nov, Dec;
1939: Jan, Feb, Mar, Apr,
May, Jul, Aug, Sep, Oct;
1940: Jan, Jul, Sep, Nov,
Dec;
1941: Sep, Nov;
1942: Mar, Apr;

1943: Mar, Apr, Aug;
1944: Jan.
Fantastic Adventures
1939: May, Nov;
1940: Feb, Mar;
1941: Jun, Sep
1942: Feb (joint).

Gaughan, Jack
Fantasy Book
1950: #6.

Gelb, Von
Oriental Stories
1930: Oct/Nov, Dec/Jan;
1931: Feb/Mar, Apr/May/
Jun, Sum.

Gilmore, H.
Astounding SF
1939: Dec;
1940: Mar.

Giunta, John
Weird Tales
1944: Mar;
1948: Nov;
1949: May.

Gladney, Graves
Astounding SF
1939: Mar, May, Jun, Jul.
*The Shadow (*covers for 1st and 15th of month)*
1939: Mar* Apr* May* Jun*
Jul* Aug* Sep* Oct* Nov*
Dec*;
1940: Jan* Feb* Mar* Apr*
May* Jun* Jul* Aug* Sep*
Oct* Nov* Dec*;
1941: Jan* Feb* Mar* Apr*
May* Jun* Jul* Aug* Sep*;
Unknown
1939: Apr, Aug, Nov.

Gross, George
Jungle Stories
1939: Fall, Win;
1940: Sum, Win;
1941: Sum, Fall, Win;
1942: Spr, Sum, Fall, Win;
1943: Feb, Apr, Sum, Fall, Win;
1944: Spr, Sum, Fall, Win;
1945: Spr, Sum, Fall, Win;
1946: Spr, Sum, Fall, Win;
1947: Spr, Sum, Fall, Win;
1948: Spr, Sum, Fall, Win;
1949: Spr, Sum, Fall, Win;
1950: Spr, Sum, Fall, Win.
Planet Stories
1943: Win;
1944: Sum.

Hadden, Ned
Amazing Stories
1943: Jun.

Hammond, H.R.
Amazing Stories
1940: Apr.

Harris, Robert G.
Doc Savage
1936: Oct, Nov, Dec;
1937: Jan, Feb, Mar, Apr, May, Jun, Jul, Aug, Oct, Nov, Dec.

Hartman, C.L.
Amazing Stories
1940: Feb, May.

Haucke, Fred
Astounding SF
1944: Jul.

Heitman
Weird Tales
1923: May.

Hilbreth, Bob
Amazing Stories
1946: Dec.

Hilkert, John C.
Eerie Tales
1941: Jul.

Holling, Lucille
Oriental Stories
1931: Aut.

Howitt, John Newton
The Octopus
1939: Feb/Mar.
Operator #5
1934: May, Jun, Jul, Aug, Sep, Oct, Nov, Dec;
1935: Jan, Feb, Mar, Apr, May, Jun, Jul, Aug, Sep, Oct, Nov, Dec;
1936: Jan, Feb, Mar, Apr, Jun, Aug, Oct, Dec;
1937: Jan, Feb, Mar/Apr, May/Jun, Jul/Aug, Sep/Oct, Nov/Dec;
1938: Jan/Feb, Mar/Apr, May/Jun, Jul/Aug, Sep/Oct, Nov/Dec;
1939: Jan/Feb, Mar/Apr, May/Jun, Jul/Aug, Sep/Oct, Nov/Dec.
The Scorpion
1939: Apr/May.
The Spider
1933: Nov, Dec;
1934: Jan, Feb, Mar, Apr, May, Jun, Jul, Aug, Sep, Oct, Nov, Dec;
1935: Jan, Feb, Mar, Apr, May, Jun, Jul, Aug, Sep, Oct, Nov, Dec;
1936: Jan, Feb, Mar, Apr, May, Jun, Jul, Aug, Sep, Oct, Nov, Dec;
1937: Jan, Feb, Mar, Apr, May, Jun, Jul, Aug, Sep, Oct, Nov, Dec;
1938: Jan, Feb, Mar, Apr, May, Jun, Jul, Aug, Sep, Oct, Nov, Dec;
1939: Jan, Feb, Mar, Apr, May, Jun, Jul, Aug, Sep.

Huey, Guy L.
Marvel Tales
  1934: Win.

Hunter, Don
Galaxy SF
  1950: Dec.

Ingels, Graham J.
Planet Stories
  1944: Spr.

Isip, Manuel
Unknown
  1940: Mar, May.

Jones, L. Raymond
Amazing Stories
  1942: Feb.

Jones, Robert Gibson
Amazing Stories
  1942: Nov;
  1943: Sep, Nov;
  1945: Mar, Jun, Sep, Dec;
  1946: Sep, Oct;
  1947: Feb, Mar, Jun, Oct,
  Nov, Dec;
  1948: Mar, Apr, May, Jun,
  Aug, Sep, Nov;
  1949: Feb, Jul, Dec;
  1950: Feb, Mar, Apr, Jun,
  Jul, Aug, Sep, Oct.
Fantastic Adventures
  1942: Aug;
  1943: Jan, Feb, Mar, Jul,
  Aug, Oct, Dec;
  1944: Jun;
  1945: Jan;
  1947: Jan, Mar, May, Sep,
  Oct, Nov, Dec;
  1948: Jan, Feb, Mar, Apr,
  May, Jun, Sep, Oct;
  1949: Jan, May, Sep, Nov;
  1950: Feb, Mar, Apr, Jun,
  Jul, Sep, Oct, Dec.

Jones, Walter Haskell
Fantastic Adventures
  1948: Aug.

Juhre, William
Amazing Stories
  1939: Jun.

Kohn, Arnold
Amazing Stories
  1946: May, Jun, Nov;
  1947: Aug;
  1948: Jul;
  1949: Apr, Jun, Aug, Nov;
  1950: Jan, May, Nov.
Fantastic Adventures
  1945: Jul;
  1946: Jul, Sep;
  1948: Nov;
  1949: Feb, Mar, Aug;
  1950: Nov.
Other Worlds Science Stories
  1950: Oct (joint).

Krupa, Julian S.
Amazing Stories
  1940: Jun, Aug (joint);
  1944: Sep;
  1947: Apr, Jul.

Kuhlhoff, Pete
Weird Tales
  1945: May, Sep;
  1946: Sep.

Labonski, Michael
Weird Tales
  1949: Sep.

Lehman, Paul
Fantastic Adventures
  1945: Dec.

Leslie, Walter
Uncanny Tales (Canadian)
  1941: Jun, Jul, Aug, Sep.

Leydenfrost, Alexander
Planet Stories
  1942: Spr, Fall.

Loehe, Richard
Amazing Stories
1949: Sep.

Long, Wilf
Uncanny Tales (Canadian)
1941: Oct, Nov, Dec;
1942: Feb.

Lovell, Tom
The Shadow
1932: 15 Oct.

Luros, Milton
Astonishing Stories
1943: Feb, Apr.
Future Fantasy and Science Fiction
1943: Feb.
Science Fiction Stories
1943: Apr, Jul.
*Future combined with Science
Fiction Stories*
1950: Nov.
Science Fiction Quarterly
1942: Win;
1943: Spr.

McCauley, Harold W.
Amazing Stories
1939: Nov;
1940: Mar;
1942: May, Aug;
1943: May, Jul;
1946: Aug;
1947: Jan;
1948: Dec;
1949: May, Oct.
Fantastic Adventures
1939: Sep;
1940: Jan, Aug;
1941: Jan, Jun, Jul (joint),
Oct;
1942: Jan, Feb (joint), Sep,
Nov, Dec;
1943: May, Jun;
1946: May;
1947: Jul;

1950: Aug.
Imagination
1950: Dec.

McKay, Hugh
Amazing Stories
1929: Jul, Aug.
Amazing Stories Quarterly
1929: Sum(?).

Mally, R.M.
Weird Tales
1923: Jun, Jul/Aug, Sep, Oct;
1924: Jan, Feb, Mar, Apr,
May/Jun/Jul.

Martin, Charles
Planet Stories
1946: Sum, Fall, Win.

Mayorga, Gabriel
Astonishing Stories
1940: Jun, Aug, Oct.
Super Science Stories
1940: May, Jul(?).
Thrilling Wonder Stories
1941: Jan.

Meagher, Fred
*Flash Gordon Strange Adventure
Magazine*
1936: Dec.

Miller, Walt
Astounding SF
1950: Jun, Aug, Sep.

Moll, John B.
Mind Magic/My Self
1931: Aug, Sep/Oct, Nov.

Morey, Leo
Amazing Stories
1930: Feb, Mar, Apr, May,
Jun, Jul, Sep, Oct, Nov, Dec;
1931: Jan, Feb, Mar, Apr, May,
Jun, Jul, Aug, Sep, Oct, Nov,
Dec;
1932: Jan, Feb, Mar, Apr, May,

Jun, Jul, Aug, Sep, Oct,
Nov, Dec;
1933: Jul (joint), Aug/Sep,
Oct, Nov, Dec;
1934: Jan, Feb, Mar, Apr,
May, Jun, Jul, Aug, Sep,
Oct, Nov, Dec;
1935: Jan, Feb, Mar, Apr,
May, Jun, Jul, Aug, Oct, Dec;
1936: Feb, Apr, Jun, Aug,
Oct, Dec;
1937: Feb, Apr, Jun, Aug,
Oct, Dec;
1938: Feb, Apr;
1940: Aug (joint);Oct;
1941: Feb.
Amazing Stories Quarterly
1930: Spr, Sum, Fall, Win;
1931: Spr, Sum, Fall;
1932: Win, Spr/Sum, Fall/
Win;
1934: Win, Fall.
Astonishing Stories
1941: Feb;
1942: Oct.
Comet
1940: Dec;
1941: Mar, Jul.
Cosmic Stories
1941: Mar.
Fantastic Adventures
1939: Jul.
*Future combined with Science
Fiction Stories*
1950: Sep/Oct.
Stirring Science Stories
1941: Feb.
Super Science Stories
1940: Nov.

Moskowitz, H.S.
Mind Magic/My Self
1931: Jun, Jul, Dec.

Mulford, Stockton
Amazing Stories

1941: Jul.
Fantastic Adventures
1940: May, Jun.

Munchausen, A. von
Astounding SF
1942: Oct.

Mussachia, John B.
1942: Sum.

Naylor, Ramon
Amazing Stories
1948: Jan.
Fantastic Adventures
1948: Jul;
1950: Jan.

Nelson, T. Wyatt
Weird Tales
1932: Aug.

Nicolson, John
Tales of Wonder
1937: #1, #2;
1939: Sum, Aut;
1941: Win, Spr, Aut;
1942: Spr.

Orban, Paul
Astounding SF
1948: Dec;
1949: May, Sep.

Parke, Walter
Amazing Stories
1946: Jul.
Fantastic Adventures
1946: Feb.

Parkhurst, H.L.
Planet Stories
1944: Fall, Win;
1945: Spr, Sum, Fall, Win;
1946: Spr.

Pattee, David E.
Astounding SF
1950: Nov.

Paul, Frank R.

Air Wonder Stories
    1929: Jul, Aug, Sep, Oct, Nov,
    Dec;
    1930: Jan, Feb, Mar, Apr,
    May.

Amazing Stories
    1926: Apr, May, Jun, Jul,
    Aug, Sep, Oct, Nov, Dec;
    1927: Jan, Feb, Mar, Apr, May,
    Jun, Jul, Aug, Sep, Oct, Nov,
    Dec;
    1928: Jan, Feb, Mar, Apr, May,
    Jun, Jul, Aug, Sep, Oct, Nov,
    Dec;
    1929: Apr, May, Jun.

Amazing Stories Annual
    1927: #1.

Amazing Stories Quarterly
    1928: Win, Spr, Sum, Fall;
    1929: Win, Spr.

Comet
    1941: Jan, May.

Dynamic Science Stories
    1939: Feb.

Famous Fantastic Mysteries
    1940: Apr, May/Jun, Dec.

Fantastic Adventures
    1940: Apr.

Fantastic Novels
    1940: Sep.

Future Fiction
    1940: Nov;
    1941: Apr.

Marvel Science Stories
    1938: Nov.

Planet Stories
    1941: Fall.

Science Fiction
    1939: Mar, Jun, Aug, Oct,
    Dec;
    1940: Mar, Jun, Oct;
    1941: Jan, Mar, Jun, Sep.

Science Fiction Quarterly
    1941: Win, Spr, Sum.

Science Wonder Stories
    1929: Jun, Jul, Aug, Sep,
    Oct, Nov, Dec;
    1930: Jan, Feb, Mar, Apr,
    May.

Scientific Detective Monthly
    1930: Apr.

Wonder Stories
    1930: Jun, Jul, Aug, Sep,
    Oct, Nov, Dec;
    1931: Jan, Feb, Mar, Apr,
    May, Jun, Jul, Aug, Sep, Oct,
    Nov, Dec;
    1932: Jan, Feb, Mar, Apr,
    May, Jun, Jul, Aug, Sep,
    Oct, Dec;
    1933: Jan, Feb, Mar, Apr,
    May, Jun, Aug, Oct, Nov,
    Dec;
    1934: Jan, Feb, Mar, Apr,
    May, Jun, Jul, Aug, Sep, Oct,
    Nov, Dec;
    1935: Jan, Feb, Mar, Apr,
    May, Jun, Jul, Aug, Sep, Oct,
    Nov/Dec;
    1936: Jan/Feb, Mar/Apr.

*Wonder Stories Quarterly/ Science
Wonder Quarterly*
    1929: Fall;
    1930: Win, Spr, Sum, Fall;
    1931: Win, Spr, Sum, Fall;
    1932: Win, Spr, Sum, Fall;
    1933: Win.

Perl, H.W.

Futuristic Stories
    1946: #1, #2.

Strange Adventures
    1946: #1;
    1947: #2.

Strange Tales (British)
    1946: #1.

Petrie, Jr., C. Barker

Weird Tales
    1926: Feb, Aug, Oct;

1927: Jan, Feb;
1931: Feb/Mar.

Powell, Bob
The Shadow
1948: Aug/Sep.

Powell, Frederic
Science-Fantasy
1950: Sum.

Quigley, Ray
Weird Tales
1938: Dec;
1940: Sep;
1942: May.

Rae, G.M.
Uncanny Tales (Canadian)
1942: May, Jul.

Rankin, Hugh
Weird Tales
1927: Aug, Dec;
1928: Dec;
1929: Feb, Apr, Jun, Aug,
Oct, Dec;
1930: Feb, Apr, Jun, Aug,
Oct, Dec.

Reynolds, James
The Thrill Book
1919: 1 Sep, 15 Oct.

Riesenberg, Sidney H.
The Shadow
1931: Apr (*reprinted from 1
Oct 1919* Thrill Book)
*The Thrill Book (*covers for 1st
and 15th of month)*
1919: Mar*, Apr* May*,
Jun*, 1 Jul, Aug*, 1 Oct.

Roberts, W.J.
Tales of Wonder
1938: Sum, Aut, Win;
1939: Spr;
1940: Spr, Aut.

Rogers, Alva
Strange Tales (British)
1946: #2.

Rogers, Hubert
Astounding SF
1939: Feb, Sep, Oct, Nov;
1940: Feb, Apr, May, Jun,
Jul, Aug, Sep, Oct, Nov, Dec;
1941: Jan, Feb, Mar, Apr, May,
Jun, Jul, Aug, Sep, Oct, Nov,
Dec;
1942: Jan, Feb, Mar, Apr,
May, Jun, Aug;
1947: Mar, May, Aug, Nov;
1948: Jan, Mar, Oct, Nov;
1949: Jan, Feb, Jul, Aug,
Nov;
1950: Feb, Mar, Apr.
Super Science Stories
1942: Aug.

Rozen, George
Captain Future
1940: Win, Spr;
1941: Fall.
Doc Savage
1949: Win, Spr, Sum.
Dr Yen Sin
1936: Jul/Aug.
Planet Stories
1943: Mar, May, Fall.
*The Shadow (*covers for 1st and
15th of month)*
1932: Jan, Mar, Apr, May, Jun,
Jul, Aug, Sep, 1 Oct, Nov*
Dec* ;
1933: Jan* Feb* Mar* Apr*
May* Jun* Jul* Aug* Sep*
Oct* Nov* Dec* ;
1934: Jan* Feb* Mar* Apr*
May* Jun* Jul* Aug* Sep*
Oct* Nov* Dec* ;
1935: Jan* Feb* Mar* Apr*
May* Jun* Jul* Aug* Sep*
Oct* Nov* Dec* ;

1936: Jan* Feb* Mar* Apr*
May* Jun* Jul* Aug* Sep*
Oct* Nov* Dec* ;
1937: Jan* Feb* Mar* Apr*
May* Jun* Jul* Aug* ;
1938: Jan* Mar* Apr* Jul* 15
Sep;
1939: 15 Jan, Feb* ;
1941: Oct* Nov* Dec* ;
1942: Jan* Feb* Mar* Apr*
May* Jun* Jul* 15 Aug, Sep*
Oct* Nov* Dec* ;
1943: 15 Jan, Feb* ;
1948: Fall;
1949: Win, Spr, Sum.

Rozen, Jerome
Dr Yen Sin
  1936: May/Jun, Sep/Oct.
The Mysterious Wu Fang
  1935: Sep, Oct, Nov, Dec;
  1936: Jan, Feb, Mar.
Operator #5
  1934: Apr.
The Shadow
  1931: Oct, Nov, Dec;
  1932: Feb.

Ruger, Jno.
Scientific Detective Monthly/Amazing
  Detective Tales
  1930: Jan, Feb(?), Mar, May,
  Jun, Jul, Aug(?), Sep, Oct(?).

Ruth, Rod
Amazing Stories
  1941: Dec.
Fantastic Adventures
  1941: Aug, Dec;
  1944: Feb.

St. John, J. Allen
Amazing Stories
  1941: Jan, Mar, Apr, May,
  Jun, Aug, Oct;
  1942: Jul, Dec;
  1943: Jan, Feb;

1944: Mar;
1949: Jan.
Fantastic Adventures
  1940: Oct;
  1941: Mar, Jul (joint), Nov;
  1942: Mar, Jul, Oct;
  1944: Apr, Oct;
  1945: Oct;
  1946: Nov.
The Magic Carpet Magazine
  1933: Jul.
Oriental Stories
  1932: Win.
Weird Tales
  1932: Jun, Nov, Dec;
  1933: Jan, Feb, Apr, May;
  1936: Oct, Dec.

Salter, George
Magazine of Fantasy and Science
  Fiction
  1950: Win/Spr, Sum, Fall.

Santry,
Astounding SF
  1949: Apr.

Saunders, Norman
A. Merritt's Fantasy Magazine
  1950: Feb, Apr, Jul, Oct.
Captain Hazzard
  1938: May.
Dynamic Science Stories
  1939: Apr/May.
Famous Fantastic Mysteries
  1950: Jun, Aug.
Fantastic Novels
  1950: Mar, May, Sep.
Jungle Stories
  1938: Win;
  1939: Sum;
  1941: Spr.
Marvel Science Stories
  1938: Aug;
  1939: Apr/May;
  1950: Nov.

Planet Stories
    1942: Sum.
Super Science Stories
    1950: Mar.

Schneeman, Charles
Astounding SF
    1938: May, Dec;
    1939: Apr;
    1940: Jan;
    1947: Jun.

Schomburg, Alex
Startling Stories
    1939: Sep, Nov(?).

Scott, H. Winfield
Doc Savage
    1938: Feb.
Unknown
    1939: Mar, May, Jun, Jul,
    Sep;
    1940: Jan.

Scott, John W.
Future Fiction
    1939: Nov;
    1940: Mar, Jul.
Ka-Zar
    1936: Oct;
    1937: Jan, Jun.
Marvel (Science) Stories/Tales
    1939: Aug, Dec;
    1940: Nov;
    1941: Apr.
Uncanny Stories
    1941: Apr.

Senf, C.C.
Weird Tales
    1927: Mar, Apr, May, Jun,
    Jul, Sep, Oct, Nov;
    1928: Jan, Feb, Mar, Apr,
    May, Jun, Jul, Aug, Sep, Oct,
    Nov;
    1929: Jan, Mar, May, Jul,
    Sep, Nov;

    1930: Jan, Mar, May, Jul,
    Sep, Nov;
    1931: Jan, Apr/May, Jun/Jul,
    Aug, Sep, Oct, Nov, Dec;
    1932: Jan, Feb, Mar, Apr,
    May, Jul.

Settles, James B.
Amazing Stories
    1942: Sep;
    1944: Dec;
    1948: Oct;
    1950: Dec.
Fantastic Adventures
    1949: Jun, Jul.

Sherry, Robert C.
Astonishing Stories
    1940: Dec;
    1941: Apr, Sep, Nov(?).
Future Fantasy and Science Fiction
    1942: Dec.
Super Science Stories/Novels
    1940: Sep;
    1941: Jan(?), Mar(?),
    May(?), Aug, Nov(?).

Sibley, Don
Galaxy SF
    1950: Nov.

Sigmond, A.
Amazing Stories
    1933: Jan, Feb, Mar, Apr,
    May, Jun, Jul (joint).
Amazing Stories Quarterly
    1933: Spr/Sum.

Slack, Dennis
New Worlds
    1947: #3;
    1949: #4.

Smith, Malcolm
Amazing Stories
    1942: Jan, Oct;
    1944: May;
    1946: Feb;

1947: Sep;
1948: Feb.
Fantastic Adventures
1942: Apr, May, Jun;
1943: Apr;
1948: Dec.
Other Worlds Science Stories
1949: Nov;
1950: Jan, Mar, May, Jul,
Sep, Oct (joint).

Sniffen
Astounding SF
1947: Feb.

Steele, Ted
Uncanny Tales (Canadian)
1941: May.

Stein, Modest
Astounding SF
1942: Nov.
Doc Savage
1943: Sep, Oct, Nov, Dec;
1944: Jan, Feb, Mar, Apr,
May, Jun, Jul, Aug, Sep, Oct,
Nov, Dec;
1945: Jan, Feb, Mar, Apr,
May, Jun, Jul, Aug, Sep, Oct,
Nov, Dec.
The Shadow
1943: Mar, Apr, May, Jun,
Jul, Aug, Sep, Oct, Nov;
1944: Jan, Feb, Apr, May,
Jun, Jul, Aug, Sep, Oct, Nov,
Dec;
1945: Jan, Feb, Mar, Apr,
Oct;
1946: Jan, Feb, Sep.
Unknown
1939: Oct.

Stevens, Lawrence Sterne
Famous Fantastic Mysteries
1943: Dec;
1944: Mar, Jun, Sep, Dec;
1945: Mar, Jun, Sep, Dec;

1946: Feb, Apr, Jun, Aug;
1949: Dec;
1950: Apr.
Fantastic Novels
1948: Jul;
1949: Jan;
1950: Jul.
Super Science Stories
1942: Nov;
1949: Jan, Apr, Jul, Sep;
1950: Jan, May, Jul.

Stevens, Peter
A. Merritt's Fantasy Magazine
1949: Dec.
Astonishing Stories
1942: Dec.
Famous Fantastic Mysteries
1946: Oct;
1947: Apr, Oct;
1948: Apr, Aug, Oct, Dec;
1949: Feb, Apr, Jun, Aug,
Oct;
1950: Feb.
Fantastic Novels
1948: Mar, May, Sep;
1949: May, Jul, Sep;
1950: Jan.

Stevenson, E.M.
Weird Tales
1926: Apr, Jun, Jul, Sep,
Nov.

Stone, David
Galaxy SF
1950: Oct.

Stone, William
Fantasy Fiction/Stories
1950: May, Nov.
Magazine of Fantasy
1949: Fall.

Stoner, Elmer C.
The Witch's Tales
1936: Nov, Dec.

Swenson, H.
Doc Savage
1948: May/Jun.
The Shadow
1947: Dec/Jan;
1948: Feb/Mar, Apr/May.

Swiatek, Edmond
Amazing Stories
1949: May.
Fantastic Adventures
1949: Apr, Oct, Dec.

Teason, James
Amazing Stories
1947: May.

Thompson
Astounding SF
1938: Sep.

Tilburne, A.R.
Weird Tales
1938: Nov;
1942: Sep;
1943: Jan, Sep, Nov;
1944: Jul, Sep;
1945: Mar;
1946: Jan;
1947: Jan.

Tillotson, Joseph W.
see under Robert Fuqua.

Timmins, William
Astounding SF
1942: Sep, Dec;
1943: Jan, Feb, Mar, Apr,
May, Jun, Jul, Aug, Sep, Oct,
Nov, Dec;
1944: Jan, Feb, Mar, Apr,
May, Jun, Aug, Sep, Oct,
Nov, Dec;
1945: Jan, Feb, Mar, Apr,
May, Jun, Jul, Aug, Sep, Oct,
Nov, Dec;
1946: Jan, Feb, Mar, Apr,
May, Jun, Jul, Aug, Sep, Oct,

Nov;
1947: Jan, Apr, Jul;
1948: Jun;
1950: Dec.
The Shadow
1943: 1 Jan.

Turner, Harry
Science-Fantasy
1950: Win.
Tales of Wonder
1940: Sum.

Van Dongen, Henry R.
Super Science Stories
1950: Sep, Nov.
Worlds Beyond
1951: Jan, Feb.

Washburn
Weird Tales
1923: Nov.

Wayne, Bill
Weird Tales
1950: Sep.

Wessolowski, Hans
Amazing Stories
1929: Sep, Oct, Nov, Dec;
1930: Jan, Aug.
Amazing Stories Quarterly
1929: Fall;
1930: Win.
Astonishing Stories
1942: Mar.
Astounding Stories
1930: Jan, Feb, Mar, Apr, May,
Jun, Jul, Aug, Sep, Oct, Nov, Dec;
1931: Jan, Feb, Mar, Apr, May,
Jun, Jul, Aug, Sep, Oct, Nov,
Dec;
1932: Jan, Feb, Mar, Apr,
May, Jun, Jul, Sep, Nov;
1933: Jan, Mar;
1937: Jun, Sep, Nov;
1938: Jan, Mar, Jun, Aug.

Marvel Science Stories
 1939: Feb.
Strange Tales
 1931: Sep, Nov;
 1932: Jan, Mar, Jun, Oct;
 1933: Jan.
Thrilling Wonder Stories
 1937: Aug;
 1941: Jun.

Wilkin, Robert A.
New Worlds
 1946: #1.

Wittmack, E. Franklyn
Weird Tales
 1943: Mar, Jul.
Zboyan
Astounding SF
 1949: Dec.

Zirn, Rudolph W.
Doctor Death
 1935: Feb, Mar, Apr.

Select Bibliography

I doubt that I could now list all of the books, magazines and articles that I have read over the years, all of which have contributed to my understanding of the development and history of the science-fiction magazine. The following is thus a selection, which I believe are the key publications for anyone interested in further study on this subject. I openly acknowledge my debt to all of the following in helping me with this history.

Aldiss, Brian W., *Trillion Year Spree*, London: Victor Gollancz, 1986.

Aldiss, Brian W. and Harrison, Harry, *Hell's Cartographers*, London: Weidenfeld and Nicolson, 1975.

Alkon, Paul K., *Science Fiction before 1900*, New York: Twayne Publishers, 1994.

Amis, Kingsley, *New Maps of Hell*, London: Victor Gollancz, 1961.

Asimov, Isaac, *In Memory Yet Green*, New York: Doubleday, 1979.

—— *I. Asimov: a Memoir*, New York: Doubleday, 1994.

Bleiler, Everett F., *Science-Fiction, The Early Years*, Kent, Ohio: Kent State University Press, 1990.

Bleiler, Richard, *The Annotated Index to The Thrill Book*, Mercer Island, Washington: Starmont House, 1991.

Blish, James (as William Atheling, Jr.), *The Issue at Hand*, Chicago: Advent, 1964.

—— *More Issues at Hand*, Chicago: Advent, 1970.

Bloch, Robert, *Once Around the Bloch*, New York: Tor Books, 1993.

Carter, Paul, *The Creation of Tomorrow*, New York: Columbia University Press, 1977.

Cave, Hugh B., *Magazines I Remember*, Chicago: Tattered Pages Press, 1994.

Chapdelaine, Sr., Perry A., Chapdelaine, Tony and Hay, George, *The John W. Campbell Letters*, 2 volumes, Franklin, Tennessee: AC Projects, 1985–1993.

Clareson, Thomas D., *Science Fiction in America, 1870s–1930s*, Westport: Greenwood Press, 1984.

Clarke, Arthur C., *Astounding Days*, London: Victor Gollancz, 1989.

Clute, John and Nicholls, Peter, *Encyclopedia of Science Fiction*, London: Orbit, 1993.

Currey, L.W., *Science Fiction and Fantasy Authors*, Boston: G.K. Hall, 1979.

Day, Bradford M., *The Checklist of Science Fiction and Fantasy Magazines 1892–1992*, revised edition, privately published, 1993.

—— *An Index on the Weird & Fantastica in Magazines*, revised edition, privately published, 1995).

Day, Donald B., *Index to the Science-Fiction Magazines, 1926–1950*, Portland: Perri Press, 1952.

de Camp, L. Sprague, *Science-Fiction Handbook*, New York: Hermitage House, 1953.

Del Rey, Lester, *The World of Science Fiction: 1926–1976*, New York: Del Rey Books, 1979.

Disch, Thomas M., *The Dreams Our Stuff is Made Of*, New York: The Free Press, 1998.

Doubleday, F.N., *The Memoirs of a Publisher*, Garden City: Doubleday, 1972.

Dziemianowicz, Stefan R., *The Annotated Guide to Unknown and Unknown Worlds*, Mercer Island, Washington: Starmont House, 1991.

Eshbach, Lloyd Arthur, *Of Worlds Beyond*, 2nd edition, Chicago: Advent, 1964.

—— *Over My Shoulder*, Philadelphia: Oswald Train, 1983.

Gallagher, Edward J., *The Annotated Guide to Fantastic Adventures*, Mercer Island, Washington: Starmont House, 1985.

Gallagher, Edward J., Mistichelli, Judith A., Van Eerde, John A., *Jules Verne: A Primary and Secondary Bibliography*, Boston: G.K. Hall, 1980.

Gammell, Leon L., *The Annotated Guide to Startling Stories*, Mercer Island, Washington: Starmont House, 1986.

Gerber, Ernst and Mary, *The Photo-Journal Guide to Comic Books*, 2 volumes, Minden: Gerber Publishing, 1989.

Gillings, Walter, 'The Clamorous Dreamers', *Vision of Tomorrow*, August 1969–September 1970.

Goodstone, Tony, *The Pulps*, New York: Chelsea House, 1970.

Goulart, Ron, *Cheap Thrills: An Informal History of the Pulp Magazine*, New Rochelle: Arlington House, 1972.

Gruber, Frank, *The Pulp Jungle*, Los Angeles: Sherbourne Press, 1967.

Gunn, James, *Alternate Worlds*, Englewood Cliffs: Prentice-Hall, 1975.

—— *The Road to Science Fiction*, 3 volumes, New York: New American Library, 1977–79.

Harbottle, Philip and Holland, Stephen, *Vultures of the Void*, San Bernardino: The Borgo Press, 1992.

—— *British Science Fiction Paperbacks and Magazines, 1949–1956*, San Bernardino: The Borgo Press, 1994.

Hartwell, David, *Age of Wonders*, New York: Walker, 1984.

Heinlein, Virginia, *Robert A. Heinlein: Grumbles from the Grave*, New York: Del Rey Books, 1989.

Hersey, Harold, *Pulpwood Editor*, New York: F.A. Stokes, 1937.

Holland, Steve, *The Mushroom Jungle*, Westbury, Wiltshire: Zeon Books, 1993.

Hutchinson, Don, *The Great Pulp Heroes*, Oakville, Ontario: Mosaic Press, 1995.

Jones, Robert K., *The Shudder Pulps*, West Linn, Oregon: Fax, 1975.

Knight, Damon, *In Search of Wonder*, Chicago: Advent, 1967.

—— *The Futurians*, New York: John Day, 1977.

Lundwall, Sam J., *Science Fiction: What It's All About*, New York: Ace Books, 1971.

Lupoff, Richard A., *Edgar Rice Burroughs: Master of Adventure*, revised edition, New York: Ace Books, 1968.

McAleer, Neil, *Odyssey: The Authorised Biography of Arthur C. Clarke*, London: Victor Gollancz, 1992.

McComas, Annette, *The Eureka Years*, New York: Bantam Books, 1982.

Menville, Douglas, *The Work of Ross Rocklynne*, San Bernardino: The Borgo Press, 1989.

Miller, Stephen T. and Contento, William G., *Science Fiction, Fantasy & Weird Fiction Magazine Index*, CD-ROM, Locus Press, 1999.

Moskowitz, Sam, *The Immortal Storm*, Atlanta: Atlanta Science Fiction Organisation Press, 1954.

—— *Explorers of the Infinite*, Cleveland: World Publishing, 1963.

—— *Seekers of Tomorrow*, Cleveland: World Publishing, 1966.

—— *Science Fiction by Gaslight*, Cleveland: World Publishing, 1968.

—— *Under the Moons of Mars*, New York: Holt, Rinehart, Winston, 1970.

—— *Strange Horizons*, New York: Charles Scribner's, 1976.

—— *A. Merritt: Reflections in the Moon Pool*, Philadelphia: Oswald Train, 1985.

Panshin, Alexei and Cory, *The World Beyond the Hill*, Los Angeles: Jeremy P. Tarcher, 1989.

Parnell, Frank and Ashley, Mike, *Monthly Terrors: An Index to the Weird Fantasy Magazines*, Westport: Greenwood Press, 1985.

Platt, Charles, *Who Writes Science Fiction?*, Manchester: Savoy Books, 1980.

Pohl, Frederik, *The Way the Future Was*, New York: Del Rey Books, 1978.

Porges, Irwin, *Edgar Rice Burroughs: The Man Who Created Tarzan*, Provo, Utah: Brigham Young University Press, 1975.

Reginald, R., *Science Fiction and Fantasy Literature: A Checklist, 1700–1974*, Detroit: Gale Research, 1979.

—— *Science Fiction and Fantasy Literature, Volume 2: Contemporary Science Fiction Authors II*, Detroit: Gale Research, 1979.

Reynolds, Quentin, *The Fiction Factory*, New York: Random House, 1955.

Robinson, Frank M. and Davidson, Lawrence, *Pulp Culture: The Art of Fiction Magazines*, Portland: Collectors Press, 1998.

Rogers, Alva, *A Requiem for Astounding*, Chicago: Advent, 1964.

Sampson, Robert, *Yesterday's Faces*, 6 volumes, Bowling Green, Ohio: Bowling Green University Popular Press, 1983–93.

Sanders, Joe, *Science Fiction Fandom*, Westport: Greenwood Press, 1994.

Seed, David, *Anticipations*, Liverpool: Liverpool University Press, 1995.

Stableford, Brian, *Scientific Romance in Britain 1890–1950*, London: Fourth Estate, 1985.

Suvin, Darko, *Victorian Science Fiction in the UK: The Discourses of Knowledge and of Power*, Boston: G.K. Hall, 1983.

Tuck, Donald H., *The Encyclopedia of Science Fiction and Fantasy*, 3 volumes, Chicago: Advent, 1974–82.

Tymn, Marshall B., and Ashley, Mike, *Science Fiction, Fantasy, and Weird Fiction Magazines*, Westport: Greenwood Press, 1985.

Warner, Jr., Harry, *All Our Yesterdays*, Chicago: Advent, 1969.

Weinberg, Robert, *A Biographical Dictionary of Science Fiction and Fantasy Artists*, Westport: Greenwood Press, 1988.

Weinberg, Robert and McKinstry, Lohr, *The Hero Pulp Index*, Chicago: privately published, 1973.

Williamson, Jack, *Wonder's Child: My Life in Science Fiction*, New York: Bluejay Books, 1984.

Wollheim, Donald A., *The Universe Makers*, New York: Harper & Row, 1971.

In addition the following academic or news magazines (not all of which are still published) have been regularly consulted.

Algol (later retitled *Starship*), editor Andrew Porter, Brooklyn, New York.

Extrapolation, editor Donald M. Hassler, Kent State University, Kent, Ohio.

Fantasy Commentator, editor A. Langley Searles, Bronxville, New York.

Foundation, editor Edward James, The Science Fiction Foundation, Liverpool.

Locus, editor Charles N. Brown, Oakland, California.

The New York Review of Science Fiction, editor David G. Hartwell, Pleasantville, New York.

Riverside Quarterly, editor Leland Sapiro, Hartville, South Carolina.

Science Fiction Chronicle, editor Andrew Porter, Brooklyn, New York.

Science Fiction Eye, editor Stephen Brown, Asheville, North Carolina.

Science Fiction Review (also entitled *The Alien Critic*), editor Richard E. Geis, Portland, Oregon.

Science Fiction Studies, editor Arthur B. Evans, East College, DePauw University, Greencastle, Indiana.

Thrust, editor Doug Fratz, Gaithersburg, Maryland.

Index